The Wonder House

Also by Justine Hardy

*The Ochre Border: A Journey
    through the Tibetan Frontierlands*

Scoop-wallah: Life on a Delhi Daily

Goat: A Story of Kashmir & Notting Hill

Bollywood Boy

The Wonder House

JUSTINE HARDY

GROVE PRESS
New York

First published in Great Britain in 2005 by Atlantic Books,
an imprint of Grove Atlantic Ltd.

This novel is entirely a work of fiction. The names, characters and incidents
portrayed in it are the work of the author's imagination. Any resemblance to
actual persons, living or dead, is entirely coincidental.

Published simultaneously in Canada
Printed in the United States of America

FIRST AMERICAN EDITION

Library of Congress Cataloging-in-Publication Data

Hardy, Justine.
    The Wonder House / Justine Hardy.
        p. cm.
    ISBN-10: 0-8021-1822-4
    ISBN-13: 978-0-8021-1822-6
    1. Jammu and Kashmir (India)—Fiction. 2. Kashmir, Vale of (India)—
Fiction. 3. British—India—Fiction. 4. Older women—Fiction. 5. Widows—
Fiction. 6. Houseboats—Fiction   I. Title.
PR6108.A733W66 2006
813'.6—dc22   2005055012

Grove Press
an imprint of Grove/Atlantic, Inc.
841 Broadway
New York, NY 10003

Distributed by Publishers Group West

www.groveatlantic.com

06 07 08 09 10   10 9 8 7 6 5 4 3 2 1

This book is dedicated to the
healers and the healing

Author's note ~

One of the results of Britain's withdrawal from India in 1947 was the division of the northern state of Kashmir between newly forged West Pakistan and India. Though, on a map, this poetic valley seems protected by the surrounding fortress of the Himalayas it has been constantly fought over by success- ive invaders, empires, and subsequently by India and Pakistan. The history of the Kashmir Valley has ever reached beyond the limits of its geographical borders. By 1989 unrest on the Indian side had reached uncontainable levels. The coveted state became an internecine warzone of guerrilla terrorism, insurgency and military control.

Ten years into the insurgency, on the 12 October 1999, General Pervez Musharraf, a senior figure in the Pakistan army, overthrew the government of Prime Minister Nawaz Sharif. On 13 October the Government of India prepared its army to go onto a war footing along the Line of Control that separated Pakistan Controlled Kashmir and Indian Controlled Kashmir. It was only two and a half months since a ceasefire had been called at the end of a ten-week war that had been fought around the high altitude border town of Kargil, Muslim by denomination, politically part of India, ethnically part of Little Baltistan, integrally a part of Ladakh.

The Wonder House

Prologue ~

Before the insurgency – Kashmir, North India, September 1975.

It broke down into a series of single images, postcards to keep, like the ones lined up at the stalls along the boulevard by the lake: single focus, captured and stored. There were his upper fingers where his hand pressed into the bark beside her head, a hand she had seen all her life without noticing the length of its joints from knuckle to nail. His face blocked out the light, dark in front of the sun. She could feel his breath but she could not separate out his features on their unlit plain. There was movement all around them: the slow irritation of his mule's tail, the way her harness shifted as she did, layers of leaves above them, trapping and releasing the light that his face had blocked out, the way the earth breathed in the heat, and how it shifted as she tried to be still.

Everything peripheral withdrew as his face moved to rest against the side of hers. He settled against the length of her body, the buttress of his hip tucking into the space below her ribcage.

The hands that she had seen scooping and wrapping the food that she had cooked, fingers she had watched flicking star anise out of her pilau as the grains stuck to his skin, moved across her. Her back slid down the tree, bark rucking up her thin cotton tunic until she was crouched at its trunk. She tasted the sweat at the sides of his mouth as his head blocked the light again.

She did not close her eyes.

The mule watched, turned towards them, part of their intersection. She threw her head up as the girl shouted out.

This pain was the only thing she had to give him and it snapped through both of them. They lay in silence under the great cedar tree, clinging in the subsidence.

The tree had been marked for timber. The boy had brought her to see it before it was felled. That was his job.

After the Kargil War, October 1999.

The Wonder House sits low in the water on the edge of Nagin Lake in Srinagar, the summer capital of Kashmir. One corner is made from seasoned Kashmiri cedar that is a little older than the wood of the rest of the boat. It panels the lakeside edge of the sitting room. At about the time when girls from Eve's Garden School paddle home across the lake in their lotus leaf-green uniforms, afternoon light crosses the room and rests in the corner, saturating the wood. After the girls have gone, the outlines of the furniture in the sitting room begin to fade and disintegrate into the sliding light. It crosses the room in a retreating diagonal until only a small table in that corner made of older wood remains suspended in the last of the day, just where particles of dust circle in the retreating bands of light.

The merchant who sold the cedar to the builder of The Wonder House had waited a long time to be rid of those timbers. He had begun to think that he was stuck with them, that they were his punishment for trying to make money from a marked tree.

When insurgents in Kashmir are shot, or when they kill soldiers, and when ordinary people are murdered in the crossfire under the thick cedars of the forests, the trees are singled out with a red cross on their bark. The foresters believe that wood is porous to emotion, to human pain and joy, and that to frame and clad a house, or to build a boat of timber from trees rooted under death is to curse the family who will live with those vibrations of violence held in the grain, the whorls and knots, like human scars.

Chapter One ~

Gracie Singh sat within the shadows of the sitting room, heavy in her skin, the light travelling across her face, picking out the down on the edges of her falling features. Her hair was cropped, pale grey from blonde, and her clothes had the local tailor's tugged fitting: tapered trousers that rose up and over the mound of her stomach, and a shirt the colour of a peacock's breast. The tailor's chalk marks were still there beside the darts that pulled in all the wrong places across her descending bosom. She was asleep.

She dreams of a smell so familiar, so thick, that it catches in her throat.

A fog of remembered sound sits on top of a voiceless sequence. Gracie is thirteen years old and she knows that everyone else in the room must be looking at her, judging her, checking to see if her vest is showing when she swings her arms up, or if her socks are falling down. She can hear the battery of tap shoes on worn-down wood in the school hall on Starbeck Road, Harrogate, memory-atrophied York-shire. She knows the mixture of sweat and the lily of the valley talcum powder that Miss Lane, the tap teacher, likes so much. She sees the deep red lipstick that Miss Lane always wears beginning to bleed into the lines around her mouth as she shouts at her pupils over the foundry of tapping. Ankles and dumb dream sound, bouncing hair and rigid faces shoot in and out of an unfixed focus.

Gracie Singh guttered on the edge of her own breathing, a real sound that woke her. She flailed in her chair, knocking an almost empty glass off a small table beside her. Droplets of gin slid down the wall behind as she jabbed at the air above her chest.

She had not tap-danced for more than sixty years. She could dream about Miss Lane's lipstick cracks but she could not remember her own mother's face any more, except as it was in the photographs she had around her, placed as landmarks in the room for her to balance between. She could not remember her mother's voice, how her Kirby Moorside used to come over a bit posh when she picked up her daughter from Miss Lane's tap class on Starbeck Road at half past four on Thursday afternoons, to prove to herself that she was as good as all the other mothers.

Gracie twitched and stared out at the lake beyond her narrowing world. There was a sound of gunfire from the city. She continued to stare out across the surface of Nagin as the separated noise bounced towards her. A small boat moved across her horizon, its shape an upward brushstroke on the water.

And in the copper market in the city beyond the lake a teenage boy fell in the street across the road from an army checkpost. The bullet that killed him entered just below his collarbone and exited under his Adam's apple. The street was empty around the body, and a young soldier behind the sandbags vomited out of sight of any of the surrounding shopkeepers as they pulled back behind their stacked copper pots, silent hermit crabs.

The lake remained quiet.

A small Kashmiri woman came to the door of the sitting room where Gracie sat. She stood watching, her pale eyes taking in the trails of gin sliding down the wooden panels, the empty glass rolled under the chair, and Gracie's tufts of chair-squashed hair.

Gracie turned to her. 'I knocked my glass over,' she said as she surveyed the area around her chair in search of her glass. 'I was dancing again.' She reached for it and held it out to the mute Kashmiri woman at the door.

Suriya sighed through her nostrils and stood watching. Gracie turned away. Suriya clapped, and then made a cup of both her hands, her thumbs and little fingers interlinked in the centre as she opened the rest of her fingers out above her palms as petals. She ignored the glass in Gracie's hand and crossed to the windows as she finished her mime. She untied and retied her headscarf as she moved to close the mosquito screens.

'Lotus root for supper,' Gracie interpreted. She waved her glass at Suriya's back. 'Can I have it masala fried?'

The small woman did not turn to acknowledge.

'The lotus gardens bloomed and died. I didn't even see them. Did I see them, Suriya?'

A merchant on the corner of Zaina Kadal, the copper market, sent his son to the house of the dead boy to tell his family. An army lorry pulled in and out of the market, collecting the body, before the merchant's son had got even halfway to the boy's house.

Gracie, the ex-tap dancer, expatriate, ex-mother and widow seemed to be fading into the Mughal-poppy pattern behind her head. Suriya reached out to take the glass from her. She stuffed it into the pocket of her *kameez,* her flowered tunic over cotton drawstring trousers. Gracie turned to look out of the window.

'The last time I tap-danced I was nineteen. I'm going to be eighty next February.'

Suriya squatted down close to Gracie and patted one of her feet.

Gracie plucked at the loose skin on her neck. 'Sixty-one years by then. Never thought I would live this long, you know. Never thought I'd have to fill up so much time.'

Suriya looked down at Gracie's foot under her hand. It was so swollen now that she could not imagine it in a tap shoe, whatever that was like. They sounded small and tidy. She got up and stroked Gracie's feathery hair before starting to rub the back of her neck. Gracie closed her eyes.

The mourners started wailing outside the Zaina Kadal police station an hour after the boy had been shot. His blood had turned dark and sticky in the road, like castor oil. The soldier's vomit had long been cleaned off his boots.

Irfan Abdullah, Suriya's seventeen-year-old cousin, was squatting underneath one of the duckboards between The Wonder House and the *dunga,* the old boat where Suriya and her daughter Lila lived and worked. He was hidden in the long shadows of the houseboat's back deck, waiting with his hand under his *kurta* for the moment when he would feel the pressure in his lower back moving to his groin, making him grab himself. Until then he crouched in silence.

He kept looking around to make sure that no one else could hear the breath that roared in his head. Just below where he waited a thin trail of soap was swirling out into the water, making islands across his shadow.

Beyond his shadow's tip Lila was washing, hunched over her scrubbing board, her rhythm rounded as she worked a thin blue lather through a hump of wet clothes. Her scarf had slipped down her head and a single strand of hair swung across the front of her face in time with her movement. She looked up to brush it away with the back of her wrist. Irfan ducked.

Her skin looked different when it was wet, paler and polished. He watched the planes of her face, studying her. Her teeth bit into one side of her lower lip as she worked. He bit his lip too. The cold water had prickled her forearms. She bent down again to scrub, the nape of her neck exposed where her hair had fallen to one side. He could see the finer wisps that curled away from the base of her plait. He pulled harder and faster and held his breath as he ejaculated, his eyes closed, his head yanked back.

He moved his hand carefully from under his *kurta* and washed his semen away in the eddies of Lila's washing, satisfied that something of himself was floating away with her suds, almost a mutual achievement.

He wanted to leave now. His legs and lower back ached and he was shivering. Looking up, he caught her profile as the same loose strand of hair fell back across her face. His satisfaction drained away.

He stumbled as he stood up. Lila looked up and stared straight at him. He scurried away, shame plucking at the legs of his pyjamas.

'Irfan Abdullah, why are you creeping around under the duckboards like a rat?' Lila shouted after her cousin.

Irfan only heard the sound of his feet and the rasp of his own breathing as he skidded over wet grass.

'Irfan Abdullah,' Lila shouted again.

This time he heard. He stopped, turned, and waggled his tongue at her before running again. Lila jumped off the back of the boat, tucking one corner of her tunic into the drawstring of her trousers. Her bare feet held the wet grass where his sandals slipped. She could hear his heavy breathing as she caught up.

'I'll beat you when I get you,' she shouted.

He was scrambling for the wooden door in the wall that separated the lake meadow above The Wonder House from the Abdullahs' garden. A cloud of cosmos around the door, full of afternoon rain, showered him as he slammed the door shut and leaned against it.

'How are you going to do that now?' he whispered to the weight of her body pushing through the wood. He could feel the edge of longing beginning again. He spat into the cosmos.

Lila leaned against the other side of the door in silence, looking at the handle. It was the shape of a chinar leaf, designed and cast by her great uncle, Irfan's grandfather, ten years before she had been born. She reached for the leaf handle and touched it, loving the feel of it, the smoothness of the stalk and the sand-rough of the leaf itself. She was running her finger down its central vein when she heard Irfan spit into the flowers. She smiled and walked away down the lake meadow. He watched her go through a gap between the two central timbers of the door, pressing himself against one of the stone portals. He pushed his mouth against the space in the wood.

'Irfan, what were you doing at the lake?' Masood Abdullah, the elder among Irfan's three uncles, called from the upper balcony of the house beyond the garden. 'Were you asked to go there? Why were you down there? Did Gracie Madam ask you?'

'I took a message to cousin Suriya from my mother.' Irfan did not look up as he replied.

'Is this the truth?' Masood leaned further over the balcony, readjusting his *topi* as he looked down on his nephew. 'What are you doing, Irfan? Come here, come to the house now. If you're lying to me . . .' he trailed off. The boy was so sullen he lost his nerve.

Gracie Singh had been living in Kashmir for twenty-two years. She had come to the Valley for the first time on her honeymoon in 1939. She returned to live as a widow thirty-eight years later. The Abdullahs were the Kashmiris that her husband's family had bought their shawls and saffron from for generations. When she returned Gracie made a deal. She would pay rent to have a houseboat on the lake edge beyond the two boats that they rented out to tourists. She paid good rent and they watched over her.

Masood had always liked her. He had first seen her in his father's study when he was six years old. Gracie and her husband had been married for exactly twenty years when they had come back to the lake for their anniversary. She drank tea while his father read out some Kashmiri love songs written by Masood's great-grandfather. Her husband had seemed bored as he sat picking invisible things off his shawl. It was the first time Masood had seen a woman in a skirt, and the shape of her legs had stayed with him.

Eighteen years later his father sent him to meet Gracie at the airport. At twenty-four he was proud in his tight blue jeans, a packet of Wills cigarettes in his back pocket. She was then fifty-seven and shapeless in a grey dress. Her legs were not on show. He was embarrassed about the flowers that he had brought for her, so he dropped them behind a bench. As they drove away from the airport Gracie told him that her husband had died and Masood regretted throwing away the flowers. They shared a cigarette and he made her laugh about his favourite hobby. He led trekking groups for his father and he liked to follow the girls up the hills, admiring the Western swing and sway as they walked ahead of him.

During the twenty-two years since then the freedom of jeans, whisky and spring-hipped foreigners had been edited out by the conflict in the Valley. For Masood, Gracie was his bridge between the old life and the new.

He leaned back out over the balcony. The tourists might have gone but Wills's cigarettes and Gracie remained. The Wonder House was where he could smoke and speak freely beyond the constraining boundaries of his family.

He would ask Gracie about Irfan. The boy worried him. As the acting patriarch of the family it was his role to worry. The boy reminded Masood of himself at that age, always sniffing around girls and jutting his chin at his father Ibrahim and his uncles. It had been safer to posture and jostle around the edges of authority when he had been that age. Not now.

A boy had been shot in the market, a mother and her son on the Barramulla Road the day before, a massacre on Monday in the village where they used to picnic when he was a boy: twelve dead, eight wounded.

Masood felt for his cigarettes in the inner pocket of his *pheran* and called to one of the houseboys to tell him that he would be going down to the lake for some time.

Irfan watched from the edge of the women's prayer room beside the kitchen as his uncle made his way down the path to the garden door. His mother, Faheema, came from the kitchen with a plate of biscuits. He shrugged her away and she clicked her tongue as she stepped back from him.

Lila was at her washing again, scrubbing viciously as Masood made his way across the wet grass, the hem of his *pheran* delicately lifted clear of the dew between his fingers and thumbs. She looked up as he approached. Her face was tight but she settled her expression as he came near, smoothing away her belligerence and adjusting her headscarf to cover more of her head.

'Salaam alaikum, good evening, uncle.'

'Alaikum salaam, it's getting dark, you should be inside.' Masood saw the gooseflesh on her arms.

'I will go in once this is done.'

'Good.' He paused.

Lila remained upright, waiting for him to finish. He continued up the duckboard. As he turned on to the deck she bent back down over her scrubbing. He watched as a lock of her hair fell across her face.

He turned away.

Gracie had not moved from her chair in the corner of the sitting room. She was expecting Suriya with a shawl for her and she barely looked up as Masood stepped down into the room through one of the open windows that ran the length of the room. Neatly removing his shoes, he balanced on the arm of the sofa below the window, and landed squarely and quietly on the carpet in front of her. He waited for a moment, unsure if she was awake in the half-light.

'You look sad, Masood Abdullah. What's the matter?' Gracie's voice came out of the fading poppies.

'No, no, inshallah. It must be due to less of light.'

'No mullah talk tonight from you, my friend.' Gracie stretched forward from the poppies. 'Sit down, Masood.' She waved to one of the chairs near her.

Masood remained standing, erect and irritated.

'Oh, come on you, I'm not insulting your god. I'm just saying none of this mawkish mullah stuff here. Do what you like within the privacy of your own prayer mat, but please respect that this houseboat is secular, a tiny pocket of success for Pandit Jawaharlalji.'

Masood did not move.

'You never did like Nehru, did you?'

He did not answer.

'I admire how your father and mother used to embrace their Pandit neighbours. How are your parents?'

He stood looking straight ahead.

'Masood, it is the twenty-third anniversary of my husband's death, I'm a crazed old widow, humour me.'

He stepped over Gracie's abandoned shoes and sat in one of the windows, the arch of his nose and his beard profiled by the pale light behind him.

'I've just read another of those ridiculous pieces in the *Reader's Digest* about Jesus Christ being buried up here.

No wonder they rubbish on about it, you could be his doppelgänger. I suppose it's the beard, and those eyes.' Gracie studied his profile. 'You were so different when you were a boy, all tight trousers, girls and fags. Thank God you still smoke, and yes, I do thank him on that count.'

Masood hunched down into the collar of his *pheran* to stop himself from laughing.

'And you laughed so much. Do you remember you used to laugh at everything and everyone – me, your parents, your uncles and aunts, life, the lakes, everything? Cigarette?' Gracie started to shuffle out of her chair. Masood nodded. 'Mine or yours?' Gracie made her way towards her walnut desk beside the wall on the other side of the room.

'Please, today let us take from my supply.' Masood pulled his packet of Wills from inside his *pheran*. 'And what is doppelgänger?'

'A double, like a twin of sorts, and it's much easier for me to buy fags without the thought-police telling on me. Have mine. Think I've got a few left. Let's smoke to my Jitu.' Gracie picked up an ivory cigarette box from her desk. 'Oh, sweet Suriya, she's filled it up. Must mean I'm being particularly pathetic at the moment.' Gracie held the full box out to Masood. 'Am I being unusually pathetic?'

'This talk of God and angels together with cigarettes, it is not a good thing.' Masood took a cigarette and leaned across to light Gracie's.

'Oh, I don't know, they sit around on all those clouds, clouds of what? Who's to say that being a chain-smoker isn't a requisite part of entry to heaven?' Gracie inhaled and closed her eyes. 'To my Jitu on his fluffy cloud.' Two thin threads of smoke trailed out of her nose and down into her lap. 'Amazing, nearly sixty years ago I jumped on a train in Bombay and went all the way to the Punjab, to that stinking palace by the river. Smelt of rat shit and death that place. Not a living thing in it apart from Jitu. Not a whole lot to show for that.'

'You had your son.' Masood inhaled.

'Yes, I suppose I did.' Gracie straightened a little.

'I need to ask a question.' Masood carefully and tidily put out his cigarette in the ashtray that he was still holding.

'Yes.' Gracie was absent.

'I have concerns about my nephew Irfan.'

'He's alive, what's there to worry about?' Gracie stared at the end of her cigarette.

Masood pinched his eyebrows together.

'What is it?' Gracie took the ashtray from Masood and put it on the edge of the windowsill.

'He tells lies about what he is doing, straight on my face he tells these lies.'

'To my face. Don't all teenagers lie?' Gracie turned back towards the lake again. 'Didn't you?'

Masood did not reply.

'I used to lie about everything. I used to bunk off tap classes to meet Jimmie the Car for a drive . . .' She dropped the words over the sill.

They sat in silence. It was almost dark. Cold air off the lake rolled up over the edges of The Wonder House as the retreating light sucked away the clarity of the mountains beyond the water and the trees.

Gracie sat up, exploring the pain in her joints in the evening chill. 'I'm not sure I would want to be that young again. I despise this decrepit wreck that I'm stuck in, but I'm pretty certain that being a bit wiser in a sagging skin is better than being an idiot in a young one. The bits I remember seem to have been all lies and desperate worry about what everyone else thought.' She leaned further out of the window. 'Suriya, is this a plan for me to die of cold?' she shouted down the boat.

'Maybe this is so, but he was down here earlier and I think he is going about things in a way that is not pleasing to Allah, or to me, and Ibrahim is not stern with him.' Masood stood up, stiff and irritated again.

'He's just a boy. He's only interested in sex and cricket. What else is there when you are, well, how old is he?'

Masood stopped and calculated on his fingers and knuckles. 'Eighteen running, and there is Allah, there is always Allah. I will hear no more on this. Cricket may be fine but the rest I will not hear. Enough.' He pulled his arms out of his sleeves and inside the body of his *pheran*.

He wanted to say more but he knew that Suriya would be coming in response to Gracie's cry. He did not enjoy being caught smoking. Suriya was an eloquent mute, her every silence a full sentence.

He got up from the window seat and walked out on to the veranda beyond the sitting room to avoid her entrance.

It was not Suriya who came to Gracie's call. It was Lila.

'Thank you. What is your mother trying to do to me? I think she wants rid of me before I get cantankerous with winter arthritis.'

Lila wrapped the shawl she was carrying around Gracie without answering, pulling the long end around her a second time, and nestling the folds up close to her chin.

'Lila, I have a date. I will have a little drink with him. He will watch over me, won't you?' She nodded to the veranda. Lila stopped fussing with the shawl and turned towards Masood's shadowed form beyond the window.

'Your mother has taken the keys to the cupboard again. Please ask her and tell her that Masood is here to mind the baby.' She wriggled her shoulders to loosen Lila's tight wrapping.

Masood tried to raise his hand in silent greeting to Lila but it was trapped, stuck inside the body of his *pheran*. He nodded instead. Lila lowered her head as she left.

She climbed up on to the roof to collect the washing from the wooden frame where a canopy hung to give shade in the summer heat. It was just to delay going back to the *dunga* to get the key. Gracie's eyes followed the sound of her feet on the roof above the sitting room.

'Tell you what worries me more than your nephew thinking about tits and arse when you think he should be mulling over the Koran.' Gracie unwound herself from the shawl and rewrapped it so that she could move her arms. Masood did not answer. She stared at him. 'I've started having a peg or two at lunchtime because I just want to be able to drift through the afternoon without spending most of it wondering what to do. Never used to drink at lunch.'

Masood stepped back into the sitting room without replying. He spent hours at a time missing the chance to be able to eat into the night, to dull the sharp sounds of gunfire from the city with the soft anaesthesia of whisky. He was glad that Gracie drank gin, colourless and uninviting in the glass. He had always preferred whisky and it would be unbearable for him to have to sit with her, resisting its earthy glow.

'It troubles me that our boys may rebel and start to drink when they are away from the home. Me and my brothers have had the time to try all these things.' He looked away from Gracie. 'To see they are wrong and that they bring violence with them, and so we leave these things behind.' His tone was flat.

'Oh, come on, Masood, what about the violence that we have all been living with for the past ten years? A few pegs here and there might calm everyone down a bit.' She sat back down in her chair. 'And don't try and tell me that you don't miss it. I can see it in your face when I'm having a drink. You loved whisky as much as I love gin and thing.' Thing was Gracie's mixer, fresh lime juice and tonic water.

Masood straightened up. Gracie cut him off as he started to protest. 'Please don't forget how many times I saw you staggering back to the house from whichever boat the latest lovely was staying on in the days of whisky, women and song.' She pushed herself back up out of her chair and went again to the cigarette box on her desk. 'Let the boy run a little bit wild.' She held the box out to Masood.

He stared at the pile of India Kings, their dappled brown filters so neatly stacked. Taking one he rolled it between his fingers, enjoying the dense feeling of the tobacco between its thin paper and his skin.

For twenty-two years Suriya had listened to the World Service news at half past six on her adored – and now crumbling – Philips radio as she ground up masalas for the evening meal. It had been the only thing she had bought with her first pay from Gracie. She had hung the transistor on the side of the *dunga* with a strip of cotton in 1977, setting it to a wavelength that had never been changed. Twenty-two years of the pungency of crushed cardamom and the musk of coriander seeds had scented reports of floods in Orissa, the murder of world leaders, nuclear testing in the desert in Rajasthan, dams dispossessing hundreds of Indian villages, the amorphous encroachment of China, Pakistan chafing at the border, terrorist attacks in the north-east, massacres just across the lake. All these daily fragments had mingled with Suriya's spices, the vocabulary of her mortar and pestle that rose up out of the narrow chimney above the fire in the middle of the *dunga*'s dark kitchen with each day's news.

Lila had brought Gracie's shawl because the news had been about to begin. Suriya had her masalas set out all around her in a semicircle of readiness, her smoothed stone mortar and pestle settled in the cross of her legs on the floor. The time pips bounced as she cornered stray cardamom and coriander seeds with her finger, pushing them towards the curve of the pestle. She snatched a finger away as she caught it under an edge. For a moment it distracted her as she sucked her bruised fingertip. She missed the even-toned remove of the opening headline. She did not miss what followed.

Pushing the mortar away, Suriya pulled herself up from her circle of spices. One of her feet was numb from sitting and she limped through the shadows on her lifeless foot towards the lights of The Wonder House.

Lila saw her from the roof and dropped the washing she had been gathering from the lines. It was unusual for her mother to run.

'*Ama*, what is it?' Lila ran too, swiping the still hanging sheets out of her way.

Masood heard Lila on the stairs and he saw Suriya from the window. 'What happened?' he asked Lila.

'I don't know. Wait for some time and then she will write.' Lila led her mother up the narrow board into the spill of light from the sitting room.

Suriya went straight to Gracie, squatting down in front of the older woman, her head bent, one hand clenched in a fist at her heart.

Gracie put her hand on Suriya's shoulder. 'Easy, girl.'

Suriya reached out, waving her fingers for something to write with. Lila put a pen and paper into her mother's hand.

Masood moved back to the veranda window, just beyond the inner circle of lamplight that held the three women, throwing their shadows tall on to the panelled wall beside him. He wanted to see what Suriya was writing but he felt held outside the circle of light. He waited as her bent figure scribbled at Gracie's feet.

Mr Marvellous, the flower man, was at the end of his evening rounds. Not a bad run; all the zinnias had gone and the roses too at the Ansari houseboat for their daughter's engagement ceremony, and they had paid a good enough price.

Now there were just gladioli left in three buckets at the back of the boat. He knew Gracie Madam did not particularly like gladioli, and they were fading a little, but he had timed his route to catch her at the end of her second drink.

He needed to make as much as he could. This latest drama would stop people buying flowers for a while. His son's medical tuition fees were due soon, and he wanted to put a bet on Abdul Saleem's Brandy, the dog-fight man's latest champion. Perhaps he could sell off the gladioli as quickly as possible, before Gracie Madam had a chance to hear the news.

He called out as he drew his boat up to the steps of The Wonder House. Gracie Madam might answer, or the mute or pretty Lila could come. There was silence. He threw the rope at the front of his boat through the steps and unwound himself from among his remaining flower buckets. He was about to call again from the top of the steps when he saw Masood Abdullah standing at the glass doors to the sitting room. He was just a blackened silhouette against the light of the room beyond but Salman Abhed, the fifth Mr Marvellous, principal flower-seller of Nagin Lake, had known Masood since they had both been boys at school, fighting it out on the same cricket fields.

The relative wealth of the Abdullahs had distanced Masood and his brothers from some of their old school friends as they had reached the self-conscious confusion of their teens. Mr Marvellous did not feel comfortable around Masood any more. The Abdullahs wore their beards long and their morals high. Mr Marvellous loved his fine moustache but he had no beard, he liked betting on the dogs, and he drank whisky when he could get it.

He raised his hand to his former friend and they bowed to each other out of silent habit. Masood slipped away from the door and across the veranda to where the flower man stood on the steps.

'This is not a good time for you to be hawking flowers, my friend,' Masood whispered over the low divide of the gate at the top of the steps.

For a moment the flower-seller considered pretending

not to know what Masood was talking about. He decided
against it. His former friend would know he was lying.
'Sometimes it is good to bring fresh blooms into darkness.'
Mr Marvellous shrugged towards his boat.

'You propose those rotting things as fresh?' Masood
straightened up above the flower man. 'Our children are
fresh, these flowers are not. The fighting poisons our children
and the stale lake water rots your flowers.'

'Masood, brother, please, this is all our strife. I am just
trying to survive. They will always take our children. Am I to
stop selling flowers every time we think there is going to be
more fighting?'

Masood bent forward from his higher stance. 'I'm sorry,
forgive me. The smell of fear in there has affected me.' He
waved a hand towards the sitting room. He did not want Mr
Marvellous to realize that he still did not know what had
happened.

'You think it will mean war again?' the flower man asked.

'Who can say? What do you think?'

'Four coups in our lives before this,' Mr Marvellous
shrugged.

Masood absorbed the information, 'And now five,' he
added, removing the question mark from his voice. 'But the
first since the insurgency, Pakistan fights India under civilian
rule and under martial law. Allah will decide.'

So there had been a coup across the border. The rumours
had been right. He had thought that Suriya had been bringing more news about the boy killed in the market in the
afternoon.

'This General Musharraf, you think he is like the rest?' Mr
Marvellous could see the women in their motionless tableau

beyond the glass.

Masood took on this further news. 'Who knows, he was the big leader behind the summer war. They say the soldiers like him, and they blamed the loss of the war on the prime minister, not on him.'

They stood in silence.

Mr Marvellous sniffed. 'A boy was killed in the market. He was not even armed. Only seventeen.'

Masood nodded.

'Same age as my elder boy, same as your nephew, the older one, I have lost his name for a moment.' Mr Marvellous was watching through the glass.

'Irfan.' Masood followed his line of sight. 'You should go now.'

'I came to greet Gracie Madam.'

'You came to sell her rotting flowers.' Masood paused before stepping away from the gate. 'But why not.' He lifted the gate latch. 'Come.' He directed Mr Marvellous across the veranda to the sitting-room door he had closed so carefully behind him. 'The flower man is here,' he announced.

'Mr Marvellous, how nice. What dying blooms have you got for me today?' Gracie did not move from her chair, nor Suriya from her crouched position at Gracie's feet. It was Lila who had broken away from the triptych. She was standing at one of the windows, her hand on the shutter as if to close it, but she was motionless.

'I have gladioli, madam, marvellous blue ones.'

'You know I hate them.'

Mr Marvellous dropped his head to one side and smiled into his moustache. 'This may have been so, Gracie Madam, but how can I tell that you may not change your mind one of these fine days?'

'They remind me of death, something about the spiky petals.'

'We use them for our marriages too, is this not so? On my way back from the market this day there was a rickshaw, a poor man's wedding vehicle, but it was stuck all over with these blooms.' Mr Marvellous smiled.

'And what are we celebrating today that I should buy spiky, spiteful glads from you, Mr Marvellous – a death or a marriage?' Gracie tried to push herself up from her chair as she spoke but Suriya's closeness stopped her. She rearranged herself in her chair. 'Oh, come on now, why all the drama? No one in this room is dead. We have been in this situation a hundred times. Bring me your filthy glads, Mr Marvellous. Suriya, give me the key to the cupboard. Lila, please shut out some of that cold night.' She turned to Masood. 'Will you stay for some lotus root? It is Suriya's first lot this year from Lotus Valida, the old lotus garden girl has apparently declared the season open.' Gracie sat in the centre of her space with the other four hovering around her.

Mr Marvellous ran back out to the veranda to grab the flowers, Suriya wiped her nose on her sleeve as she fished around in her pockets, and Masood made his excuses about going back up to the house to tell his family the news. Lila still remained by the window.

'How will you get the details unless you wait for a bulletin from the *dunga* news-on-a-string?' Gracie reached out for Masood's arm as he made to leave.

'I have kept my small radio from the trekking days. I can still get BBC when it is needful,' he smiled.

'Smart boy, always a smart boy, and maybe watch Irfan a

bit, the rabble-rousers will be at the Jama Masjid tomorrow trying to whip all the boys into a frenzy. Perhaps you could just go to the mosque at the top of the road. All of you could go, your brothers and the boys too.' Gracie gripped Masood's hand as he tried again to extract himself.

He raised his free hand to his lips and closed his eyes as Mr Marvellous bustled back into the sitting room, the flowers dripping in his arms.

Gracie nodded. 'Thank you for coming to see me. Give Naseema my warmest greetings. She's a fine woman.' She held on to his arm. 'How long have you been married now?'

'Nineteen,' Masood replied flatly.

She let go of his hand. 'So many and you're both still young. You must celebrate.'

Masood looked down at the carpet.

'We could share a party next year, your twentieth anniversary and my eightieth birthday. Did you know I was going to be eighty next year?'

'How could we not know this?' Masood laughed as he climbed back out on to the running boards beyond the window next to Lila. 'There is a coup just beyond our border and you are thinking of parties?'

Gracie turned away from Masood. 'So, how much are you going to steal from me for this sad little collection?' she asked the flower man. Her voice followed Masood down the duckboard and out on to the wet grass.

He lifted his *pheran* higher than before. The grass was sodden now with layers of rain, evening dew, and the roll of twilight mist off Nagin. It drifted in a fine band over the surface of the meadow where Mr Marvellous and he had played so many games of cricket as boys and adolescents, fighting over who had been the better player between the captains of the Indian and Pakistani teams. Masood had always sided with Pakistan, while the flower-seller-to-be had usually wanted to be India's latest spin bowler. He stopped for a moment as he saw them both again as they had been.

He was slipping over the edges of his sandals as the leather softened in the wet. He would get his new shoes out soon. They would be better for the cold weather than these soft-soled camel-hide *jutees*. He had bought them in Delhi, sitting happily trying them on in the shop; four different kinds, all with varying swoops and swooshes, go-faster stripes, pumps up, vents down, all sorts of paraphernalia. To think that they all used to run around in Indian Army keds when they were boys, just thin slips of brown rippled rubber where now there was the promise of inner arch lift, a place on the Asian Games squad, and what all. He could just sit and drink *chai* and let them do it all for him.

He imagined them nestling in their box, wrapped in white paper, with tiny bags of silica to keep their marvels fresh and dry. He smiled at the thought of opening them up, at the idea of the clean orderliness of them.

Before opening the garden door he stopped. His mood was lighter than it had been when he had walked out through the heavy cosmos an hour or so earlier, and he had not even known about the coup then. He would have to compose himself to break the news to his family. Masood felt a pang of time passing. Playing cricket as a boy did not seem forty years ago. He turned the chinar leaf handle, clasped his hands behind his back, and walked up the path.

Chapter Two ~

The heartland of a mother and son lies in shapes of glass on a road, pieces that make a pattern where they have exploded on to the tarmac, a map of fragments. Gracie sees herself reflected in the shards, younger but broken too, below her is her boy, almost a man, shattered among the surfaces and viscous darkness on the road around.

She woke herself as her neck lolled against her shoulder.

The curtains across the doors to the veranda were still open. She could see herself, her image rippled by the flaws of the glass. She closed her eyes again. How had she got as old as this, so diminished and softened at the edges?

A pair of cold hands pressed down inside her and she began to cry in the same way as she had on an afternoon on the edge of the old city twenty-two years ago, more than a year after Jitu had died, when she had finally understood that she was a widow.

It has been just after people had stopped calling to see

how she was. In the dark gap that followed she had been faced by her husband every time she had closed her eyes, and by her son, Hari, her golden mango boy with his freckled ochre eyes and his kiss curl so perfectly independent that people had always tried to tidy it away, even when he had been a grown man.

Hari Singh had been killed in a car accident in 1972 when he was twenty-three. Gracie's dreams had kept his death current for twenty-seven years.

Irfan lay between his two brothers, his body rigid. The news of the coup in the evening had made his face hot and he had turned away from his mother's watching eyes as his uncle had told them. He thought again about Lila's neck as she had leaned over the washing. He did not dare masturbate. If Shabeer, his youngest brother, was awake he would tell the others in the morning. Shabeer was too young to understand. His other brother, Omar, was thirteen, only he understood. Irfan rolled on to his stomach, and tried to sleep.

His hands were crunched into his chest in tight fists as they used to be when he was a baby, when he used to push his mother, Faheema, away when she was trying to nurse him.

Gracie believed she had the right to tamper with the news. The only time she ordered a paper was when she felt she needed back-up information. She could not stop the World Service but she could contradict the stories that were causing Suriya to burn or over-spice the food.

As ammunition Gracie used what she believed to be the irreproachable resources of the *Indian Express*. It had been easy to establish that the broadsheet was beyond question because of its proprietor's bravery in standing up to Mrs Gandhi's broad-slash censorship during the State of Emergency, a period Gracie thought of as the darkest time in Indian history since Partition. Suriya had been easy to convince. She had never liked Mrs Gandhi, mainly due to the lacquered and daunting bouffant nature of her hair, something that Suriya felt reflected the true nature of the late prime minister, or at least her hairdresser. A person's hairdresser said a great deal about them in her view, though she had never been to one herself. She cut her own hair with a razor blade beside the lake. Gracie had taught her that split ends made the hair look dull.

The *Indian Express* arrived the afternoon after the news of the coup with the cabbages, chillies, tomatoes, and Irshad Butt, the vegetable-seller.

He pulled his flat-bottomed boat up to the edge of the *dunga* and nodded to Suriya. He was one of those who felt he hardly needed to speak to the mute woman. Like so many others he assumed that stupidity was a side-effect of silence.

'Where's Lila?' Irshad asked, and then cleared his throat into the lake.

Suriya waved her hand in a non-committal fashion. She did not like Irshad, his *topi*, his little prayer cap, was always dirty, and he spat too much. His mother had been worse. It was a family trait. His mother and she had tried to out-spit each other once when they were girls, running back from the bazaar and trying to launch spittle beyond the weeds on the edge of the canals coming out of town. Irshad's mother had won by lengths. Suriya missed some of what the son was saying as she remembered those two young girls beside the canal.

'. . . with her about new prices. It will be harder now with this.' He waved the *Indian Express* at Suriya.

She snatched the paper from him.

'Tell Lila that I need to speak to her about money.' He spat again as he pushed off from the cooking boat.

Suriya turned away. She looked at the picture on the front page of the paper and refolded it carefully underneath a plate of hot spinach and potato pakoras, smoothing out a large photograph of a man in Pakistani military uniform that took up most of the front page.

She sniffed at him even though his face seemed too approachable for a man who might upset the balance of their walled-in world. His centre parting looked funny to her, like a wicked Hindi *filmi* father, the predominantly evil kind with a thin line of moustache.

It was ten years since Hindi films had been shown at the Regal Cinema Hall where she and her brother had gone as teenagers. They used to throw puffed rice at the screen as those centre-parted demons had threatened to keep their daughters from their fine fleshy paramours who danced so vigorously among Swiss meadows, Kashmiri landscapes, and along acres of marble and chandeliers.

Suriya pushed his folded face further under the pakoras.

Gracie was not in the sitting room. Suriya put the tray on the table beside her chair and listened. There was no sound of movement above the familiar in-and-out breath of the boat in the water. She knocked on Gracie's bedroom door, pressing her head against the wood to listen. Gracie was neither in her bedroom nor her bathroom. Suriya stood in the corridor and thumped on the wall.

Gracie was predictable in her patterns. Four o'clock meant she would be in the sitting room waiting for tea.

Suriya thumped harder.

'I'm on the roof.' Gracie's voice came down over the edge of The Wonder House.

She had not been up on the roof for a long time. Suriya hitched up the front of her tunic and climbed the stairs.

Gracie had propped herself between the carved rail at the edge and one of the summer canopy struts. Suriya walked around in front of her so that she could look into her face. They stood face to face; Gracie stooped between her two supports, Suriya with her hands on her hips, posing her silent question.

'You weren't about when the post arrived. Farouk brought it when he came to collect Lila,' Gracie replied. 'My *Reader's Digest* came. Two weeks late the *Digest*, I've been waiting for the next part of that story for bloody weeks. That poor boy has been dangling off the edge of some ice-shelf since when? About the beginning of last month and where are we now?'

Suriya flicked her chin.

'It's getting to halfway into October, isn't it? Coup was the twelfth, wasn't it?' Gracie grabbed the strut to pull herself up. Suriya reached out and wrapped her arm around her back.

'I can manage.' But Gracie did not push the proffered hand away.

'When was the last coup?' Gracie asked.

Suriya held up her free hand to make the number with her fingers.

'1977, as I was moving in. How could I forget that?'

Suriya nodded.

'So what's this one a harbinger of then?'

Suriya puffed the edges of her nostrils.

Below them four children from the Elvis Presley house-boat further up the lake paddled past. Gracie called out to them and they waved in unison.

'Such nice manners those children, you know.' Gracie leaned her full weight back against the strut. 'Hari had such . . .' she drifted.

Suriya made a cup with her hand and pointed towards the stairs.

'Yes, I know, I smelt the pakoras but this bloody coup made it feel hard to breathe down there.' Gracie tried to push herself away from the strut but she could not. Suriya helped her.

'Where's Lila?' She began to make her way towards the stairs.

Suriya waved down the lake.

'Oh, tea-time, end of school, collecting the Abdullah girls, I suppose. I thought they might close the schools today. Perhaps they don't think it's that serious, as coups go. Let's have some tea now, perhaps I can manage pakoras too.' Gracie was unsteady on the first steps. 'Make sure you send Lila to me when she's back.' She paused. 'They're a good bunch those Elvis Presley children, such lovely manners.' She took the next couple of stairs. 'I have to go and get that boy off the ice-ledge now, about bloody time.' She stopped again, turning back to Suriya. 'Perhaps this will be a good coup, seems he might be a better man than Zia. That's a thought.'

Suriya waited for a moment on the roof.

Some of the summer cushions were still out, piled up at

one end under the washing line. She would get Lila to help her bring them down. Most of the wood needed revarnishing. The boy had done a bad job last time. There were blisters of varnish where he had not sanded old layers away properly. They would find someone different to do it this time.

The paddle of a boatman's oar was discernible to her even though it was still five houseboats further up the lake. She could see Lila and the two girls beyond the erect squat of Farouk, the Abdullahs' boatman. Raising her arm she waved to them. She could get Lila to help her with the cushions when she got back. Perhaps Farouk could come up as well if she gave him some tea and pakoras. The lock on the big storage trunk under the water tank was so hard to manage.

No response from Lila and the girls. Perhaps they had not seen her. Suriya stopped waving and watched the small boat for a while.

Lila had blurred her vision into a series of hazed concentric circles as they moved in silence through the water. She played with the unfixed images, ghosts of fading greens over the tops of the chinar trees, the stretched reflections of the houseboats, reaching out long and thin towards them. She focused again on a point of movement ahead of them. She could see her mother on the roof of The Wonder House, waving to them. Lila felt somehow ashamed and tried to distract the girls' attention.

'See the cockscomb-cutters are coming in.' She nudged Safoora and Zubeeda, Masood and Ibrahim's daughters, both seniors at the same school as the Elvis Presley houseboat children.

The girls turned to look without interest at the line of

people on the path beside the lake: three women, two men and a pack of children. Each of the adults carried baskets on their heads, piled high with Kashmiri cockscomb, its red velvet-topped stems staining the foreground. Lila saw that the girls were not interested. She searched beyond the baskets.

'They're exercising the horses from the palace, see, under the chinars.' Lila ducked to the eye level of the two girls so that they would follow the line of her finger.

She made up a story about the men who rode the horses, about how they rode with no hands, and could stand up on the horses' backs, even when they galloped. The girls looked on, still without interest. Lila glanced back at the distant roof and saw that her mother was no longer waving, just standing now, a small figure on a houseboat roof.

She felt ashamed and turned back to the horses.

Farouk sucked his cheeks in a way that made his old face seem to turn inside out, and spat into the lake.

Masood's back was aching even though he had been grinding his fists into it in the way Dr Hamid had shown him. He got up from his desk. He could try lying on his back, his knees pulled into his chest so that he could roll across the clenched muscles, another of Dr Hamid's suggestions, or he could go out on to the balcony and call for Naseema. It would be better to call Saqeena, his elder daughter, to bring a hot brick for him to sit against but she was at the Jama Masjid market with Irfan. It had been simpler to just send the boy with her than to try and stop her going. It would be good for him to have a sense of responsibility, to have to think about his older cousin.

He did not want to disturb Naseema. His wife would be resting before going back down to the kitchen again to begin the afternoon's cooking. He pushed the window open further and the smell of burning turmeric came in, softened by distance. It would be from The Wonder House *dunga*. Suriya cooked with *haldi* more than his wife and sisters-in-law.

Gracie had such a taste for hot *desi khanna*, home food. Naseema called it Hindu cooking. She would puff as she said it. Even she seemed to have forgotten how it had been before the insurgency, that time when there had been a constant exchange of food from Hindu to Muslim kitchens, house-to-house, undivided, the same spices simply applied in different ways. The Kashmiri Pandit and Muslim festival foods had marked the quarters of the years of his boyhood, Eid-ul-Fitr chasing the year ahead of or behind Diwali, tied together by the exchange of flavours. He could remember how the hot sweets used to feel in his hands, and how the syrup had burnt the palate of his mouth.

He liked those pakoras though. He wanted to show Gracie his new trainers. She would laugh at them and he could have pakoras and *chai* with her.

Masood smiled as he bent to lie down on the edge of the carpet. The muscles clamped tight around his lower spine and the pain stabbed down into his right buttock.

What did Dr Hamid know? Old fool would not have been able to get down on his own back for who knows how many years to try out his own worthless exercises.

Masood limped through the open window on to the balcony to call Naseema. It was getting cold. He should have shut the windows and then the cramping might not have started. He leaned on the rail to call out but stopped. Just the change of angle and the support of the rail eased his pain.

He could leave Naseema alone. It was satisfying, a moment of relief. He could sense his house around him and his family beneath him, the garden stretching away in front of him to the uneven line of trees.

He had planted the poplars inside the wall with his father Gulam when he was fifteen. Now they were as high as the roof gables. They shut out the fear.

There was always danger now. Masood could no longer remember what it had felt like not to sense its presence creeping across the lake from the city.

He closed his eyes and gripped the rail in search of something of the time before the troubles began: a night on the back of a houseboat with a Danish girl who had tasted of pineapple when he had kissed her. Another, an afternoon pelting his youngest brother Rafi with apples from the old tree against the wall in the orchard. The faces that triggered the images came and went but now all of them were curtained off by the pall of tension that hung around every action.

He could not think of a sura in the Koran, or an article of Sharia law that could help him in making sense of this generation of fear.

Perhaps the general across the border would not be as corrupt as some of his predecessors. The army liked him. That must a good thing. It could be that he was a man of discipline, a good Muslim.

Masood leaned further over the rail, pushing it into his belly to release his back. Someone was waving on the roof of The Wonder House. He could not see who it was, but he wondered what the figure was waving at, or to. He liked watching the intimacy of the gesture. He pushed himself up from the rail and nursed his hands into his lower back again. In the distance he saw the waving hand drop and the figure became isolated. He recognized Suriya's defeated posture.

Light came through gaps in the wooden flanks of the Jama Masjid, the Friday Mosque, on Ganderbal Road. The great hall was almost empty after prayer. Dust spun in the lattices of light among the pillars where there had been the recent rise and fall of the rows of the devoted. In one corner of the hall the muezzin was arguing with a mosque-sweeper about the amount of dirt that lay in a permanent grey sheen on the red carpets scattered among the pillars. His voice was padded down by the scale of the hall. Two soldiers sat on the stone threshold of the great mosque, their AK-47s across their laps. They were talking, one of them bouncing his foot off the wall, his toe hitting the words of a sign: 'Footwear Not To Proceed Beyond This Gate. Signed Secretary Irfaq', the same message in Kashmiri looped underneath. Beyond the two soldiers the quiet of the mosque courtyard ended where the rabble of the Friday market swelled up and over the gate.

There were more soldiers than usual behind the sandbags of the surrounding military posts, their rifle snouts combing the crowd, but no one had stayed away, the scrum was as thick as always.

Three women in full *burqas* at the ribbon stall pushed Irfan out of the way as they barged to get at a pile of sequined hairbands. As he lost his balance he was righted by the press of people from behind. Bowing his head, he folded his hands to an older woman whom he thought he might have fallen back against. She ignored him as she pushed past to reach for some unseen pretty. He ducked down into a squat and backed out of the ribbon-stall crush through the flock of black hems and leggings.

He could smell the women in layers, the most familiar being the claggy rankness of fresh sweat on old. The others were more subtle, more complicated. He could not identify them as he wove his way out through the bumping and nudging of legs all around him. They only separated themselves in his mind later in the stillness of his room as he listened to the breathing of his younger brothers in the night.

As he stood up again at the back of the crowd he was taller than most of the women, so he could still see his cousin Saqeena. She was pushed up against a trestle table at the front of the stall, her body half-bent over by the weight of the women behind her. She was bargaining for a length of pale yellow chiffon ribbon. Even from where he stood Irfan thought it was an ugly colour, the same as his youngest cousin Feroz's vomit had been with summer fever, but Saqeena obviously liked it enough to be crushed for it. He would not say anything.

If they could get through the afternoon without fighting they could walk back by the golf course, and maybe stop for an ice cream at the place near Broadway Hotel. He liked Jamoca Almond Fudge too much. If Saqeena could bargain with the ribbon-seller, and then get the cloth that Aunt Naseema needed for a good price, they would have enough left to get one each, maybe two scoops. He would back her up when it came to haggling for the cloth but, from his new position, he was not going to be able to fight his way back into the throng of flailing arms to help her in her quest for vomit ribbon.

'Irfan Abdullah, playing with the girls again.'

The sun was hard in his eyes. He could only see the silhouettes of two figures behind the railings of the mosque.

'I'm here to be with my cousin Saqeena. Who is asking?'

'Did you pray here, Irfan Abdullah?'

'Of course, it's Friday, why would I not?' Irfan still could not identify the speaker. If he moved he might lose sight of Saqeena. He checked again to see where she was.

Waving her ribbon around she was still pressed against the table.

'Who is it? I have the sun in my eyes, I can't see you,' he called out.

'Come over,' the voice called.

'My cousin is at this stall.' Irfan moved to try and get out of the glare of the sun. As he bent down out of the direct light he identified the voice. 'It's Sidi, isn't it?' he shouted back.

Sidi Saleem was the son of the dog-fighter, the same man whose prize brute Mr Marvellous, the flower man, was keen to back. Sidi had been two years above Irfan at school. He had never liked any of the Abdullah boys. He thought they were spoilt and rich. Once he had picked a fight with Irfan about nothing, a no-ball in a game of cricket. The other boys had cheered when the fight had started, but there had been silence as Sidi had pinned Irfan into the dust on his belly, sitting astride him and grinding his face into the dirt until Irfan's cheeks and lips had bled and the skin had been grated off one side of his nose. Irfan had made his brothers and cousins promise not to tell the truth about the fight. The boys had told their fathers that Irfan had fallen from a tree while trying to pick the first of the walnuts for his mother, Faheema. Irfan had still been beaten.

'It is Sidi, come.'

Irfan looked for Saqeena. She was now arguing with the ribbon-seller. It gave him perhaps a minute. He crossed to the railings and stood directly opposite Sidi, looking straight at him with the confidence of a small dog facing a larger one through a solid fence.

'We have a meeting here tomorrow afternoon, the house behind the mosque with the blue window. You will come.'

Irfan remembered the smell of Sidi's breath from their fight, bile and bad digestion. He started to move back from the railing but Sidi reached through and grabbed his collar. Irfan could feel the material biting into the back of his neck as Sidi pulled, but his attention was held by a shawl on a windowsill in his eye line. It was the colour his mother loved, a washed-through blue, and it moved on the afternoon air, swelling, subsiding and filling again.

Sidi relaxed his hand a little but he did not let go. 'It's time for you to leave the girls and become a Kashmiri.' His voice had changed, and was now smooth with self-confidence.

'What time should I come?' Irfan asked. It sounded to him as though someone else had asked the question.

'Five o'clock and if you are not here I will send someone for you, or perhaps I will come.' Sidi pulled tighter again. 'You even smell like a girl.' He forced Irfan's face against the railings and then let go.

Irfan turned slowly back to the crowd, feeling as though he too was the shawl on the sill, fluid and disembodied. Sidi Saleem presented no threat to him as he moved with this sense of weightlessness through the mass of bodies that he had first crawled through. He felt untouchable as he looked around for his cousin. When he looked back to the railings Sidi was watching him with the same confidence that had been in his voice.

Saqeena was waiting for him beyond the main hum of the ribbon crowd, her arms crossed, her prize already somewhere in the folds of her *burqa*.

They walked to the material shop on Ansari Marg in silence. It was as they waited for the lengths to be folded and packed that fear began to crawl up on Irfan. He felt the muscles on either side of his neck tightening where his collar had cut into the skin as he had been pulled through the railings.

He did not suggest going via the golf course or to the ice-cream shop, even though they had enough spare change. They walked back to Nagin by the shortest route below Hari Parbat Fort.

Later in the darkness, lying between his brothers, Irfan remembered the smell of Sidi's breath again, and he wondered how he would be able to leave the house and reach the meeting without being seen. It made him sweat. Closing his eyes he escaped into the other layers of human scent in the crush at the ribbon stall. One was musk, rubbed on by some of the devout before their Friday prayers, warm and sacred, a safe smell. There had been spices layered into fresh sweat, cardamom, turmeric and chilli inhaled by skin as the women cooked. He could not identify the one underneath all of those that had made him think about them again. He tried to find a sea he had never seen, the touch of oil on dry skin, and he saw Lila's wet forearm again as she washed. She did not smell like that. She smelt of the smoke of the *dunga* kitchen and of star anise. Irfan lay rigid in the dark between the breath of his brothers.

Naseema, Masood's wife, was alone in the kitchen in the afternoon lull of the following day. That was rare. To be there in the quiet was a chance for her to feel wholly in control of her household among the trays of sorted rice, sifted dhal, the mounds of carefully chopped onions, garlic, peppers, potatoes and okra. She stood very still and inhaled the recently ground spices in the air, the sharper edge of chilli against the green-scented flavour of cut vegetables. She always deseeded the chillies herself before cutting them as fine as grass. She had been doing it since she had been a young bride of eighteen years, a little less than half her lifetime.

It was not even her job any more. She was the senior daughter-in-law now. It was the newest bride into the family who was supposed to cry over the stripped chillies, but Naseema did not trust Kudji, Rafi's wife, the junior of the three Abdullah wives. She could be so slovenly. Naseema liked that English word; it felt round in her mouth as she used it, soft and hard.

She had told Kudji that morning that she was being slovenly about her rice-sorting. There had been a small pile of stones and grit beside her hunched body as she had sifted through layers of rice on a white sheet, spread out on the grass outside the front of the kitchen in the clean morning sun. The grain had been running through her fingers, the grit dropping first to be picked out and piled up away from the good clean rice. Naseema had watched the bits of dirt that Kudji had missed as she hummed absently

to herself. Naseema had used the word and Kudji had
looked up at her gratefully with her great big cow eyes that
could look so beautiful and so stupid. She had accepted the
word, dropped into her sister-in-law's flow of Kashmiri, as a
gift. Naseema had a tone that made even her insults seem
complimentary.

Naseema looked at the rice now in the paler light of the
late afternoon. Of course the girl had no idea what the
word 'slovenly' meant. Naseema was not sure herself. Lila
had used it about a woman in the bazaar who sat in a
corner of the Friday Market in clothes that were always
damp and dirty. Naseema collected the English words that
Lila scattered through her language, words that she in turn
had collected from Gracie and the books she read. Naseema
could not imagine how someone could be so interested in
reading.

The quiet time would be over soon. The younger children
of the house would wander down to the kitchen in search of
food. She had a few more moments to admire the com-
pleteness, the sense of order, among the small mounds of
production around her. She bent down to pick some of the
remaining bits of grit from Kudji's heaped rice.

Irfan edged along the low wall outside the kitchen. He could
feel the sweat at the base of his spine even though the
afternoon was already getting cold. He knew that there was
just one slice of time to pass by the kitchen windows, to get
to the back wall of the courtyard while there was no one to
see him go. It was that same moment of stillness in the late
afternoon before the whole household woke up again, when
his youngest cousin Feroz would make his punctual way

down the stairs to ask for something sweet, his hair in damp tufts from his afternoon dreams.

Irfan clung to the corner of the window as he balanced on the wall. He rolled his face around the frame to see in without being seen. Shanks of light divided the room. It seemed to him that all the sections of light and shade were empty.

He straightened up, jumped off the wall and ran across the courtyard, pulling himself up easily into the lower branches of the walnut tree. As he scrambled for the top of the wall his right foot jammed into the fork of his balancing branch. He yanked it away hard and cried out as he landed. He had ripped the bottom of his trainer away from the sole and the muscles around his ankle shot pain up his leg as he tried to run.

The risk felt pathetic, child-like, and now painful. He stopped as he reached the road.

Why would Sidi come to the house if he did not turn up to the meeting? His uncles and his father looked down on Sidi and his father, the dog-fighter, and Sidi knew that. He carried his contempt for them like a shrivelled talisman. He had held on to the time before the beards when a couple of the Abdullah brothers used to go to his house and put bets down with Sidi's father. One of them had been Irfan's father. Sidi remembered and so did Irfan. It had been what their fight at school had been about, not a no-ball in a game of cricket.

He kicked at stones in the road with his good foot and tested the bad one. If he rolled on to the edge of his instep and jutted his left hip out he could manage a slow swaying jog. He limped on. If he could get there as it started then he could leave quickly, once Sidi had seen him. They would not even notice at home. He wanted to hear Sidi for a while, just the beginning, to see what he said.

Naseema looked up from the rice at an animal sound in the courtyard. She bent out of the sunlight and saw a pair of legs hoisting up over the wall from the walnut tree. She pulled at the window to open it, to call out, but it stuck. She was about to bang against the glass but stopped. It was Irfan. She recognized his *kurta*.

She stood by the jammed window, plucking at her lower lip, wondering whether to call for Masood. As she turned to step back over the rice she was almost knocked over by Feroz, her six-year-old nephew, grinding one of his fists into his eyes, the other held out to her for food. She had not noticed him.

'Why did Irfan go up the wall?' he asked, plucking at her tunic.

'He has gone to do something for me.' The lie came easily.

'But why did he have to go over the wall?'

'Because it is quicker that way,' she snapped, realizing her lie meant that she could not go and call Masood.

Feroz dropped her *kameez* and stared at her.

'Come, today we will have special honey, the honey man brought it down from the cloud mountains while you were sleeping.' Her voice was soft again.

'Where are they?' Feroz grabbed her again as she crossed the kitchen.

'As high up as you can go, where the lake spirits live now.' She reached up and took one of the small, flat, round loaves from the basket that hung over the stove.

Feroz only let go of her as she began to drip honey from the new pot on to the bread. He reached up to break the sweet thread. For a moment he was involved, laughing as the honey fell on to and over his finger, and down on to the bread. Then he pulled his hand away and licked his finger.

'But why would Irfan be faster to go over the wall when the gate is beside the tree?'

'I asked him to test the tree, the branch might be good for hanging things from.'

'What things?'

'This will have to be a surprise for you.' She passed the bread and honey to him. 'Here, take it.'

'When will Irfan come back?'

'Soon, he will be back soon.' Naseema turned away, unable to lie to the boy's open face any longer.

Would she have lied if Irfan was her own son, would she have tried harder to stop him, calling Masood, running out into the courtyard after the boy?

She reached up to untie and retie her scarf. 'Go and find your mother. I need her help,' she asked without turning to look at Feroz.

He seemed surprised, swallowing his mouthful like a dog and looking up at his aunt. Naseema shooed him out.

Suriya missed the news on the World Service on 13 October because Gracie knocked her teacup off the small table beside her chair. She did so just at the very sacred instant that Suriya was assembling her spices. She did not immediately call for help, trying instead to pick up the shattered cup herself, and then cutting the palm of her hand on one of the broken shards. Her cry as she cut herself was loud enough to carry

clearly over the familiar tune that Suriya had turned up to
hear over the pounding of her pestle. It took her almost an
hour to clean up both the china and Gracie, and then to
settle her back in her chair. The news had long gone by the
time she went back to the kitchen. It did not cross her mind
to listen to a later bulletin. She never had.

Gracie had fallen asleep again when she went back to
collect the second pot of *chai* that she had taken to her. She
thought to wake her but her hand stopped just before
touching Gracie's shoulder.

She watched as the sleeping woman's breath stuttered in
and out over her bottom lip. If she slept through until supper
then perhaps she would eat, perhaps Suriya would not have
to hand over the cupboard key. She had hardly eaten the
night before, wasting so much of the first of the lotus root,
but it had been a black evening. Now there were special
masalas for the evening, soft pungent ones that would chase
away the sadness that was filling the air from across the
border and across the lake.

Suriya left the sitting room almost silently.

Gracie is standing at a window within the mute frame that
she has inhabited so many times. The moon is reflected on
the grass, though it cannot be. Grass is not glass or water, but
the moon floats between the squares of dark and light that it
makes on the lawn of a Delhi garden that she knows but
does not own. They are coming at her as they always do –
three men, two tall, one somewhere in between, their
shadows thrown behind them by the moon. She is in both
places, up and down, at the window above and on the lawn
too, just at the edge of one of the squares made by the moon.

They move towards her on the lawn while she looks down on them from the window as well. Their mouths move but there are no words. She knows they are telling her about a water buffalo and broken bodies and glass on tarmac.

Now she hovers over the tarmac scene on frantic humming-bird wings. The water buffalo has deflated, its skin draped over its haunches, peeled open in parts, its blood black on the white road, its legs west and east, southeast and southwest, unconnected. A single shoe is there, lying on its side, empty. It is not a shoe just as the moon was not reflected in the grass, nor the buffalo's legs compass points. They are all her, just as the shoe is Hari, empty in the road. When she wakes she will have to sit still for a while to pull the present in from the past so that her body does not automatically go into a spasm.

She kept the newspaper clipping of the accident, folded away in a copy of the Bible that her aunt and uncle sent to her when she married Jitu. The words down the crease of the article have worn away.

New Delhi, 7 Feb: A spee   ng jeep lost the road
at the Khelgaon Corner i   he early hours. There
were no survivors when it   ollided with the cart
of farmer Dan Singh, 46.   expired later as a result
of injuries sustained with   s elder son Prabhu Singh,
16, second son Rampul S   h, 12. His wife, the water
buffalo and two daughter   were killed too. The driver
of the jeep, Hari Singh, 2   Simla, son of Raj Kumar
and Raj Kumari Jitendra S   gh of Firozpur. The father
of the deceased is the ses   ns judge at the high court
in Simla. Hari Singh was th   nly son.

It had been reported in that order, the farmer, his sons, his wife, his buffalo and his daughters. Hari had been given a section of his own. The girl who had been in the car with him had not been mentioned in the report. She had survived anonymously. The police had been well paid by her family to remove her name from the accident report before it had been filed.

Chapter Three ~

Next to the bank a pair of dragonflies fretted the water beside Lila's hands as she rinsed Gracie's clothes. The distance between the pair seemed fixed, like magnets repelled to just such a point. Then the male broke through the field as they hung over a small patch of Lila's suds. She stared as he entered the female, holding her static and throbbing.

Lila wiped her nose, admiring the silence of the pretty penetration.

'Lila!' Masood was standing a few feet away from her at the edge of the duckboard that ran from the *dunga* to her washing place. She had not heard him, and he was now looking directly at her.

'Yes *ji*?' she hoped that he had not seen her watching the dragonflies.

'Where is Gracie Madam?' Masood stared past her as he spoke.

He tried not to look at her. She was Suriya as she had

been at Lila's age, fine-boned but strong, with the same sliding curve at the base of her throat. It agitated him.

'Isn't she in the sitting room? She was there for tea.'

'I have just been there. She was not.' He stepped up on to the duckboard and then off again. 'You must find her for me now.' He had moved his focus to the edge of the plank in front of him.

'Did you call for her?' Lila asked.

'Did I call for her?' He seemed confused.

'I didn't hear you calling for her. I will go and try.'

He looked grateful. Lila began to gather up the washing around her.

'This can be done later.' He came up the duckboard and began to pull the washing out of her hands.

She grabbed it back from him and one of Gracie's nightdresses fell into the wet dirt beside the bucket. Masood turned away, one hand in the air, his upper body slumped forward as though to defend himself. He looked smaller than usual, bent over and slight. Lila followed him down the duckboard, the washing left where it had fallen.

Gracie was making her way down the passage from her bedroom to the sitting room, singing 'My Man's Gone Now' from Porgy and Bess, one of her regular lavatory tunes. She bent over her cardigan as she buttoned it, bumping gently off the corridor walls as she concentrated. Masood and Lila were standing at the side entrance into the hall, but she did not see them. Lila stepped back as she approached so that she was presented with Masood, face to face. He had to put his hand up to stop her, pulling his fingers just short of making contact with her bosom.

She sucked in air. 'God, you're like a lurking criminal.

Why all the creeping about?' She stepped back into the wall behind her.

'You have misdirected a button.' Masood waved the same hand that had stopped her in the direction of her cardigan.

'Oh, doesn't matter, who's going to notice? And you try doing it with one mangy hand.' She waved her bandaged palm at him. 'Anyway it's supposed to be lucky, isn't it?'

'To cut your hand?' he asked without smiling.

'You look cross, should I unbutton and start again? Lila, is that you skulking back there as well?'

'Just waiting to come in and close up the sitting room, not skulking.' Lila pushed her head around the side of Masood. He took another step forward so that there would be no contact.

'Get me the key to the cupboard and some Thing, would you?' Gracie did not look at Lila. 'It's a rather wonderful evening, you know, the bulbul chicks by the old kennel are trying to fly. I can see them from my bathroom window, all flap and no fly. They're terrible. Mad George would have barked them out the nest weeks ago if he was still here, poor old sod.'

Gracie had named the dogs she had owned in India in rotation after her brothers George and Arthur. It had been confusing to everyone but her. Mad George had been the third of the Georges.

Gracie paused. She was watching Masood. 'You're still looking at my buttons, do they distress you or are you flirting with me, Masood Abdullah?'

He looked up, finally, but it was almost as a delayed reaction.

She peered at him. 'Come with me, come and join me for

a while.' Her tone was gentle and questioning as she set off down the corridor, past the pantry, and through the dining room to the sitting room. 'Do you remember when we cremated Mad George and you argued that he should be buried?' she called back over her shoulder.

Masood nodded to Gracie's back.

'Probably the only religious argument we ever really had, still can't remember why you decided Mad George should be Muslim.' Gracie stopped by her chair and turned back to Masood. 'He never kept a day of Ramadan in his life.' She smiled and sat down hard.

Masood stopped just inside the sitting room and Lila waited behind him.

'Lila, Thing and the key please,' Gracie asked again without looking up from her chair.

Lila turned to leave.

'When he was a young dog you said he was a Muslim because he was too proud to be a Hindu and too rude to be a Christian,' Masood said.

'Puppy,' Gracie corrected.

'It is getting dark, what time is it?' Masood's expression was fixed.

'Probably just after seven, why?'

'He has been gone more than four hours now,' Masood spoke quietly.

'I can't hear you, who's gone?' Gracie leaned towards him.

'Irfan has gone.' He stared at shifting, unfocused water beyond the window.

'Gone where?'

Masood turned to look directly at her. 'Why do you ask me where? If I knew this don't you think I would be there to find him?' He pushed his palms into his eyes.

Gracie reached out and patted the air in front of him. 'When did he leave? Do you know when he left?'

'More than four hours ago. I have told you this.' He kept his hands pressed into his sockets. 'Naseema saw him climbing over the wall from the kitchen side but she waited so many hours to tell me.'

'Why did he climb the wall? What's wrong with the gate?'

'Nothing wrong but sometimes it is locked in the afternoon when most of the house is sleeping. That was the time he left. He would have known it was most likely to be locked.'

'Perhaps he went to town for something, sneaked out. You've been quite restrictive on them since the latest fuss, haven't you?' Gracie plucked at a loose thread on her sleeve.

'He went yesterday only with my Saqeena. I have not stopped him. Would you climb a wall if you only had to ask?'

'Maybe for fun I would, just to prove I could. How hard is it to climb that wall? Would you have done it at his age, just for fun?'

'That is there but Irfan is more fearful than I was at his age.'

'So, what are you hoping I might say?'

'I am not asking this for you to say something that I want to hear. I have come to share this weight in my heart with you that I cannot show to my family, as I have shared with you for so many years.' He waved his hand towards the direction of the house, his language fracturing with his anxiety. 'For them I have to have all the answers for all the questions. If I ask questions to them they think I am weak, that I am not strong enough to be the head of the family with the blessing of my father. With you this is not so. You do not ask for answers.' He took his hands away from his eyes and looked at Gracie. 'Please do not ask this now.' In the silence his breath pressed up into her collarbones.

There were footsteps on the duckboards. Lila was at the window. She stayed outside the room, balanced on the running board.

'Even in this light you can see how the whole boat is beginning to peel. We should have it done again before the winter. See, it's a great snake shedding its skin up and down its whole length.'

'Ecdysis is an expensive habit,' Gracie waved her into the room.

Lila and Masood stared at her from inside and outside.

'The shedding of skin − word of the day. The Wonder House is an ecdysiast.' She stopped and looked from one to the other. 'Though it can also mean a striptease artist.'

Lila moved to step in.

'I was taking my leave,' Masood said as she crossed the sill into the room.

'You were not.' Gracie reached out to him again.

Lila put a small jug of lime juice and tonic water on the desk and the key on top of the cupboard.

Masood lifted his head half towards her. The fine hair on her forearms was hardly there, so much paler than the thick stuff on Naseema's arms.

'I must go back to the family now.' He turned away from her.

'Stay a little longer, we've hardly talked,' Gracie said.

He waited until Lila left. 'A few minutes more, just two, three.'

'Well, please sit for just two, three then.' Gracie waved at the sofa beside her chair. 'I've got a few pegs of whisky in the cupboard, just in case.'

'In case of what?' he asked.

'Something like this when a little softener would be no bad thing, and certainly not an offence to Allah.'

'So I will go back to my family with my breath all smelling of whisky and demand that they respect my wishes?'

'Something like that.' Gracie levered herself up out of her chair with her good hand. 'Won't push you. I'll pour my own as only a lady in such circumstances is forced to do.'

He watched her as she went to the cupboard, her actions so familiar, the key to the lock, the bottle, cap, pouring and recapping, the flow of movement only marginally stilted by one-handedness. She did not put the bottle back in the cupboard or shut the door.

'I would take a peg if I did not have to go back to the house so soon. I am not so much of a hypocrite as to say never-never after how many years of enjoying so much of whisky? But I am not strong enough to defend the accusations they will have in their eyes.'

Gracie made her way to the desk and added lime and tonic to her gin. She turned and lifted her glass to Masood. 'To my fine friend, the reformed lover of whisky.'

Masood watched her neck as she swallowed, how her skin fell away on either side of the movement in her throat like the lizards' backs as they puffed in and out on hot rocks in the garden through the summer. 'Now I must go because I cannot stay.'

Gracie did not try to stop him. She saluted him with her

glass as he made to leave. 'It's only four hours, he'll be back when he's hungry.'

'He's not a dog,' he replied as he climbed out through the sliding sitting room window.

'All children are part-dog,' Gracie called after him.

He did not think about Irfan as he walked away and crossed the meadow towards his garden. The dilapidated Gracie depressed him. She had seemed young and strong when he had first seen her in his father's study, even though most adults had looked old to him then. He did not want to feel that he was getting old yet; maybe today, maybe this was understandable, but not all the time.

As he opened the gate to the garden he saw Irfan's mother at one of the upstairs windows, watching, waiting. Masood tripped on the corner of one of the stone slabs of the path as he looked up at Faheema, almost falling and staggering to right himself. He heard his youngest niece's laughter from near the side door. He shouted at her. The sound of his anger stopped him. The younger children did not even know that Irfan was missing. Masood never shouted at them. He pressed his palms into his eyes again, and stood in the cold, waiting for breath.

Lila waited until Masood had gone before she went back to the sitting room. As she took off her shoes outside the pantry Mr Marvellous, the flower man, was sliding between the back of The Wonder House and the *dunga* boat, his *shikara* low in the water with the weight of unsold flowers. He whistled her over and lifted a bunch of zinnias to her. Some of their pollen stayed on her nose. She waved him to be silent and he flapped his hand back to her, imitating her, his face screwed tight, his lips pursed. She laughed and it sounded too loud. She pointed towards the sitting room. Mr Marvellous tilted his head in reply. He knew that Gracie was there, that was why he had come with his unsold flowers at the time of the cupboard key.

'What's so funny?' Gracie called from the sitting room.

'Mr Marvellous is here,' Lila replied.

'That's not funny.'

'Will you see him?' Lila asked.

'Not if he's going to flog me filthy glads. What else is there?'

Lila looked down into his boat. Cosmos pressed against the deep red velvet frills of Kashmiri cockscomb. Four buckets of gladioli and one bucket of roses, the petals creamy with darker tips, as though just dipped.

'Roses,' Lila called.

'Good, tell him to bring his roses as long as they're cheap.'

Lila looked at Mr Marvellous. He scooped the roses from the bucket.

'No dripping on the carpets,' she said.

He put them back into the bucket and lifted the whole thing, following behind Lila through the dining room, checking behind him to see that the bucket was not dripping.

'Mr Marvellous, roses for a change.' Gracie was standing by the desk as she had been since Masood left, her glass still in her hand.

He looked at her, at the glass, and he lifted the bucket up to her so that she could see the roses. Lila went to close the curtains. He watched her move and Gracie watched him. He caught Gracie's eye and changed his mind about the price, asking for less than he had meant to.

'They're pretty, you should get more of these,' she said, waving the bucket towards Lila.

'Very hard to find, Gracie Madam, most unusual and very expensive.' He held the bucket out to Lila.

'So I see.' Gracie took one from the bunch as he passed them to Lila. 'Very elegant, not the usual fare. I'll pay you next time, my money's all locked away for the night.'

'Just some small small thing, just for good luck,' Mr Marvellous asked.

Gracie held the rose carefully between the thumb and finger of her bandaged hand.

'You are hurt?' he asked.

'Only by old age.' Gracie called to Lila who was taking the roses to the pantry. 'There might be some in the jug on the shelf, Lila.'

She and the flower man stood opposite each other, neither one looking at the other. Gracie watched his feet as they shifted between the woven lotus buds in the carpet. The nail beds seemed to have squeezed the toes out so that they reminded her of chameleons with their bulbed grips. Staring at his feet on the corners of the pale pink carpet buds she willed them to change colour so that even the dirt under his nails might go pink too. She smiled, for once enjoying her obscure mind-routing. Mr Marvellous took it to be a shared smile and he returned it as he heard Lila coming back from the pantry.

'Won't be much if there is any, couple of fives if you're lucky.'

'Anything is good luck,' he looked at the rose she held. It was dripping on to the carpet so he put his hand under the stem to catch the drops, turning so that Lila would see him.

He left as soon as she had passed two five-rupee notes to Gracie, and she had passed them on to him.

Gracie was still standing by the desk, her glass still in one hand and the single stem in the other, when Lila came back again with the roses in a blue jug.

'They are unusual, aren't they?' she said as Lila put them on the desk beside her.

'They are.' Lila stood back from the desk as though she was looking at them for the first time, her head to one side. 'Yes, unusual.'

'They all watch you. They're frightened of you. He was catching the drips off this to ingratiate himself.' Gracie handed the stem she held to Lila.

'That's not true. It was to please you.' Lila took the rose, bit the end off the stem and crushed the new tip between her back teeth. She put the flower into the middle of the jug with the others where it stood out, a little taller. She reached to take it out again but Gracie stopped her.

'Let it be. Sit down for a moment.'

Lila helped her to her chair and sat on the arm beside her.

Gracie put her glass down and took Lila's hand. 'Be careful with them, they don't know how to be with you.' She turned her head towards the vase. 'They will all want to take you out, bite a bit off to make you the same length as the others.' She squeezed Lila's hand. 'I've made you into something they want but don't understand.'

Lila pulled her hand away gently. 'What time would you like to eat?'

'When it suits.'

Lila nodded and left. She could feel the heat in her face as she ran back to the kitchen along the duckboards. Her mother's quiet rhythm over the kerosene stoves meant that she could slide in among the shadows and shapes of pans and jars in the blue flicker. The radio was off, the news finished. Suriya's face was passive and loose, her expression suggesting that there had been no further developments from the new military order in Islamabad.

'She is sad, it would be good to have the food ready before too long,' Lila stood above her mother.

Suriya looked up, her eyelashes tipped with flour. Lila laughed and reached down, pressing the top of her back with her thumbs. The little woman closed her eyes and dropped her head forward at her daughter's touch. The two tongues of hair that came up on either side of the nape of her neck were almost completely grey, and her upper vertebrae strained against the skin. Suriya was forty-two but there was already the fragility of age about her. It shocked Lila. She stopped pressing so hard, her fingers simply stroking her mother's shoulders. Suriya reached up and held her hand for a moment.

Gracie ate with her fingers using a scoop of warm *kulcha* bread as her spoon. The power was low and the light fell as lace on the table around her through the carved screens between the sitting room and the dining room. Lila had made her napkin into a swan. It arched in from her side plate, swimming on the patterned light.

She had learned swans, tulips and pagoda napkins from the houseboat boys in the hotel-chain houseboats at the top of Nagin. There had been a lot of time to teach napkin-folding since the tourists had stopped coming.

Gracie looked down at her hand covered in curd and age

spots. It looked foreign to her, someone else's hand with a wedding ring on the little finger because arthritis in the left one had swollen the joints, pushing up a map of veins that made her hide it in her lap whenever she remembered to.

Jitu would be so shocked to see her wedding ring on her right hand, and covered in curd. His hands had been long and fine, wet otter skin, elegantly fitted, carefully hung.

Those long fingers of his – the first time she had noticed them had been in the instant that they had met. A day in May when he had been sitting in a high-backed chair, his clothes draped on him, his hand arranged on his knee. She had never met an Indian before. He was dark but not as dark as she had expected. She had not been able to stop staring at his hand on his knee as they had been introduced. Jitu had thought she was being English, demure and shy. Gracie had wanted to lick his skin, to see if it tasted different.

When, two weeks later, they had gone in a taxi to Woodstock, with a friend of his and a friend of hers for appearances, she had sat behind him, her hand on the back of his seat to stop her pressing against his friend. Tariq had been a socialist from Lahore whose breath had smelt of cloves and bad temper. Jitu had turned to tell Tariq about the Capability Brown grounds at Blenheim Palace, an edge of show-off arrogance in his voice. As he had turned back again he had seen Gracie's hand on the back of his seat and he had leaned gently against her fingers. The edge of his shoulder blade had been like a hot tongue on her skin.

Gracie sniffed.

Strange to have experienced erotica on the Woodstock Road, probably the first time we touched, or did we shake hands when we met?

She could not remember. Odd to remember Tariq's name and his breath but not to know whether Jitu and she had shaken hands when they had first met. Tariq must be dead by now too.

She looked down at her hand again. This was not willing Mr Marvellous's feet to change to pink on the lotus buds, this was the variety of wandering dialogue that made her sad.

In the quiet she made her way to her room, guiding herself along the wall in the weak light. She sat down on the end of her bed and did not move, her hands braced on her knees, her shoulders hunched, her eyes squeezed shut. She said his name, just once, and then lay down on her bed, curled up on her side like a little girl.

He had not expected it to be a bus, at least not a local bus. They had flagged it down on the road to Sonamarg. Sidi Saleem had just stepped out into its path with enough determination to send the driver off the road as he swerved. It had been done with the same bullying conviction that he had used at the meeting when they had all raised their hands as he had challenged them to be men.

Irfan had been standing at the edge of the crowd, five or six deep away from Sidi, though it had still felt that the whole speech had been shouted just to him, every vowel spat into his face, but he had missed some of it as he had tried to keep his balance when two other boys started to fight behind him. He had been distracted by their shoving at the moment when Sidi had called them to take up arms, to cross the Line of Control, to become men. Irfan had moved as part of the crowd, simply doing the same thing, raising his hand with the others because his uncle had made him ashamed, because he wanted to have sex with his tainted but beautiful cousin, and because anger presented itself as a virtue in a place where, in the shape of his future, he could see no exit from the shuttered-in conflict. To leave was obvious. The taste of blood in his mouth had made it seem the right thing to do. He too would be a soldier of Allah.

But the bus had been a surprise.

There were four of them crushed into two seats over one of the front wheels, and because they did not know one another they were acutely aware of each other's smell. Irfan was beside the window, his nose turned towards the dirty glass, vibrating on the smears of his own skin as the bus bounced. The boy next to him had started eating *chana jor*, flattened fried chickpeas, while they had been waiting for the bus, throwing the pieces up into the air and trying to catch them in his mouth, his lower lip jutting out as he shuffled with bent knees to line up for the catch, his hands reaching out behind, his fingers spread wide. Irfan had watched him from the end of the line of waiting boys by the side of the road.

He was hungry now and the boy beside him had moved from *chana jor* on to dried apricots. Irfan did not want to ask for any and the boy did not offer.

He wished he had planned for this. There was always food in the kitchen, bread in the basket above the stove, and biscuits in jars, freshly made on Tuesdays and Thursday by his mother or one of his aunts. He could have taken supplies while everyone in the house had slept. He could have brought more money than the 108 rupees that he had in his wallet. There had been so many chances on the way to the meeting to have stopped for dried fruit, walnuts, cashews, *chicki*, the jaw-locking peanut brittle that he loved, anything, but he had not known, so how could he have planned? There were so many other things that he would have thought about bringing: his knife, a shawl, his notebook, the pictures he had drawn of his sisters that he had pinned to the wall by his bed, the one of Lila that he had in his copy of the Koran, folded so small, so sacrilegiously neat and forbidden between the suras. His head cracked against the window again as they hit another pothole.

The boy beside him was reaching across to the window. As Irfan realized what was happening it was too late for him to move. The boy grabbed his shoulder while Irfan tried to struggle away as partially digested *chana jor* and dried apricot splattered his chest and lap. He stared down at himself, looking at the stranger's vomit with a mixture of surprise and disgust. The boy had managed to reach across to the window, forcing it further open, his heaving body pressed against Irfan, his sick splatting against the glass beside Irfan's face, and flying back down to the other windows, some closed, some open.

Irfan was pinned down. Through the sliding particles of food he could see the walnut orchards where he and some of his male cousins had earned their first money picking and shelling until their fingers had been stained black, and their muscles had tied up. Lila had made them samosas, potato ones, speckled with smoky cumin. She had left them on the steps of the kitchen with a note saying that they were for the walnut-pickers.

The smell and the weight of the other boy on his chest made Irfan feel sick as well, though he willed himself not to retch.

This was how they were travelling to be soldiers of Allah — jammed together for hundreds of miles in each other's filth. It was not what he had envisaged as he had jumped up from the kitchen yard.

He turned his head further towards the window and traced the outline of one of the walnut trees in the dirt on the glass.

Lila was waiting at Dal Gate, a small sack of rice between her feet. She was being watched by a group of boys sitting on the bakery steps across the road. They leaned across to each other, looking out at Lila, and then huddling back together again. Four off-duty policemen stared from another angle inside the *chai* stall next to the bakery. She looked down at the water beyond the tips of her shoes and willed Gulshan to come.

When Farouk, the old boatman, had no time beyond his work for the Abdullahs, Gulshan was stand-in boatman for The Wonder House. He was twenty-one and he wore his *topi* on the very back of his head, more Hassidic than Muslim, and his curly hair kept it there. He liked to have his *kurta* overshirt shorter than most men, and his trousers a little longer, so that they almost covered his feet. He was conscious of how they spread and of how his toes had splayed because he walked barefoot most of the time, right up to the edge of the winter freeze. Sandals and shoes made him feel trapped.

He had known Lila for as long as he had known anyone. She was the first girl he could remember who had not been a member of his family. Suriya had been the first mute that he had met.

When he reached Lila, she snapped at him.

'Where were you?'

He slid his *shikara* on to the steps below where she stood.

'I was waving as I came across.' He was surprised by her tone. He was not late. He was never late for Lila.

'Come, we have to go.' She bent to pick up the rice.

Gulshan reached into his *pheran*. 'Gracie Madam asked your mother for these things.' He handed a piece of paper to Lila.

Lila bumped the rice into the boat and sat down. 'Come on, we're leaving.'

'But this list?' He held the boat on the step.

Lila took it from him. 'She wants macaroons. It's Monday, they will only have the stale ones from last week.' She crumpled the paper.

Gulshan pushed away reluctantly from the ghat steps. It was not until they were further out that he saw the staring groups on the bakery steps and in the *chai* stall. He bent over his paddle and pulled them hard across the neck of the lake, and back towards the lotus gardens.

They moved in silence across Nagin, time that felt stretched and empty to Gulshan, but quiet to Lila. To her they eased through each point where their shadow had just been on the surface of the water. To Gulshan the boat sank with each stroke, heavy and inept. They crossed the lake divided by their perceptions.

He tried to judge the distance between the front of the boat and the duckboard as they approached the *dunga*. It sounded crude to him as they bumped alongside. Lila did not notice. Gulshan reached for one of the stakes that supported the boards. He could feel her moving in the boat as he turned away.

'So you think he has gone across?' he asked.

'Across?' She humped the sack of rice from under the bench and on to the duckboard.

'Irfan, so you think he has gone across?'

'He's stupid enough to go.' She was out of the boat, the rice lifted from the duckboard on to her head, before Gulshan had finished tying up.

'Will you need me tomorrow?'

'Gracie Madam may want to go to the city. I'll send a message.'

'And you?' Gulshan held on to the duckboard to pull the boat closer, bringing his face just in front of Lila's feet.

'I'll send a message.' She did not look down as she turned to go. The rice would have slipped.

He would have to lie to his mother about where he had been for the afternoon.

Irfan's mother Faheema waited by the kitchen door throughout the whole of the following day. In the evening Naseema gently led her away to sit and eat with them.

Faheema loved food. She ate when she was happy and when she was sad, she ate when it was too hot and when she was cold, when she was tired and when she felt exuberant. And when she was not eating she was cooking. She had not gone for a day without eating since she had been carrying her son, Shabeer, eight years before. The sickness had been all-defeating and she had been reduced to sucking ginger for most of the first six months of her pregnancy. She had become slightly anaemic as a result. This had given her a reason not to have to keep the Ramadan fast with the other women. Through the long month of stinking fasting-breath, and fragile afternoon tempers, she ate with the smaller children and drank tea in the corner of the kitchen on her chit from Allah. She never felt any guilt and the food tasted sweeter to her for being eaten while so many others were hungry. It was not malicious, just a dedication to food. By not eating Faheema moved herself into a place of isolated suffering.

Naseema had been watching. She had not tried to make Faheema eat with them the first evening after Irfan had gone, but now it was more than twenty-four hours, twice as long as anyone kept during Ramadan.

'Not taking food will not help.' She bent over Faheema so that the others would not hear.

Faheema did not respond.

'You think Allah will hear the shouting in your belly and bring him back that way?'

Faheema hit out at her, flailing her arm at Naseema's legs, but she had no strength. Naseema bent further over her and gently adjusted her sister-in-law's headscarf.

'Come, Faheema sister, come and eat with your children and family.' She kept her hand on Faheema's head, pressing softly into the base of her neck.

When Faheema looked up, Naseema took her hand and led her to the eating place as though she were a child. Kudji and the houseboys were laying plates and bowls of food out among the children who crawled over one another, puppy-fighting, bickering, pinching and pulling, oblivious to the grey loss that hung over Faheema, veiling her in spite of her scarf with its flowers in the blues and greens of cornflowers and wet grass.

She sat down as soon as Naseema let go of her hand, and

she stared without seeing as the household moved around her. Naseema waited until they were all eating before she took the last plate. She made small mounds around the soft curve of a piece of Kashmiri naan: red lamb curry, chilli-spiked aubergine, glossy rice tinted with saffron and dotted with raisins and star anise. She pushed the food towards Faheema where it sat untouched in the space that the children had left around her without knowing why they had.

Naseema nudged the plate into Faheema's crossed leg. She knew she was pushing with the pressure of her guilt at having let her nephew climb over the kitchen-yard wall without having called out to stop him. She took her hand away and waited while Kudji and the children finished eating. In twos and threes of chatter and intimacy they separated again and filtered out into the rest of the house. Naseema tore off one small piece of naan and folded some lamb into it, bringing it carefully to Faheema's mouth, coaxing her with the same soft sound she had used with her children when they had been too young to be interested in eating. Faheema opened her mouth and chewed the food slowly without tasting it.

The three brothers, Masood, Ibrahim and Rafi, ate later and separately in the winter sitting room after their mother and father had finished their food and gone to bed, Gulam Abdullah holding on to his wife's arm, rumbling and complaining that Kudji cooked with too much chilli, and that it kept him awake all night with wind. They did not know yet that Irfan was missing. In a family household of seventeen, twenty-one including the four houseboys who slept in a room at the back of the house, it was easy not to notice an absence.

'It will give us indigestion if we speak of this thing now,'

Masood said to his brothers as they sat down again after their parents' departure.

They put food on their plates in silence, and when they had finished Masood wiped his mouth with the back of his hand, and pushed his plate away.

'We will not speak to people about this. Only Farouk knows now,' he said, though they all knew that this in itself was a risk.

Farouk believed that the only real secret was the sight of his wife's body by oil lamp, as it had been when they were young. Every other secret had a journey to take.

'I had to tell him because he will go with me tomorrow to look for the boy.' Masood justified his decision.

Rafi and Masood looked at their brother Ibrahim, the boy's father, but he said nothing.

'Naseema tells me that Faheema will not eat. This will frighten the other children. You must tell her to eat.' Masood shifted on the carpet in discomfort.

Ibrahim looked up at this elder brother. 'She is the boy's mother, I cannot make her eat,' he replied.

Masood looked down at his fingers digging into the silk of the carpet. He could not think of anything to say to his brother, so he shifted again, pushing one of his hands into his lower gut to ease his creeping indigestion.

Chapter Four ~

He moved as though through smoke, the mist wrapping around his edges, seeping over the collar of his woollen *pheran*, as his boat sank and emerged. Gulshan's melting and reforming figure loomed beside the old kennel beyond the *dunga* boat. The bulbul chicks flapped at him with their skinny wings.

He could hear Lila's voice from the kitchen, rising and falling in circular rhythms. He sat in silence listening, not to hear what she said but to memorize the sound shapes that she made. Irfan's name surfaced and Gulshan began to separate the words.

'Someone bullied him. He wouldn't have gone otherwise. I'll sort the rice later, the mist's even come in here, I can't see properly.' Lila was spreading cupfuls of rice on to a wooden tray.

Suriya looked over her daughter's shoulder and began flicking through the rice, her fingers finding grit that Lila could not see.

Lila pressed her cheek against her mother's. 'So, you can sort the rice then, and I'll do breakfast. You think scrambled eggs? She didn't eat so much last night, eggs will be good.'

Suriya flicked her chin to one side.

Lila reached up to the egg basket at arm's length above her head. 'Is there enough butter?'

Suriya's chin flicked again.

'Scrambled eggs and toast then.' She sniffed. 'He'll get killed.' There was a pause. 'And then he'll become another Nagin martyr like the Butt boy who was shot near Uri. Nothing heroic about that, just boys all of them.' She wiped her hands down her front. 'I have to go to the bazaar today. We need a new small pan for Gracie's hot milk.'

Suriya tapped Lila's chest and then drew her hand across her throat to stop her theme.

'It's the truth, though, you know that.'

Suriya closed her eyes.

'He was a fine boy but now he's always creeping about.' She saw that her mother's eyes were still closed. 'I'll go this afternoon, do you need anything?'

Suriya pulled at her *kameez* to show a hole under her armpit and made a threading gesture.

'We have needles, you want thread?' Lila stuck her finger through the hole. 'It's worn out, we should get you a new one.'

Suriya shook her head vehemently and pointed at her daughter's eyes.

'Blue thread then.'

Suriya pinched Lila's cheek and she squirmed away.

'Stop!' She yanked Suriya's hand away.

Her mother looked back down at the rice. Lila put her

hand to her cheek where she had been pinched, then she kissed her palm and placed the flat of her hand against her mother's face. Suriya dropped the weight of her cheek into Lila's hand. Constant forgiveness was a requirement in their daily life.

Gulshan knocked his boat against the side of the *dunga* and waited. Lila's face came to a small window just above where he held the edge of the deck.

'Salaam alaikum,' he swallowed the greeting.

She screwed up her nose at the smell outside.

'It's not me, it's Nagin's sewage.' He flicked water at her.

'It's not the lake's sewage, it's ours,' she smiled down at him. 'What do you want, stink boy?'

'There's a letter for Gracie Madam.'

'There often is.'

'It's from England.'

'I think all her family there are dead now. What's the writing like, old and shaky?'

'Not really.'

'Young and English or young and Indian-in-England?'

Gulshan shrugged, 'How would I know that?'

'Indian-in-England would be small and apologetic on the envelope.'

'And English?' he asked.

'Would be cocky.' She said the word in English.

'Cocky?' he repeated.

'As though he owned the paper, the whole supply of it, and the mill too.'

'He, can you know it's a he?' Gulshan pulled his boat in closer with both hands.

'No reason, come, show it to me.' Lila pulled back from

the window so that she could stick her hand through.

Gulshan stood up on the seat of the boat in order to be able to reach up to her height from the water. His face was almost level with hers. He teetered, smiling up at her.

'So where is it?' she asked, her face darkened by the interior, her hand reaching further towards him.

He reached down and pulled up a lily pad, flopping the wet leaf into her palm. She threw it back at him but it hit the inside of the window.

'Come and get your love letter from your Angrezi boyfriend then.' He bounced on the seat so that his boat slapped up and down in the water.

Lila was out of the *dunga*, and she had grabbed the front of the boat, even before he had a chance to get his balance.

'I'll tip you in.'

'Then it'll be wet.' He went on bouncing.

'You said it was addressed to Gracie Madam?'

'It is.'

'So how can it be to me from an Angrezi lover then?'

'Lover is he now?'

Lila jumped on to the back of the boat and pinned Gulshan's arms behind his back, pinching his thumbs together and pushing them up his spine. He butted back against her with his hips. Stepping back she used her full weight to keep his thumbs fixed. The boat rocked, Lila pushed more.

'Stop now,' Gulshan cried out.

'Why? Is it hurting?'

He struggled. 'Yes, happy now?'

Lila let go as she hopped back on to the *dunga* deck. 'So give me the letter.'

He sat down, shaking out his thumbs and wrists. She

stood above him, her hands on her hips. Bending under his seat he pulled out a rucksack and passed her the letter.

'Young, definitely young and a man,' she said, studying the writing and then sniffing along the edge of the envelope. 'And nice features too.'

Gulshan stared. She laughed.

'How?'

'I can smell his skin,' she said, with her eyes closed.

'The skin is not a feature, it's an organ, you told me that.' Gulshan looked away across the lake. 'Will Gracie Madam need me today?'

'I will send a message if she does.'

He waited.

Lila turned back. 'You were kind to bring this.' She went back into the *dunga*.

He stared at the space where she had been.

The letter sat on Gracie's desk in the sitting room all day. She had no reason to look. Her cigarettes were there but Masood had not been down to smoke with her since just after Irfan had gone. Lila did not have the chance to tell her about the letter before she went to the bazaar.

The lentils sucked in around her hand as she sank it into the first in a line of sacks, right up to her wrist. She pushed further in, almost to her elbow, watching the pulses sliding and rolling against her skin.

'You think they're better at the bottom?' A woman beside Lila bent over, lifting the front of her *burqa* to free her hand before dipping it into the sack. 'They're smoother, aren't they, best for dhal.'

Lila smiled at the latticed mesh of the woman's *burqa*.

'It's Zubi's mother, Lila.' The woman moved her hand next to Lila's among the lentils. 'How is your mother?'

Zubeeda had been at school with Lila. They had not been friends. Zubi was from an orthodox family.

'She is keeping well.'

'And you?'

Lila shrugged.

'Inshallah, I hope this means good things. Always different, Lila, always wanting brighter feathers than the rest.' Zubi's mother withdrew her hand from the sack and stood up. 'Perhaps I won't buy the green ones this time.' She dusted off her hand carefully on the inside of her *burqa* as she turned away.

'Please give my best to Zubi,' Lila asked.

The woman did not reply.

Lila bought yellow lentils. They were cheaper than the green ones.

She was asked for her papers at the checkpoint on the corner of Zaina Kadal bridge, at the edge of the copper market in the old city. The soldiers usually just checked men but barefaced women caught their attention.

The young man who stopped her just wanted to look for a while. His leave had been cancelled because of the red alert since the coup, and he simply wanted to look into a softer face for just long enough to forget.

Lila waited while he looked at her papers, her eyes fixed on the dirt of the road at her feet.

'You are from Nagin side, what is your business here?' the young man asked in Hindi. His voice was softer than the question.

'I have to buy pans.' She did not look up.

'The best ones are here.' He stared at the point on her head where her shawl made a line above her widow's peak. He could see where the damp air had curled the fine strands at her hairline.

'This is why I have come.'

He held her papers out. 'I hope you find what you want. You speak Hindi very well.'

Lila reached out to take them and he held on to them for a moment as she pulled them away from him.

'I can only think that you must be a very fine cook,' he said into the space she was trying to make between them.

She did not reply.

'My misfortune is that . . .' he tailed off.

Lila lifted her head as he looked down.

'May I go, please?' she asked in English.

He looked up as she spoke but she had already turned away.

'Thank you, Miss.' His voice was higher in English, surprised too.

His fellow soldiers laughed at him as she walked away.

'Fit arse on her,' one of them called to him.

'Shut up, man,' he shouted back.

'Too beautiful these women, what to do?' a second chanted at him.

'No point chatting up the locals, forget it, *naar*,' another laughed.

The young man went to the other side of the sandbags so that he was out of earshot. He watched Lila as she turned away around a corner into the copper market. He felt homesick.

She stopped for a moment when she knew that the

checkpoint was out of sight. He had been polite and clean-shaven too, rare for a soldier, always those self-important little moustaches.

Burnt-out houses in the Hindu quarter of the old city framed the street on either side of her, with their broken faces, empty windows hanging in cracked walls, nothing behind them but the dank sky. Lila did not come to this part of the old city much any more.

On the opposite corner of the street that she had turned down was a house with wooden casements like so many others. Its character was marked by a Juliet balcony that hung out over the intersection of two streets. Rani Kaul used to hang over the edge of it, her chin on the rail so that her plaits hung down, misquoting the balcony scene that they had spent so long learning by rote at school. It had made Lila laugh every time as she had crouched at Rani's feet, watching the streets for cousins or parents through the carved spindles of the balcony, as Rani called down into the movement on the streets, pleading with a faceless lover for chocolates and a new shawl.

They had written their own play, their story starring them, but it had not been finished.

Rani and her family had left the Valley in 1990 when the trouble had begun to empty out the Hindu quarter of the city. Only part of the Kauls' house had been burnt out. The Juliet balcony remained, clinging at the juncture of the two streets.

Lila looked up at the house before she moved on. She always took the same route into the old city when she came, just to check.

The copper merchant argued with her about price. She

wanted the smallest pan he had to warm Gracie's milk for her coffee as the winter mornings chilled her.

'There's more work involved when they are this small,' he complained.

'This is what you charged me for one three times the size.' She leaned forward to look.

'More work, I told you, the detail is finer, look.' He pushed the pan at her, pointing to the rough welding at the handle.

'It's not such fine work.'

'Don't wave your hands at me.' The copper merchant pulled the pan away from her.

'I don't need it.' She began to walk away.

'But you came here to get it.'

She walked on. He dropped his price in an abusive tone and she turned back to him.

She decided to leave the old city by the next bridge down from Zaina Kadal. She had heard the other soldiers at the checkpoint taunting the clean-shaven boy as she had walked away. They would probably do the same thing if she went back that way. She cut down a side alley in a deserted area where the Pandit *mithai* man used to have his shop, where Rani and she used to run to buy Diwali sweets and eat them sitting on the step. He was a cousin of Rani's cousin so the girls were family to him.

Rani had married a Punjabi who worked for a cruise company. They lived in Florida, and the elder of their two daughters was called Lila. Rani and Lila did not write to each other. They had promised that they would as Rani's family had bundled their life into big cotton bags that the girls had been sent to buy at the Friday market.

The alley was grey and quiet.

Their voices came first, but she did not have time to react before two hands clamped over her mouth and her eyes. One of the side walls cracked against her head and back as she was rammed against it. She fell and a man came down on top of her. There were two others, she could hear their feet around her head in the dirt as she was crushed down. Something tore inside her left knee as the first man straddled her hips. One of the others tied something around her eyes, the other held her arms up over her head. Her eyes stung. The cord of her *salwar* tightened as it was torn at. It bit deep into her back until it was cut with something.

She could smell diesel but she could not make any sound. The man on top of her rammed at her hips and thighs without entering her. She felt the spread of warm sperm on her belly as he pulled himself away.

Another body thumped on to her. The second one cut her *kameez* and yanked her bra away, grabbing at her breasts and biting her nipples, his finger digging into her as though flailing in clay.

She was unable to make any sound, though noise battered to get out from inside her. Short sentences that the men shot at each other seemed to be yelled in her ear. The second man on top of her pushed her face to one side and kicked one of her legs further open, crashing down on to her again and again, trying to steal, trying to destroy.

Then it stopped.

They were gone, their feet kicking dust into her mouth as they ran.

Lila lay in the dirt waiting for something else to happen.

They had been shouting Hindi at each other.

She pulled the blindfold away from her eyes. It was an engine rag still wet with diesel.

A boy stood at the end of the alley. They must have seen him.

'Who were they?'

'Soldiers,' he called, and then he turned and ran as well.

Lila sat in the silence, her attack mapped in the damp dust around her. She grabbed a handful of dry dirt and scrubbed at her belly where semen stuck to her skin. She rubbed until her skin was raw. The knee that she had fallen on to was beginning to swell with its own pulse beating under the injury. She knotted her ripped *salwar* over her raw stomach. Her shawl was stamped with their footprints. Rolling on to her good knee, she pulled herself up against the wall to reach for her shawl. She tested her left knee. The pain yanked through her thigh and into her groin. She thrashed her shawl against the uneven bricks, harder each time, panting as she beat it. Stepping back she held it up to a thin strand of light that came down through the burnt-out walls of the houses above her. The footprints had gone from the dark blue wool. Folding it along its length she carefully wrapped it around the back of her neck and then crosswise over her chest where her *kameez* had been slashed open.

Her left shoulder had been cut, a deep point opened by a stone as she had fallen. She noticed it as she tied the shawl ends behind her back, and she saw where the blood had seeped down her arm inside her sleeve. It had marked the back of her hand in two dark lines. Some of the yellow lentils from the market had spilt out of their bag. She began to pick them up and then stopped, tipping what remained into the small saucepan, clinging to the handle.

Using the wall to lean against, she walked out of the alley eight minutes after she had turned into its grey silence. A square block of light at the end stopped her, framing her within its starkness. She held on to the corner, sucking air like a surfacing diver.

The young man at the checkpoint by Zaina Kadal waited beyond the end of his duty. He told the soldiers on the next shift that he had been ordered to stay on. He waited until they began to ask him why he was still there. He waited until hunger made him hail a jeep heading back to the barracks. He had hoped to see the barefaced girl again on her way back from the copper market, he had hoped that she might smile at him.

The fishwife from Wular Lake saw a broken shape making its way back along the edge of Nagin in the leached slats of late afternoon light. It was not until she was much closer that she realized it was Lila.

The fishwife had known her since she had been a little girl. She had taught her to gut fish with two sweeps of a knife, one to the belly, the second dragging the tip of the blade down the exposed spine taking all the entrails with it. Lila had learned quickly and she could scale fish as fast as the fishwife. The fishwife was proud of her pupil. She came to The Wonder House once a week to talk and to listen to the news with Suriya.

She had some fresh river trout, one of Gracie's favourites, pan-fried in butter with a little fresh masala, the smell bringing the ribbed and manged cats of the neighbourhood out to sniff the air.

It was Lila's profile that she recognized but the stoop was

wrong. She waited until the half-familiar figure was close enough for her to be sure.

'Lila?'

The figure stopped but did not reply.

'Lila, I've fresh fish, all the best ones saved, still wet in the basket, eyes still clear.'

Lila stood in silence at a distance from the fishwife.

'And river trout too for Madam. What is it, Lila-baby?'

Lila raised her head. She had not been able to see the blood on her face, nor had she felt the skin torn off one side of her cheek.

'What happened to my little girl?' the fishwife shouted, dropping her basket and running. 'Lila-baby, what happened?'

Lila stood silently as the old woman examined her, the small saucepan gripped tight in her hand.

Putting a hand to Lila's undamaged cheek, the fishwife looked at her. 'Who did this to you?' She turned, looking around for someone to come and help. 'Hey brother, come here, hey brother.' She waved to another figure crossing the meadow.

Masood had seen the two women from the top of the meadow. He had watched the fishwife dropping her basket and running towards the hunched figure. He had stood still, not wanting to interfere, wondering whether he should turn back towards the house. Then the fishwife had called. He started to walk towards them and then he ran, falling on the downward slope just before reaching them. His legs shot out in front of him, planting him just in front of the fishwife. He laughed a little as he picked himself up.

'Lila has been attacked.' The fishwife stepped to one side to show the girl to Masood.

She had turned away, hunching over even more, one hand covering the cut on her shoulder.

The fishwife reached out and turned her gently towards Masood. 'See what they have done to her.'

He saw the dullness in her eyes before the blood and damage. He wanted to touch her face and shout at the sky, but instead he reached out and put a hand on her arm. The fishwife stepped away. Lila stood catatonic between them.

'What happened, Lila, what did you do?' he spoke to her in English. He started to uncurl her fingers from the small pan that she clung to.

She lurched out of her stupor. 'What do you mean, "what did you do?" What did I do, Masood Abdullah?' She seemed to shrink. 'What did I do? I am a woman, that is all that I did.' And now she grew as she shouted at him.

'I'm asking what happened, Lila. You must come to the house, we must call the doctor.' He turned to the fishwife and spoke again in Kashmiri. 'Help me.'

'I should tell Suriya,' the fishwife said.

'Wait for some time. Let's get her to the house and call the doctor. Come.'

'I can walk, I have walked here from the city.' Lila tried to turn away. 'I will go to the *dunga* now, leave me.'

'You will come to the house.' Masood stepped in front of her to block her.

'Why do you want me to come to the house? So people don't see me? So there is no shame for you? What will you say to your women?' She tried to step around him but she lost her balance. 'That you found wicked Lila broken in the road and you have brought her to the house to mend her.'

Masood reached out but she fell instead of taking his

hand. He bent down to her, a hand on the back of her shoulder. 'Come Lila.' This time he spoke in Kashmiri.

She folded herself down towards the earth.

'Who, Lila? Was it men in the city, were they *jawans*? Soldiers or policemen?' he asked.

She did not need to answer.

He turned to the fishwife. 'Help her. I will go ahead now and call for a doctor. The kitchen-yard gate is open, bring her that way.'

'Will you carry my fish then?' Her abandoned basket lay where she had dropped it.

Masood looked at it with distaste. The circumstances required him to bend. He nodded to the fishwife.

He had been carrying a copy of a news magazine, an excuse to see Gracie, an article about the coup had excited him. A gentle argument on the subject was what he had been looking forward to. Now he opened the magazine, flicking through the pages until he found the story and pulled it out of the binding, folding the pages and stuffing them down into his *pheran*. He spread the rest of the magazine over one edge of the fish basket that he would have to hold close to him. He lifted the basket, his bottom sticking out to keep his body away from the fish. At any other time Lila and the fishwife would have laughed at him, just not that afternoon. He stopped and bent to pick up Lila's pan, and he placed it carefully on top of the fish.

Kudji was washing Feroz's hair in the kitchen courtyard. She had left it until almost too late in the day, and he might get a chill from having damp hair in the evening cold, but Naseema had said it needed to be done. Kudji had only remembered when she had noticed him scratching like a dog. She was trying to be as quiet as she could but Feroz was squealing because she had not had time to heat the water properly. It was a bad idea but his head was full of soap now and it had to be rinsed.

Naseema would criticize her if she did not.

Kudji reached out to hold the boy's head. Feroz twisted away and scampered towards the gate. She picked up the bucket and ran after him, throwing the water as she came into range, aiming for his lathered head. He dodged and the water flew out through the gate. The shout from the other side made her drop the bucket. She peered through to see Masood, a basket fallen at his feet, fish spilling out on the earth around him. She stood with her hands in front of her face.

'What were you thinking?' he shouted at her.

'So, so sorry. I was washing Feroz's hair. He ran from me.'

'I would do the same. You were using ice water, what kind of mother are you? Get your boy and go into the house and tell Naseema to come.'

Kudji backed away from the gate.

'You've brought so much fish, are we having a party?' Kudji asked.

'Go and do as I ask, quickly now, run, Kudji.'

Her mouth was open as she turned and ran to the house. Feroz was crouched in the corner of the courtyard, ready to run as his mother came towards him, but his uncle's voice stopped him. As Kudji picked him up he opened his mouth to protest, but he made no noise as he stared at Masood, bouncing against his mother's shoulder as she ran back into the kitchen.

He watched as his biggest uncle stooped down and

gathered fallen fish back into a basket as though he was a servant, and he wondered what was wrong with all the grown-ups.

Masood filled Kudji's abandoned bucket from the court-yard tap and threw it over the fish. Then he spread the soggy remains of the magazine pages over them, and put the basket under the walnut tree beside the wall, before hurrying back to kick away the spilt lumps of melting ice just as the fish-wife and Lila came around the outer edge of the courtyard.

'Did you call the doctor?' the fishwife asked, looking down at his feet scrubbing in wet dust.

'No doctor,' Lila pulled away from her.

'There has been no time, too many people were here. I am going now. Naseema is coming to help you.'

Lila held on to one side of the gate, jamming herself in the entrance with her good leg. 'No doctor.'

'Come, Lila-Baby, you must see a doctor, you can hardly walk, your face needs to be cleaned and your shoulder will need some stitching.' The fishwife put her arm around Lila's waist, but she pressed herself more tightly into the gateway.

'Naseema can do these things. She stitched my eyebrow when it was split at cricket. There is no scar, look.' Masood stepped closer to Lila and ran his finger across his eyebrow. As she looked at the smooth line of hair he could feel her breath on his face. He did not move. Her rigid body softened enough for the fishwife to be able to lead her across the courtyard.

Naseema watched the trio from the kitchen, her husband walking backwards, coaxing Lila, the fishwife and the bloodied girl huddled together, hip to hip. Her sisters-in-law, Kudji and Faheema, were behind her at the door.

'Close the door now,' Naseema whispered without turning. They pulled it halfway.

'Shut,' she hissed.

The latch clicked behind her as Masood took the steps up to the kitchen door in reverse, a small pan in one hand, the other extended out to Lila in a way that Naseema could not understand.

After nineteen years of marriage her husband still had the ability to surprise her.

Lila stood in the middle of the kitchen, her body divided by afternoon sun into the sections of her damage. Naseema moved around her in silence. Masood and the fishwife stood back, watching.

Naseema waved her husband away as she guided Lila towards a low stool. She beckoned to the fishwife to hold the girl's head. Masood opened the kitchen door. Kudji and Faheema were pressed against the other side, his older nieces lined up behind them in a tight group. They bumped against each other as they tried to scramble away.

'What are you doing?'

'In case Naseema needed help.' Kudji did not move.

'If she needed help she would call. Now go, all of you go.'

They scattered as he stood with his back against the closed door. Kudji was the first to stop, and she stood watching from the gap between the winter sitting-room door and the wall.

Lila remained rigid as Naseema put ice on her shoulder, sliding it over the broken skin. The fishwife tried to make her turn her head away but Lila stared straight ahead.

'Come, Lila-Baby, look here now, hold my hand,' she whispered.

Lila hardly even seemed to be breathing as Naseema

threaded her needle through the two tears of skin. She cut one end and knotted both pieces together. The fishwife looked away.

'She's as neat as you are at gutting,' the fishwife patted Lila's hand, hoping that she would not feel how hers were shaking.

Masood moved closer to the door.

Sweat ran off dust-matted tendrils of Lila's hair around her temples. It dripped on to Naseema's hand as she took another stitch. In her concentration it made her twitch the needle as drops of sweat hit her skin. Lila swallowed her cry. The fishwife gripped her hand harder.

Masood put his hand against the door and closed his eyes. Kudji watched him from her gap behind the door, her eyes wide.

When Naseema had finished, the fishwife took Lila back down to the *dunga* because she refused to rest at the house. Naseema had made her a small pack of ice wrapped in a cloth to hold to the torn and bruising skin that she had stitched, and another for her swollen knee, and she had made Lila put on one of her own *salwar kameez* so that Suriya would not see that her daughter's had been ripped and slashed. It swamped Lila, falling around her as though she were a child.

The fishwife told Suriya the parts of the story that she knew as Lila retreated to a corner of the *dunga* and sat with her knees pulled to her chest, her small pan of lentils beside her. When the fishwife had gone, Suriya went to her daughter and held her head, smoothing her hair, rocking her back and forth until Lila began to loll against her shoulder. Suriya went on rocking her, her fingers working through her hair, gently rubbing away the blood and dust between her finger and thumb, strand by strand.

When she went back up to the house the fishwife thumped about on heavy feet by the kitchen gate for a while, grumbling about her ruined fish.

He had even tried to hide his mess by covering it with some filthy magazine full of pictures and unreadable writing.

She could see where print had come off on to the dulled scales of some of the fish. She raised her hand to knock on the kitchen door. Normally she would have hammered and demanded that Masood pay for what he had done, but the circumstances required her to bend. She looked into her basket again. If she washed them down properly she could still sell them in the city at the late market in the failing evening light.

Gracie had walked twice to the sitting-room window to see if Suriya was bringing tea. Her watch had detached itself some time during her afternoon sleep and she had given up looking for it among the tangle of bedclothes. Finding out the time meant going to the other end of the houseboat to see her bedside clock.

Suriya would have to help her find it.

It was the last thing that Jitu had given her, her fifty-seventh birthday present. Three words were engraved on the casing, one above the other – 'meri jane jigar', 'light of my heart'.

At least she could remember the words. All was not lost.

Why was Suriya so late? It was almost evening. Was winter closing in so fast?

She sat down and tried to find where she had got to in the book that she had been reading, a new novel that someone had sent her from Delhi; all names with too many syllables and sentences that melted one into another, the characters too.

She got up again and went to the window for the third time, calling for Suriya. She waited but there was no sound, no reply from Lila to tell her Suriya was coming.

Now she was hungry. Putting the book down she made her way down the corridor. Suriya was at the side entrance just as she got there.

'What happened to tea, it's late isn't it? I lost my watch.'

Suriya lifted her wrist to Gracie. She wore one of Jitu's old watches. Gracie had given it to her twelve years earlier when she had taught her to tell the time.

'It's quarter to six, so what happened to tea?'

Suriya bowed her head.

'Where's Lila?'

Suriya put her hands together on one side of her head and closed her eyes.

'She's sleeping, why, what's the matter? Is she ill?'

Suriya flicked her chin.

'Does she need to see Dr Hamid?'

Suriya shook her head, her eyes down. She pointed to the sitting room and made the gesture of tea.

'I'm coming to see her.'

Suriya shook her head more vehemently and pointed again to the sitting room. Gracie went ahead of her back into the room. Suriya waved towards the desk and picked up the letter that had been sitting there all day. She held it out to Gracie. Lila had told her to give the letter to Gracie when she had woken on her mother's shoulder, just as Suriya had been trying to move away, inch by inch.

'A letter.' Gracie took it. 'From England, don't recognize the writing.' She held the envelope up to the light. 'Don't worry about tea. Look after Lila. Perhaps some pakoras in an hour, or when there's time, and bring some Thing too, would you? Don't need supper tonight. I'm getting dumpy again, bit of banting required, bit of stringency.' Gracie smiled and took Suriya's hand. 'Go and look after your girl, off you go. If she gets worse, make sure you tell me, bug of some kind, is it?'

Suriya looked down.

'Off you go then and give her lots of liquids. I've got some aspirin in the bathroom; that might be an idea. Come on, we'll find it, probably take a bit of digging about. You could have a dekho for my watch with those sharp eyes of yours. Probably all tangled up in the sheets. Wonder what I was dreaming about.' She turned to go back down the corridor. 'The bugger is, if it was exciting I wouldn't remember anyway.' She turned to check that Suriya was following her. 'Strap's broken again, I should think. Lila can hunt one out for me in the bazaar when she's up and about.' She took Suriya's arm and they shuffled along together, Gracie half a step ahead to allow room for both of them in the corridor.

Suriya crushed four aspirins into milk that she warmed in the little pan that Lila had been clutching when the fishwife had brought her back to the *dunga*. She added saffron and shaved almonds. Lila drank it without asking what it was, curling back under her blanket. It took her perhaps a minute to put the half-full glass to one side, guiding her hand because it was shaking so badly. She did not want her mother to see.

Suriya missed the news again. Setting the oil to heat as far as she could from Lila, she spread her spices around her and lifted the mortar and pestle into the cross of her legs an hour later than usual.

She thought her daughter was asleep by the time she took the hot pakoras to Gracie. Lila opened her eyes as she left and stared as her mother's figure diluted into the night beyond the single electric bulb of the *dunga* kitchen. The shapes around her were familiar, pots and bowls that she had scoured all her life with handfuls of mud from the lake bank, tins that she opened to take pinches of rough cracked pepper, cumin, nutmeg, Hindu turmeric and saffron, secular cloves, and Kashmiri green tea. She wanted to wrap herself in the habitual minutiae of the cramped space that she had so often longed to escape, to be pounded down in her mother's mortar and pestle, among the sweet dark cardamom and coriander seeds, to be submerged in the smooth voices of the evening news.

There had been a story when they had been at school, just at the time when they had been sitting on the edge of puberty, peering at themselves in constant fascination, as though seeing themselves for the first time. It was the time when they used to sneak out and find backstreet tailors to have their shapeless tunics taken in to fit more closely to their changing shapes.

They had not really understood the story when they had heard it. 'The Raped Village' it had been called, where the security forces had lost control and attacked the women they were there to protect.

Just a routine house-to-house check for militants they had said, but thirty women had been raped: women whose husbands had then left them, girls who then could not get husbands because they had been stained, and a seventy-year-old woman who had been thrown out of her house by her family in case she brought more bad luck on her sons and grandsons.

Someone in their class had a cook with a sister in the village. The story had been that the boys of the village were taunting the violated women and girls: 'Did you enjoy it, do you want more?' they were said to have shouted at them in the streets.

Their Urdu teacher had asked them what they understood about the militants. They had sat in silent rows. One girl had put up her hand, and they had laughed when she had told them that her mother kept shaving her brother's chin when he was asleep, so that the militants would not be able to see his first wisps of adulthood and tempt him with a gun. Rani Kaul had said that there were good and bad militants and good and bad soldiers, just as there was good and bad in all men. Lila had stared at her friend in amazement.

The story had sat somewhere for years, kept out of the light. Lila could see Rani's face again, a hand on each of her plaits, tugging as she had spoken, two deep lines between her eyebrows. Not even the teacher had spoken after Rani, or perhaps Lila had just forgotten what she had said.

She turned on to her back again to readjust away from the burning pain in her shoulder. There was a lily leaf in the window, hanging from its stalk that had stuck between the sill and the frame, the leaf that she had tried to throw back at Gulshan in the morning mist.

A sound came from somewhere inside her that she did not recognize, a thin, penetrating cry.

Gracie looked up from her book as Suriya arranged the pakoras beside her.

'The bulbul is crying. Her chicks must be about to fly.'

Suriya closed her eyes as she slipped shiny pink paper napkins under the chutney bowl.

'Such a beautiful, sad sound.' Gracie opened her book again. 'That letter, some boy wants to come and talk to me about being a *farangi* wife and widow before and after Independence. He wants to come out from England. What do you think?'

Suriya looked up, her face blank.

'I rather agree. Did you give Lila those aspirins?'

Suriya tilted her chin.

'You go and keep an eye on her, and if there are any stale rotis, break them up and throw some up at the bulbul nest, cheer the sad mother up a bit.' She looked up but Suriya had already gone. Gracie closed her book, and took the letter from the inside back cover, opening it again as she picked up one of the pakoras. It was still too hot and she dropped it on the letter, the oil seeping into the paper and mixing with the ink.

So, he wrote with an ink pen. How nice. Can't read most of it now, though.

She scooped the pakora off the paper, dipped it in chutney and bit into it, dripping mint, curd and some of the soft, hot potato centre back on to the page. Making a cone of the letter she tipped the spilt food back into her mouth.

The cold had soaked into every part of him, pulling muscles tight on bones, shortening his ligaments and tendons so that

every part of him ached as he rolled over on the hard
ground. He kept his eyes closed, longing for the sound of his
mother's voice calling him for food, but it was the metallic
whine of the call to prayer and not her voice. Even when his
neighbour kicked his rump Irfan kept his eyes closed, just a
few moments more. As someone opened the tent flap it
made two triangles of light through his eyelids. He rolled
away, back into smooth darkness. Boys around him were
pulling on more layers, struggling into clothes, tying cords
and pulling sleeves over sleeves, numb and raw, stumbling on
cold-dead hands and feet.

'He'll make you run through the river again if you're
caught.' Irfan's neighbour stuck his foot under his hip this
time.

'I ran through it yesterday, so I'll be better at it today.' Irfan
still did not open his eyes.

He had missed all but one of the firing targets the day
before. He had been made to run through the glacier river as
a punishment.

He only moved as the other seven boys left the tent,
pulling his blanket around him, but it felt as cold and heavy
against his aching body as the ground was beneath him. He
pressed his forehead into his knees. Every part of him was
numb, except his mind.

Someone pushed the tent flap aside. 'What are you doing
here? Why aren't you praying?' It was the broad brow of one
of the camp cooks.

'I could ask the same of you.' Irfan lifted his head from his
knees.

'I am going, inshallah, but you're still in your night things,
are you sick?'

'I am.' Irfan dropped his head back on to his knees.

'I heard you ran through the river yesterday, and you did not eat last night. What kind of sick?' The cook did not like many people, but Irfan was the only boy who had ever thanked him each time he gave him food.

'Mind-sick. I can't feel my body, so if it's sick I wouldn't know?'

'Irfan, it's Irfan, isn't it?'

Irfan did not reply.

'Come to pray, Irfan. Allah will guide you.'

Irfan did not move but he knew the cook had gone as the tent was dark again. He pulled his knees more tightly into his chest and tried to remember the faces of his family. The grinding exhaustion of the past thirty-two days was pushing him into obsessive patterns. He could only complete the next task if he could clearly see his sister's and brothers' faces before he started. He would only allow himself to eat if he could conjure up his mother and father, every detail exact. He could only let himself sleep once he had re-created Lila, even her fingernails, the little white crescents at the base of them, the shape of her eyebrows, the way one wandered a little, and the finer hair that caught the light at her hairline. He uncurled himself back on to the cold ground, willing it to freeze him, to deaden his mind as well as every other useless part of him. He pulled the blanket up over his head to muffle the single sound of a hundred and five voices in prayer.

He was caught and made to run through the river again. The training commander waited until the sun began to be cut away by the peaks, dragging the temperature down with it, before he metered out the punishment. Irfan was taken back to the same place by the river as the day before. His hands were tied to either end of his gun so that he had no choice but to hold them up over his head as he forded the river. If his gun dropped down below his head, the other boys from his tent had to throw stones at him until he lifted them up again. One of the other boys was made to take his shoes from him before he went down to the river. It took the boy a while because Irfan triple-tied his laces, the way Masood had taught him when he had given his first pair of trainers for his eleventh birthday.

He stood barefoot by the river, his gun above his head, waiting for his commander to fire. He looked for Lila on the other bank in her blue *salwar kameez*, the one cut square at the neck where it sat on her collarbones.

A shot came, a blank just over his head, and he slipped into the water, falling on to his knees as the iciness punched him down. He flicked himself up and searched out footholds among the shifting stones. There was another shot over his head.

'Move faster,' his commander yelled at him.

The freezing water attacked him, cutting into him so that he could not stand up. He slipped again and fell, his arms reaching up to try and keep the gun aloft. He saw stones hitting the surface around him as his head went under. They slowed and swung down around him in the clear rolling water. The cracking of the stones on the riverbed seemed so loud as the world above the surface receded. His left knee hit a rock. The pain made him suck for air and he swallowed a lungful of river. Spitting and gasping he surfaced back into the noise above.

'Get up, get up,' came the voice from the bank.

A stone hit him in the back of the neck as he found his foothold again. He lifted his arms higher and, closing his eyes, he ran to Lila.

He lay still on the opposite bank, his ribs pushing down into the cold ground beneath him as he laboured for breath.

'Now back across the wire. Untie your hands with your feet,' the voice shouted from across the river.

Irfan stared at the stunted grass in front of where he lay, the way it grew up out of the frozen ground.

'You have five minutes until the stones start again.'

He inhaled the wet turf of the bank and pushed himself back on to his knees. The left one burned under the pressure. His hands were so numb from the river that he was able to slip the left one out of the tie. The right was easy once he had a hand free. Using his gun to help him stand, he hobbled downstream to the wire. Standing for a moment in front of the concrete post he had no idea where to put his gun.

'Move, now,' came the yell across the water.

Irfan pushed his gun down the back of his dripping *kurta*, tucking the barrel tip into the back of his pyjama, and he turned away from the voice. He jumped for the wire, grabbing it and swinging his legs up in front to cross over the top of it. He moved along the wire, hand over hand, his legs pulling in behind him, the barrel of his gun pressing into the groove of his buttocks as he moved. He had not even checked whether his safety catch was on. He did not care.

Being shot in the arse would be light relief, lying on his belly in the tent and dreaming of Lila and fresh roti with melting butter. He might blow off his balls too, that would be a waste. That really would be a waste.

He had no more strength in his hands. If he fell into the

river he would have to start again from the other side, the whole pathetic pattern again. Wrapping his forearms over the wire he held his arms, elbow to elbow, and thrust them back behind his head. The twist of the steel cut through his sleeve and scoured into the soft skin on the underside of his upper arms. He turned his face away, his cheek pressed against the wire. Stones lay on the riverbed below, clacking as they had when his face had been just above them under the water. The barrel of his gun jammed into the inner curve of his left buttock as he slid his legs again towards his arms.

'You have thirty seconds and you will pray when you reach the other side.' The training commander's voice seemed close enough now for Irfan to drop his legs back down from the wire.

He uncrossed his ankles and let go without caring whether the river was below him. He closed his eyes to find her.

Chapter Five ~

Banked fog blotted the call to prayer even before it began to bounce across the reflecting surface of the lakes. The emptiness of the bulbul nest above the old kennel was padded with snow, the earliest fall since the insurgency began.

Farouk stopped paddling to readjust the *kangri* under his *pheran*, the little firepot was pressing right against his stomach and burning the hair around his navel. Even as he stopped, the sweat on his back began to freeze while his belly hair curled more tightly in the heat.

He would have to pull in close to one of the canals where the filth from the city's spread stopped the water from freezing over. The ice surrounding The Wonder House frilled out around her.

Even if he tried to pull in there, he would have to skulk past the duckboards. He would be seen as an unwanted emissary of the Abdullahs. The women of The Wonder House and the Abdullahs had closed in on themselves since

Irfan had gone missing and Lila had been attacked in the city before Ramadan. Layers of trust between the two households had been separated and pulled apart.

Farouk was bringing dates from Iraq, dried figs from Afghanistan, and apricots from Pakistan, all via Abu Azim's dried-fruit shop in the bazaar. It was Eid-ul-Fitr beneath the snow, the end of Ramadan. He was delivering to the Abdullahs for the final breaking of the fast. Lila would probably shout at him if he tried to tie up near The Wonder House. He would just have to walk further from the canal mouth.

He lifted his paddle and turned the *shikara* for the canal. Another boat was moving along the edge of the lake from the canal opening, looping around the skirts of ice that spread from the houseboats. Farouk lifted his paddle in greeting and the other *shikari* raised his as well. Farouk swore as icy water ran down his arm from the paddle on to his chest and down into the *kangri*, making it spit under his *pheran*. The other *shikari* was moving fast, younger and fitter on the water. Farouk recognized Gulshan. He would be delivering to The Wonder House, carrying the same dates, figs and apricots from Abu Azim's shop.

Gulshan had seen the older man struggling with the cold wind that was pushing across the lake. It was why he had taken the canal routes from the city, so as not to have to sweat and freeze on the open water. He hugged his *shikara* in as tightly as he could to the ice to stay in the lee of the houseboats. He thought about what Lila might give him from the *dunga* kitchen. His mother would beat him if she knew that he wanted to break the fast with Suriya Abdullah's girl. They had once been friends, Suriya and his mother, he knew that, and the mute woman's story, he knew that too.

Masood stood by the window of his study. When he put his fingers to the glass it felt as though ice penetrated from the outside. He would go back down to the winter sitting room as soon as he was done. The kitchen used to be the only place where there was any real warmth during the six frozen months, but now there was this second haven, its thick stone floor warmed through from underneath by bricks that were heated in a fire in the kitchen courtyard and then placed, with long tongs, in the space between earth and floor.

He needed a little longer to finish the accounts, to be separate from the fuggy excitement downstairs as they watched for sunset.

When he looked at his hand on the cold glass he could see dried blood still under his nails. He had cut a goat's throat in the morning, its chin warm in his hand, its demonic eyes fixed and staring as he had held the knife against its skin, the blood then pulsing out thicker and faster than he had expected, making dark holes in the snow.

Every time he got blood on his hands, every year the same, on his hands and under his fingernails. He would not make a son of his cut *bakra*. If he had a son. He would not make his nephews do it, but for his brothers it was a rite of passage. Their sons had to learn to spill blood as they had.

Why teach them? Why encourage them with the sense of death in their hands? His brother Ibrahim had made Irfan cut the *bakra* last year and now what? Now where? Enough of killing.

He pressed his forehead to the glass and rolled it left to

right, numbing the noise inside. Two *shikaras* were out on the lake below. He knew one of them would be Farouk bringing more food for Eid. He watched the second boat moving towards The Wonder House as Farouk moved away from it in the direction of the canal opening. He realized it was Gulshan carrying supplies.

It would be the first Eid that he had not seen Gracie since 1977, twenty-two years of sharing a cigarette and a few dates before he went to his family to break the fast with them. He had always taken dishes from their kitchen to the *dunga*, and Suriya and Lila had always sent back something in return. Last year it had been soaked dried figs that Lila had roasted, their insides stuffed with walnut and almond paste that had melted into the flesh. Gracie had tried to make him have a peg of whisky that some guest of hers had left behind. He had sniffed it, drawing the smoked honey in, before pushing it back at her. That temptation and the smell of the figs had made him eat one on the way back up to the house.

He could remember the taste now, the warmth of the scented memory in the saliva on his tongue. He remembered how the fig, still hot from the roasting pan, had seemed to explode and melt in his mouth at the same time. The heat of the paste in the centre had burned the back of his palate, sweet pain that had made him open his mouth and suck in the cool evening air, and the fig seeds had stuck in the gaps between his teeth. He had still been flicking them out as he had lain in the dark at the end of that night, even after so many hours of eating other things.

Masood closed his eyes, pressing his forehead harder against the frozen glass.

His smile had made Naseema so suspicious, and she had

prodded him during the course of that evening, asking him
again and again whether he had broken the last day of the
fast while his family had waited for him. The way he had
tried to drop his smile had given him away the first time she
had asked, but he had not admitted to it. She had continued
to ask until he had grunted in the darkness as they lay with
full bellies, their breath puffing above them in the cold air,
and she had rolled away from him, triumphant in her dis-
covery of his treason, refusing him access to her warmth
when he had asked forgiveness.

A year since that forbidden fig had been eaten in the
meadow.

'Uncle.'

Masood turned. His young nephew Feroz was standing by
the door, his knees squeezed together in the cold. 'Auntie
sent me. Farouk has not come with the fruits. What is she to
do?'

'He is coming now, tell your auntie that.' He held out his
arms to the boy who ran at him, hurling himself into
Masood's stomach, making his back spasm. He gasped but he
did not push the boy away.

'Why are you here? It's so cold.'

'I had some things to do.' Masood wrapped the spread of
his *pheran* around the boy, folding him in towards the
warmth of his stomach.

'Can I come with you to wish Gracie Madam for Eid? I
am seven running, old enough now to come and wish her.'
Feroz buried his face into the core of his uncle.

'Maybe not this year.' He rubbed the boy's back.

'Why? Every year you go, every Ramadan.' Feroz looked
up, his face small and direct.

Masood was silent, not because it was better than lying, but because his mind was blank.

'Is it because of Irfan and the hole in Lila's shoulder that Auntie mended?' He was still looking up at Masood.

'Come, we will go down into the warm. You're right, it's much too cold up here to be able to do anything more. See, I can't even feel my hands. I think they're rubbing your back but I can't feel them.'

'Of course you can,' Feroz laughed. 'I can feel it, you must too.' He wriggled away as Masood rubbed harder and harder.

'I can't, nothing, nothing at all.' Masood clapped his hand. 'See, nothing, can't feel anything.'

Feroz jumped up and down, clapping his hands as well.

'And see, we are warmer now for all this.'

The boy laughed more, hurling himself again into Masood's stomach. His back buckled into another spasm. 'Come, I think you are right, I will go and wish Gracie Madam. You can come next time. Go and tell your auntie that Farouk is here.'

'How do you know?'

'Because I am taller than you.'

Feroz looked up at his uncle. He was not a tall six year old and his head was still only level with Masood's navel.

'How tall is that?'

Masood had no idea. He had not been measured since he had been at school. 'As tall as the apple trees at the end of the garden.'

Feroz was trying to see out of the window, jumping up to get his head above the sill. Masood pulled his chair over from the desk and lifted his nephew.

'Is Allah taller than that?' the boy asked.

'He's taller than the trees.'

'Even the so huge chinars on the road, the ones as high as houses?'

'Yes, taller than that.'

Masood and Feroz stood at the cold window. The square of light from the study fell out on to the snow below.

'He's taller than anything we can imagine.'

Feroz did not reply.

'We're all just tiny dots in comparison, smaller than a stitch on a shawl, so small you can hardly see it at all.'

Feroz looked up at his tall uncle, who was claiming Allah to be taller than a tree, and that they were both as minuscule as a stitch. He looked down at the sleeve of his little *pheran*. There were stitches on the cuff that were barely visible. Uncle Masood was not a stitch and Allah could not be taller than the chinars on the road, nobody could be. He realized that he probably knew more than the adults. He accepted the weight of this understanding with a small sigh. Reaching out, he took his uncle's hand and pulled him towards the door.

Masood turned back at the end of the garden. His footprints had made a clean track from the house – the evidence. No one had seemed to notice him leaving. Farouk had arrived from the canal path, bearing the last things needed for the intense activity in the kitchen. Naseema had been waving clouds of steam away from a huge pot on the stove, hissing at Kudji, while Faheema and the two kitchen boys had retreated into a safe corner to sort dried fruit. The door to the winter sitting room had been closed, a ripple of heat coming from underneath. Masood had felt it on his ankles as he had passed.

He was standing in the snow where Irfan had been the last time he had spoken to him from the balcony outside his study, picking on the boy, shouting at him. Had it been that?

He stared at the darkening hollows of his footprints. Irfan's face was no longer clear. He closed his eyes to try and find the details that had faded.

The snow had been scraped away from the main duck-board to The Wonder House, leaving two dirty lines on either side. Masood waited for a moment and considered the idea of turning back. Suriya's head appeared around a thick blanket that hung in the entrance to the *dunga* boat. He raised his hand to her. She nodded in reply and her hand came around the edge of the blanket, waving him towards the sitting room. He could feel her watching as he took tentative steps up the duckboard, testing for ice. He looked up to check whether she was still there, but the blanket hung straight in front of the *dunga*.

The back of Gracie's chair was facing the door, turned towards the belly of the stove. Masood could not see whether she was there. Again he waited, conscious that he was trying to breathe quietly.

'Suriya, I'm sitting here in the gloom, waiting and watching for the sun to go down. My soul and liver have been purged enough now, thank you.'

'Mine are eight years and eleven months more purged, imagine that?' he replied.

'Masood.' Her voice flew up. 'Is that the man I never see?'

'*Ji*,' Masood smiled from the entrance.

'Is our cold war over then?'

'Is that how it has been?'

'I think so, and very cold too, no tan-ta-tan, no artillery, no cavalry, no medals, no lovely uniforms, just too many weeks of lonely smokes. When did I become the enemy?'

Masood did not reply.

'How is everyone then? How is Naseema?'

'Fit and fine.' His voice was flattened.

'And you, how are you?'

'Fit and fine, and you?'

'Old and angry, thank you. Are you going to stay by the door and talk to me like a cross schoolboy?'

'I came to wish you.'

'Wish me what?'

'Eid-ul-Fitr.'

'Oh that, the month of suffering. Suriya has been honing her skills of torture. A month on the wagon, and you know she even managed to make me stop smoking for ten days?'

Masood was watching how the snow had changed the colours across the lake. There were no lights showing from the boats on the other side.

'Everything is dark now.'

'You have no idea, life without pegs and nicotine is one long haul through the pitch black, contemptibly dull.'

'The boats.'

'Contemptible or dull, or both?' she asked.

'They are all dark, the ones across from here. Last Eid there were still some lights.' Masood could feel the warmth of the burner moving around the wings of Gracie's chair. He took a step into the room. 'Now every one of them is in darkness.' He was close to the back of her chair.

'Do you remember how it was before all of this? The Pandits, they loved Eid almost as much as you. Do you remember that Kaul girl who Lila had such a crush on?'

'From Zaina Kadal?'

'Yes, yes, she used to keep the fast with Lila and come for Eid every year. Those things she used to bring from that *mithai*-wallah of theirs, the cream horns and that special *pinni*. Suriya used to heat it up for me piece by piece for weeks afterwards. With cream, oh God, the ghee used to melt through the dhal flour and go crunchy.' She sighed.

'We were better then.' He reached towards the back of her chair.

'Were we, or is that just how it seems now?'

He did not reply and his hand dropped to his side. He could see his breath in the cold air above where the warmth of the fire had reached him.

'We lost our way, Masood. Somewhere between Nehru and your children we lost our way. Cigarette?'

The familiar pattern of conversation hung between them, for a moment. Masood lifted his hand to her chair again. She turned as she sensed him so close behind her.

'Oh look, Lila, look who's back.'

Masood had not heard her coming. She stood at the entrance, a terracotta dish held out in front of her. Even with a cloth over the top he could still smell the sweetness of the figs.

If he could freeze the moment, he could lift the cloth and take one, eating it slowly, just biting a small hole in one side so that he could test the hot paste inside and not burn himself. And when he had sucked all the seeds out from between his teeth, and wiped his mouth, he could reanimate the scene, the cloth replaced, the dish as it had been in Lila's hands.

'I came just to wish you. I cannot stay. I must go back to

the family. The sun will be fully set soon.' He half-turned, as though to leave.

Gracie began to pull herself up out of her chair. Lila lifted a corner of the cloth. He stopped, almost expecting to see a space in the dish, but the figs sat in fat uninterrupted rows.

'Have an Eid fig,' Gracie said, one hand stretched towards Masood.

Lila pushed the dish towards him. 'Have.' It was the first thing she had said to him since she had cried out at him in the meadow over a month before, her body curling away from him.

There were hardly any marks now on that face he knew so well, just some paler spots edged with greyish-blue where the skin was still healing. He looked away, raising one hand between them.

'Have one,' Lila said again, pushing the edge of the dish against his raised hand.

'Go on, please have one.' There was a sadness in Gracie's voice. She held Masood's forearm with both her hands.

'Are they still very hot? I burned my mouth last year and had so much drama from Naseema. She knew I had broken the fast without them.' He dropped his raised hand.

Lila smiled. 'They are still hot but not so hot as to burn.'

'Put it on one of these.' Gracie held out one of the silver coasters that sat in a pile on the table beside her chair.

Lila lifted one of the figs out of the dish, looping it around to catch its own drip, and put it on the coaster in Gracie's hand. Masood could not stop himself from watching as she licked the thick sweet juice off her fingers. Gracie held the fig up to his face. He took the coaster and bowed slightly to Lila and then to Gracie. Both women smiled.

He carried it up through the meadow, his hands inside his *pheran*, one hovering over the fig to feel its warmth. He realized he was nervous and, like a boy with stolen fruit, he waited until he was out of sight of The Wonder House before lifting it up through the neck of his *pheran* and biting into it. The juice slid down his chin in a hot dribble. He closed his eyes, lost his balance and fell into the bank of snow at the end of the meadow that rose up to the garden gate. Lying on his back in the snow he laughed and ate, digging through the warm flesh, scooping out the hot paste and sucking it off the ends of his fingers too.

He was still brushing snow off his *pheran* as he reached the kitchen courtyard gate. He inhaled the last of the sweetness in his mouth as he reached for the door. Naseema opened the latch before he could.

'Someone is here to see you,' she said. Her eyes were fixed.

'Who is it?'

She did not answer, though her eyes opened wider and rolled to one side. Masood looked around her. There were two soldiers standing in the kitchen. Kudji and Faheema were huddled into the corner opposite them. The young men turned at the sound of Masood's arrival. One of them pointed his rifle directly at him and then flicked it towards the door, his head making a similar movement. Masood asked Naseema with his eyes. Hers did not move. The first soldier waved his rifle again.

'How can I help?' Masood asked the first of the young soldiers in his oversized uniform.

The boy flicked his head again. Masood stood his ground for a moment, but Naseema narrowed her eyes. He turned and walked between the soldiers and his sisters-in-law.

Ibrahim and Rafi were standing in the hall beyond the kitchen, their faces in a shadow pool directly under a light on the wall above them. Masood could not read their expressions. The door to the winter sitting room was open, something that never happened until the last late-winter frosts had gone. There was a voice from inside, a one-way conversation on the telephone in English, smattered with Hindi. Masood stood at the door of his own sitting room, his hands folded in front of his chest.

A major was sitting on one of the window seats, his back to Masood, the telephone cord pulled to his ear so that its spirals were straight. He was looking out over the garden, his head hunched to the side to hold the receiver in place as he fiddled with one of his eyebrows. Masood coughed from where he stood in the doorway. The major turned from the window, waving his hand to usher in Masood. He did not move. The major turned back to the window. Masood took a step into the sitting room. The major turned again. Masood stopped. It felt like a game.

It was clear that it was an STD call to Delhi, long distance, at peak time. The major was in no hurry.

The sun had dropped, leaving pale stains under the line of clouds just above the mountains. The fast had ended. Masood's body tightened as the intimate moment between him, his family, and their god passed.

In the kitchen Naseema swallowed down her tears as the light fell away from the courtyard wall beyond the window. The soldiers were pushing around the Eid dishes that had already been put out on the kitchen table, knocking lids on to the floor, spilling a bowl of *pulav*, the rice, cashews and raisins scattering around their boots.

Masood's head dropped.

Now their fast had been abused twice over: the first time as he lay on the snow bank in the meadow, and now by the soldiers he could hear among his family. In the moments between the noise from the kitchen and the end of the major's telephone call Masood felt control slipping from him. Every corner of his world had been invaded, every dish at their table putrefied. He lowered his head and prayed for the strength to be as pure and cold as the snow that he had fallen into.

The receiver banged down and the telephone cord recoiled around the end of the major's revolver holster. He yanked it away, pulling the receiver off the hook again. Part of the mouthpiece splintered away as it hit the floor. Masood did not move and the major did not pick up the broken piece.

'There is a curfew, where have you been?' he asked.

'I have been on my land, sir.'

'I use English as I heard you using it a while back.' The major looked directly at Masood. 'Is Hindi better?' he asked.

'Whichever makes you comfortable.'

'Two educated men, we can use English. Be free to change at any time.'

Masood did not reply.

'The sun has set now, the curfew is in place. How many family members are there living in this house?'

'Seventeen.'

'And they are all in the house now?'

Masood did not look up as he replied. 'My nephew is out of station, he is in Delhi with relatives.'

'How old is he?'

'Eighteen running.'

The major worked one of his eyebrows with his left hand. 'How long has he been with your relatives?'

'More than one month.'

'Why is he away from your family for Ramadan?'

'He has been keeping the fast with our relatives and now he will be making the celebration of Eid with them.' Masood looked up at the major for the first time.

'You can contact these relatives? They will vouch for him?'

'They will.' Masood now looked beyond the major's shoulder to the afterglow on the mountains. 'The sun has set for curfew, sir. It is also the end of our fast. May I be with my family now?'

'I have no wish to keep you from your family at this time. Do you have another telephone here?' The major ignored the broken receiver at his feet.

'There are telephones in neighbouring houses.' Masood looked down at the damaged instrument.

'Are you asking me to leave?'

'No, sir. I am just informing you that there are other telephones that you could use.'

'So you think it suitable that I take my men and disturb the Eid of others so that you can carry on with your own festivities.'

'It is more prayer, sir, than festivity, and this is not what I am saying.' Masood looked at the bulled tips of the major's boots. One was still mirror-buffed, almost sharp enough to reflect the major's sprouting nasal hair, the one unrestrained part of his appearance. The other was scuffed, the glassy finish scratched by something it had hit or kicked.

'This is the only line you have in this house?' The major waved towards the telephone.

'There is another one upstairs in my study, but you will find it very cold up there. We have no method of making warmth in that part of the house.'

'You have a study? And what is it that you study in this study of yours, Masood Abdullah? Lists of the names of people we would like to have perhaps? Newspapers from the enemy, full of lies?'

It was the first time the major had used his name.

'Not at all. I have a business to oversee. It is my office.' Masood inhaled. 'You are most welcome to go and see, and to use the telephone there. I was thinking just of your comfort, sir.' Masood stepped aside to show the major to the stairs.

'No one in this valley thinks of the comfort of the security forces. We are abused and attacked by those we are trying to protect, so you will forgive me for finding your sentiment unusual.' He turned to look out of the window again. 'Cuckoos you call us, unwanted in your nest. But, Abdullah, I am sure I do not have to inform you what the cuckoo does to its host in the end.'

They watched each other's reflection in the window, waiting in the darkening glass. Queues of replies formed in Masood's mind but he did not speak.

'One of your neighbours, who perhaps does or does not have a telephone, has been helping the militants. You could ask him if there is any uncertainty on his part as to the outcome of the cuckoo hosts.' The major moved to the door, turning his body away from Masood so that they would not touch.

Masood followed him up the stairs, listening to the sounds from the kitchen. Bowls and pans were being pushed around, though the women were silent.

At the end of the alley that cut off from the road in front of the Abdullahs' house another group of soldiers was in Masood's neighbour's kitchen. The man's wife was kneeling on the floor among a splattered pattern of slowly cooked white rice, the grains now in cooling lumps that were splashed with spills of lotus root, their revolver chambers glistening with ghee. A piece of star anise dug into the woman's knee, imprinting its six points into her flesh, but she did not notice. Her *kameez* had been cut away from her body, and she had been forced to hold up her soft breasts to make it easier for the soldiers to beat them with the wooden ladles that she had been using all day to stir rogan josh and lamb meatball curry for Eid.

As she knelt in the kitchen her husband and her two elder sons lay on their bellies in the back of an army lorry, their thumb joints bound together with wire behind their backs, their faces pressed down on the metal ridges of the floor. Three soldiers had one of their boots on the side of each of the father and sons' prostrated faces, pushing down a little harder when any of them tried to move.

The major did not stay on the telephone for long in Masood's study. It was too cold. His point had been made. He left the room quietly and stood on the landing, listening for family noise, hoping to hear a moment of normality in which he could rest.

There was none.

He inhaled the scents of the interrupted Eid feast preparations. They were the same spices as those used at his favourite meat haven under one of the walls in Old Delhi, the place where he met up with his old college friends during leave. They gathered to escape the chit-chat of the women at home, and they would sit and eat *malai* kebabs and *koftas* until the onion and garlic began to bubble back up their throats, laughing at old stories that they had shared over and over.

He breathed in and came back down the stairs.

He looked at the three men in front of him, their beards to their chests, their moustaches cut back to stubble. Their eyes still looked young but the hair made them seem old, greying, worn out. He hated what they did to their moustaches to mark their journey to Mecca.

'You have all been for Haj?' the major asked, plucking at his own full, dark-dyed moustache.

Masood, Ibrahim and Rafi bowed their heads.

'Quite a thing that, the whole family. Have your children been too?'

'Some of them, the older ones,' Masood replied.

'Has your absent nephew been?'

'He has.'

'I have no doubt it inspired him.' The major had stopped on the last step to give him height above the three men. On the level they were all taller than him.

'It is a most profound experience for all who go – king, soldier, beggar, all are equal for the Haj.'

'You must be doing very well to be able to afford to take your family.'

'We have been blessed, inshallah.' Masood's head remained bowed as he spoke.

'Very blessed, a thing that can change at any given moment, you know, Abdullah.'

Masood lifted his head to look past the major.

'We can pick anyone up at any time. Remember that as you run your business and whatever else from your study. Ask your neighbour. He will have wise advice for you.' The major waved the brothers out of the way of the kitchen door. 'I realize that we have interrupted your Eid, not something that I enjoy having to do, you understand.' He stopped to look at each of them. 'You did not even offer us tea. A sad thing not to be civilized enough to have offered *chai*.' He pointed at the kitchen door.

The three brothers looked without replying. The major stepped forward and rapped on the door. There was a pause before it was opened. The soldier on the other side snapped to when he saw that it was his officer. The major surveyed the kitchen, lids on the floor, plates and bowls scattered, two women in one corner, a third opposite them, two houseboys sheltered behind her, the pungency of the spices hanging over the cornered women. A long-bladed knife lay on a white cloth in the middle of the disarray on the table. There were dots of dried blood on the linen, perfectly lined up with the edge of the blade, undisturbed, untouchable.

He waved the soldiers out of the kitchen ahead of him, and turned to Masood as he picked his way over the food scattered on the kitchen floor. 'You will have your nephew report to the nearest police post when he returns. I will leave his name with them. He will be expected. They will have orders to send the information on to me, Major Kumar.'

Masood nodded. Major Kumar waited a moment. Masood stood silent in the doorway.

'There is something you have kept from me.' Major Kumar's hand rested on his revolver case.

Masood's body tensed, though his face remained empty.

'He has a name, your nephew? You have not given me his name.'

'The name is Feroz, sir, Feroz Abdullah.'

Major Kumar nodded and left, leaving the kitchen door open.

His soldiers were in the corner of the courtyard. There was something childish in the way that they stood and whispered. It annoyed him. He waited until he heard the door close behind him.

'Are you two bum-fluffs too frightened to touch a *bakra* knife? Only brave enough to throw around rice and vegetables in front of women, are you?' He pointed to the gate beside the walnut tree in the courtyard and both men ran to open it.

'Are you mad? What do you mean taking Feroz's name.' Kudji erupted from the corner as one of the houseboys closed the kitchen door, her head thrust at Masood.

Naseema stepped between them.

Masood moved back. 'It's not so mad. Feroz is too young to have papers but he is listed as a member of this house. We can have papers made in Delhi with one of the cousin's pictures and Feroz's name. It will be possible, you will see.' He turned to his wife and put his palms on either side of Naseema's fidgeting hands.

She snatched them away and covered her face. 'Our faces were not covered. They just came in and spread their filth all over our food, all over our home. And now they have made my husband into a liar. Why did you say this thing?'

Masood moved one of his hands towards her face, shielding her mouth without touching her. 'You are not to say these things.' He caught and cradled her hand again as she lifted it to push him away.

'We had done nothing wrong until this. We were clean and now you have made us dirty. You have made us criminals. We are just like them now.' Naseema started to pull her hand away from Masood but his grip tightened.

'Where are the dates?' he asked.

Naseema looked at him, her forehead crinkled in surprise.

'Bring the dates. We will break the fast now together. Then we will pray. You will throw away the food that was touched. There are other dishes, ones they did not see. You always make so many more than this.' He turned to Kudji and Faheema. 'All of you, you make so many wonderful dishes. Come, we will do this together.' He stopped and bent to pick up one of the bowls of rice. 'Where are the children?' he asked, looking from Faheema to Kudji to Naseema. 'Where are they?'

'They went to get the Eid rugs from the cupboards in the roof room. They went up before all this.' Faheema flapped at the food scattered on the floor. 'They must have heard all this and stayed hidden.' She looked up, her face beginning to collapse.

'Go and get them.' Masood pushed Naseema gently towards the door. He realized he had touched her four or five times in the few minutes since the soldiers had left. He rarely touched his wife in front of other people. He looked at his offending hand in surprise as Naseema went to call the children by name.

They came out of the cold above, lining up along the landing, their faces pinched. Masood smiled up at his daughters and nieces and nephews, his arms reaching out towards them. They smiled down at him, their faces opening.

'What did he mean about our neighbour?' Rafi asked Masood as the children ran down to them.

'We will not think on this now. Let us take dates and water.'

Gracie twitched among the pale poppies.

Fuses blown, synapses shrivelled away, beginnings of sentences, almost ends, subjects, verbs, no buggering objects, no objectives, no point, no tidy ends. Like falling down a hole, everyone I've ever known standing around giving advice, but I can't hear what they're saying.

In her half-consciousness she tried to hold on to the image, looking for names to match the lifespan of faces standing around the hole she seemed to be in.

Alice, I've become Alice, down the hole and this lot are about as much use as the flamingos. Good, remembered that, or was it storks. No, storks are for babies, flamingos were croquet mallets with their legs all tucked up. Masood is looking old. How old is he? How old would Hari be? '49 born, '59, '69, '79, '89, '99 – my God fifty, how could my boy be fifty? Sixty Eids gone. Where's Lila.

She surfaced from the grey space just above sleep. The dish of figs sat beside her, the only gap being where Lila had taken the corner one to put on the silver coaster in Gracie's hand for Masood.

Where was he?

She looked around the room, staring into the fading corners.

He left, of course he left. Went to his family as he should. Eid, end of fast, sunset, family time, stupid woman. Suriya and Lila. Must go and break their fast with them. They won't come to me. Asked them to, every year for what? '87, '97, twenty-two years and still they won't come.

Jitu, Hari and Gracie, her husband, her son and she, had spent one Eid on Nagin in 1953. Jitu had just won a big case and he wanted them all to be together. He had been away in Calcutta for nearly six months. Hari was four then and he had fallen off their houseboat – or a six year old from another boat pushed him. Jitu dived in after his son, crowning himself in the sludge, while their houseboat boy lowered himself gingerly over the edge to help. Of the three of them in the water only Jitu had been able to swim. Hari had been silent as he was pulled from the freezing water. Masood's mother wrapped them all in shawls warmed in front of the kitchen fire, and fed them dates mashed with hot ghee. She had spooned the mixture lovingly into Hari's mouth as though this part-Hindu, part-foreign child was one of her own.

Too many Eids since then.

Gracie stared at the wasting light on the mountains.

Sun all set, day done, Rama-done, gin, gin, gin and Thing. Mother's milk to her it was. Bit the bowl right off the spoon she did. *My Fair Lady*, must have been 1962. Not bad, got the date. Lovely Audrey, all that neck under those huge hats, and delicious Rex Harrison, so like Jitu – only paler.

She heard her own laughter in the silence and wished there was someone else there to witness her life, a presence to stem the overflow of past on past.

Someone must come. Someone is coming. Isn't someone coming? Not now, not right now, but quite soon. Just can't remember who or why.

~~~

Hal surveyed the world on either side of the road. From the air the gap between the airport and the swell of Delhi had seemed barren, on the ground what had looked empty now teemed with tightly packed life.

Every flat space was a pitch. Anything was good enough for the wicket: battered oilcans were stumps, or a large pot-hole and a twisted bicycle tyre. The taxi turned down a side road to cut away from the traffic and, as it turned, it was hit broadside by a leg drive from a small boy wielding a broken shovel handle with a liquid stroke. The batsman stared at Hal's face the other side of the taxi window, the boy's expression puckered with the frustration of his interrupted shot.

Hal clapped, raising his hands so that the young batsman could see the applause for his leg drive.

The boy smiled as the taxi nudged its way through the rest of the game, taking a careful detour around the wicket keeper, who refused to move from his place behind his twisted bicycle-tyre stumps.

Hal had forgotten how they played cricket, every boy dreaming his way out of the dust. As they drove on the bitter smell of the open sewer in the back road mixed with the warmth of a string of jasmine flowers that hung from the driver's mirror, swinging above Ganesh on the dashboard. The little elephant god was perched on top of a row of red flashing lights, the pot-bellied disco king of Hindustan Motors.

Two hours later he was on a domestic flight to Srinagar. The man in the window seat next to him was wearing a striped shirt and checked trousers. His fingers were covered in stones; emerald, cornelian and lapis lazuli, all variously promising to be the only sure answer to his peptic ulcers and marital strife. He intrigued Hal with his constant movement, scribbling figures on a piece of paper even as they juddered in and out of the air pockets above the city's bilious haze. As he wrote, his left hand kept flicking up to rearrange a stray slick of hair that continuously broke free from his heavily oiled helmet.

He had not acknowledged Hal as he had pushed past him to get to his window seat. He had still not spoken when a neat stewardess with plum-outlined lips had offered him fresh lime-water. When she returned, her matching plum fingernails flying over the trays in her trolley, proffering veg or non-veg, he simply waved to show that he wanted non-veg. Again he did not show any sign of having noticed Hal, even as he helped pass across his tray.

The man's two drumsticks had been neatly stripped down by the time Hal's food had been delivered, the flesh pulled deftly away in long strands, whipped through a small bowl of mint chutney, and folded into his mouth. He continued to scribble, changing his pen from his right to his left hand, balancing his paper between the tray and his knee. Hal tried not to stare and concentrated on a decorated cream twirl on the top of a solid square of orange mousse on his tray.

'It's the stigma of a crocus,' the scribbling man spoke to the back of the seat in front of him.

Hal turned to him. 'I'm sorry, are you talking to me?' he asked.

The man waved a chutney-covered finger at Hal's mousse. 'On the top, stigma of crocus, saffron from variety of crocus *C. Sativus*, making the creamy go orange, saffron, hence the name, you understand.'

'Oh, I see, thank you.'

'Italian ladies used it for dyeing their hair, they were so keen for the same blondization as their northern neighbours. You are not enjoying this taste?' asked the scribbler.

'I was just fiddling.' Hal put his spoon down.

'You are English?'

'Partly,' Hal replied.

'Good enough. You have a town in your part-country, Saffron Walden in your state of Essex. Do you know this place?'

'I know where you mean but I haven't been there.'

'It was grown there for hundreds of years. A pilgrim carried it from Asia Minor to his native place. The name of that place was just Walden then, you understand. But I am told it is all gone now. Saffron is only grown in my valley and in one place in Spain, I am forgetting the name.' The scribbler raised his pen for a moment. 'In Kashmir you will drink *kawa* tea.' He separated the fingers of his right hand. 'Green tea, cardamom, *dalchini*, what is that? Cinnamon, yes, that's it.' He folded down his middle finger. 'And almonds and saffron.' His other two fingers closed over his thumb. 'It takes 170,000 flowers to make one kg of it. This is why it is so expensive.' He held out his hand. 'Sanjay Dhar.'

Hal took his hand.

'Oh sorry, sorry, you now have my lunch in addition to your own.' Sanjay Dhar laughed at the chutney that he had passed from his hand to Hal's, and Hal looked for his napkin. 'You may find the refresher wipe in this very-hard-to-open packet more effective.' Sanjay Dhar waved the salt and paper and refresher wipe packet at Hal. 'It is your first time to India?'

'No, I spent some time here after university, but that was ten years ago.'

'Ah yes, after university, of course. This is your first time to Kashmir?' Sanjay Dhar was managing to eat, scribble and talk.

'Yes, it is. I wanted to come ten years ago but it was winter, a minister's daughter had been kidnapped, and people told me that it was not a good time to go to the Valley. I've come to write about the changes.'

Sanjay Dhar laughed. 'Now it is the start of the worst of winter, we have just finished a war, Pakistan has a coup, and you think it is a better time to come? Why?'

'My timing's not great.' Hal had not meant to try and explain his numbness. He concentrated on his tray again.

Sanjay Dhar pushed his face up and under Hal's. He stared for a moment and then nodded. 'This I see.' He leaned back and folded the last strip of chicken into his mouth. 'The lotus gardens are finished, the fruits are finished, the only thing my valley has in abundance now is cold. But there are other things to find.' He turned his attention to his mousse. 'It's still a strange time to come to the Valley. You will be watched.' His fingers prodded the creamy top. 'You see what is sad about this little stigma that is making this cream all saffron, the saffronization of the *malai*?'

'I don't think I do.' Hal stared at the single piece now stuck to the back of his spoon.

'This small, small thing is grown by Muslims, planted, watered, all the needful, and then plucked by Muslim hands in the fields beyond Pampur, not so far from Srinagar, maybe ten, fifteen kilometres. Then where does this little thing, picked so carefully by Muslim fingers, end its journey? You tell me?'

Hal still stared at his spoon. 'Here on some ungrateful foreigner's lunch tray?'

'No, no.' Sanjay Dhar waved an erect index finger in Hal's face. 'As a tika on the foreheads of the priests in our Hindu temples, but more than this, as tika on the foreheads of the Shiv Sainiks and other extremists who want nothing more than for every last Mussulman to be hounded out of India. So you see, my friend, perhaps this is the only secular thing you will see in India, from Muslim hands to Hindu foreheads, Pandit Nehru's great dream only possible in this little flower part.' And Sanjay Dhar whipped the cream twirl off the top of his mousse with his index finger and popped it in his mouth.

Chapter Six ~

As December passed the first freeze backed away.

It was warmer. The previous night had been sealed in by cloud that had lifted with the early mist. By late morning The Wonder House's ice skirt had softened enough for Lila and Suriya to be able to break it free from the sides, pushing it out into the lake, some of the pieces floating away with whole lily pads intact inside. They pulled all the windows open and hung blankets and carpets out on the roof railings.

There was no wind on the lake and fish came up to the surface. Kites hung just high enough above the water for their shadows to be distorted, diving and grabbing as the fish jumped. It was the first day that the scar on Lila's shoulder had not ached.

When Gracie finished lunch Suriya tidied her out on to the front of the boat. She was going to clean the sitting room and dust out Gracie's musty temper. Gracie did not try to help as Suriya pulled a *pheran* over her head, gently easing

Gracie's arms into the sleeves. Piling cushions around her, Suriya stuck a thin pillow between Gracie's stomach and the *kangri*, the little fire pot, that she put into her hands inside the *pheran*.

'If the *kangri* cancer hasn't got me by now I don't think it ever will,' Gracie said, pulling the protective cushion away and sticking it behind her back with the others. 'And it's bloody cold out here. Don't think I want anything between me and this hot pot.'

Suriya shrugged and set about her task in the sitting room with her carpet beater and duster.

'Did you know that we have the highest rate of stomach cancer in the world from these fellas?' Gracie patted her *kangri*.

Suriya plumped cushions.

Gracie settled herself. For a moment she fussed that she had been shoved outside without anything to read, then she felt the sun. She could not remember when she had last sat outside. It seemed months ago. Now, in late December, she could feel it on the gap above her ankles where her trousers had ridden up a little. She leaned down and pulled them up further. Her skin absorbed the heat and she could feel the patches of cold where the shadow of the carved struts of the deck veranda canopy fell across her legs.

The water-lily gatherers were out, moving among the melting ice, all women, their bodies hunched to their knees at the front of the boats, thin lily-vultures pulling their flowered loads of cattle and goat fodder across the water. Gracie watched as they moved. Some of them raised a hand to her and called out. She nodded and returned their call.

Some of the women's heads were uncovered, their hair caught up in a knot or a long plait. It cheered Gracie. The creeping spread of the *burqa* and the *hijab* through the city and across the lakes depressed her. Even the youngest of the Abdullah girls, the ones who were hardly more than babies, were covered up now as if they were old married women.

Who had decided that the *hijab* meant that they should be black shades moving around the streets like half-people? That lovely man from Aligarh, think he came to help Jitu on a case of a Muslim divorce in Simla, the professor with twice as many teeth as most people. He had said that the Arabic word '*hijab*' just meant modest covering, nothing about obliterating every feature of a woman. The women of Kashmir were hardly running around in polka-dot bikinis. How much more modest could you get than the *pheran*? It was a *hijab* in its own right. Since when had modest meant a black sack? And those little girls, shrouded in black, just their little faces out to stop them from being like the other crows. Need to talk to Masood about it. Perhaps not immediately, maybe wait until the waters have become a bit more honeyed. Water gets ruffled, honey just shifts a little, better to be honey than water. Sweeter too. Yes, that's right.

Gracie punched the pillows around her back, righteously indignant at the satisfactory end of her one-sided argument. There was so little sound that she could hear the grebes on the lakes as they fluffed their feathers against the water. In the distance was the hum of the traffic from the city, hyphenated by longer blasts from rude freight lorries bullying their way through.

Gracie pulled her hands in through the sleeves of her *pheran* and moved her fingers around the *kangri*. She could almost stretch them out fully. Even her arthritis seemed to have retreated a bit with the ice.

One of the lily women pulled in between The Wonder House and the next houseboat, leaning down into the water to pull up the lily leaves that were free of the ice. She sang as she worked, a song that Gracie recognized but could not remember, in the same way that she knew the woman's face but could not remember her name.

Probably asked her a hundred times. Would rather hear her sing than ask her name to forget it again as soon as she's gone.

Gracie fell asleep to the sound of the lily-gatherer singing a Kashmiri nursery rhyme that Masood's mother used to sing to Hari when they had come for Eid to the lakes, when Hari had fallen in, or been pushed.

She was woken by the gentle rocking of the front of the houseboat as someone climbed up on to the steps below the deck veranda.

'Who is it?' a mottled voice called down to Hal as he crossed from the *shikara* to the bottom of the broad-stepped ladder up to the houseboat.

He climbed up to find the voice sitting in a pile of cushions, dressed as a Kashmiri, her head covered with a shawl, though the voice sounded English, its brittleness eased at the edges by something else. Her shins and feet stuck out from under the same kind of thick woollen tunic that almost everyone he had seen so far had been wearing. Her exposed skin was pale and dry, almost translucent. She seemed to have no arms. He began to introduce himself.

He was standing in front of her almost unchanged, no older, just as beautiful. As Gracie cried out, she tipped the *kangri* over and some of the coals fell against her leg. She felt nothing.

'Hari,' the woman shouted out, interrupting his introduction, her face flushing from the point of her neck that Hal could see above the collar of the tunic and her shawl.

'I'm Hal,' he said.

She seemed to struggle under her tunic, repeating the name again and again until it became an hysterical stream of sound. A slight woman rushed out of the room behind. Hal tried to speak again, but the second woman hushed him, a finger to her mouth. She pulled up the seated woman's tunic and yanked out a small smoking pot, half-basket, half-bucket, but it was not the pot that was smoking, it was some coals that had spilt out and were now smouldering against the woman's trouser leg.

There was a blanket on the seat of the *shikara* that he had come in. Hal jumped back down the steps to grab it, dragging it through the water as he climbed back up. As the slight woman flicked the burning coals away with her hands he flung the blanket over the older woman's smouldering trousers.

'What are you doing, Hari?' she asked, her voice apparently separated from the drama below.

'Trying to put out this fire.'

'What fire, my darling?' She tried to reach out to him.

Hal could now see that she did have arms but that they were trapped inside her tunic.

Lila had heard Gracie shouting. It sounded as if she was repeating the same thing over and over, calling in panic to someone.

She stopped as she reached the edge of the veranda. A tall man, his hair as dark as a Kashmiri, was bending over Gracie, as though trying to hear what she was saying, a blanket in his hands. Her mother was flicking coals from an overturned *kangri* across the carpet, her fingers constantly moving them so that they would not burn the silk. Gracie seemed to be half-conscious, her head lolling to one side as she continued to mutter the same word, but now Lila could separate out the words. Gracie was repeating a name, her dead son's name.

The man bending over Gracie stood up to face Lila. Then she understood. He was olive-skinned, blue-eyed and dark-haired, with the kind of soft curls at his neck and temples that made you want to wind your fingers into them. He looked like the pictures of Hari that Gracie had all over The Wonder House, not identical but close enough.

Lila leaned towards Gracie as the man stood up.

He saw her as he lifted his head.

Another woman, younger than the other one, much younger, almost a girl, finer featured, paler and more delicate than the round-faced girls that he had seen in the city. She was taller too, quite a bit taller than the other woman, but she was also silent in her response to the older woman's demented state. The girl's body was also engulfed in a tunic but she looked thin under the heavy wool. Her hands were rough, though the fingers were long. She wore thick grey socks, the big toes knitted separately from the rest.

Pretty local girl, very pretty, no, beautiful.

Then she did speak. 'Who are you?'

'I'm so sorry, I'm Hal, Hal Copeman. I wrote.' He held out his hand to the girl but she ignored it. He was conscious of his hand in the air between them and he dropped it.

'What do you mean you wrote?' She turned away from him. 'No matter now, what happened here?' Her voice was as complicated as the older woman's, but in reverse, the accent was Kashmiri but layered with an English exactness to most of the words. Her question was directed more to the other woman. As she listened to the girl she scooped up the coals from the carpet into her hands before throwing them over the edge. They hissed as they hit the water. Her hands were thick and callused but there were already blisters on her palms from the coals. She made no sound as she wiped them down the side of her *pheran*, and then waved them in front of the girl. For a moment Hal did not understand until the woman's movements began to make a pattern, a language. She was signing to the girl.

'My mother says that you came from nowhere and frightened Gracie Madam. She knocked over her *kangri*, and now you have to explain, but I have to look after Gracie Madam. Can you wait for some time?'

'Of course, can I do anything to help?' Hal stood uncomfortably between the three women.

'I think not for now, but you can take this cold blanket away before it gives her fever. It is not ours.' She pulled the sodden rug away from Gracie's leg.

'It's the boatman's.' Hal took it from her.

'Then you must give it back to him. You can wait or are you going to push off now?'

He realized that she did not mean to be rude, that it was just the way she used language. Hal turned away towards the *shikara* so that she would not misread his smile. He went back down the steps to pay the boatman, and to apologize for the state of his soaking blanket.

Gracie opened her eyes again. 'Lila, he was here, he came back. Did you see him? He was standing here talking to me. Hari, he came back.' She stared around the veranda, pushing herself away from the cushions. 'Where did he go? You frightened him away. Did you frighten him away? Hari, Hari?' She swung her legs down from the seat, screeching with pain as she moved.

'You've burned yourself with the *kangri*. We have to see how bad it is. Sit now.' She lifted Gracie's legs back on to the seat, gently separating them with Suriya's help.

'Where is he?' Gracie was crying.

Hal sat at the bottom of the stairs with the *shikari*, listening to the scene above.

Should he stay where he was or offer to help again? Would the old lady go even loopier if she saw him again? Or perhaps it would calm her down.

The lake was so still, and the *shikari*'s face beside him seemed placid, unmoved by the drama. Three small grebes lifted from the water, running along the surface, kicking up their own wake, until they had beaten hard enough to take off. A kite flicked its tail feathers, changing direction, then folding its wings to dive, grabbing a fish as it pushed back up from the water, paralysing the tiny silver thing in its grip. A houseboat roof of pigeons took off as the kite passed, surging away from it, changing direction as one to circle back to where they had started. The kite settled on another roof and slid its feet to either end of the small fish before tearing through the scales.

Hal gave the *shikari* fifty rupees more than they had agreed at Dal Gate. He climbed silently back up the staircase as the boatman pulled away, the blanket dripping showily over the edge of the boat.

Gracie Singh was poised in the doorway of the veranda, her back to him, supported between the other two women.

The younger one turned, closing her eyes as though to ask him not to speak.

He waited beyond the doorway, looking into the sitting room, partly furnished with carved Kashmiri pieces and the heavily crewel-stitched material that was already becoming familiar to him. The walls were panelled and carved with the same flowers and swirls that were embroidered on to the cushions and curtains. Where the walls and the ceiling met there was a fretted screen that petticoated the top of the room in a wooden frill. The other pieces of furniture, two armchairs and a desk, were Chippendale design, though they looked Indian-made in their flourish. Everywhere there were tarnished silver frames – under lamps, beside vases, on the desk and the low tables. He wanted to go in and look, to see if he could find a photograph of the man who Gracie Singh had mistaken him for, to see if he could begin to put pieces of her story together even before he spoke to her.

There was a smell to the room.

He was six years old, standing in the doorway of his Spanish grandmother's sitting room outside Seville. The same shadowed interior after the hard light outside, the same moment of adjustment as his eyes found the edges of the furniture, the same breath of old age hanging in the dust of the light-filled windows. His hand lifted to reach out for his mother, to follow her into the grey world, and listen to her as she lit the shadows with her excited explanations of who the people were in the clumps of photograph frames that filled every surface.

Her lightness had been spoilt when his grandmother had come in, her spine as rigid as her face. The grip of her cold hand had been as frightening as the smell of decay in the room. When she had bent to kiss him, Hal had fixed her in his mind as a vampire, hunching his shoulders up to his ears to try and close himself away from her touch. She had pinched his nose hard enough to make him cry, though he had told his mother later that it was because of the dust in the room.

Hal stepped away from the glass door.

When the girl had said to wait, did she mean on the veranda or in the sitting room? It was warmer in the sun. The coals had burned neat holes in the cushion covers where Gracie Singh had been sitting. She was a surprise, somehow he had expected tweeds, a bun, lace-up brown shoes with school ma'am heels, somewhere between Madame Arcarti and one of Paul Scott's remnants. But that would make her a cartoon.

Hal sat down on the opposite side of the veranda to where Gracie had been, but it was too cold out of the sun. He moved back to her side and arranged himself away from the coal scars and the damp patch where the wet blanket had been. His view was divided into vertical parts by the struts of the veranda, each portion framing the mountains, the naked chinars and poplars, the houseboats on the other side of the lake, and the water. The afternoon was already losing its warmth in the mist. Three *shikaras* were coming together from separate directions, moving towards each other. They met in the middle and then turned across the lake.

There was a heaviness to everything around Hal. The idea of moving any part of him seemed exhausting. He managed to reach across to some of the cushions that had been piled around Gracie. Even that seemed too hard. He fell back against a bolster that he managed to pull from the pile. It was as though he was being drawn into the views.

It had to be jetlag.

The *shikaras* had reached the steps of The Wonder House and three faces came over the low veranda gate at the same time, two of them almost identical twins in *pherans*, their skull caps pushed back on their heads, their faces shaven though grey with stubble around their moustaches.

'Hallo, welcome.' They spoke together and leaned over the gate at the same time.

The third man was much younger, no stubble and no moustache. His face was softer. As the other two climbed over the gate he stayed on the lakeside, watching rather than participating in the performance.

'My name is Pete, Pete Touche.' The first over the gate thrust his hand towards Hal. 'You are enjoying Kashmir? You are having a good time?'

'It is lovely but I've only just got here. I arrived yesterday and . . .'

But Pete Touche, who had hijacked his name from a rock guitarist he had once taken in his *shikara* for a whole day, was not put off. 'You want to see papier-mâché? I have very beautiful pieces. You have wife?'

'Not yet,' Hal replied.

'No problem, inshallah you will. You have girlfriend?'

'Not at the moment.'

'You have mother, sisters?'

'Yes, I have both of those.'

'This is good, and they are all fit and fine?'

'Yes, as far as I know.'

'So, you will buy gifts for them so that they will have

memento of your happy time in Kashmir.' Pete Touche folded his arms in satisfaction as a boy appeared behind him, hidden by two large wicker baskets that he was carrying.

Identical salesman number two had settled himself in the opposite corner of the veranda, his legs and arms pulled up inside his *pheran*. He seemed happy to wait his turn.

Pete Touche pulled a white cloth out of one of the baskets and laid it out on the carpet, carefully smoothing it at each corner. Then he began to arrange his pieces in family groups: flowery boxes in the top left-hand corner; rabbit and chicken-shaped boxes below; candlesticks on the right; box sets of coasters in the middle; and the space beneath Hal was reserved for the stars of the show. Pete Touche slowed down as he revealed two larger boxes with highly detailed scenes: the first a courting Mughal couple in a rosy bower, their lineage obvious in the heavily outlined and swooping noses that almost met, hook for hook, as the billing pair intertwined; the second was of Krishna in blue romantic mode, legs casually crossed as he leaned against a tree, trilling on his flute for radiant Radha, the queen of the milkmaids among her heavy-uddered herd.

Hal looked at them. Sanjay Dhar had been wrong with his plane parable. It was not just the crocus parts that were secular, this papier-mâché salesman with his stolen name was too; his Hindu love-myth box cheek by nose with the Muslim love birds.

Hal settled into the rhythm of the banter, the waving hands, the click of the boxes, candlesticks, rabbits and chickens. It was the same sound as the backgammon pieces used to make when he had played with his father on his good days, when he had been home from hospital for long enough to have a routine. The thlak, thlak as they had made their moves and talked about things that were not very important, but that had grown to become immense to Hal within the structure of that time.

'Does anything say "hallo" to you?' Pete Touche was tugging at the hem of Hal's trousers.

'Say "hello"? I'm not sure. What happens when one says "hello"?'

Pete Touche looked at him and put a hand gently on his knee, guiding a fool in the ways of the world. 'Sir, it is when a piece speaks to you, maybe many pieces, inshallah. See this?' He picked up the box of the courting noses. 'How beautiful it is, *asal* we say, *asal*. How can this not speak to you? It says "hallo" to you in any language.' He held out the box.

Hal took it, lifting the lid and replacing it to make again the sound of the backgammon pieces. He stopped mid-stream, his hand static on the second mildly erotic piece when Lila spoke.

'I see you have brought all the sales-wallahs with you.' She was standing in the doorway. She could have been there for any length of time.

Hal pushed himself up on the bolster. 'They just came across the lake.'

Gulshan stepped up from where he had been sitting behind the gate. 'Is he the one who wrote the letter? Is this that man?'

Lila flicked her tongue against her front teeth. It made a hard hiss as she jutted her chin at him. 'If you want to speak to him, ask him in English.'

'My English is bad.' Gulshan squatted back down.

'Why are you hiding out there? Are you ashamed that you came with these two, landing on the first white face you see like so many vultures. Step over, come and join the crowd, why not?' Lila spoke quickly, her eyes fixed on Gulshan.

He got up and moved the wooden keeper down, pushing the gate gently. It stuck on the floorboards of the veranda. Lila stepped around the back of the papier-mâché man and pulled the gate hard. Gulshan climbed in and squatted down again, just inside the edge of the veranda. He pulled his hands inside his *pheran* and lowered his chin into the collar.

'I'm sorry, have I caused some kind of problem?' Hal tried to make sense of the contrast between Lila's careful English and the ricochet of her Kashmiri.

'It is not a problem. This boy was asking me if you were the one who wrote to Gracie Madam,' she replied.

'I did, but how does he know that?'

'He brought the letter.'

'So you did know I was coming?'

Lila turned to Gulshan and screwed up her face at him, but the corners of her mouth were softer than her eyes. The boy smiled down into his *pheran*. Hal watched her, and Pete Touche and the carved wood salesman watched as well.

'You will take tea?' Lila turned back to Hal.

'How nice.'

'*Kawa* or *chai*?'

'*Kawa* would be delicious.'

'You have had it before?'

Hal held up his hand. 'Cardamom, cinnamon, almonds, saffron and . . .' He counted off. 'I can't remember . . .'

'Tea, you passed by the tea.' Lila looked at him, the foreigner trying to sit so upright against the bolster, and she laughed. 'I will leave you to the good attendances of these fine gentleman.'

'Shakespeare?' Hal was surprised.

'Yes, you know we read here too.' She turned away. 'Gracie Madam is resting now. She will need some time.'

'I am sorry. I think she must have been asleep when I arrived and I just . . .'

'She thought you were her son.' Lila cut in.

'Amazing reaction, he must be a popular man.' Hal leaned against the bolster again.

'He was killed in a car accident many years ago.'

'Oh God.' Hal stared at Lila, both his hands lifted in question.

'She had been asleep, who knows what she was thinking or dreaming. She needs some time to rest.'

'How old was he?'

'Hari, he was twenty-three, I think.'

Hal stared at the array of papier-mâché in front of him, realizing how open the conversation was to the three men.

'I think it would be better if you could come back again to talk to her perhaps tomorrow. Would that cause a problem for you? Do you have time?'

'Yes, I have time and it's no problem. Will I be able to get a boat back from here?'

'Gulshan can take you, he is a *shikari*. Where are you staying?'

'Residency Hotel.'

'Of course you are, all the journalists stay there.' She had already turned and began to speak to Gulshan.

He nodded without lifting his head as she spoke to him.

'He will drop you at Dal Gate and then you just take a

rickshaw to Hotel Road. They call it Maulana Azad Road now but most of the old rickshaw-wallahs still call it Hotel Road. Take an older driver. The younger ones can sometimes cause a problem.'

'Thank you.'

'There is no rush but when the sun goes it will become very cold. I will bring *kawa* now for you while you shop.' Lila disappeared through the sitting room.

Hal and Gulshan's eyes followed her. They caught each other watching, and they both looked away.

Pete Touche held the second box up to Hal. 'Krishna and Radha, very beautiful love story of a god for a simple woman.' He handed the box to Hal. 'Very strong woman.'

The other salesman laughed from his place across the veranda.

Sidi Saleem was hunched over a steel beaker of *chai*, his back and head all part of the same curve. He broke flat dry bread into the tea, prodding the hard pieces under the surface until they softened, then he scooped them up with his fingers. Sodden crumbs and *chai* spilt on to the rug and down his *pheran*. The boy crouching next to him told him not to dribble.

Sidi turned to him. 'So you want me to eat like some foreigner, all "oh thank you so much", and shit?' he spat the English phrase with more of the bread.

Irfan had been sipping his *chai*, his head pulled down into his *pheran* to hold in his own warmth. He broke the flat bread and dipped it into his beaker until the tea had reached his fingers. Turning his head to one side to catch the drips he dropped the bread into his mouth, enjoying the mixture of the wet, warm softness and the dry crunch of the end held between his fingers. He pushed his head back out of his *pheran* collar when he heard Sidi.

'Ah, Irfan, got something to say?' Sidi launched another soggy handful into his mouth.

'How would you know about the way foreigners are? Most of us are too young to remember what it was like when the houseboats and hotels were full.'

'And long may they stay away from our valley.' Sidi hunched back down over his tea.

'What do you mean by that?' Irfan rolled forward on to his knees. 'It's the main reason we're all sitting here on this filthy blanket, freezing alive because there's no work for us back at home. All this is not the tourists' fault. We all had it good when they were here. What do you have against them?'

Sidi lifted his head slowly. 'And why exactly are you here, Irfan Abdullah? I don't think your mother or your sisters have been raped?' Sidi waved his hand at the boys on either side of him. 'As far as I know none of the big Abdullah brothers has been arrested, taken into custody, tortured until his bollocks didn't function any more. Am I wrong?' Sidi stuck a finger in his mouth to fish something out, and examined it in the palm of his hand. 'Feeding us stones now, trying to harden us up on the inside too,' he laughed into the silent circle and threw the small stone from his mouth at Irfan. 'Your family don't seem to have suffered at all, no badge of humiliation to qualify you for this brotherhood. What have you all done? Sold carpets to rich foreigners, hawking our crafts all over the world, taking rent from that old Angrezi bitch and her two whores.' He rocked back on his haunches.

Irfan caught Sidi as he shifted, knocking him off balance, grabbing his arm and flipping him on to his belly. He bounced his full weight on to Sidi's back, winding him.

The other boys moved in closer. Irfan reached for the mulch of spilt tea and bread on the blanket and rubbed it into the side of Sidi's face. He knew that Sidi would not be able to move until he caught his breath, and he bent over him, his mouth close to his ear.

'I'm not fighting you, this is so that you hear me. And in case you have forgotten it was you who told me to come here.' He pushed his weight down into the small of Sidi's back. 'My father says that you and your father are like your dogs, always trying to find a fight. There will always be one there if you go looking.' Irfan pinned Sidi's other hand down with his knee as he began to struggle. He bent closer to his ear so that his mouth was almost against the lobe. 'Do you think it's a braver thing to start a fight or to stop one?' He jumped off and out of range. 'Which of the Suras tells us to go out and find fights in the name of Allah?' Irfan realized that for the first time he had said something that his uncle Masood had tried to instil in him across the years.

The other boys were edging away, separating themselves from Irfan and Sidi.

There was a third voice. 'Tell me where in the Koran it says that we must lie down like broken dogs and allow our fathers, our brothers and sons to be taken away, beaten, and ripped apart so that we can no longer recognize them? Where does it say that we should quietly watch while our mothers, our sisters, and daughters are raped in front of us, the seeds of the enemy planted in their bellies. What are we supposed to do then, oh Maulvi Abdullah? Are we supposed to say 'thank you*ji*' and let them deface our valley with their Hindu filth?' The training commander spoke from the opening of the tent.

Sidi was pushing himself up from the ground, sucking in air in great gulps, making more noise than he needed to. Irfan stood in the middle of the widening circle, facing the commander. He was wrapped in a scarf that covered his head and the whole of his face, leaving just his eyes and forehead exposed, and muffling his voice. He flicked the front of his *pheran* with one end of his AK-58 and levelled it at the space between Irfan's eyebrows. 'Why do you think we are keeping you here for so many months instead of just turning you back across the line after a couple of days of gun-training like the rest of them?' He moved closer to Irfan.

'So that we don't get caught or shot down so fast,' Irfan replied.

The commander brought the muzzle of his gun right up against Irfan's forehead. The cold circle of metal pressed into his skin.

He will not shoot me.

Irfan did not move. He did not blink.

'This is why.' The commander lowered his gun. 'So that you learn the difference between when a man is going to kill you, and when he is trying to scare you. So that you learn to kill him before he kills you. Then you little boys might be ready to go back into our valley to fight rather than just to make noise and show off to your friends.'

'He attacked me.' Sidi was back on his feet.

The commander flicked his gun around and pushed Sidi with the butt. 'And to stop you from being whining women too.

'It is 6.30, there is no call to prayer, the border patrols are listening in tonight. Come to prayer, you bunch of little girls.' The commander turned away.

Irfan smiled somewhere inside his chest. Sidi had accused him of being a woman when he had threatened him through the bars outside the mosque. The irony had a good taste.

The camp cook was behind the commander, and he waited while the other man walked away, and then spoke. 'If you were women you wouldn't make such filth.' He looked down at the blanket covered in spilt tea and mashed *kulcha* bread. 'Babies playing with food, all of you. If there is so much spare that you can play I'll give you less.'

The boys huddled around him, dropping their cups into the plastic washing bowl that he was carrying. They rubbed his back and pressed his legs.

'It was a fight. Your *chai* was too good. I'm dreaming about the next lot already.' One of the honey-tongued boys took the bowl from the cook.

'Ah, so not babies then, my error, you're dogs, a pack of pi-dogs. All of you, get out, go and pray.' The cook smiled as he bent down to pick up the edges of the blanket.

Irfan squatted down to help him. Sidi kicked him hard at the base of his skull as he passed. Irfan bit into the tip of his tongue as he fell forward.

The cook caught him. 'No damage, just more shit from you puppies.'

Irfan sat down as the impact became a hammering headache at the front of his forehead. 'Do you really believe that Allah wants us to carry the gun and to kill in his name?'

The cook was folding the blanket, flicking the sodden bread away. 'And do you think those Hindu boys think that their wavy-armed, animal-headed gods want them to kill Muslim boys in their names?'

Irfan wrapped his hands around the back of his head. Closing his elbows in on either side of his face, he lowered his head to his knees and cried as silently as he could.

The cook finished folding the blanket and threw it into the corner of the tent. 'You'll have to drink the next lot in your own filth. Nothing will dry outside now.' He turned to Irfan and saw the blood at the corner of the boy's mouth being carried down his chin by the tears. He put his hand on Irfan's back. 'If you think, if you try and find reasons, you will get a bullet in your head. It's the thinkers that get killed, the idiots that survive.' He got up and helped Irfan to his feet.

Gracie was sitting as she had been the first time, propped up among the cushions, but not asleep this time.

Hal began waving from the boat as soon as he could see her.

Lila had sent Farouk to collect him from Dal Gate. The return journey was much easier than the previous evening when Lila had sent him back to the city with Gulshan.

As they had cut away from The Wonder House, Gulshan had set his face and it had not changed for the whole hour that it had taken them to get back to the city, as the evening freeze tracked them through the dying lotus gardens. Hal felt the young *shikari*'s irritation bearing into him from behind as he flicked his paddle out of the water, over and over again.

There had been no point in trying to speak to him. Hal sat, first with his feet just over the edge of the deep seat, the way he had on his grandmother's chairs twenty-five years before, upright and ungrounded, but as it got colder he edged back against the cushioned seat and pulled his legs into his core. He sat for a while with the memory of how he used to itch to escape from his grandmother's furniture. Gulshan misconstrued the silence, stabbing at the water with renewed anger. The exchange of money at Dal Gate had been almost furtive, neither one of them looking at the other. Gulshan pushed away from the ghats as soon as Hal's feet were off the boat. Hal raised his hand to the dark shape at the back of the *shikara* but there had been no response.

It was a different daylight journey with Farouk. He offered his hookah before they were even out of sight of the ghats, and by the time they reached the lotus gardens Hal knew how many sons and daughters he had, and he had also sympathized over Mrs Farouk's problems with her sugar disorder.

'She cannot see you as yet,' Farouk told Hal as he started to wave as they approached The Wonder House.

'I just want to make sure that I don't start another fire.'

Farouk did not understand. 'You know Gracie Madam?' he asked.

'Not really, not yet.'

'Lila was telling me that you know of her.'

'I only met her yesterday, but it wasn't quite the first meeting I had hoped for.'

Farouk smiled without understanding.

As they moved closer Hal called out. 'Mrs Singh, it's Hal Copeman. I've come back, I hope you don't mind.'

There was no reply.

'It is still too far.' Farouk nodded in time to the dip of his paddle.

A young girl with cropped hair was standing in a houseboat garden opposite the *shikara*. She wore a short checked dress over a pair of leggings, the back of her skirt tucked in so that her bottom stuck out too far. She was pulling frost-bitten chrysanthemum heads off their stalks and throwing them into the water. She worked with the determined air that seven year olds have. Someone called out to her from the *dunga* at the back of the houseboat garden. Turning towards the caller, she saw the *shikara* on the lake in front of her. Hal waved and smiled at her. She threw the remaining flower heads at him with a fierce expression.

Hal turned to the old boatman. 'What was that for?'

'People here are angry. There are many things to be angry for.'

'But she's just a little girl.'

'They are taking the anger from their mothers now.' Farouk lifted his head towards The Wonder House. 'She will hear you now.'

Gracie did not hear, or she did not seem to hear. She waited until Hal was at the top of the steps.

'Haven't been called Mrs Singh for years. Couldn't think who you were shouting at.' She waved him over the gate. 'Come, let's meet again without the pyrotechnics.'

Hal held out his hand to her and she took it, not to shake but to hold between both of hers. Her skin felt empty.

His hand so alive in hers.

'You look very like my son. That was the confusion.' Gracie nodded to the seat beside her, still holding on to him. Her tone lifted. 'Come and sit down. What would you like? Not a lot to choose from at this time of day. *Kawa* or *chai*, though I think there are pakoras coming. Been smelling them on the breeze.'

'How's your leg?' he asked, trying to work out how he could sit down without pulling his hand away from hers and seeming rude.

'Oh fine fine, silly thing to happen. You're not all English, are you, something else in there too?'

Hal propped himself against the edge of the seat. 'Half, my mother's Spanish.'

'How nice, all that bull-fighting and tango.' Gracie squeezed his hand a little tighter and then released it.

'Flamenco,' he said.

'Exactly.' She patted his hand before releasing it. 'Where in Spain, where is your mother from?'

'Seville.'

'Oh.' Gracie sank back into her cushions, her hands in the air making castanets with her fingers. 'I always wanted to go to Seville. Read *Death in the Afternoon* while I was pregnant with my Hari and just wanted him to come out quickly, grow up and take me to dance thingy in Seville at Easter time. You know what I mean, all that dancing and fighting?'

'The *fiera*, when the whole city is full of orange blossom if Easter's early. The smell is breath-taking.' He paused. 'Madrid,' he added.

'They have a thingy there too?' she asked.

'No, I'm sorry I meant that Hemingway's obsession with the bullfight started in Madrid.'

'Hal, that's not a very Spanish name either.'

'It was that or Alfonso.'

'Alfonso, same as our mangoes, beautiful name.'

'Not when you're trying to get into the school football team.'

'You could have cut it down to Alf, very Yorkshire, very

tough.' Gracie stuck her finger in her ear and wiggled it, making a strange growling noise in her throat at the same time.

'Hal came first, my parents argued about it for two months until the local priest told them they had to decide because if the flu epidemic got me then I couldn't be buried on hallowed ground. My father bribed my mother with a beaver jacket she'd been hankering after. So Hal came first, Hal Alfonso John Copeman.' Hal made the sign of the cross.

Gracie took her finger out of her ear. 'Alfonso of Seville, Alfonso the mango-orange man.' She closed her eyes. 'Better than John, very dull name John – the Baptist, the Baker and the Candlestick maker. Men called John, very dull.'

'Hence Hal.' He sniffed and then settled to watch a woman just beyond the boat pulling up the water-lily leaves. She raised her hand to him as though she knew him. He raised his in reply.

'He was an alcoholic,' Gracie said.

'What?'

'Hemingway, did most of his writing off his head. Probably why I liked him so much.' She opened her eyes. 'You look terribly proper sitting on the edge like that. Why don't you sit more comfortably?' She waved her hand towards the cushions at the back. '*Chai* or *kawa*? Can't remember what you wanted?'

'*Chai* would be delicious.'

'That might upset the girls, think they'll probably have made *kawa* for you. Let's see.' Gracie gave an odd little-girl giggle.

Elfin, that was what she was like, with a scheming quality that turned her face into a walnut broken clean across, more

Tolkien than Hans Christian. There was a bit of Bilbo Baggins about her.

Hal pushed himself back against the warmth of the cushions that still had the sun on them. '*Kawa* would be delicious too.'

She was already in motion, calling out, arms waving. She turned back to Hal and looked at him with the same expression. 'All this literary chit-chat and I don't even know why you're here. Why are you here? Are we related? Have you come to wrest my home from me?'

'I wrote to you,' Hal laughed.

'So we are related?'

'I don't think so, though it would be a great bonus if we were. I wrote to say that I was coming in the hope that I could talk to you for an interview.'

Gracie sat and watched him.

'It would be part of a series on how the Islamic conflicts have affected those just trying to live where they have always lived. We're doing Bosnia, Palestine, Iran, Kashmir and Afghanistan. I got Kashmir.'

'Who's "we"?'

'My paper.'

'You own it?' she asked.

Hal turned at the sound of feet behind him.

Lila was between two of the veranda struts above his head. He leaned over the back of the seat to see what she was standing on. Her feet were on running boards that stretched the full length of the belly of the boat, right back to the *dunga* duckboards. She was wearing the same grey socks with the separate big toes, one of them gripping the edge of the running board. He pushed himself back so that he could look up at her without looking straight up her nose. He smiled and half raised a hand. She nodded as she turned to acknowledge Farouk who was moored at the bottom of the steps.

Gracie Hobbit elbowed into their silent conversation. 'Lila, this is my cousin Hal Alfonso John, dull John, who has come for tea. He would like *chai*.'

Chapter Seven ~

The determination of the two women pressed in on Hal.

It eased away as Suriya came sideways through the sitting room doors, carrying a large tray with a samovar, a thermos, a chafing dish, a bowl of fresh chutney, and two thick white cotton napkins.

'Your mother has the instincts of King Solomon. The children bicker so she brings both *kawa* and *chai*. We even have the best linen for the prodigal pup.' Gracie paused. 'But we'll go inside. It's too cold out here now, and Lila you will light the *bukhara*.' Her will imposed, Gracie sat back.

Suriya reversed into the sitting room, and Lila stepped over the edge of the veranda from the running boards and into the space between Hal and Gracie. She thumped between the sitting room and the veranda, carrying Gracie's cushions, and then putting her arm firmly under Gracie's elbow to support her.

As they moved inside, Hal tried to talk as Lila began

crashing the *bukhara* lid up and down, and striking matches without managing to light the stove. He gave up in the face of the sideshow, though Gracie carried on through it, settling herself into her chair and waving him to the nearest sofa.

Hal felt that his next error was to choose *kawa* tea instead of *chai*. It seemed as though both Gracie and Lila slightly adjusted their opinions of him as he took what he thought would be the diplomatic route, the tea of the Valley. Gracie ignored his choice, poured herself *chai* from the thermos, and took the lid off the chafing dish. She ate two pakoras with steady deliberation before offering them to Hal.

'Just checking that Suriya is not trying to poison my newfound family.' She smiled as she passed them to him, her mouth still full.

When he only took one of the hot battered pieces, she shook the dish at him so that several more slid into his lap. Lila passed him a plate and a napkin as he picked the pakoras out of his crotch, each one leaving a small oily patch on his trousers. She turned away before he could tell whether she was laughing.

'Didn't anyone in London or Delhi tell you that perhaps it was not such a good time to come up here?' Gracie wedged the dish between her thighs. She took one at a time in a steady stream, dipping them into the chutney and then straight into her mouth. She offered the chutney to Hal as an afterthought.

When he did not answer she looked up.

'Sorry, disgusting manners, but I missed lunch. Weren't sure whether you were coming for lunch or tea so I held off. Oldies aren't supposed to have much of an appetite. Not me.

Always hungry.' She popped the largest pakora in the dish into her mouth and then offered what was left to Hal.

He took two.

'So didn't anyone warn you off?'

'They said it would be very cold.' He helped himself to chutney.

Gracie laughed.

'Bloody cold, but then I don't think I've ever been as cold as I was in Oxford. I remember the fountains freezing in one of the quads. Which one has a fountain? Never mind. It was as cold as Yorkshire and that's bloody cold.'

'The House?'

'Oxford boy then?' She reached across and patted his hand with her chutney-oiled palm. 'I'm an Oxford girl too.' She laughed again.

'Yes, there seemed to be a whiff of blue-stocking.' He licked the mix of spices and mint off the end of a pakora before it dripped.

'No, a black stocking; cooking and secretarial college, the totty-typists I think we used to be called.' Gracie was laughing so hard that little pieces of pakora flew out of her mouth.

Hal tried not to move when one of the larger bits landed just below his right eye. Lila seemed to fade out of the room between them, lifting the empty chafing dish out of Gracie's lap as she passed.

'Are we going to get some more?' Gracie spluttered.

'I think this is all.'

'Please ask her to make some more. We're so hungry, aren't we?' She looked to Hal for support.

He lifted his remaining pakora and waved it without much enthusiam. Lila walked away without answering.

'Have I annoyed her?' he asked.

'Don't think so, it's much more likely to be me.'

'She looked pissed off.'

'How wonderful – lovely slang – strange to think one could miss hearing it.' Gracie wiped her hands. 'She's an angry girl, that's all.'

'About what?'

'Growing up here.' Gracie picked something from under a fingernail and examined it. 'Now, where are you staying?' She looked up from her investigation.

'Residency Hotel.'

'And how is it?'

'Well, it's a hotel.'

'It's where all the journalists stay when they come to town, when we're the biggest circus going and everyone comes along to hitch a ride. They said that it was so full of journalists when the troubles started that they were paying room rates to have a bathroom to sleep in. It was packed again in October after the coup next door. Think everyone really thought the two new entrants to the nuclear playpen would blow each other up. Supposed to be a million of the Indian army along the LoC at the moment, but then you know all this border stuff. Seems so absurd, I can't even imagine a million men. You know this poor little valley has more military in it than any other volatile area in the world? But you know all this stuff already or why else would you be here?' She looked at her wrist. 'So, you must come and stay here. What time is it, I've lost my watch.'

'It's just after four.'

'Ideal, Farouk can take you back before it gets dark, you can pack your bags and get a rickshaw back here. He'll meet

you at the jetty just across from here and bring you back.'
Gracie looked at Hal. 'It's not entirely appropriate but you
had better take Lila. Farouk will have to stay with the *shikara*
and you'll probably get lost in a rickshaw.'

'That's so kind, but it's fine at the Residency.'

'Fine is not good enough, we have a huge houseboat here
with three spare bedrooms. Why waste your money when it
would be so easy for you to be here?'

He was about to resist again but stopped. The hotel was
depressing and cold, and there was a sense of life in the
sitting room of The Wonder House. He would be right with
his subject, but then his subject would be right with him too.

Gracie was waiting.

'That would be lovely, thank you. A few days here would
be a real bonus.'

'A few days, rubbish.' Gracie shouted for Lila through the
dining room. 'She probably won't hear with everything all
shut up. Could you go back to the *dunga* and tell her?'

'Of course, how do I get there?' he asked. 'And why
would it be inappropriate for her to come with me?'

'The mullah crowd wants women to always be accom-
panied by a male member of their family. Suriya and I are the
wrong sex for that. Stupid anyway.' She puffed with annoy-
ance. 'Oh, and it's just out through the side after the dining
room, duckboards, follow the path, *dunga* on the right.'

Hal got up and Gracie raised a hand to stop him.

'Local girl, code of behaviour . . .' she stopped.

He nodded.

As he climbed out through the sliding window beyond
the dining room he knew why Gracie's use of English was
familiar; a memory of cold mornings on a drill square, puffs

of breath around his Cadet Corp commander's yelling mouth, the abbreviated form adopted by those who gave orders, by people who did not have many conversations, who had cut away the paraphernalia of language and spoke in just the bare bones.

The chrysanthemums on either side of the path had been bunched together with grass ties, their rotting heads pressed against each other. Two boys were running across the flat meadow beyond, one of them waving a cricket bat, trying to catch the other boy with it as they ran up to a grass bank towards a gate in a high wall. Hal turned towards the *dunga* boat.

Suriya's face and the smell of frying spices came around the edge of a blanket that hung in the open entrance as he approached. She disappeared and Lila's face came through.

'What do you want?'

'Gracie sent me. I'm sorry, she wants me to come and stay here and she asked if you could come back to the hotel with me.'

Lila stared at him.

'I'm sorry, I'll try that again. Gracie has kindly asked me to stay and insisted that I go and get my things now. She thinks that I will probably get lost in a rickshaw on the way back so she suggested that you might be able to show me the way.'

She smiled. 'You are sorry a lot.'

'I'm English, we're apologizing to the world.'

'I thought you were half Spanish.'

'I am, but the education damage was done in England.' He noticed the freckles along the line of her cheekbones.

'Could you wait for some time?'

'Of course.'

It was the second time she had asked him.

'Shall I wait here or go back?' he asked.

'Could you take these, please?' Lila handed the chafing dish through the blanket. 'My mother made more.'

'Thank you.' He took the dish.

Her scalp was so pale through her dark parting.

The blanket fell across the opening and he stood on the deck, the chafing dish in his hands.

The sky was in the water as Farouk paddled them across Nagin – a candy-painted one. Lila watched Hal put his hand on the sky and it was as though he touched her. Farouk watched her as she looked away.

'There is not much light now,' he said.

Lila had been sitting opposite Hal and she climbed past him and over the back of his seat to squat in front of Farouk. She picked up the second paddle and began to work in time with his stroke.

'There's a blanket here for you if you feel cold,' she called to Hal.

He turned. 'I'm fine, thank you,' he said, though the wet air off the water was beginning to freeze.

'As you wish.' Lila pointed to their right as they turned out of the lake. 'That's Hari Parbhat Fort where the sun is going.'

The structure squared off the top of the hill that rose up out of the spread of the city.

'Akbar built it.' She rested her paddle across her knees. 'Great builder he was. It's said that he put a goat of gold into the walls so that the people would be able to afford to rebuild them if ever they fell.' She waved her paddle to the left of the city. 'And that's Shankaracharya Hill over there. He was one of the great saints of Kashmir, the one who taught everyone in the Valley to be a Hindu. He lived up there, and now the TV tower does.' She started to paddle again. 'There used to be so many Pandits going up and down all the time to the temple, but not now.' She turned back to Hari Parbhat. 'There are almond groves below the upper walls. In the spring it looks as though the fort floats on their blossom.'

'Can you go up there?' Hal asked.

'Not now, the army is using it as a fort again.' She changed sides with her paddle. 'And a helipad.'

'So you don't get to see the blossom any more?'

'You can see it from Nagin side.'

They moved on through sinking lotus plants.

Masood was drinking *chai* on the steps of the tailor's shop above Dal Gate. Mohammed the tailor and he had been to the mosque and now they sat together in easy silence, watching the buses dropping and collecting below them. Masood laughed.

'What happened?' Mohammed asked.

'See this bus, it says on its side "genuineness inside". What does this mean?'

'Genuine discomfort.' Mohammed gurgled into his tea.

The bus moved off with two boys in the door pushing each other to get on. 'Look with Love' and 'Be careful as you take seat, no tension please' were the messages on the rear of the bus, and above them a line of heads with prayer caps bobbed on top of the back row of seats.

Mohammed stopped gurgling. 'Each year I find the fast

harder. This time I broke it, I think, six times because of headaches and feeling so much weakness.' He started breaking a small round of bread into his cup. 'I am still trying to catch up but I keep forgetting how many days I have fasted. Each time I think I am done, Sahida tells me I have more days to go.' He spooned some of the bread out of his tea.

'Who is more likely to be right, you or your wife?' Masood asked.

Mohammed thought for a while as he ate the hot wet bread. 'I think Sahida. I am at heart a lazy and greedy man.'

'Not lazy, inshallah. Every time I come to take tea with you I have to drag you away from your work, you're always bent over your machine like an old crow.'

'I did not choose to be the crow. It is because neither of my boys show any wish to do tailoring work, and little pleasure it gives me sewing clothes to hide our women, black, black, black. It is the colour of death in so many places in this world.'

Both men sat in silence, their tea in their hands.

Two buses came at the same time from different directions and made enough noise to distract them.

'But not just black, this pretty piece here is different.' Masood reached up to a length of material draped in the doorway, a paler shade embroidered with little sprigs.

'Black with a few flowers for the girls with fancy ideas – see how I hang it, just so that they can imagine it on themselves.' Mohammed ran his hand down the material as though it was hanging on a body.

Masood looked back down at his tea.

'See, as I said, a lazy man, happier for the hang of the

material to make my sales for me than to have to get up off my end and be a salesman. More *chai*? Have some *kulcha* too.'

'I have to go, my friend, it is getting dark now and I won't be able to find a rickshaw to take me to Nagin if I stay on.' Masood passed his cup to the boy who had brought it, and who had been waiting as they drank and talked. 'Have a good night.'

'And you too, inshallah.' Mohammed waved his cup at the boy for more.

As Masood walked towards Dal Gate he saw a foreigner coming up the ghat steps and stopping on the road beside the houseboat post office, a tall man with dark hair and good clothes. For a moment he closed his eyes and thanked Allah. If there was a foreigner taking a *shikara* ride then perhaps things were not so bad. Then he saw Lila behind the foreigner, pointing him towards a rickshaw, hurrying him. Masood crossed the road without looking. A jeep swerved and blared at him. Hal and Lila looked up. Masood was beside them on the pavement as they turned.

'Lila, what are you doing?' He took her arm.

She tried to pull away. 'You're hurting me,' she replied to his Kashmiri in English.

'What are you doing with this man?'

Hal had climbed back out of the rickshaw. He tried to pull Lila away from Masood. An officer and two of his men from the swerving jeep separated Masood from Lila and Hal.

'What is this?' The officer shouted at Masood.

Masood weighed out the words with care. 'This is my niece, sir, and we are about to take our *shikara* to our home.'

'Where is your home?' The officer was still shouting.

'Nagin Lake, Zadibal side.'

Hal was now being held between the two other men. They had local faces but he could not tell whether they were army or police.

They all wore the same khaki and they all carried guns. A police or army bullet would feel the same. Lila seemed calm. Perhaps it was not so bad.

The men were good-looking, the kind his sister liked, all big brown eyes, long lashes, open faces. What were they doing dressed up to fight?

He heard the man who had grabbed Lila saying Nagin, a familiar word.

'Excuse me, sir.' He reached towards the officer and one of the other men pushed his hand away. 'Excuse me, sir, do you speak English.'

The officer turned to him. 'A little.'

'This lady is my guide and we are here to collect my things. I am going to stay with her employer on Nagin Lake. I do not know who this man is.'

Masood was staring at Hal.

The officer turned back to Masood. He did not understand.

'He said that my niece is his guide and that he has come to collect his belongings because he is going to stay on Nagin Lake,' Masood translated.

Hal watched Masood carefully as he spoke.

His mouth was gentle but the beard, the cap, and the orthodoxy were severe.

Hal turned to look at the men on either side of him again. They were both listening to what was going on between the officer and this other man. Their safety catches were on. Hal inhaled more fully.

'My name is Masood Abdullah.'

'Where are your papers, and hers too.' The officer shouted at Masood, waving at Lila without looking at her.

Masood and Lila reached down inside their *pherans* and handed over their papers. Hal saw that the three men were wearing shoes, not boots. The officer's were more highly polished, though there were cracks in the surface. The others were scuffed and they all looked so small. Kashmiri men seemed to have such little feet. He looked as his own trekking boots. They looked enormous.

They must be policemen.

'I know your brother Rafi. We studied together.' The police constable smiled up from Masood's papers. 'I have been to your house. I came just after his son was born to wish him and Kudji.'

Masood smiled. 'I'm sorry I did not recognize you.'

'Easy to do, I would not have been in uniform then.' He patted Masood's shoulder. 'We must have all played cricket together in the meadow below your house when we were boys. Masood, I think I remember you, a leg-spinner?'

'I used to think I was.' Masood's body relaxed a little with his voice. 'You must have been away for some time?'

'I have been in Jammu for most of my years in the force. I am newly back with promotion. Yes, absolutely I remember. You were the only Abdullah bowler. Rafi and your other brother were no good, much better batsmen.'

Hal picked up the English cricketing words that scattered the exchange. Lila remained motionless, her posture passive.

He turned to her. 'What's going on?'

'They're talking about cricket.'

'I realized. Is this standard arrest procedure – a bit of sport and then perhaps the weather?'

The policeman between them pushed Hal further away from Lila.

The constable turned to him. 'So, you have to tell me what is your good name?' His English was foundering.

'Hal Copeman.'

'Where are you from?'

'England.'

'Which place?'

'London.'

'Show me your passport.'

'I don't have it with me. It's at the hotel.'

'What hotel.'

'The Residency.'

'At all times you must carry your passport. It is illegal elseways.' The constable turned to Masood and spoke to him.

Lila translated. 'He's sending one of his men with you to the hotel to check your passport. I have to go back with Masood.'

'Why did he pick on you?' Hal asked.

'Gracie Madam rents the land that the boat is moored on from him. His family house is just above the meadow.'

'Is that a good reason?' Hal tried to move towards her.

She turned away.

'We will drop him at the Residency,' the constable told Masood.

'I'm sorry. Could you tell Gracie?' Hal asked Lila.

Masood stepped towards Hal. 'Please forgive me that our

first meeting was this way. I hope we will meet in happier times, inshallah.'

Hal nodded without looking at Masood as he was led away.

Forty-eight hours in Kashmir and he was already in the back of a police jeep.

He watched through the jeep flap as Lila and Masood disappeared over the top of the ghat steps. The constable was in front and the other two men sat opposite him, looking at him with unblinking concentration. One of them managed to take a single cigarette out of his top pocket, light it and pass the matches to the other one, without once shifting his attention from his slow scrutiny of Hal.

Farouk had missed what had happened on the street above the ghat. He had just started to move away as Masood called to him from the top of the steps. He pushed back through the smaller boats that had paddled in as he had left, ramming the front of his boat hard up on to the bottom step. Masood was holding a handful of the back of Lila's *pheran* to stop her. He did not want to talk in front of the boatmen on the ghats.

'Why is your head uncovered.' He spoke in English.

She did not pull away. She was tired. 'There wasn't time.'

'How much time can it take to pick up a shawl?'

'We were hurrying to get to Dal Gate before it got dark.'

'You are always out with your head uncovered. Why won't you wear *hijab*?'

'I'm not one of the women of your house.'

'What do you mean by that?'

'Why should I cover myself up in shame and fear?'

Masood saw that he was gripping her *pheran* in his fist. He let go. Lila moved away down the steps.

'I am all covered. Why should I hide my face as though I don't exist? Who for? Does it make you more comfortable?'

The boatmen on the steps were listening.

'Maybe if you had been more covered that day in the city . . .'

Lila cut across him. 'I had a shawl, a dark shawl covering me, you saw me with it in the meadow. A dark blue shawl, almost black.' She ran down the rest of the steps towards Farouk.

Masood's focus clung to her as she ran, and he prayed that she would not fall in the dusk. The eyes around him moved with her, enjoying the swing of her plait against the pale grey of her *pheran*.

He hated them for it, for wanting her. He wished that, like his friend Mohammed, it was the fast that he found harder each year. He thought of Naseema, his wife, and he wished that he did not think of her as more of a sister now, whose warmth he turned to in the night only when it was too bitter to lie turned away from her, the cold air between them crawling up his back.

He looked across at the rows of vacant houseboats around Dal Gate. Some of their wooden shutters were screeching on runners as they were pushed together after the day's airing, curtains were being drawn, the process repeated over and over like a talisman, as though if it stopped hope might drain out of the lake through a plug-hole the size of the dome on Hazratbal mosque.

Masood shrugged in the cold and followed Lila down the steps.

The jeep was parked by the hotel, right outside the door, and

Hal was standing by the front passenger window being lectured by the constable.

'There is no need for passport. Masood Abdullah has vouched for you,' the constable said.

Hal was trying not to explode away from the lecture.

A businessman with a plastic briefcase, his barrel-belly tight inside a cheap suit, pushed past the hotel doorman in order get closer to the show by the jeep. Hal was now the subject of an increasing and fascinated audience: the businessman, the hotel doorman in his filthy uniform, two girls wearing sunglasses in the twilight, their *salwar kameez* almost hidden under jelly bean-coloured fake fur coats, and a gathering number of people from the petrol station next door.

'You will carry your passport with you for all movements from this place.'

'Indeed I will, sir.' Hal's tone was earnest.

'And I wish you most happy visit in Kashmir.' The constable was as serious.

'Thank you.'

'Thank you, bye, bye.' The constable flapped his hand at the driver. 'One thing more, when you shift you will leave Nagin address with hotel.' The constable gave what seemed to be a salute.

'I will.' Hal returned the salute.

The businessman, the doorman, and the girls in sunglasses all resumed their original courses, the girls giggling over their shoulders as they went.

Masood and Lila crossed Dal Lake, the lotus gardens and Nagin in silence. She moved to the back of the boat to paddle with Farouk. Masood was cold and his hands were shaking from the encounter on the road. He would have enjoyed the warmth of paddling but he sat in front, conscious that he was sitting where the young man had been. He could smell the charcoal of Farouk's *kangri*, but he was not going to ask for it. Pulling the collar of his *pheran* up around his face he prayed. He prayed for Irfan, for his beaten neighbour with his smashed ribs and broken toes, for the man's sons who had been kept for further interrogation, for Naseema who loved him and their children, for things to go back to how they had been before Irfan had climbed the wall beside the walnut tree, and Lila had gone to the city in a dark blue shawl. He knew that he was praying like a child but he could think of no other way.

Gracie's initial reaction was petulance. She crashed the cigarette box back down on to the desk before she had offered it to Masood. Then she began to laugh, dropping down on to the sofa, a little stream of farts popping through her laughter.

'So it's you and the Gestapo at Dal Gate with Masood playing the morality police.' Her face was pulled tight to the centre, concentrating the effort of laughing.

Masood wanted a cigarette but she had banged the box down so hard he did not feel he could ask. He did not have any with him as he had gone to pray and to meet Mohammed for *chai*.

He never took cigarettes into the mosque. It would make him feel uncomfortable, and if they fell out of his *pheran* pocket as he was bending in a *rakha*, then what? Gracie was still laughing. Enough.

'Who is he?' Masood spoke loudly enough to make Gracie look up.

She stopped laughing a little too quickly. 'Who's who?' she asked.

'The man Lila was with.'

'I will clarify this for you, Morality Police Sahib Sir.' Gracie pursed her lips and saluted.

Masood hated it when she tried to sound Indian. She sounded like a cheap shopkeeper who had been drinking.

'He has come to talk to me. What's the word?'

'Interview.' Lila began to collect the cups and plates of the tea that Hal had hurried away from.

Gracie was watching Lila. 'I asked your mother to go to the house to see if we could beg some chicken for the return of the prodigal foreigner.'

'He is to come back?' Masood was loud again. 'When was he here before?'

'Masood Abdullah! First you accuse Lila of prostitution in public, and now you are behaving as if our visitor is another runaway militant.'

There was silence as Irfan's absence sat back down between them. Masood dropped on to the arm of Gracie's chair. Lila picked up the tray.

Gracie cleared her throat. 'His name is Hal and he is coming to stay for a while until he has done his interview.' She was gentle. 'But obviously not tonight.'

'You must not speak of the boy with this stranger.' Masood looked from one woman to the other, one fist pressing into his chest

Lila hitched the tray on to her hip so that she could open and close the sitting room door behind her.

'Will you have a cigarette with me?' Gracie reached across to the desk. She opened the box and held it out to Masood.

He looked in at the comfort of the neat stack. He could smell the tobacco.

'You alienate her a bit more each time you lecture her.' Gracie pushed the box closer.

He took a cigarette and sat with it in his hand, staring at it, seeing just the white paper, the brown filter and the lines on his palm – the two deepest ones met between his thumb and his index finger, and were bisected at the bottom, just above his wrist. Feroz's new game was to open out his uncle's hand and draw over the upturned 'V' and its crossbar with his finger, so that he made an 'A' tipped on its side.

'A is for Allah, so that we always remember,' his little nephew would chant.

Masood closed his hand over the cigarette.

Lila approached the telephone with caution. It seldom rang in the morning. Most people gave up after a few rings if it was not something important. It was ringing persistently.

Hal was sitting on his bed with the receiver in his hand, waiting. He had started counting when it had rung enough times to be answered, and he had counted ten since then.

How long could it take Gracie to get out of her chair and to a telephone? He had not seen one in the sitting room but the number was ringing so there must be one somewhere. If she was asleep how long could it take Lila or her mother to get from the *dunga*, even if they had to put shoes on, walk backwards down the duckboards, crawl along the path . . .

'Hello.'

Hal sat up.

'Hello, Mrs Singh?'

'No, this is Lila speaking. Who is on the line?' She knew.

'Hal. So you got back?' He stopped. 'In the dark and everything?'

'Yes.'

'Good.'

There was a pause.

'I had an interesting ride with the constable and his boys.'

There was another pause.

'Hello?'

'Hello,' she echoed.

'Hello.'

'Yes,' Lila replied. She was winding the cord around her finger, unwinding it, rewinding it, uncoil, recoil.

'Is Gracie there?'

'She is sleeping.'

'So late?'

'I think she did not sleep so well in the night.'

Lila's voice sounded faint to Hal, as though she was holding the receiver right away from her mouth.

'Oh, I'm sorry.'

'It's not your fault, so why sorry?' Her voice sounded stronger.

'Okay.' Hal paused. 'I'm ringing because . . .' He faded. 'Perhaps I'll ring back a bit later. When do you think Gracie might wake up?'

'No telling. She is expecting you soon.'

'That's really why I was calling. I wasn't sure when to come and also what to tell the taxi driver.'

'You should take a rickshaw,' she said.

'Okay, I'll do that. I have to do a few things here. I need to make some calls and go to the bank. Is there anything you need from here?'

'What sort of things?'

He wanted to put the phone down. Talking seemed too hard. He wanted to ask her why she was being so difficult.

'Are you always this difficult, Lila?' It had been a thought, he had not meant to say it. He hunched up around the receiver.

'Not always, I'm not so good on the telephone. Why talk to plastic holes?'

Hal laughed. 'I was just asking if you wanted anything from here, to save you a trip.'

Lila could think of so many things. 'No, we are fine.' And then she outlined the route.

Hal looked around to find something to write with, but there was nothing within reach. He tried to memorize the five main points of the convoluted verbal map she was giving: 'At the end of Lal Chowk there is a small shrine on the right, locked up now, and the flags have all been torn or pulled down. There are great big padlocks on the front of it. Do not turn here, carry on until . . .' She sounded like his sister. She sounded like every other woman who had ever given him directions.

'And you will be here at what time?' she said at the end of her long description of the journey from the hotel to Nagin.

Something ticked below Hal's throat. It took him quite some time to tell her that he thought it might be by late afternoon. He put the receiver down very carefully and sat looking at it.

Lila put the receiver down and went to help Suriya sorting the rice. Her mother put her hand to Lila's forehead as she crouched down beside her in front of the tray of rice. She looked as though she had a bit of fever. Suriya signalled that she should drink some water and rest for a while. Lila bent low over the rice, tilting her head so that her plait slid across and hung down beside her warm cheek. She concentrated hard on the grains and pushed her mother's hand away when she tried to feel her forehead again.

Hal started trying to explain where he was going to a rickshaw driver. The doorman was staring at him again, every detail and gesture studied. Hal changed his mind and asked to be taken to Dal Gate.

He was still a tourist and he wanted to take the ride across the lakes again in the light, while he could still see the land and lakescape without the weight of stories he would hear. And he knew the way to The Wonder House by water.

The length of Boulevard Road was lined with soldiers in tin helmets and khaki: long-faced Sikhs in olive turbans; big-nosed Rajputs with show-off moustaches; flat-browed Ladakhis; even flatter-faced Assamese. Some were in big boots, some in just green plimsolls with webbing around their ankles, but all were united by their camouflage flak-bibs and their rifles, standard issue SLRs, barrel down, butt up, safety catch on, but close enough for comfort.

Your own comfort, that is, if it were you standing on a long road facing a hillside of alleys and shadows, every one of those shifting shades a potential militant; to you, that is, if it was you on that pavement, barrel down, butt up, safety catch on.

Halfway down the road there was a space hemmed by alleys, dusty hopeful shopfronts, and empty or army-occupied hotels. Khaki underpants, olive long johns, and once white vests hung from the balconies in continual layers of requisitioned-barrack bunting. The space between was fronted by chinar trees as tall as Feroz's Allah. Behind the trees were two great houses, garden to garden. The second was set too far back to see properly but Chinar House was on view, its ochre-washed roof, gabled windows, lace-carved balconies and verandas, its state of anachronism, an image of how this part of the city had once sat beside the lake, charmed and sedate.

The boatmen at the ghats recognized Hal. They had all watched as he had been driven away in the police jeep the evening before. Hal waited at the top as they stared.

Their faces were stage-lit as they lay in the backs of their boats with their hookahs. Hal stood with his luggage, enchanted by the line of *shikaras* at the bottom of the steps, their fringed curtains and flowered cushions wrapped around by thick wedges of late sun. Flirting for all their worth they bobbed: Serious Moonlight, Lovely England, Miss America with her deluxe sprung seats and music too; but queen of the flirts was Sppeedy Ghazales with her supa-delux, supa-wide seats, bobbed a little apart, temptress of the lake. He wanted to lie in all of them.

Then they came at him, their voices calling him, coaxing him down. He looked for the face of the man who had taken him when he first arrived. He had been almost silent, not needing to know where Hal was from, or why, or how and who. He was there at the corner of the All J&K Shikara Owners Association Office Central, quietly sliding in among the other boats while their owners bounced on to the ghats to tout for the foreigner.

The boatman knew that Hal would come to him. The English formed habits and attachments so quickly.

Hal walked through the other men and put his foot on the front of the boat he knew. There was no exchange as the boatman took his backpack and hauled it over the seat to the back of the boat. A boy on the steps with bare feet helped to push the boat out as Hal settled against the seat. He noticed that the blanket that was passed to him was still damp from when he had used it to put out Gracie's fire. He turned and smiled at the boatman. The *shikari's* mouth did not move, though the lines at the corners of his eyes lifted. He pulled a second blanket out from under his small seat and passed it over. Hal took it and arranged it over his legs, releasing the smell of moth balls and unwashed feet.

The other boatmen on the ghats pulled their hands back inside their *pherans*, and huddled back together, angles of skin on bone in fluid light. Their heads moved together to gossip again about the foreigner, Lila, the policemen and Masood Abdullah on the pavement the day before, arguing for all to see.

Dal spread itself out around him as they moved. Hal watched the big fronts of the boats on the main lake as they crossed towards the channel beyond the small island that was Nehru Park with its ugly café on square legs. The New Chez Henry No. 392, The Bangkok and Savoy, all empty and shuttered down. The Taj Palace, for let! Best Price! Every fiddle-front of interwoven lotus petals and flowers within flowers seemed more lovely, more intricate than the one before.

Three *shikaras* came at them. There was a young cuddling couple in one, she was pretending to be asleep, he was wondering quite how far his hand could get, hidden, as he thought, under her shawl. The second was a jewellery-seller, his head bent over his book. A middle-aged couple was in the third, she was fat and blacked-out except for her eyes – he was thin and diminished by his cheaply made Western clothes, apart from the flourish of his astrakhan hat – she really was asleep but he did not notice.

The Leeward Hotel sat at a corner ahead of them. Its windows framed stray drying garments hung up and outlined by single hanging bulbs. Hal turned to watch as they passed.

Was it the one where young, disenchanted Naipaul had stayed? Had he hung his underwear in the bathroom while he wrote about the mess of India? He would ask someone, Gracie would know.

Two women came out of a *dunga* boat just beyond, one of them carrying a baby comfortably balanced on her broad hip. Half of their faces were lit up as the men on the ghats had been. The women smiled back as he smiled, and then turned away laughing and talking.

How tall, how nice, how foreign, *asal*, beautiful, *asal* man. Good to see a tourist. Is he a tourist?

All the shops on legs on either side of the canal were shut up, padlocks on chains on top of corrugated iron, as though the papier-mâché man on the right might steal from the papier-mâché man to his left, or the shawl man on the other side. The gas man was open, rolling three clean red cylinders across his narrow deck and down into a filthy boat below, the boatman catching them, his *shikara* dipping further, just cheating the curve of the water at its edges each time a cylinder dropped.

On the corner of one water route and the next, a stand-alone shop was open, This and That, though not much of either except for tiny coats, with rabbit-fur collars and bunny-tail pompoms, dangling in the doorway. The butcher beyond the corner was looking out over the water and weed, his curved blade beside him, chopped into his block. Anuses and ears for sale, racked up beside ribs and tails with their dangling pompoms too, more corpses, suspended, waiting.

Hal moved the blanket around to cut the chill of the wind between his thighs.

A bread-seller had his boat pulled against the bank on the other side. Ducks and geese gobbled on a piece of escaped floating garden in between, surrounded by their own peaks of olive shit, colour-matched to the Sikh soldiers' turbans. A pretty woman squatted by the bread boat, her scarf a bright rebellion against the mud brown of her *pheran*. She held eight small flat loaves, counting them over and over as her six children stood around her. They all waved at Hal as though rehearsed and on cue. The smallest boy at the end was wearing just a dirty jersey and a pair of short red plastic boots. As he waved, the ragged hem of his jersey lifted to show the tip of his tiny penis.

'Hello, hello,' Hal called to them.

'Angrez, Angrez,' they called back, their waving arms getting wilder.

He was not quite sure whether it was an accusation or a good thing. He waved again. 'Yes, English.'

'*Baksheesh, baksheesh,*' called the brood mother.

Shit. He was just another tourist.

As they pushed through the thickening weed and the dying lotuses he felt cold, a post-coital chill after the first prettily lit intercourse with the people of the lakes. As they came into Nagin, the houseboats around seemed like the sad items hanging beside the butcher's block, all the life dripped out of them, a ring of mausoleums around a lake.

Hal's hands felt so cold that he could not feel where his fingers met under the blanket. He closed his eyes, wishing he had taken a rickshaw, that he had not tried to make some romantic gesture to himself about life on the lakes.

When he opened his eyes he saw Lila.

She was standing on the roof of The Wonder House collecting sheets off a line between the summer awning struts. The sky was back in the lake again, as beautiful as the beginning of a film that is probably going to make you cry.

Gracie was there when he came to the steps for the third time.

'Hello you, we've all been hanging about waiting,' she called out.

'I'm sorry, Mrs Singh. Banks, bills, phone calls, it takes so long when you don't speak the language.'

'Oh rubbish, everyone speaks English perfectly well. And if you don't call me Gracie I'll call in the cavalry.' She reached her hand out to him. 'None of them left up here any more, all intelligence and artillery bullies. Glamour of the Cav all gone.' She took his hand between both of hers again. 'Come on, blue-eyed Hal, let's go and find you a room. You've got three choices.'

He helped her up and followed her slow swaying progress through the sitting room and the dining room and into the dark corridor beyond.

'I'm in the honeymoon suite at the end.' Gracie waved

ahead. 'And this is your first choice.' She pushed a curtain aside and opened the door. Even as she started she changed her mind. 'Actually no, this is where all my husband's and son's stuff is kept.' She shut the door again. 'Desperate sort of shrine really.' She closed the curtain and moved on to the next one.

Chapter Eight ~

The lights went out as Hal got into the bath. He sat for a while, waiting for them to come back on, and he went on sitting as the icy air cooled the water around him.

His bathroom was on the side of the room that faced the corridor so that he did not even have the pale reflection from a window to show him the outline of where things were. It was black and wet, and now becoming unpleasant.

He thought about calling out. The door to the bedroom was open and he was naked. He continued to wait, hoping that he would get used to the nothingness and that it would become something, but it did not. He tried to remember where things were in the bathroom. He knew where the basin and lavatory were, and he could remember the large orange bucket and the green scoop between the two, but he had no fix on a towel.

He got up with his hands against the wall beside him and the full force of the cold sucked on to his wet skin. Both shins hit the edge of the bath as he climbed out. Swearing did not help, nor did it stop his balls from hiking right up inside as the cold gripped. He stood holding the front of the basin, trying to remember where he had put his torch.

A towel rail should naturally be above one of the ends of the bath. The shower was to the east and the towel was obediently to the west.

Looking from the bathroom into the bedroom, he began to see shapes lifting out of the obscurity in the reflected light off the water beyond the windows. He would probably be able to find his torch if he trod carefully through the obstacle-filled blackness.

As he made his way from the bathroom to the bedroom a circle of light came to the door. He shielded his wide-open irises.

'Who is it?' He thought the door to the corridor was closed.

'I didn't know you were here, the door was open.' Lila's voice remained stationary.

'I shut it.'

'It swings open unless you turn the key. Was there enough hot water?' It was conversational.

Hal could not see that she had turned her face away.

'It was fine until the light went out, and I don't like locking doors.' Hal noticed that he was standing in the spill from her lamp, trapped by the light, rabbit in a towel.

'It always goes out about this time. Didn't Gracie tell you? You should have taken a lamp with you.'

'No, she didn't tell me, and no, I do not have a lamp.' Hal pulled the towel more tightly around himself.

'I will go and get one.' Her voice came from behind the lantern halo.

'Could I have yours while I wait?'

'How will I find another lamp then?' she asked.

'Okay, I'll sit and wait in the dark.' He sat down on the edge of the bed.

'I'll be back.' Her voice was moving away.

'Fine.' He felt that she was smiling as she went along the corridor.

Then he stood up in a state of panic, trying to drape the towel again as he thought it had been when he was standing in her light. He held both ends in his teeth and felt down to where the bottom reached; quite high up on the thigh but nothing showing, not quite the muddy boy with no pants and the tiny bits beside the lake. He sat down again and began to shiver.

Every movement in the half-light seemed to take so long, and it was almost an hour before he managed to feel his way, lamp in hand, down the boat.

Gracie was in the sitting room, in her chair, waiting for him. In contrast to the hard corners of his bedroom and bathroom in the semi-darkness her edges had softened in the diminished paraffin lamplight.

'You took so long,' she said.

'My power-cut skills are not good.'

She caught the irritation. 'I'm sorry I forgot to warn you. Lila told me off. Come and sit down. Have a drink.'

He sat on the sofa where he had sat the last time, before the lake journey and the jeep ride.

'I've got gin, think that's about it apart from something in a bottle from somewhere odd that someone brought me years ago when people still used to come and stay. They came all the time then, bearing bizarre things in bottles when they all knew that I only drink gin. People go mad when they're buying presents. Think there's a tiny emergency supply of whisky too. '

'I'm not a big gin fan.'

'Well then, it's buggery in a bottle, a whisky sniff, or *nimbu pani*.'

'I bought some whisky at duty-free.' Hal had imagined for some reason that she would disapprove of alcohol. He had bought it to have quiet drinks in his room, alone, away from the tin-canned joviality of the hotel bar.

'Hooray for Hal, bearer of a bottle.' Gracie clapped. 'Gin and Thing for me, how do you have your whisky?'

'Thing?'

'Lime juice and tonic, a sad old woman's euphemism for how she takes her poison.'

'I love whisky with lemon juice and soda, but I got into the habit of having it on the rocks. The hard-drinking journalist crowd apparently found the lemon juice thing a bit gay.'

'Are you?' Gracie looked up.

'Am I gay? I don't think so.'

'Hardly convincing, and why should lemon be homo-sexual? Most men's aftershaves are based on lemon and all those woody smells, and the rutting stag one, what's it called? Jitu had his sent from London, from Trumpers. Can you imagine?' Gracie's hands fluttered in her lap and Hal saw that her fingernails had been painted, a hard red that sat on the ridges of her nails. It had been carefully applied, freshly done. 'And my husband was certainly not a homosexual.'

'No euphemism there then?'

'No, I reclaim gay and queer as words I like to use

regularly when not discussing rear entry. I shall drink to that when I have Thing and you have your homo-mix.'

'I'm not a homosexual, and it's musk.'

'The lady protesteth. What do you mean "musk"?' She smiled.

'The rutting stuff.' They sat in the buzz of their conversation. 'Why is it okay for people of your generation to ask that, but not for my peer group?' Hal leaned away from the sallow lamplight to see Gracie's expression better. 'The gay thing.'

'You look so like my son now.'

'I'm sorry.'

'Not your fault, not your fault at all. Let us drink to the reclamation of gay and queer from deviants.' Her lightness was brittle.

'So you think it's wrong?' asked Hal.

'To use those words?'

'No, to be gay?'

'Stop now, get your whisky before I start to regret that I'm housing a nancy boy.'

'Aha, euphemism.'

'Hush you, get your whisky, go and ask Lila for my euphemism and yours, now, quickly, quickly.' She folded her arms.

Hal put his hand on her shoulder as he passed. 'Yes, ma'am.' He clicked his heels behind her chair. 'And I'm not, by the way.'

'I know,' she said. 'We wouldn't have had this conversation if you were.' Gracie felt the warmth of his hand through her shawl, and the space when he took it away, and she felt a sadness. She tried to hum, proud that she had been able to spark so quickly back into real conversation, but the sound faded.

It took Hal a while to get used to carrying a lamp below eye level so as not to lose his balance in the glare. He had almost fallen off the duckboards twice before he began to time his steps with the backward swing of the lamp in his hand. Suriya appeared at the *dunga* blanket to see who it was. Lila came behind her. She was a whole head taller than her mother. There were the burbles and gaps of a conversation behind them in the *dunga*.

'I'm sorry, have I interrupted you?' he asked.

'What is it?' Lila spoke over her mother's head.

'Could I have some of Gracie's stuff for her gin, and also some soda.' He felt embarrassed about asking for himself.

'The soda is for you?'

He nodded.

Suriya reached behind Lila to pull the blanket to one side, waving Hal in. An electric bulb hung from the central beam inside. It was working.

'You've got power.' He did not move. 'How come you have it here and the houseboat doesn't?'

'Someone wired this to the emergency supply that goes to the nearest army barracks. Taking any more than this would make it easy for them to trace.'

'Clever lad.' He guessed that his unenthusiastic boatman of the first evening, Gulshan, had been the tapper. 'Does Gracie know?'

'She does.'

'Wouldn't she like power too?'

'She thinks we workers need it more. She would rather eat than read.' Lila waved him in as well.

He followed them both into the kitchen, treading between girthed cooking pots stacked by height below the windows and Suriya's centrally placed stone mortar and pestle, surrounded by brown paper bags of spices, the openings carefully rolled down like tiny gunny sacks. A double kerosene burner was roaring with large pots on each blue ring of flame. Hal ducked to avoid the single bulb and he looked for somewhere to stand that would not be so obviously in the way. The entrance to the next room was the only place. The conversation he had heard was coming from a tired old radio hanging from a piece of dirty cloth above the circle of spices. It was the news in English.

'The World Service.' Hal nodded at the radio.

Suriya's face opened, the first smile of hers that he had seen. It changed the shape of her, making her a younger, prettier woman. They were much closer in age than he had thought at first.

She patted her hand down, inviting him to sit.

'It's her talisman. If she hears the news from pukkah BBC the rest of all this has an order she understands.' Lila wrapped her mother in her arms and kissed her forehead three times.

It seemed the wrong way around.

'You are okay now, you've passed. Sit.' Lila repeated her mother's gesture.

'I think Gracie was hoping that I would be hurrying back with the tonic and stuff.' Hal ducked down to an uncomfortable squat.

'And the soda?' Lila asked.

He was left crouching, embarrassed again.

'I will bring it. You'd better go back. She's still the burns patient to be humoured.' Lila raised her hand, signalling him away.

'Thank you.' He picked his way back through their industry as Suriya pulled a pot off one of the rings and balanced it on its side in another, mouth down. She leaned back from the cloud of steam that rose off the draining rice, but it caught Hal's hand. He swore, and Suriya clicked her tongue behind her teeth. He apologized and she smiled again, but not in the same way as before.

'You can listen to the news with my mother some other time, any time, half past six every night unless the radio tower is blown up. You can help her make masalas too.' Lila held the blanket aside for him to pass.

He did not know if she was teasing him.

'I will, thank you.' He walked out into the cloud of her breath, pausing in it.

Lila watched him going down the duckboard, stepping cautiously in and out of the circles of light from the lamp he carried.

He was so tall.

Suriya tugged at the back of her *pheran* to get Lila to drop the blanket back.

'Is there soda?' Lila asked.

Suriya shrugged, though Lila knew that her mother always kept a check on what they had in stock.

As he reached the security of the path between one duckboard and the next he stopped. The call to prayer had begun from Hazratbal mosque. The one in Lal Bazaar replied. Makhdoom Sahab mosque called back from the foot of Hari Parbhat; surround sound and around again. Hal stood and listened. From the *dunga* the radio was faint now but he could still just hear it. Someone was visiting Delhi to lecture the government about joining the nuclear race. From Hazratbal's minaret there was background sound to the call, a throat being cleared, a door opening and closing, ordinary sounds caught on the recording.

The calls continued as Hal looked through his bag for the whisky. Thinking about Islam and looking for alcohol, the punishment would be medium to high. Gracie was calling out for him and Thing, her own call to prayer. He found the whisky, buried at the bottom between a clutter of spare films and a dictaphone that he had not even thought about using yet.

'They took my baby and stuck him on someone else's tit.' Gracie hit the flat of her hand, the one not holding her glass, against her bosom. 'Wet nurse, isn't that a disgusting expression?'

Hal was as drunk as she was, the edge of his thumb in his mouth, chewing the skin. He had been on antibiotics the week before India for a small lump behind his ear. These had been his first drinks for more than two weeks.

First drinks: five of them, three before chicken and whatever it was that came with it, and now two more. Gracie was heavy-handed when she poured.

He tried to pace them, drinking his first one very slowly.

Gracie was quick, three glasses to his one. They talked about Naipaul at the beginning. It was the same Leeward Hotel, but she had not read him. She saw no point in reading books by someone who apparently loathed India while she had made it her choice. Hal asked how she had met her husband in the course of her second drink. They compared

Oxford and Cambridge, mainly the quality of cooked break-
fasts in the cafés and the superior attitude of the college
debating societies. Her opinion was based on the inability of
the members to flirt, while Hal's dislike was for their habit of
huddling together in the dining hall, always at the same place
on the same table, transmitting signals of higher intellect
even when asking for the salt. She had her third over this
topic, during which time she began to slide out of the
amusing and into the arcane and archaic. Her repeated and
underlined generalizations made Hal chew the edge of his
thumb. They started to argue because Gracie kept saying that
the English had forgotten how to flirt.

He wondered why an old woman on a boat in Kashmir
was just as boring as any other drunk. It was only half past
eight. Lila came in and asked when they would like supper,
and Gracie sounded momentarily sober when she said that
in an hour would be fine. He smiled at Lila over Gracie's
head. He knew that it was the same smile he used for
restaurant staff when he was eating with people who
thought that being rude to waiters was clever and grand.

Another hour before dinner – a great stretch of grating
comments before they could eat.

Hal poured himself his second drink after Lila had gone,
and then he too began to fall away at the edges. Halfway
through his third it became magnificently easy to sit with his
legs stretched out, his bottom on the edge of the sofa, his back
arched with just the top of his shoulders against the cushions
behind. They dissected communism, toy dogs, men who
lisped, women who were devoted to shopping, and penknives
with too many blades promising too many things, particularly
the one claiming to be a can opener, yes, particularly that one.

He had noticed himself reiterating and underlining his own generalizations, and he had laughed out loud.

Their uneven journey from the sitting room to the dining room now seemed a long time ago. He could not remember whether Lila or Suriya had brought it or what he had eaten, except for the chicken.

Now he was wholly with Gracie in sympathy with the disgustingness of wet nurses. The idea was sickening. He should have another drink, Gracie first, ladies who were not allowed to breastfeed first.

He took her glass but he could not remember where she had put her gin, nor could he remember where the whisky bottle was. Gracie gave a racing commentary on his search around her chair, under the sofa and the desk. Both bottles were sitting on top of it.

He had to pour. She made them too big, he had to make them lesser, smaller, less of. His muscles were gone. He had to prop his arm as he poured.

As he sat down again he remembered that the clear gap at the top of the whisky bottle had been too big.

So what. Great drink, lovely woman, great night.

'I wouldn't let them have my boy for long. Fought them off. No one sticking their tit on my baby's mouth except me.' She was staring at Hal which meant looking right down her nose as he had slid so far down the sofa that he was now sitting on the floor at her feet.

'You know they beat women's tits here.' Gracie slapped her hand on her chest again.

Hal made a sound.

'The army, they do it. Cavalry wouldn't do that, Cav aren't tit beaters.'

'Dib dib.' Hal slopped his drink as he saluted with his glass.

Gracie grabbed his hand.

Lila came to put out the lights but she stopped just outside the room.

She saw Hal sitting at Gracie's feet, his arm yanked up into her lap as though he was helpless. Gracie looked as if she was crying, her glass tipped sideways, though there was nothing to spill. If she had been alone Lila would have helped, half-carrying, half-supporting Gracie to her room as she had done so often in the past. Each of those times she had undressed her like a child, peeling her clothes away and rolling her under the quilt as Gracie had burbled about tap dancing and Hari, her brilliant sponge cakes and Hari, Jitu and Hari. It was in that darkness that Gracie had told Lila that she loved her, so many times, her babies, Hari and Lila, lovely lovely Lila.

Colours were playing through his eyelids. Hal waited while the first wave of nausea rolled through. Every muscle was tensed to get him to the bathroom, the door to the left, the lavatory immediately to the right, left and then right. The wave passed and he let the light in by sections, filtering it through his eyelashes to start with.

The colours were not part of his hangover. Curtains covered most of the bedroom windows but there was a large triangle of stained glass above. He closed his eyes quickly, the combination of green, red and yellow was too strong. Water was the most important thing. He tried to breathe more deeply, knowing it would make him feel worse in the short term before the oxygen got to where it was needed. He wanted to be sick.

He was, clinging to the edge of the bath.

It gave him the reprieve to be able to go and look for water. Brushing his teeth could wait. He could not remember how safe the tap water was. He started singing feebly.

The curtains along the corridor were closed. He pulled one aside, shrinking from the whine of the metal hooks on their rod. Mist sat uniform and opaque across the lake. He pressed his forehead to the cold glass and tried to look into the haze. A single *shikara* emerged and disappeared, the figure on the front and the lifted line of the boat made themselves into the first brushstroke of an Arabic calligrapher. Hal traced the shape in the condensation of his breath on the glass.

There was someone further up the corridor in the galley kitchen, trying not to make too much noise. Hal could smell his breath off the window and he did not want to meet Suriya, Gracie or Lila at that particular moment. He stood very still in the pause between his in- and out-breath to try and find an idea through the noise in his skull. It would be just three or four steps to get back to his room, to close the door and turn the key.

Lila had heard him in the corridor as she washed the plates and bowls from the mangled dinner of the previous night. Gracie always announced herself and she never opened the curtains, especially when she had drunk too much. Lila stopped with her hands over the basin, the water and congealed rice running off her fingers. Without moving, without breathing, she waited until the corridor was again quiet. When she let go of her breath she saw that her hands were shaking, and she washed the last dishes slowly in case she broke anything. A door closed quietly. She knew what he had wanted.

He stood by the door listening. There was no more sound from the galley, and then there were footsteps taken toe first as they came down the corridor to his room. They stopped outside and then retreated. Then they were on the duckboard, treading normally, perhaps even making a little more noise than usual. He waited until they faded and then turned the key. Two bottles of water were outside his door with a glass.

He drank them sitting on the edge of his bed, lowering the bottles between each long gulp and sucking in air, his eyes closed against the light. Lying back with the second emptied bottle still in his hand, Hal's headache let go enough for him to realize that he was wearing only a pair of pyjama bottoms, and that he was as cold as he could remember being. Numbness was beginning to creep up his body. Tunnelling back under the quilt he thought about his electric blanket and central heating at home.

No mist there, no lake, no mad old woman, nothing surprising in a basement flat that had once been the scullery and kitchen of the big house on top. Nothing unpredictable on the surrounding streets of London in a neighbourhood where women sat at cafés with babies in three-wheeler buggies, discussing how much they paid their nannies and how to fix up people like him with their neurotic single friends. That was why he had left.

There was hot water. He jumped up and down in front of the basin while the water ran, to the extent that his head would allow. He wrapped one towel around his waist and the slightly damp one from the night before around his shoulders. Soaking his hands in the hot water until they were warm enough to shave, Hal thought about how many layers of clothes he had that he could wear at the same time.

In the sitting room he found pale sun beginning to push through the cold air. There was a second sofa under one of the windows on the morning side of the room, and it was absorbing the weak warmth. He wanted to lie on it, his feet on one end, his head pushed up by cushions at the other, waiting in the expectation of fresh coffee, and diluting the light through closed eyes. Instead he sat back down on the sofa that he had sometimes managed to sit on the night before. He could smell stale whisky and raw onions from one small plate of them that had been left on the dining-room table. A bookcase on the other side of the room was piled with photograph albums, books about birds, and a thick one on wild flowers of the subcontinent that was too big to fit on either of the shelves. It was too cold. He needed to walk.

Hal climbed out through the corridor window, down the duckboards and away from the houseboat towards the meadow. The cold pinched the skin across his forehead and behind his ears so tight that it overrode his headache. It was better outside. He stamped his way through the frost towards another group of houseboats at the further end of the meadow.

There was a man under an almond tree just in front of Hal as he came over a hummock, sitting on the frozen ground, his hands resting on the grass on either side of him as though it were a warm day. His head was shaven and uncovered. Hal nodded to him. The man raised both his hands and began to chant in a high piercing voice. Hal stood and listened to the winding sound, realizing that he had been just the trigger to his song, and his presence was no longer required. He left the man, still with his hands raised, transported by his own sound.

'He does not feel cold or heat. He thinks he is a *Pir*, a holy man, directly in touch with Allah. He is always singing me lectures.' The voice behind Hal was gentle and persuasive. He had heard it before. 'He is a little touched, he thinks it is by Allah but the doctors say it is in the head.' Masood stopped.

Hal had turned to face him.

'Good day to you and I am most sorry that our first meeting was unfortunate.' Masood extended his hand for the second time. 'Will you now accept my apologies? It was a misunderstanding, you see.' He looked down at his empty hand between them.

Hal took his hand out of his pocket. Masood took it.

'But your hands are so cold. You must come in and have tea. Where is Suriya?'

'There was no one about and I didn't want to disturb Gracie.'

'So nice of you. We are like animals at this time of year. Many people sleep so late in the morning that half the day is gone before they are up and out. It is hibernation season in Kashmir.' Masood was smiling.

Hal stuck his hand back in his pocket.

'I think you are cold, we must get a *pheran* made for you.' Masood pulled his own hand back into his sleeve. 'You are so tall it will take more wool than normal, but they are so warm, you will see.'

Hal could not be so conversational. 'The police constable told me that he was effectively letting me off because you had vouched for me. How could you vouch for me, you don't know me?' He knew that his nose was beginning to drip, but he kept his hands in his pockets, pushing them down further.

'But you are a friend of Gracie Madam's. If you are a friend of hers then I know you.' Masood's tone reached out again.

Hal wanted to stop, to respond to Masood's warmth, but he felt trapped in the pattern that he had set. He stared at the ground without replying.

'You will please come and take tea with me and my family. It would be an honour for us.' Masood's hands bounced on his stomach inside his *pheran*.

The dripping was too much. Hal sniffed and wiped his nose. 'Thank you.'

Masood turned towards the top of the meadow but he did not move. They stood side by side watching a boy in the lee of the bank above them, a labourer's son, kicking an empty plastic engine-oil bottle; a thin boy, perhaps only seven or eight, Bihari dark, a frayed jersey over filthy trousers that were torn at the back, showing one small, slightly paler buttock. He kicked the bottle up into the air with the side of his foot, and then again and again. Each time the bottle veered to one side he twisted and caught it in his hand, and then started again. Masood and Hal stood and watched.

'*Asal*,' Masood said, more to himself than to Hal.

'He's good, I'd love to give him a decent pair of trousers though.'

They moved forward together.

'I keep hearing '*asal*'?' Hal asked.

'*Asal*, perhaps our favourite word here. Sometimes I think we should be asking for *Asali* instead of *Azadi*. It means beautiful, pretty, lovely, anything that is good. We use it so much in my language that it is like a common call. We would then be asking for beauty, for things to be good. Perhaps this would be a better thing to hope for than freedom. What do you think, Mr Hal?' He stopped and turned to him.

They looked directly at each other for the first time. Masood saw an open face that was not as hard as the voice. Hal saw the same large brown eyes that held the common pain that he had seen in the streets of the city.

'It's a good word.' Hal sniffed again and they moved on towards the boy.

'And for him it is that I'm admiring his footwork.' Masood half-smiled and, as they reached the boy, he pulled one hand out of his *pheran* and pushed something into the boy's hand.

It was so quick that Hal only saw him pulling his hand back in through his *pheran* sleeve. The boy looked up, his face as empty as the plastic bottle in his hand, and he stuffed the money in his pocket.

There were two strands of sound, one was his own breathing, the other a group of men having morning *chai* in the cold. Irfan tried to separate himself from both strands. He visualized the rapid heartbeat that felt as if it was choking him, seeing it again as the diagrams that he had hated so much in tenth grade: the aorta thick with blood, the pulmonary vein full of empty blood heading back for refill, left atrium, right atrium, left and right ventricles, cuspid valves, bi and tri, so hard to copy, his pencil sitting heavy on the paper as he had stared at the diagram, willing it to transpose itself during his final exam assessment.

It had not been so long ago, only months.

He shifted his weight, his movements slow and exact so as to be soundless.

The soldiers below having *chai* made the same morning sounds that Irfan had heard all his life: in Srinagar, by the lakes, the men of the J&K Shikara Owners Association gathering at Iqbal Wani's tea stall to spit, drink and argue while Iqbal patiently brewed, stirred and poured. Here was just another group of men doing the same.

Depersonalize them, do not absorb their names, they are just words, listen to where they are, wait until they are easy, vulnerable.

A Sikh appeared at the edge of the bunker below Irfan, his turban not yet tied, the back of his neck exposed where his hair was pulled up into a double knot. He took a mouthful of tea, gargled it and spat it out, clearing his lungs at the same time. Irfan saw the smear of heat that came up from where the Sikh's spit hit the frozen earth. The young man laughed at something someone was saying from inside the bunker and disappeared back inside.

Irfan had heard four names: Singh the Sikh, Gupta and Lal the Hindus, and Batapa, probably a Ladakhi, probably a Buddhist, Batapa the pacifist. Irfan tried to make them into words but he still heard four men, gathered up from around the country. They were being trained to believe that these men came only to stamp all over their land, that each of those four men, and the hundreds of thousands beyond them, were the rapists of the Valley, non-believers, destroyers.

There were four of them as well, four trainees watching an experienced unit perform, watching Singh, Gupta, Lal and Batapa's names being taken away.

'You will watch and you will learn.' Their training commander had told them. 'And you will lie on the ice bank above the bunker with this unit and wait. They will not see you. They have basic thermal imaging now but not the new stuff as yet, not the kind that can pick up a cold body on ice. Ten men leave the bunker as it gets light to get rations and water. They are away for half an hour. You will then watch the unit operating.'

Fear had pinned the four boys to the ice. The unit they were with was just two men, one of them not much older than the trainees. They both had goatskins to lie on and burning charcoals in tin-lined boxes to hold against their bellies. The four boys had not been given either. They breathed with their hands around their noses to cut the chill on the inhalation, exhaling through their mouths into their cupped palms to warm both their hands and faces.

Irfan had been the furthest from the two men on their skins with their warm bellies.

'Weren't we taught that they only use thermal imaging at the high-security border posts?' he whispered to Yasin, the boy beside him.

Yasin did not reply.

'This isn't high security.' Irfan tried.

Yasin wrapped his arms around his ears.

'And if they are using thermal imaging why have our teachers got *kangri* boxes?'

Yasin glared. A lump of hard snow hit Irfan from the other end of the ice. He stopped whispering.

In this wan early light fog moved in banks. The bunker emerged as Singh spat; it disappeared as he went back inside to finish his tea and tie his turban. They were speaking

Hindi, two of them teasing Singh about his fiancée in Delhi whom he had yet to meet.

'She might be a pig Singh with big fat teeth and no tits,' one of them laughed.

'Pigs try harder,' a second voice added.

'But maybe she's Aishwarya Rai's twin, and I'll ask you all to the wedding and you can cry while I get the movie star sister to sleep with for the rest of my life.' Irfan smiled at Singh's optimism.

No name, just a word, no name, no face. Irfan shifted.

In the next blank of fog two grenades went in through the opening of the bunker. Only one of the four men inside saw them as they landed, and there was not even time to scream.

The boys ran directly uphill from the attack, separating in four directions after the first explosion to regroup when they had stopped to listen for counter-attack. Irfan moved hard left, his heart roaring in his ears again. His checkpoint was a rock about two hundred feet above the bunker. He lay behind it until he could breathe without gasping. There was no sound below. He pulled one arm out of his sleeve, sticking his gun through it and pushing the sleeve out beyond the edge of the rock. No one fired. He looked out around the other side into the whiteness.

The fog moved. The whole top of the bunker had been blown off. Lal, Gupta, Batapa and Singh had been scattered with the bunker roof. Irfan vomited behind the rock, both of his hands over his mouth to muffle the sound of his retching. He saw the unblinking black eyes of a yellow-bellied marmot watching him as he kicked frozen earth over his bile before running on to the regrouping point.

Lila must never know that these things happened.

'The lakes don't freeze over any more.' Gracie was drinking coffee propped up in bed, two shawls wrapped around her shoulders.

Hal was perched on the end of her bed like a hospital visitor.

'So Masood and his brothers were telling you tales.'

'If I had known I could get coffee here I wouldn't have strayed so far.' Hal bounced gently on the bed.

'Stop it, I'll spill this and I'll tell Lila to deny you coffee privileges.' She held the cup up to weather the bouncing.

'Is this how you control people? With bribery? Have you too fallen for the Indian way.' Hal bounced again.

'If you were less good-looking and older I would ask you to leave. And their stories about cricket on the frozen lake are their romantic time slip. Everyone would love it to be so but the pollution stops them freezing, bar a bit around some of the houseboats.'

Hal sat still and listened.

'Did they lecture you about the evils of alcohol and the awful influence of the old drunk on The Wonder House?' Gracie looked straight at him. 'They'd have smelt the whisky on you, surprised they let you into the house.'

'Not a word.'

Gracie waited.

'Really, they said nothing. They sat on the opposite side of the room to me while each of those wrapped-up girls popped their heads around the door to have a look.'

'You were on show,' Gracie sniffed.

'That's what it felt like. Amazing floor in that room, the way it's warmed. Ibrahim gave me a long scientific chat about how they do it, really clever and simple. I think the *kawa* tea rehydrated me.' He made the next bounce smaller.

'Will you stop, what is it, why are you so sprightly? Have you been making love to Lila?'

Hal looked at his hands in lap, how the fingers curled in as Gracie said her name. He did not reply. His father had used the same expression for flirting.

Gracie waited. 'I meant in the way you managed to get coffee from her without having to beg.' Gracie swirled what was left in her cup.

'I could try and get some more,' Hal said quietly.

'You could, and some dry biscuits would be a good idea. Don't normally eat in the morning but some lining is required today. You might like the same.' She readjusted both shawls and Hal was faced by a gap of stretched skin and fallen bosom through the opening of her nightdress.

He turned away. He had lied to her. After he had drunk tea with the three brothers and Gulam, their almost silent father, Masood walked with him back to the garden gate. He asked him if he could try and encourage Gracie to drink less. Hal said that he did not know her well enough to start being her alcohol conscience. Masood shook his hand warmly and asked him if he could just try. Hal nodded.

'Nagin and Dal did used to freeze right over at one time, thick enough for a car to drive on. Old Suffering Moses, the Shi'a papier-mâché king, used to drive his jeep out into the middle of Dal.' Gracie lay back into her pillows. 'There were cricket and football games, twenty years ago, though, the lake was alive then. Dal is half the size now that it was fifty years ago. It'll be just a bog soon, just a bog, and then Kashmir will really be on its last gasp.' She kicked Hal under the blankets.

'Go on, coffee.' She passed her cup to him. 'I plan to be dead a long time before that starts, and if I smell the bog coming while I'm still around I'll jump into it, glug glug, Gracie Singh died with the lakes, may she rest in sludge.'

Hal got up. 'So, it's dry biscuits and coffee.'

'Yes, yes, off you go.' Gracie waved him away.

Hal thought about opening lines to Lila. He needed some way of being humble about the drunkenness without sounding weak. 'Thank you for all you did last night.' No, no. 'As a journalist I fail by not having the drinking capacity enjoyed by my fellow scribblers.' Pompous. 'My capacity is pathetic, sorry, Lila.' He turned to the sliding window at the end of the corridor.

Suriya was outside, putting a tray down so that she could open the window. He pulled it across for her. She nodded and lifted the tray. There was a pot of coffee and a small copper saucepan of hot milk.

'Oh Suriya!' It was surprise, and disappointment. 'Thank you, I was just coming to beg for this. Where can I find another cup?' He blurted to cover his first response.

She lifted her chin towards the galley kitchen behind him. He reached to take the tray from her but she pulled it back. The wooden sill divided them. Hal turned to the kitchen to find a cup. Suriya was already at Gracie's door by the time he had found the right cupboard.

He called after her. 'Hang on, I'll come and open the door.' But she had put the tray down and knocked.

By the time Gracie had answered, Hal was behind Suriya, cup in hand. Gracie looked at them in the doorway: Suriya, coffee and Hal. She laughed and clapped them into the room.

From his study Masood watched his wife coming along the path at the top of the meadow, her head bent over inside her *burqa* against the cold. Checking that no one else was in the hallway he ran down the stairs.

Now Naseema stood at the kitchen door, the front of her *burqa* lifted, her face framed in black. Her eyes were red-rimmed from the freezing air outside. She kicked her shoes off on the step and bent to pick them up, her neck arched back to stop her *burqa* from falling forward again. One of the kitchen boys closed the door behind her. She held her shoes in one hand and a letter in the other.

She had been to her sister's house further along the lake. They had arranged for forged identity papers covering Irfan to be sent to her house. Naseema's sister had three daughters and no sons. The police and security forces would not be so suspicious.

The letter had come, he had been able to tell by the way she walked, a stiff nervous shuffle under her *burqa*.

She held the letter out to Irfan's mother, Faheema. Masood had reached the kitchen door as the letter passed between the two women. He wanted to snatch it but he kept his hands inside his *pheran*. Faheema looked at the envelope and then carried it over to the carpeted corner of the kitchen where they ate. Masood turned to leave, aware that he had encroached. But he stopped and waited on the other side of the kitchen door.

It was the time when the women and children had their afternoon *chai* and *kulcha* bread together, their time while Masood and his brothers went to the mosque. It was when the boys threw their weight around, ordering their sisters and

mothers about, even Feroz became a mini-martinet, his chin
stuck out as he slurped his tea the way his father did. The
women laughed at him and pinched his cheeks, covering
him with kisses, and making him slurp even more.

When the brothers came back from prayer the kitchen
changed, the laughter died down and the activity became
centred around the three men while they drank tea and
asked the children about their marks at school. At this time
the three women moved among their children, pulling *hijabs*
back into place that had slipped as the younger girls played
over their *chai*, pushing escaped hair under the sides,
pinching the material tighter together under their chins so
that it might not slip again.

As the women and children's *chai*-time began Masood
could hear his wife from where he stood in the corridor, but
he could not hear what she was saying. He leaned in towards
the door. They were whispering. He had another fifteen
minutes until he should be at the mosque. He opened the
door again. Naseema and Faheema were sitting together in
one corner, away from the others. They were bent over the
contents of the letter.

'Have they come?' Masood stood by the step up to the
carpet where they ate.

'They have come,' Naseema replied without looking up.

He held out his hand. Faheema reached out to pass the
papers to him but his wife snatched them back. Masood did
not move his hand. The children stopped talking. Masood
looked at his wife, his hand outstretched. He flicked his eyes
towards the children and then back to Naseema. She passed
the papers to him.

Kudji was making *chai* at the other end of the kitchen,

dipping a ladle into the large pot and peering into it to check for lumps of milk skin; Masood's eldest, Saqeena, was pulling the breadbasket down from above the stove, knocking against her aunt and laughing. Her younger sister, Safora, was rinsing out a carefully balanced pyramid of cups that they would need for *chai*. They were beyond the atmosphere at the other end of the room. They had not seen Masood coming back. Their noise and chatter made them unaware of the silence on the crowded carpet. Kudji called out for the younger girls to come and help carry the tea. No one answered her. She turned from the stove, the ladle still in her hand, and then she saw Masood. She turned back and lowered the ladle carefully back into the *chai* pot. Everyone in the room watched in silence as Masood took the papers and left the room again.

He went with one of the cousins to the police post at the corner of Lal Bazaar four days later.

Mushtaq was a few months younger than Irfan, and his moustache was beginning to show in the same way as Irfan's. They were both late growers. Most of their classmates had fine beards by the time they had finished their last term, while Irfan and Mushtaq still had only a light shading on their upper lips. It was a good match, and Mushtaq was a brave boy, braver still once Masood had offered him a new cricket bat and a pair of trainers for going to the police post with the forged papers. They practised for three days, going through all the trick questions that could be thrown at Mushtaq. Masood made him come to stay at the house and everyone had to call him by his forged name, Feroz, while he stayed. Kudji refused and the real Feroz kept forgetting until Masood made it into a game for him, with prizes.

Masood went with Mushtaq as far as the *chai* stall on the corner of the street before the police post, and then he waited nervously, turning a cup of *chai* around and around in his hands without drinking it. Mushtaq was gone for less than five minutes. There had only been a junior officer at the police post. He had not asked any questions. He had told the boy that Major Kumar would come to the house again if more information was needed.

Mushtaq and Masood sat opposite each other in the *chai* stall. Masood continued to turn his cup in his hands, trying to make a plan for when Major Kumar might come again, and how quickly he could get the boy to the house if he did. Mushtaq wondered why his uncle seemed so worried when he had done exactly what he had been asked to do. He jiggled his knee and thought about his new cricket bat and trainers.

Chapter Nine ~

On both sides of the lake different things happened on New Year's Eve, but they were threaded together.

Gracie did not have a drink during the day for the first time for five years, barring when she had been ill, or the times when Suriya had banned gin during Ramadan. She wanted to be clear-witted to justify to Hal why she had fought so hard to stop Jitu from joining the Congress party in the 1940s. He had wanted to be part of India's Independence movement. She had wanted him to stay out of prison. She was planning a longer version of these two simple facts.

She had not noticed what day it was.

Across the meadow, in an upstairs room, just down the corridor from Masood's study, Faheema gave in to the creeping depression that had been lapping around the edges of her every action since Irfan's disappearance. There was no reason to get up. The shape of the day did not interest her. Her daughter, Zubeeda, and her two other boys, Omar and

Shabeer, sat on her bed at various times during the morning, crying and begging her to get up, to come and cook for them, to come and have *chai*, even just to come downstairs. Their tears did not move her, even though she was aware of the action. She just lay with a photograph of Irfan in her hands, staring at the web of cracks in the ceiling above her, as if she might also find his face written among the lines in the plaster.

As Faheema lay following the line of one crack to where it met the next, a wailing sound started from the house at the end of the alley that cut off the road beside the Abdullahs' house.

Masood's neighbour died just after half past three from pneumonia. It had been complicated because his right lung had still been so weak. One of his ribs had punctured it during three days of interrogation at the Fairy Palace above the lake, the place he and his sons had been taken to on Eid night, and where the two boys were still said to be.

Zubeeda was sitting on her mother's bed when the keening started. She saw the tears that began to slide down Faheema's cheeks, but her mother made no effort to wipe them away. Zubeeda starting crying again too, for herself rather than for their neighbour's widow.

Hal was on his way back from the city. He had gone to call his mother. She wanted to know when he was coming back. He told her that it was taking longer than he had thought. It had taken him a week to rouse himself from the creeping lethargy that had taken over after his arrival at The Wonder House. He settled on the reason that his body needed the time to get used to the severity of the cold. His recent pattern had been to get up just before midday and crawl back into bed straight after supper. Gracie seemed happy to indulge him. He had only started taking notes over the past couple of days.

He had not told his mother this. She cried when he wished her Happy New Year and century. She just started telling him that her boyfriend, the supposedly reliable retired diplomat, had gone back to his ex-wife, and then the line was cut. He tried to call back but he couldn't get through. It was too cold to wait around in the phone booth. He crossed the road to the Punjabi café, where he drank to the scattered remnants of his family with a cup of relatively good coffee, huddled on a wooden bench with two Sikhs. He sat and sipped to his separated sister, his freshly single mother, and his dead father, as he looked out over the main bunker on Lal Bazaar that dominated the front of what had once been the busiest cinema in town.

He asked the rickshaw wallah to drop him on the edge of Zadibal Bazaar above Nagin. The potholes along the last stretch were too much for his back and he had wanted to walk for a bit before submitting himself to more of Gracie's life.

The cows were on their way back from the meadow. Hal knew them, they were there every day, chewing the dry grass around the stumps because the cricket fellowship was not in session. There was the chestnut lead girl, her white streak spreading over one eye so that it looked as if she was winking, her hindquarters perennially shit-smeared. A clever cow, she knew how to open the gate into The Wonder House garden, and how to shut it behind her so that she could eat the chrysanthemums and the soft silvery rabbit-eared leaves of the salvia while her sisters stood on the other side of the fence and watched. Hal had named her Estanza after his aunt, his mother's sister, who also had a habit and skill for opening apparently locked doors. Estanza was now leading the ladies home, their heavy udders swinging between their hocks, driving them back to the hands that would milk them. Hal greeted her as she approached past the alley that turned down beside the Abdullahs' house. He bowed to her and Estanza turned away.

He thought she was making the noise when it began, a low animal sound that moved and swelled until it became a continuous aching cry. As Estanza passed by she draped her tail gracefully over one side of her rump and a jet of green capped both her hocks before splattering on the road. The boy who pushed the charcoal barrow around the bazaar was wheeling his way in the opposite direction to the cows. Both parties paused before manoeuvring in slow motion out of each other's way. Hal and the boy nodded to each other.

'Where are you going?' asked the boy.

'Nowhere really,' Hal replied. 'I'm just waiting here, listening.' He cupped his hand to his ear in the direction of the sound.

'Man is dead,' said the boy. 'Man is dead, ladies make noise.' He leaned back down over his barrow and pushed on past. 'Bye bye now.' He raised one hand.

Hal lifted his in reply to the boy's humped back.

Lila was lugging a steaming metal bucket around the edge of the *dunga*, her back to Hal as he reached the gate that Estanza liked to open, her body bent to one side by the load of wet clothes she carried. As she stepped on to the last duckboard she slipped. Her other hand was inside her *pheran* and she had no counterbalance to stop the full weight of her body coming straight down on to the edge of the bucket. She did not cry out as she fell but Hal heard the sound of her hip against the bucket's hard rim.

He stumbled and slithered towards her across the tufted, stiff grass, calling out to her. The clothes had spilt in a trail around her head on the frozen ground. She was picking herself up as he reached her. He took hold of her shoulders from behind to help her up but she squirmed away from him, one hand clasping her left shoulder. They stood facing each other, the clothes steaming on the ground between them: Hal's shirts, a pair of jeans, his socks clumped together in a pile on the rim of the bucket. They spoke together, stopped at the same time, started again, stopped again. Hal opened his hand towards her.

'It's your washing.' She pointed her bent elbow at the clothes on the ground.

'I can see, thank you, I'm sorry.' His hands felt useless, untaken, so he dug them back into his pockets, hunching his shoulders against the cold so it would seem that he was doing it to warm his hands, not because they had been rejected. He was looking at her shoulder. 'Did I hurt you?'

Lila flicked her chin.

'Did you hurt it just now?'

She shivered.

Hal swayed backwards and forwards, trying to find his way out of the static between them. He looked up as he rocked back. 'There's a nest up there.' He pointed above the old dog kennel.

'Bulbuls,' she replied.

'Okay.'

Lila bent to start collecting the clothes, her hand still to her shoulder. He bent too. She came up, hitting him with the back of her head. His hand went to his forehead and he smiled.

'She had two lots of eggs. A cuckoo laid hers in with the first clutch.' Lila almost smiled and her hand dropped from her shoulder. 'I watched the cuckoo chick hatch and push the bulbul eggs and chicks out.' She began pairing socks, turning the wet ends into each other. 'It squatted right down into the nest until the other chicks were pushed up the sides of the nest and on to its back.' She hunched down, her elbows out as wings. 'Then oomph, over the edge.' She threw two pairs of soggy socks into the bucket.

'How revolting.' Hal looked from the nest to the socks.

'It's clever.'

'Usurpers usually are.' He passed her the one sock that he had managed to pick up.

She matched it with the singleton that she was holding. 'And the bulbul had another clutch. No cuckoo the second time, they hatched.'

'Did they survive?'

'Who would know? They were beginning to fly not long after the coup.'

The clothes were gathered.

'They're not there now so they must have made it.' Hal smiled.

'Or been eaten.' Lila pressed her hand into the hip that she had fallen on, bending with the pressure.

'You did hurt yourself.' He reached down to pick up the bucket.

She did not resist.

'Somebody died,' he said.

'The neighbour in the alley, he died perhaps an hour ago. It takes the mourners about an hour to get going.' She reached out to take the bucket from him.

'Was he old?' He did not let go.

'Not old enough.' Her hands went to her scarf and she retied it in the way that Hal was beginning to love. 'He was beaten by *jawans* and he never got his strength back. They will say on the certificate that it was pneumonia but it was the army.' She pressed her hand back into her shoulder.

'What happened to your shoulder?' he asked.

'Something . . .' She stopped and reached out to take the bucket away from him.

They pulled it in opposite directions, both of them bending over a little more to cover the fact that they were smiling down into his soggy clothes.

Suriya watched from the *dunga*, both her hands pressing into the middle of her narrow chest.

Lila turned away and stepped carefully on to the duck-board. Hal's hand went out, as though to help her, but she had passed and again his hand was left empty in the air. He walked back to The Wonder House, his thumb rubbing at the mark of the bucket handle across his palm.

The years were being cut loose. When Gracie tried to line them up she found them wandering around in random island groups. Sometimes they were linked by a person: the Hari-was-Mine island years; the Purple Era clump when Jitu had decided to move away from his family, when they had been able to make love for the first time without palace servants listening at the door to report back to mother; the

Black Island between Hari's death and when she had got up from the bed in the Abdullahs' spare room to watch the ribs of The Wonder House being filled out by cedar planks that she had bought for such a good price. People surfaced from other island groups and scattered the one she thought she was just beginning to negotiate. They had become water on lotus leaves, the way the drops rolled around on the waxy surface like mercury, rushing together, separating, and sucking back together again.

She had been trying to find an order to the 1940s since lunch so that she could explain them to Hal. Not having a drink had helped, but she was stuck now, irritated by the space that had opened up between Partition and having Hari, two bloody births with a blank between.

She wanted Hal to help. The years seemed to line up more obediently around him. He had been away all day. She wanted him to come back, and he did, calling out as he pushed the side window open down the corridor. Gracie settled in her chair, nice and easy, as though she was just sitting there, not waiting.

Hal was at the door of the sitting room. 'My mother has been dumped by her latest boyfriend.'

'How old is she?' Gracie asked.

Hal dropped on to the sofa opposite her. 'She lies. I think she says she's fifty-eight, or she might just have pushed it up to sixty now, but I'm thirty-four and she was thirty-five when I was born, so . . .'

'Not far behind me, and she still has boyfriends?'

'Does she ever, my God, she clocks about one a year.' Hal undid his coat but he did not take it off. 'Shall I light the *bukhara*? It's very cold in here.'

'Where does she meet them?'

He got up and went to the *bukhara*. 'Where all the sexy old widows hang out, in over-sixties dating bars.' He lit a match.

'They have those now?' Gracie noticed a smear of dhal on her cardigan and picked at it.

'Of course. We'd have to get you into something a bit more clingy, bit more décolletage, and you'd be right there with them.' The *bukhara* would not light. He dropped the first match and lit another one. 'They're very well designed, they have very tasteful areas tucked under the stairs where people can leave their Zimmer frames before they hit the bar.'

Gracie looked up from her cardigan. 'I believed you until that last bit. It won't light, by the way. It ran out of kerosene after lunch. I was waiting for Lila or Suriya. Too lazy to do it myself.'

'She fell over.' Hal shook the match out.

'What?'

He looked at the match end glowing in his hand. It broke off and he bent to pick it up off the carpet.

'Who fell?' Gracie asked again.

'The match, got it now.' He proffered her the retrieved end. 'We could start them, though. How do you think it would go in downtown Srinagar? All the old widow folk giving it a bit of a go somewhere on Residency Road. We could do blind-date bingo, no money obviously to respect our Muslim brothers' sensibilities. Win win, *chai* and cookies instead of cash.'

'The widows here aren't old.' Gracie pulled the blanket she had over her knees up over the dhal stain. 'Where does your mother meet them?'

Hal put the matches down. 'Through friends, that's how it works with the widows in London.' His voice flattened out. 'I'll go and get more kerosene.'

'Don't, Lila or Suriya will be here soon, it's teatime isn't it? What time is it?'

Hal reached into an inside pocket of his coat. 'Obviously my wrapping is not the most elegant.' He passed a small bag to Gracie.

'What's this?'

'It's New Year's Eve and I didn't give you a Christmas present.'

'Well, neither did I, and I don't have anything for you.' Gracie clenched and unclenched her hands.

'Please, it's nothing, just a little Happy New Year, the millennium.'

'I wish you hadn't. I'm embarrassed now. It didn't cross my mind. What happened to Christmas?'

'It was the day I came to stay here.' He was still holding the bag out to her.

'Did we do anything? Didn't you want to be with your family?'

'We got drunk, that's fairly traditional, and I would hardly have come this far if I had wanted to do the whole festive marathon with what's left of my family.'

'But did we even notice it was Christmas?' she asked.

'No, that was the best thing about it.'

'Do you hate Christmas?'

'Loathe it. My father died on Boxing Day.'

'So you run away?'

'You married a Hindu to get out of it.' He pushed the bag at her.

'So why are you giving me this?'

'Oh Gracie, just because.' He put it in her lap.

'We'll have to make some effort this evening then. We can't just sit and slide out of one century and into the next without some kind of acknowledgement. Vast parties all over the world, that absurd bloody thing in Greenwich like a hairdresser's tinting cap, and we were about to just let it slip past.' She folded her hands over the bag.

'I was planning to say Happy New Year when the time came.' Hal sat down.

'We're all in bed so long before midnight. I suppose we'll have to try and sit it out tonight.'

'What did you do other years?' He now regretted the present.

Gracie opened the bag.

'Thank God, I thought I was going to have to use brute force.' Hal clapped.

'Oh no, it's in a box. What have you done, Hal? Did you buy me diamonds?'

'Nope.'

She opened the box. 'A watch, you lovely man, a watch. Did you know I'd lost mine?'

'I did.'

'Did I tell you? How rude.'

'No, you just keep asking me the time.'

It was a man's watch, just a plain, clean man's watch.

'I always have men's watches. Did you ask Lila?' She turned it over in her hands.

Hal was happy. He had bought it at the airport, without any real idea of who it was for, because it was elegant. 'Put it on.'

She held her wrist out to him and the watch. He did it up too loosely, worried about pinching her skin where it fell away from the bone above her wrist. She pulled it further up her arm so that it was tight.

'Happy New Year, Gracie Singh.'

'Happy New Year you.' She looked at the watch on her arm. 'It's grand, thank you.'

'A great pleasure.'

'Is that it then?' She looked at her new watch. 'Only quarter past four, wonderful, teatime. Call Suriya or Lila, would you? We need tea.' She pushed on through her embarrassment.

Hal went back out into the cold. Gracie sat looking at her present. She had not been given anything by a man since Jitu had died, twenty-two years ago. She cried quietly as she heard Hal leave the boat, her hand over the new watch on her wrist.

For each of them midnight came at a different time, the moment separated by eight minutes.

Gulshan was bent over the back of his family's *dunga*, his watch in his hand, trying to see the minutes by the reflected light of the moon on the water. There was no power. His brother and mother had gone to sleep because it was too cold to stay awake, and they had said that it wasn't their new year anyway.

He thought it looked as though the second hand was hard on twelve, two arrows, straight up. He had been holding his breath. For what? Nothing happened. Nothing changed. The air in his chest had been hope, a tiny optimism that something would change; that the sky would dissolve on to him, the stars settle all around the *dunga*, light perpetual; that he would be robed in new blue jeans, sandblasted and tight, and a distressed leather flying jacket too, as worn by the Bollywood stars they were not allowed to watch any more; that his mother's stomach cancer would be sponged away by the melting sky; that he would have a motorbike, unoriginal perhaps, but again like the leather-clad movie stars; that his brother would leave and find a home of his own; that he could have Lila.

But the sky stayed where it was, and he could smell the sewage coming off the water.

Masood lay in the dark.

It was not their new year.

But it was, they were all part of it, part of the same mass of people praying, shouting, kissing, holding each other, the expectation of a billion-strong scrum across India.

The house was quiet. He had hoped that some of the children might stay awake, that they might rush into the bedroom as the century flipped over, so that they could feed his small pockets of hope with their energy. He picked up his watch again to make sure that he had seen the right time, lifting it silently from under the bed so that he would not wake Naseema. She was lying on her back, the blankets and quilt pulled halfway up over her face, the bulk of her body rising up from where her wrung-out breasts hung to left and right of her, each nipple suspended from trellises of stretch marks.

It was hard on midnight. The emptiness rose up inside. He was about to reach across to his wife, to wake her, to roll into her so that they could be warm together while the other billion roared. His hand stopped. He would let her sleep.

~~~

Faheema lay in the same position that she had been in all day, still staring at the cracks that she could no longer see, Irfan's picture gripped tight in her hands. She did not know the time. She only knew that she had to hold on to his picture because if she let go then bits of her would start to fall off.

He was not as he had been in the picture. He was thinner and darker. The cold altitude had turned his skin the same colour as the jacket that Gulshan was hoping might fall from his melting sky. There were black rims under each of Irfan's nails, even when he scraped them out with his knife. Now the longing for his mother had become real, almost strong enough to transmit through the captured, framed moment that she gripped so hard.

He lay awake. They had been told not to celebrate. They would cross the river if they did, back and forth, back and forth, until they understood that this was not their new year. It was for the poisoned West. So he lay awake and waited. He had seen a watch at quarter to eleven as one of the commanders had taken it away from his neighbour, just to make sure. He had been counting since then, seventy-five times sixty. He was only four minutes out when he leaned over as he got to fifteen in his last set of sixty. His knife was beside his boots, his new boots, the ones he had been issued after seeing Lal, Gupta, Batapa and Singh scattered on the snow. He opened it as he got to forty-five, turning over on to his belly, his blanket pulled up over his head. On sixty he cut away the first few hairs of his beard in silent rebellion.

~~~

Gracie had fallen asleep at eleven, her chin dropped on to her chest, her breath ruffling in and out of her cheeks. Hal knew her pattern now. With one drink she was funnier. So she travelled via garrulous, argumentative and maudlin, to number five and deep sleep. He had only had one whisky and he was cold and tired, but he was still waiting. At five to twelve by his watch, seven to twelve by the one he had given Gracie, he poured another whisky, neat.

When he had been at school they had all talked about where they were going to be at the millennium. This had not been his plan. Thirty-four had seemed old at fourteen, life almost gone. He had said he would be successful, and at fourteen that meant cars, a fleet of them, a wife, family, and deference from everyone, though no clear route had been marked to the point where deference might be due. And here he was on a cold sofa, opposite a woman who seemed as old to him now as thirty-four had seemed to that fourteen year old.

His job had gone stale on him, the last promotion to section editor missed because he felt too numb to play the politics. There was too much fallen hair on his pillow every morning, and he was paying a mortgage for a basement on the other side of the world where the plumbing was even worse than on The Wonder House.

Summary of his life to date: a static job; eight ex-girlfriends, only one of whom really sat deep in his memory map; an increasingly volatile mother; a sister at decree nisi; a dead father; a car from a time when he thought having one mattered. So he had escaped to a place where he wanted every part of a woman – no, more a girl – who worked for an old woman on her houseboat on a dying lake. Not very promising.

He got up and crossed to the dining room, waiting by the table to make sure that Gracie was still asleep. Her breath whistled. A large bowl of *gajari halwa* was on the table. Suriya had bought it in after supper.

The Wonder House kitchen did not usually serve up sweet things, but Suriya sometimes produced them instead of words on days that needed expression. *Gajari halwa* for New Year: shards of optimism grated with carrots into a pan on the *dunga* floor; her longing for security melting with the ghee as it slid among the carrots; her dreams of money dissolving into the sugared milk. She stirred her language of hope into the lava surface of her pan.

She had brought it to the table, the bowl hugged to her breast as her offering. Gracie had held her hand, thanking her and stroking her wrist, telling her how lovely it looked, as though she was talking to a child. Suriya had stood over her bowl of wishes for a moment before turning away.

Gracie had not even tasted it. Her appetite and sensitivity had both gone with her fourth gin. Hal had tried a little, the warm sweetness of the carrot flooding his mouth, making him want to have more than the small spoonful he had taken, but Gracie had got up and made her way to her chair in front of the *bukhara*, her unsteadiness demanding his support.

He reached out now and took a large spoonful, pushing the bowl of the spoon right into his mouth. It was cold, the soft richness now a coagulating greasiness that coated his palate. He swallowed it like a dog and swilled his mouth with whisky to cut the grease on the back of his tongue.

The bowl was still almost untouched. He wanted to please Suriya. She gave her disapproval voice in the way she pounded her masalas when he went to the *dunga*, and in her shortened gestures of response when he asked her for something. He looked at the bowl again, and then he put enough on to a side plate to make it look as though both Gracie and he had eaten some, resting the spoon back against the bowl so that it made no sound. He crept to the side entrance, keeping to the far left of the corridor where he knew now that the boards did not creak.

The night air bit as he opened the roof cover, the cedar whining on its runners as he pushed. His watch said two minutes to midnight. It was two minutes slow.

Straight up and down, on top of each other, on his wrist, perfect, clean, exact. Major Kumar's watch was split-second accurate. He had left the Mess at eighteen minutes to midnight. Ten minutes to talk to the family, three minutes to get to his room, three minutes to get ready, and two to spare. His wife's voice had sounded as though she had been asleep, his daughter had cried about being kept in for the evening, and his son had been at the party she had been denied. His wife had ended with her inevitable question mark. He did not know when he was coming back, leave cancelled in October, and now again at New Year. He had called her 'baby' in their secret way, and promised they would have next New Year together; maybe in Goa, maybe at one of those fancy resorts that she could show off to her 'kitty party' ladies about. Nitu Kumar had smiled down the phone, her lips pressed thinly together as she sat on the edge of her bed in her night sari, her long hair in a braid over her shoulder.

Major Kumar sat on his bed too, looking at his side-by-side shoes placed under his uniform, the jacket buttoned right up to the empty collar. He still wore his socks under his *kurta* pyjama, and a shawl that his mother had given him, wrapped around his shoulders. He got up to get a bottle of whisky out of the cupboard under his barred and razor-wired window. A glass had already been set out on the table beside his bed, exactly between his alarm clock and a picture of Nitu and the children. It had been taken at Diwali two years earlier; his wife was smiling out at him while both the children stood hunched and unenthusiastic.

Three fingers of whisky, exact, precise, the hands of his watch straight up and down, exact, precise. Sashi Kumar pulled his shawl tighter around his shoulders and raised his glass to the photograph, and then he drank the three fingers of whisky to fill the hole inside.

'What are you doing?' she asked as Hal threw small lumps of *gajari halwa* out into the lake from the roof. She was standing on the bank, her hands inside her *pheran*, her head wrapped around in a shawl.

'Happy New Year.' He put the plate and his glass behind his back.

'Is it time?'

'I think almost exactly, just a bit past.' He wondered how long she had been standing and watching.

'Then Happy New Year. Has Gracie gone to bed?'

'She's asleep in the sitting room. I was going to help her to bed in a while.'

'Did you drink as much as she did?'

'About a quarter.'

'Are you drinking now?' She ducked her head, trying to see what was behind his back.

He produced the glass. 'Just for the millennium.'

'Can I try some?' She lifted her face.

'What?' He laughed, amazed.

She did not repeat it. He knew what she had said. She half-turned.

'Lila, here.' He reached his glass down towards her.

She stood on the bank below him, still half-turned away. He knew he had about two seconds to stop her going. Squatting down, he leaned over the edge of the roof, the plate of *gajari halwa* still behind his back in one hand, the whisky in his other. He could not keep his balance and he tipped backwards on to the plate. She laughed.

'My mother's *gajari halwa* all over your backside.'

He scrambled forward on to his knees and came back to the edge. 'If you knew why did you ask?'

'I didn't know why you were throwing it. Clever of you to manage not to spill your glass.' She walked away.

He was not going to call after her. Gracie might hear, Suriya certainly would. He stood up on the roof, looking about over the lake, longing for her to turn back. She did not.

The flat water looked back as he took a mouthful of whisky. There was still a lot left. He had poured too much, but as it scoured down into his chest its warmth was immediate and clarifying.

He would leave. He could finish the article in a couple of days and move back into the city while he researched the other pieces for the series. It would probably mean making up some story for Gracie. Then there would be the flight problem and changing the ticket. The office would be shut on New Year's Day. It would probably mean another four days. He could be back in London by perhaps the sixth or seventh. He could go to Ned and Annie's for the weekend, muck about with his godson, get drunk with Ned, detach himself. It would be simple.

The boat spoke into the cold silence. He listened to see if it was Gracie moving down below but it was quiet again. A depressing string of fairy lights drooped across the front of one of the boats across the lake. Most of the bulbs had blown, presenting a melancholy, toothless smile.

'It really is all over your backside.' She was a few feet behind him, her head and shoulders above the opening on to the roof.

Hal could not see that her hand was shaking on the stairrail below the edge.

'I sat in it.'

'I know, I saw.' She did not come up any further.

He held his glass out towards her. 'Would you still like to try some?'

She pulled her hand back inside her *pheran* as she climbed up the last two stairs. He followed each of her careful steps, the way she picked the planks that would not creak. She was opposite him, her face level with his hand and the glass. He did not know how to give it to her as her hands were inside the body of her *pheran*. She made no move to take them out. He put the glass to her bottom lip and lifted his hand. Her head tilted and he saw the movement in her neck as she swallowed. She stepped back and coughed, both hands coming up through the neck of her *pheran* to cover her mouth and the sound she made.

'It's like fire.' Her eyes were watering.

'That's what's they say.' He adopted a thick Glaswegian accent.

'What?'

'Scotch from Scotland, it was the accent, it doesn't really work in Kashmir does it?'

'Turn around,' she said.

He turned and felt her picking *gajari halwa* off the back of his coat and trousers. He shouted out silently at the lake as she touched him. She stepped away again once she had finished.

'They'll need washing. It will have to wait for a warm day.'

A pause seemed to expand.

'Why is your English so good?'

'Gracie sent me to Miss Mallinson's.' She stood with one hand still inside her *pheran*, the other holding a small mound of her mother's *gajari halwa*.

'Is that a school?'

'The best one in Srinagar, and she made me read plays and biographies and novels with her when I came back in the afternoons. Sometimes some poetry, but she doesn't like that so much. She thinks it's the condensed version of all that's bad about language and sentimentality.' She threw the *gajari halwa* over the edge and wiped her hand down the side of her *pheran*.

'We called it dictionary diarrhoea at school. I hated it, except for Pablo Neruda, but that was probably because he wasn't English, and hadn't been dead for over a hundred years.'

They stood in the silence after their whispering. Lila wiped her mouth.

'Love and bicycles,' she said.

He stared at her.

'I read a poem of his about love and bicycles, the word

"velo", rolling down a hill faster and faster until the letters changed around to be "love". I didn't understand it until Gracie explained that it was half in Spanish and half in English.' She stopped and sniffed. 'Like you.'

Hal held the glass out to her again.

She looked at his hand. 'You first.'

He drank and then passed it to her. One hand came back out of her *pheran*.

'He wrote in both the languages that I grew up speaking. My mother says that all poetry should be written in Spanish because it curls itself around the shape of the poems. His real name was Neftali not Pablo.'

She took the glass, a finger touching one of his. It startled him.

'So you could leave and get a job somewhere else?' He stopped and took a breath. 'With that level of education.'

'I cannot leave my mother. She has only me.' She spoke so softly Hal could hardly hear. 'Your mother was Spanish, so where do you belong? What are you?' She turned the glass to drink from the same place as before and, closing her eyes, she took another small sip. Her eyelids were paler than the skin around her eyes, and there were two darker smudges underneath. The rest was smooth, almost unmarked except for a small scar below her left eye, and little handfuls of freckles, thrown on to the tops of her cheeks, two fine paintbrush flicks of them.

'Half and half,' he said.

'Good halves or bad halves?'

'Just two different halves.'

The space between them was cubed, solidified by pressure pushing in from both sides. Her hand movements seemed restricted to one side, Hal's to the other. He knew he would go over it, again and again, using different words in the replay, less lumpen, less clunky, polished and rephrased until they had an elegance, a finely tuned balance. He felt the fragility of it, a bird's skull between his hands, easy to crush, easy to let it go. Lila moved on the other side of the pressure chamber, passing the glass back to him, her hand then retreating into her *pheran*.

'Which half do you feel?' Her body shifted.

'Stuck halfway, probably somewhere around Andorra.'

She lifted the front of her *pheran* and passed her *kangri* to Hal.

'Have this for some time. You must be cold.'

He did not have the chance to answer because of a thud and the sound of falling furniture from below. Lila put the *kangri* at his feet and ran to the stairs.

He looked at the coals pulsing from glow to grey knowing that he should follow her down.

Gracie had beached herself, belly down, on the edge of the sofa after tripping on the table beside her chair. She was singing as Lila lifted her up. Lila liked the tune but she could not remember the words. She hummed as she turned Gracie right side up on the sofa, then picked up the glass, books, mats and photographs that had fallen with the table.

She knew that the burning between her collarbones was the whisky, and that it softened her towards Gracie and her ambling song. She put her arm around Gracie and tried to hoist her up. She came halfway and then slumped back down, giggling and still singing, her hands flailing about, conducting her own song. Lila tried again but Gracie was laughing too much to help at all. Her hair was pushed up on one side of her head from sleeping against the wing of her chair. It stood on end, her pink scalp showing underneath.

'You look like a mad chicken,' Lila was laughing now.

'I am, I am, the mad chicken I am,' Gracie waved her arms and sang on.

That was how Hal found them when he came down from the roof with Lila's *kangri* hidden inside his coat; two women on a sofa babbling about a mad chicken. He helped Lila to half carry Gracie to her room, the *kangri* burning his stomach as Gracie's weight slumped against him. Lila waved him away once they had put her on the bed.

'Happy New Year, Gracie,' he said.

'Happy happy to you,' Gracie sang, clutching his hand.

Lila stroked the old woman's peaked hair back into place. Gracie turned to Lila and exchanged Hal's hand for hers. He left them, Gracie singing, Lila trying to undress her while Gracie still clasped the girl's hand to her breast.

He could hear her from his room as he lit his *bukhara* and changed. She was still singing when he went to the bathroom. He stopped as he put his toothbrush into his mouth, taking it out again and putting it beside the basin. He leaned in closer to the mirror. He had not looked at himself carefully for days, maybe even since he had been in Kashmir.

His skin was now perhaps just one shade lighter than hers but his face seemed old in comparison to her smooth pale darkness. She was probably ten years younger than him. She didn't even look twenty-four, maybe only twenty-one or two. The virgin of the lake, young in one sentence, worn out in the next, but she'd learned from an old woman. His eyes looked red to him even though he was sleeping such long nights, nine or ten hours every time. He wanted to look younger than he did, and he wanted to not have lover's balls all the time.

He stepped back from the mirror and pushed his hand down into his aching groin. It was too cold to go back down the corridor to get his whisky. He wanted it now, just to help him sleep. He could still hear Gracie, and Lila's voice, sometimes admonishing, sometimes laughing. Her *kangri* was on the floor beside his bed. There was heat left in it. He turned it in his hands and then put it into the corridor outside his door. He used the curtain that hung in front of his door to jam it shut so that he would not have to lock it.

When he was ten he had locked himself into his bedroom in his grandmother's house in Seville and the lock jammed. They were forced to call a locksmith. His grandmother made him drink curdled milk as his punishment. Twenty-four years later he still remembered the taste of that fetid milk.

There was a thin line of cold air that was cutting across the warmth from the *bukhara*. He had not shut the window fully and latched it. Lying in the dark he thought about getting up to close it. Wind was pushing water against the sides of the boat but it sounded like a small boat sliding along the edges of The Wonder House, looking for an unlocked window. He pushed himself further down the bed. In the grey space on the edge of sleep it was too hard to get up, and, in the same unfixed space he felt her, and so he let himself fall over into the dream that was beginning in the cocoon of warmth around him.

He was pulled back out of it without coordinates, spun out into the dark room, the edges of his consciousness trying to calibrate, to know what was happening. He lay in a rigid block listening. The space beyond him was not empty.

There had been someone in a *shikara* at the window. They had broken into the room.

It was as though air contracted as the other body took a step, its every muscle drawn tight to move with minute control. A foot tested the floor in front of it to see if a board under the carpet might give it away, might take away the edge it had in the black.

'Who is it?' His voice was hardly there.

Breath was pulled out of his lungs, lobe by lobe, deflating in his hard exhalation as a body lay down on the bed beside him and she put her hand to his face.

He could smell her, cooking oil and spices in her hair, her breath acid and sweet, fear and excitement, a bit of the whisky she had tried. He felt the cotton of her *salwar* and the softness of her shawl. Rigid they lay facing each other, the breath between them short and harsh. She did not move her hand from his face as he pushed himself up on to one elbow.

Their faces were an inch apart but they could not see each other. Hal pressed his cheek against hers. Her hand did not move from the other side of his face. Her eyes were wide open. He could feel her teeth clamped together through her cheek. The muscles in her neck contracted as he covered the whole of her right breast with his hand.

In the dream he had crashed straight into her. There had been no clothes, no clamped jaw, sheets or blankets, no jammed muscles. He had just pushed his way in without any overture.

She let go of his face and he pulled the quilt and blankets from underneath her stiff body and folded them over her. Then he took her face in both of his hands and kissed her on the forehead.

~~~

Suriya woke up in the *dunga*. She could hear Gracie singing to herself in her room at the end of The Wonder House. She reached out to where Lila would be beside her and felt the flatness of empty blankets. She stared into the dark and felt the movement of her daughter's heart in someone else's hands.

Chapter Ten ~

When the separation came it cut down into his sleep. He felt her rolling away from him in fractions until she sat on the edge of the bed watching the space that he filled in the dark. He tried to breathe as though he was asleep as she began to feel around for her clothes. He did not want to stop her, or to make her have to explain that Suriya was waiting for her on the *dunga*, counting the time since she had been away in quarters and halves of pain. Her *salwar* and *kameez* were at his feet at the bottom of the bed. He heard her movement and breathing stop as he stretched down inside to retrieve her clothes. Reaching out for her hand he passed them to her. She took them and he heard her feet pushing against the cotton as she stepped into the legs of her *salwar*. She stopped and took them off again.

The bathroom door shut quietly behind her and she ran water into the bucket, holding it right up against the tap so that it would make less noise. He knew it would be cold. He had used all the hot water from the geyser for his bath the previous evening. He got up to tell her, to ask her to turn the geyser on again, and to wait with him until it was warm enough for her to wash away the smell of them for her mother's sake. The idea of icy water on her skin upset him.

He pushed the door open. The bulb was on above the basin and it highlighted the bones of her spine as she crouched in the bath, pouring cold water between her legs. She ducked lower when she saw him, grabbing a towel from the rail above her and wrapping it around herself.

'I'm sorry,' he said, and stepped back into the darkness of the bedroom, realizing that his own nakedness had probably shocked her. He pulled the door closed and stood in the cold thick black, seeing just the lit image of panic in her face. He heard her pouring cold water again as he got back into bed and sat in their warmth.

The smell of semen seemed trapped in her nostrils, and with it came the suffocation of diesel. Water would not wash it away. Lila turned the light off as she dried herself so that the dark wrapped itself around her. None of her clothes were in the bathroom. She knew that her *pheran, salwar kameez* and shawl were by the edge of the bed. She needed to cover herself.

Hal waited until she was by the door. She was pulling on her *pheran* when he whispered to her.

'Lila, nothing changes.'

Her head was inside her *pheran* and she could not hear what he was saying. She did not want to speak, to ask him to repeat himself.

When he heard her opening the door he whispered again, 'I left your *kangri* outside the door.'

She did not reply.

'I have to go to meet someone near Jama Masjid tomorrow. She doesn't speak English. Would you be my translator?' He tried as the door opened itself again behind her. He heard her bend down and pick up her *kangri*, but she still did not reply.

'I wanted to go in the afternoon if you can come,' he said without whispering. It sounded so loud.

She stopped and waited in the corridor for any movement from Gracie's room and then she tiptoed away without replying, still wondering what he had said as her head had been muffled inside her *pheran*.

He lay on his back, knowing that he had managed to frame their act in that one sentence in a way that made it sound as if it had been a mistake.

Nothing changes.

Boxed in by words, well done.

Happy New Hal.

He rolled into the smell of her on the pillow, inhaling until he lost her scent.

Lila crept on to the *dunga* from the far end, her shoes in the same hand as her *kangri*, the other reaching out into the blank air to find things to hold on to as she made her way up the duckboard at the back of the boat. Instead of going into the central warmth of the kitchen where her mother lay, she went through and curled up in the corner of the empty room beyond, between the winter piles of onions and potatoes, her *kangri* pulled against her stomach, her arms and legs drawn up inside her *pheran*. She was shivering, trying to push away stored images from the alley that had rolled over her again with the water that she had poured between her thighs.

She thought that she would lie awake in the cold all night, reworking each part, each shift of the fulcrum of her balance. In the silence she blocked out the alley and drew herself back to a point where she could see her hand again, shaking on the rail of the stairs to the roof, and she could smell the whisky as she stood opposite him in the cold, watching the clouds of their breath meeting and falling down between them. Curled among the cold vegetables she played over again the weight of his body on hers, the way his fingers drew down into her skin, and how it had seemed as though it was someone else's body he touched, another woman who responded. Her face was hot as she found the image of his back rising up in front of her when he moved to her navel, wrapping her thighs outwards as the muscles around her tailbone clamped down.

She thought that shame would rise up and straddle her, punishing her for having cried out into his neck as she had snapped between her pubic bone and her belly button when her whole body had jerked into his. It did not. Instead of shame there was a small sweet knot, just below where the implosion had started, tied up again as it had been when she had walked back from Gracie's room and seen the curtain in his door, holding it shut but not locked. And, as she had almost passed by she had decided, in that moment, to go in, just to watch him as he slept.

She tucked both her hands into the heat of her thighs and spun the evening back to the beginning again, back up on to the roof, Hal throwing her mother's *gajari halwa* into the lake, so tall and open.

Suriya lay on her back, her knuckles pushing into her eye

sockets as she listened to her daughter's short breathing. Her tears ran down her temples and into her ears.

She too had curled into the dark like that, away from her own mother, clutching her secret to herself between her tight knees, trying to smother her electrified skin under the dead weight of heavy blankets. She pushed her hand right into her mouth so that she could bite into the silent scream to Allah to leave her daughter alone, unsacrificed. When she heard Lila's breath become softer and longer she carried the empty blankets beside her and put them, inch by inch, over her sleeping daughter, her prayers shouting from her in the silent shapes of her breath.

A pile of leaves was burning at the western entrance to the Jama Masjid, its smoke sitting between the grey sky and the same grey on the ground between dirty trails of lingering snow. Two women in black *burqas*, one with her face veil pulled down, the other with hers thrown back, walked past a pile of rubbish in front of the burning leaves. Two boys in school uniform, their trousers blending with the smoke, the sky, and the ground, pushed bicycle tyres with sticks backwards and forwards beside the slower progress of the two women. Brown tiers of brick rose up behind these small movements on the road, the layers of the eastern entrance diminishing the figures below as they lifted up beyond the women, the boys, the smoke, the road and the sky.

Lila walked straight past, her head turned away from the smoke. Hal stopped to look. He had to run to catch up with her when he saw that she had reached the edge of the market, and that she was about to disappear into the spate of scarves and *pherans* between the stalls. Then she stopped,

leaning down into a huddle of women. He waited outside
their circle, watching as they chattered and laughed over
baskets of charcoal-blackened fish. Two older women
presided, following hands that hovered and pointed, slapping
them away before they prodded.

Hal saw Lila making the same faces as the other women,
gesticulating as they did. He saw her as she was among these
people, arguing and laughing. The night before they had
been encapsulated, and now she looked as all the other
women in the crowd, their language so hard and rapid,
imperative and angry. She was one of them and they were
foreign to him.

She stood up from the group. One of the women turned
to her and said something, taking her hand and pressing it to
her cheek. Lila walked on and Hal followed, trying to
understand what it was about the ordinary group of women
that had seemed extraordinary. One of them called out to
Lila as she walked away and pointed to Hal. She turned and
smiled and called back.

It was their laughter that had made them different, the first
he had heard out in the streets of the city.

'What were they saying?' he asked.

'Just talking about fish,' her voice softened into English.

'Weren't they saying something about me?'

'They just wanted to know who you were, any foreigner
is interesting now.'

'And what did you say?' He was about to touch her arm
but she dropped back so that he could not reach her.

As they had started out from the lake to the rickshaw
stand she told him that she was taking a risk in going with
him right into the city.

'Foreigners move around with male guides. They will assume one thing,' she said, looking down at the road between her feet.

'It wasn't just Happy New Year,' he said as they passed by the tailor's shop where he was having a *pheran* made.

It was already three days overdue. Lila stopped to lecture the tailor.

'Not just the New Year, Lila, not just that,' he continued as they walked away from the man huddled in his tiny shop over lengths of black cloth.

'I can't do that again,' she said as they had passed the bread man, his bicycle piled high with baskets layered with loaves.

'What do you mean?' he asked.

'I can't be with you in that way again in the place where I have lived and worked all my life, separated from Gracie by just a thin wall, and from my mother by just a few steps,' she whispered as two women she knew crossed to the opposite side of the road. 'And you must not touch me in any way while we are outside. Nothing, not any kind of touch. Please.' Her whisper had been urgent.

'Do you understand what I was saying?' he asked as they got closer to the rickshaw stand.

'It is why I've come with you today,' she replied as she had dropped two or three steps behind him.

And now, within an hour, he had failed to do what she had asked, trying to reach out and touch her among the crowd of women outside Jama Masjid.

'I'm sorry.' He stopped so that she could walk past him again.

'I said I was your translator.'

'And?'

'They laughed.'

'Why? Because you're a woman?' He pushed closer to her again, finding it hard to pick out her words in the market noise.

She stopped by the main entrance to the mosque. ' Yes, that, but more so because it's hard for them to believe that someone who looks as poor and crushed as them can speak English well enough to be a translator.'

'You don't . . .'

She cut across him, 'Come.' She lifted her head towards the arched gateway of the mosque.

'Am I allowed to go in?' he asked.

'Why not? This is a gentle religion when it's not carrying a gun.'

A girl stood by the entrance holding a large red plastic bucket. She was slight, about eight years old, but even in her little girl's dress with a pair of dirty grey leggings under-neath, there was already something old about her. She had been playing with her bucket, taking out the shoes that she was minding and lining them up in mismatched pairs. She stopped to watch Lila and Hal. Her hands went up and she untied and retied her scarf in the way that she had copied from her mother and grandmother.

Weak sun began to break through the grey.

A man wearing a *pheran*, his white prayer cap on the back of his head, stepped up over the low dividing wall that separated the front courtyard from the entrance. In one connected movement he lifted the side of his *pheran* and reached down to pick up his shoes with the other hand. For a moment he looked at the little girl, the shoe minder, but decided to take his shoes with him through the Mughal arch.

Hal bent down to untie his bootlaces and the little girl watched him, the skin between her eyebrows smooth as though she was going to smile, but her mouth did not move.

The doorkeeper had pushed himself back against the wall at the gate, his legs tucked up inside his *pheran*, creating a tent to hold the warmth of his *kangri*. He stared at Hal and then Lila.

Lila pushed a hand out through one of her sleeves and waved Hal towards the left as she turned right amongst the shadows of the arch.

Beyond the interlocking bands of grey light in front of him there was a bright fall that flooded an interior courtyard. Two men stood on the grass turned towards Mecca, one in western clothes that were just too tight, trapping and restricting his body, the other man moved easily in his *pheran*. They lifted and fell in prayer, their faces tilting up into the sun each time they rose. Sometimes they moved in unison, then one of them would move faster, his head bobbing away from the other until their rhythm balanced again and they became one.

Their movement was echoed in the shadows among the rows of great wooden pillars by the rise and fall of other figures moving through dusty angles of light from the windows set high into the great walls.

Hal stood just to one side, almost among them, and no one came to move him away or to tidy him to the side. The ripple of backs in front of him was not rigidly disciplined nor dressed as one. Prayer caps sat at all angles and in all colours. Among the greater spread of *pherans* moved shawls wrapped tight around fallen shoulders, dirty anoraks, army surplus jackets with fur collars spiked and pointed by damp errse

and dirt, and sleeveless tweed coats over scarves, over jerseys, over *kurta* pyjamas in padded layers. He knelt among them, drawn down by the fluid movement around him and its unbroken flow, as though these men did this all day long as part of a process, oiled, tuned and unending. He wanted to move with their cycle, but he stayed on his knees, his fear of being picked as an outsider keeping him low to the carpet. He bent his face to the ground as they did.

There was a smell of longing, an ashy scent of stratified prayer.

As Hal came up he saw a man beyond the rows of people, out in front. He sat on his knees, his toes curled under, his shape undefined beneath his *pheran*. His pale prayer cap and his raised face were picked out in a shaft of light, and his hands were raised up into the same sun. It was an act of ecstasy. Hal's logic wanted to discover that it was a set-piece, that the man in the light was part of a contrived scene that would crack open and prove to be just empty choreographed theatre, but the man stayed in the light, unmoving in his prayer. Hal buried the image in a small space inside, and coloured it with a sense of possibility.

From the same space came the memory of the smell. It was the one that had pushed down on him as he had longed to hold his mother's hand, standing beside her in a great frozen church where their desiccated hymns had seemed to reach no further than halfway up the aisle towards his father's coffin. There had been no sun through glass, but the smell had been the same – faith and fear bound into a mixture that could be confused with dust and decaying books.

Hal bent back down towards the carpet to inhale. The voices of prayer muttered around him, the words familiar

250

without being understood, and he waited, bent low, until the image of his father's coffin had passed and he was just a stranger again among believers.

He crawled backwards from his place and then out into the courtyard where the girl with the red bucket was still rearranging shoes. He leaned against the wall beyond her and she stared at him again. It took him a while to realize that she had fixed on his feet because he was still barefoot.

The alleys beyond Jama Masjid climbed away through stalls selling plastic shoes, huge bags of carousel-coloured sweets, and bicycle parts. They turned further into the interior beside a copper shop where a man stood at the entrance in dirty jeans, a *pheran*, and a prayer cap. Lila said a woman's name to him. He nodded and pointed further into the coldness of the alley.

Lila had nodded in the same way when Hal had told her the name of the woman he wanted to meet. Her name seemed to require no conversation. A girl at a gate just pointed when Lila used the name again at the next inter-section of narrowing walls.

She came to the door of her house and opened her arms to Lila, holding her close and kissing her cheek again and again with her eyes closed. She stood holding Lila's hand in both of hers as Lila explained why they had come. Zamruda Parveen led them into a dark room and sat down under a picture of two young men on either side of a fine-looking man with a close-cut beard and pale eyes. The two boys in the picture had inherited their father's jug ears.

Zamruda pointed to three lit *kangris* in the corner of the

room, offering one to Lila, passing the second to Hal without looking at him, and putting the third under her own *pheran.*

'Did she know we were coming?' Hal quietly asked Lila.

'News of foreign faces runs on fast legs here.' Lila drew the *kangri* into her belly.

Hal looked away. 'But they've been lit for a while.'

'We're hospitable people.' Lila smiled down and put her hand over Zamruda's on the floor beside her.

Zamruda reached out for a plastic bag that was on top of a little mound of files below the picture. Unfolding the bag she took out a large stack of business cards and put them on the floor in front of Hal, all the time talking to Lila. Hal began to go through the pile as Lila translated for Zamruda. Every card was from a familiar-sounding journalist: television, radio, newspaper, magazine, Indian, French, German, American, English, Spanish, every nation, every medium, they had all been to see Zamruda.

'She says that every one of them has come and every one of them has interviewed her and heard her story, but not one of their stories has brought her even a finger closer to finding her husband and her sons.'

As Lila spoke, Zamruda reached up and took the photograph from the wall above her. She put it into Hal's lap. Three faces stared out from in front of a blank wall.

Imran, Ja_ved and Parvez Parveen,
disappeared 14 June 1991.

The words and numbers underlined their three faces in Times Roman italics, the 'v' of Javed's name dropping like a falling arrow in the middle of the empty information. Imran was trying not to smile in the picture, his father was staring towards the camera, though one pupil was out of focus as it flicked towards his younger son. Parvez's expression managed to separate him from his father and his brother. It was contained and unsmiling, removed from the intimacy between the other two.

Zamruda talked as Hal looked at the picture. From the tone of her words and the room around him Hal began moulding the shape of the story he would write, even before Lila had translated.

'She wants to know why your story will be any different from any of the others?' Lila put the *kangri* Zamruda had given her to one side and lifted the woman's hand.

Hal's working rhythm stopped.

'And I want to know what this has to do with your story about Gracie?' Lila asked.

'It's nothing to do with Gracie.' He looked at Zamruda.

'Then why?' Lila asked again.

'I didn't come just to write about Gracie.'

'Then what?'

'About the damage.'

'The damage?' Lila let go of Zamruda's hand.

'Yes.'

'So does that mean that we are damage, Zamruda, her husband, her sons, my mother, me?' Her voice was low. 'Are you researching all of us?' She took Zamruda's hand again. 'And as what? Part of that phrase we hear about ourselves — collateral damage — is that what we are?'

Hal turned back and leaned towards her. 'I can only write what I can understand. There is so much of this that I don't.

Even if I spent years here I would still not be able to write well enough to express the reality. So I write from within the limitations that I have.' He stared down into the coals of the *kangri* in his hands. 'To bear witness.'

'How pompous. Can you hear yourself?' A fine spray of spit came from Lila's mouth as she flared in reply.

Zamruda lifted her head and spoke. She grabbed the picture of her husband and sons from Hal and waved it in his face, turning to Lila as her words crowded together.

Two young boys came to the door of the room and hung against the jambs to hear Zamruda's rage. As they listened they stared at Hal, studying his clothes and his discomfort at having to sit with his long legs crossed among others who found it easy. They smiled at each other and left. Hal heard their laughter in the narrow lane beyond the house.

'She says that every one of these people promised to help her bring to justice the officers who took her husband and sons.' Lila translated and then waited for Zamruda again.

He watched her as she spoke, seeing the shadows of her sons in some of her features. Lila turned back to him to translate, but he interrupted her.

'Were any of them militants?' He knew the different versions of Zamruda's story as it had been told in various languages and voices, some poetic, others hard, but all embellished by each individual's impression of how they had found this woman in her empty home.

Lila was silent. Zamruda rubbed her hand across the picture. She looked up at Hal, and put her finger to the side of Parvez's face, beside his bitter mouth.

'He took up gun.' She spoke in English and her hand spread out on the picture to cover her elder son's face. 'Not my husband, not my Imran.' She stopped and put the picture on the floor in front of her. 'Other persons telling *jawans* at interrogation place not my Javed, not my Imran, but *jawans* telling to them to shut. These persons who have seen this thing face death for saying these things on my face.' She stopped and looked at Lila.

He watched as Lila let go of Zamruda's hand and touched her face, her palm cupped around her cheek. Zamruda tilted her head into Lila's touch.

'There were other militants at the interrogation centre who recognized Parvez, and they tried to tell the *jawans* that her younger son and her husband were not militants. She found these men once they had been released from prison and they risked their lives by giving her this information.'

'How did she find them?' he asked.

For the first time Zamruda looked at Hal as she spoke from the cup of Lila's hand.

Lila translated. 'She was married to Javed when she was twelve years old. She had not left her home since then until she was thirty-seven and they took her husband and the boys. She knew she could sit at home and weep like the other women or that she could go out and try and find them. She has spent almost nine years looking for them.'

Zamruda curled into Lila's side, her head now on Lila's shoulder. The Kashmiri half-widow closed her eyes as she gave the same facts that she had given to every name in the pile of cards in front of Hal, rocking backwards and forwards as she spoke: every prison visited; every legal implication; the slide across nine years towards the realization that the army protected its own, that the officers who had taken her family had been absorbed back into the oblivion of a million men;

and how finally she had begun to weep with the other women who had also lost their sons and husbands.

Lila held her, kissing the side of her face and stroking her head as she spoke, and Hal watched the gap that closed between her lips and the curve of Zamruda's temple. He stared at the skin of her inner wrist as it stroked Zamruda's shawl-covered head, and he looked back down at the three faces in front of the rocking woman to stop himself thinking about the shapes of Lila's body.

He knew that he was looking at three dead men.

Zamruda opened her eyes and looked at him, breaking off in the middle of one of her sentences and, lifting her head from Lila's shoulder, she sat up. She spoke in Kashmiri but directly to Hal.

'She's asking if you have ever lost someone?' Lila translated.

'My father.' He looked at Zamruda as he replied.

She understood.

'You know small, small part then,' she replied in English, and her hand went back to the picture at her feet. Then she held out the same hand to Hal, and he took it.

They sat without speaking, Zamruda kneading Hal's hand as she began to rock again.

She wanted them to have tea. Hal thanked her and asked Lila to explain that it would be getting dark and that he wanted to be able to get her back to Nagin while there was still some light.

Zamruda came to the gate in the wall of the alley with them, and spoke to Lila, hugging her, whispering into her ear, kissing her cheek over and over as Lila had done to her. As they left she reached out and took Hal's hand, kissing it and then holding it to her cheek.

'Make good story for me,' she said.

He raised his hand to her as they went through the gate and back out into the alley, and Zamruda turned back towards her empty home, the pile of names, and the photograph on the floor.

'What was she saying to you?' Hal asked as they turned out of the alley.

Lila was wrapping her shawl around her head. 'Just what she said to you, about a good story.'

'A lot of words just to say that,' he said as they reached the mosque on the corner of Zamruda's street.

She had not said that.

She had told Lila that the foreigner liked her, that he seemed to be a good man, and a rich man in his expensive clothes, and that she should go away with him from the Valley because there was nothing for Lila in this place any more. When she had spoken in her ear as they left Zamruda had told her to lie down with him because then he would want to keep her.

Lila drew her face down into her shawl as the men across the street began to go in for afternoon prayers.

On the way to Nagin in a rickshaw they looked out on to opposite sides of the road. Hal saw empty faces hurrying to be off the streets ahead of the evening cold and before the shadowed light made the checkpoint soldiers flick off their safety catches. The rocking head of a galloping pony lunged out of the gloom, drawing a cart out of the mist. The driver stood as a charioteer, high above the pony at the front of the cart, one side of his *pheran* raised up so that he could hold the reins aloft and swing his whip in full circles. He rattled past in solitary energy along the sickly road.

On the other side Lila looked out at the barrows along the pavement beyond Jama Masjid, watching the colours of mounded vegetable and fruit flying past, wondering if they were cheaper than at their market.

Hal stopped the rickshaw at the beginning of Zadibal Bazaar.

'Do you mind if we walk from here?' he asked. 'The ruts in the road . . .' he faded.

'Why not?' She waited as he paid the driver.

'Don't give him any tip, he took a bad route.' She turned away. 'We can stop at the tailor again. He said he would finish your *pheran* by this evening.'

'So you bullied him?' Hal had already tipped the driver.

'No, I just said that he was already three days late and you would deduct ten rupees for each day.'

'Could you stay with me tonight?' he asked.

She stopped on the road far enough away from the tailor's shop and the checkpoint on the corner not to be seen. 'Are you mad?'

'No, I want you to stay.' Hal wiped his nose. 'Very much.'

Lila was looking down at the road beneath her feet. 'I had a very good Pandit friend here before the problems started. She's in America now. In her people's stories they have a line they call the Lakshman Rekha.' She drew a line in the dust with the end of her shoe. 'It's from the *Ramayana.*'

'Ram's brother, wasn't he?' Hal had started to bounce in the road to keep warm.

'You know the story?' She looked up from the line.

'Just the broad sweep of it, and the jumping monkey, but not the detail.' His voice juddered as he bounced. 'We're told that all the sharing of Muslim-Hindu stories is long gone, but you still know them?'

'We all had Pandit friends.' She ran her toe up and down the line, marking it deeper into the dust. 'The stories haven't changed, just us.' She hunched her shoulders up towards her nose, her hands still inside her *pheran*. 'Ram, Sita and Laksh-man were in the woods. The demon king Ravanne wanted Sita so he turned himself into a golden deer, cavorting in front of her until she was enchanted. Ram went to catch the deer for Sita because he loved her, leaving Lakshman with the strictest orders to look after her at their little forest hut. Ravanne then took on Ram's voice and called out to Lakshman, saying that he was wounded in the hunt and needed help. Sita begged Lakshman to go but he told her that he had sworn a brother's promise to Ram that he would protect her.' Lila looked up, but past Hal. 'She went on and on, in the way of women. Lakshman gave in.' She looked down again. 'As men do. So, he drew a line on the ground with the end of his bow and told her that she would be safe if she stayed within it while he went in search of Ram. He knew that if Ravanne tried to cross he would be destroyed by the purity of his loyal promise to Ram, but that if Sita crossed she would be lost.' Her toe stopped. 'That is the Lakshman-Rekha, the line that should not be crossed.'

'And being with me takes you across?' he asked.

She walked away towards the tailor's shop, stepping over her line in the dust.

There was nothing in the *chai* stall to detract from the cold. The blue heat from two kerosene burners below the kettles blew out and away through the open front. The power was off, leaving the stall's two tables unoccupied, except for one figure. Masood pushed his back further into the wall and wrapped the outer edges of his *pheran* in across his thighs. He had forgotten to bring his *kangri*. A glass of tea that he had been warming his hands around was now cold. Even when he leaned towards the entrance he could hardly see to the checkpoint as the light fell down. Every day he came to the *chai* stall, ever since Mushtaq had gone to the checkpoint with the false papers from Delhi. The *chai* stall owner had known Masood since he was a boy. He did not ask him questions, his business was welcome, three cups of tea every afternoon, each one only half drunk, and the same question every day, disguised among others.

Had it been a quiet day at the checkpoint?

Each day had been the same. No changes to report to Masood, but still he sat and drank tea until it was almost dark.

The stall owner sat absently winding the end of his beard with his fingers while Masood watched for Major Kumar. In another ten minutes an officer would come to the post, every day the same. Every day he waited in case it was Major Kumar carrying the papers for an invented boy.

Lila and Hal did not see Masood. He picked them out as soon as they had reached the edge of the checkpoint, both of them walking closer to the sand-bagged gun slits than he would ever dare.

Hal nodded to one of the soldiers, a Sikh, his long forehead pulled smooth by his turban. He asked Hal a question and they talked for a moment while Lila stood and waited. Masood leaned across the table to try and reach for any of their conversation. The *chai* stall owner misunderstood his movement and thought he might be about to ask for his fourth *chai*, a record. He pushed the pan back on to the burner, filling the stall with noise.

Masood held his breath and pulled himself further back against the wall in case the two figures moving up the road heard the noise and looked into the *chai* stall. He knew that the tea-seller must know the outline of Lila's story, as did everyone within the radius of two decades of gossip. He would also know that Lila was Masood's cousin. He could give Masood away, simply calling out to Lila to tell her that he was there. He might want to see the reaction. Probably he would have heard the story of the foreigner, the police, and Lila and Masood Abdullah on the road above the ghats.

Hal raised his hand to the *chai*-wallah as they passed and called out to him, not the Islamic Salaam but a Kashmiri greeting. The stall owner was surprised, though he returned the greeting, and Lila and Hal passed on towards the tailor. Masood waited in the ensuing silence. He paid and walked away with a sense of purpose that might make it seem that he was trying to catch up in order to walk back to Nagin with them. Behind him he sensed the *chai* man leaning over the edge of the stall watching. He heard their voices in the tailor's shop and he hurried past, his chin pulled down into his *pheran*. Lila's tone was so easy to pick, the lilt she used when she was getting something from someone. Masood wished that it did not make him smile into his collar as he hunched into the grey of the evening beyond the spill of light from the tailor's window.

Gracie was trying to convince herself that she was not waiting; simply sitting as she always did at that time of day, at that time of year. They had been away for almost four hours. She could tell now that she had a watch. She picked up the thicker millennium edition of the *Reader's Digest* for the fourth or fifth time, but put it down as soon as she heard the entrance window in the corridor opening.

'Who is it?'

There was no answer except for the closing of the door. It was Suriya. She came in with *chai*, a chafing dish, and two cups.

'He's been having *kawa*, why didn't you make *kawa*?' Gracie asked.

Suriya put the tray down on the low table in the middle of the room and turned to face Gracie, but she made no replying gesture. She took one of the cups, filled it, and then placed it carefully on the table beside Gracie, adjusting the spoon in the saucer.

'I'll have it when he's back. He's not back yet, and will you turn up the *bukhara*.' Gracie pulled her hands inside her shawl and ignored the tea beside her.

Suriya turned away and began pulling the curtains, tugging them hard so that the metal rings rattled on the rods, but Gracie still heard the voices on the duckboard outside above the rasping.

'You knew he was back, didn't you?' Gracie spoke to Suriya's back as she bent over the stove.

She did not have to turn around to know that Gracie was stroking the feathery wings of her hair into order, pushing herself up in her chair a little, and reaching for the *Reader's Digest* once again.

Gracie picked up the cup of tea that Suriya had put beside her as Hal came into the room.

'And how doth I find my lady on this fair new century aft?' He bowed in front of her, his right hand reaching to her feet through the sleeve of his *pheran*.

Grace smiled into her cup. 'Half parched for waiting on my tardy lord.'

'He was waylaid in matters sartorial upon the way. Come, madam, tell me your thoughts upon my vestige?'

''Tis a sorry colour, my lord, prithee tell why thou did chooseth the hue of the muck of geese that shitteth close by yond lake?'

'To match my lady's mood, madam.'

Gracie shook her head a little as she laughed, a slight movement that she had not made for twenty-eight years. Suriya studied its unfamiliarity as she poured from the thermos, and handed the second cup to Hal without a spoon. He was turning in front of Gracie, his hands holding out the sides of his *pheran*, his cheeks sucked in and his eyes rolled up, the same way he had cartooned women when he was a boy. Suriya waited beside the tea tray with the cup in her hand. He realized she was holding out tea to him as he finished his twirl.

'Oh, thank you, Suriya, I've been looking forward to this all the way from Jama Masjid, taking no other tea but yours.' He smiled and bowed over the cup as he took it.

She did not react.

'And what have you created for tea?' he tried.

Suriya lifted the lid of the chafing dish.

'Pancakes, Scottish pancakes, you are the queen of the kerosene stoves.'

She sucked her lower lip to bury her smile and passed him a plate, making him wait as she buttered two of the pancakes, moving the butter slowly on the hot surface of each one until it melted. She passed them to Gracie who in turn passed them to Hal, taking his empty plate in exchange and handing it back to Suriya.

'So, what took you so long?' Gracie asked.

Hal drank some tea and bit into a pancake, licking the melting butter as it slide down his wrist. Gracie leaned towards the tea tray and waved her hand at the napkins beside the thermos. Suriya took her time to pass them. Gracie held the napkins out to Hal who had retracted into his *pheran* to take it off.

'It's warm in here, and my God these things really work.' He sat down on the sofa with his cup and plate.

Gracie saw that the hair on one side of his head had been pushed up as he took off the *pheran*. One of his curls was stuck across the side of his temple. Her hand just lifted from the side of her cup, as though to rearrange the stray curl. She stopped the movement over her plate and played with the edge of one of the pancakes.

'Did you find her?' she asked.

'We did. Incredible woman.'

'They're gritty these women here. They have no choices. It's choice that rots people.'

Suriya moved the tea tray closer to Gracie and turned to go.

'Do any of them leave?' he asked.

'And go where?' Gracie stared at him.

'I don't mean just leave on their own. Do any of them . . .' He bit and chewed, slowly finishing the mouthful. 'Have any of them gone off with foreigners to get out of it?'

'It wouldn't work.' Gracie put her plate down hard.

'Why not?' he asked.

'They're mostly uneducated or under-educated women who don't know anything beyond the inside of their homes, the kitchen, and producing child after child. They can't even think beyond the Valley.'

'Zamruda has, she's been all over India to every prison where her husband and sons might have been, and she's been to a conference in the Philippines to talk about the disappeared of Kashmir.'

'There's only one Zamruda Parveen.'

'I didn't mean it so specifically.' He looked down into his cup.

'I know you didn't, that's why I am being more specific. It doesn't work.' She reached towards her plate again. 'And has all the rushing about got her family back?'

'Not yet, you know that.'

Gracie took another pancake and bit. 'So, you see, it didn't work for her, doesn't work for anyone,' she said, her mouth full.

'You did it, just the other way around, Harrogate to Srinagar.'

She gulped the pancake. 'There is no comparison, it was sixty years ago, the Brits were still in charge, Jitu and I met at Oxford, no comparison, none at all.' She coughed as the pancake stuck in her throat. 'And it was Harrogate to the Punjab, Mr Spanish Pedant Tango,' she snapped.

Hal noticed a real edge of Yorkshire in her voice for the first time.

'But you were . . .' he stopped.

'Were what? What were we?'

'Young enough to be able to adapt.' His voice dropped.

'You were going to say we were different classes, weren't you?' Her fingers knotted in her lap.

'No,' he lied.

Gracie seemed to diminish. She put her plate down and picked up her cup, wrapping her hand around it. 'We were different classes, the prince and the tap dancer. Not bad for a girl from a market town up north, but it was not that glamorous. That palace on the river was a mausoleum. You're a journalist, you've been asking all the questions, surely you've worked out that every part of my marriage and my life here with Jitu was another fight, another battle with his clinging family, their traditions, and the courtiers they used to do their muck-racking.' She snorted, making ripples on the surface of her tea.

'But you got him away from them.'

'I did, but it didn't stop them sending their missiles from that mausoleum in the Punjab to Simla. I told you they sent that bloody milk nurse up when Hari was born, didn't I?'

He nodded.

'And because of some misplaced, bitterly entrenched filial loyalty to that woman, Jitu and I fought about it for, God, I can't even remember how long. I left and went and stayed with some colonel's widow, in hiding from him and the bloody wet nurse.'

'You told me,' he said gently.

'I know I did and I'm telling you again.' She put her cup down. 'That's the second time. They say you have to tell people a thing five times before they really hear.' She picked up one of the pancakes from her plate and it dripped across her lap. 'That's either Confucius or the *Reader's Digest*, can't remember which, or maybe the Dalai Lama.'

Hal passed a napkin to her.

'It doesn't work.' She ignored the napkin and licked the butter off her fingers.

'What doesn't?'

Gracie looked at him, the way his eyebrows tugged together when he was trying to work out something.

So like Hari, especially now that he was darker from the sun.

She forgot what she had been saying. 'So like him.' She now took the napkin that he was still holding out. 'So like him.' Her voice slid down towards her bosom.

Hal watched her. 'What doesn't work?' he asked again as she began to drift.

She refocused. 'I will always be a stranger here, didn't matter if I learned the language and wore the clothes, if I knew the scriptures better than they did, if I had my child here, if I lost my son and my husband, I will always be a *farangi*, different, not quite clean, and ultimately never to be trusted because they still think I can up and leave whenever I want.' She tore the pancake in half and ate one piece slowly, watching him as she chewed. 'But I never did. It would be the same for her,' she said, with a mouth full of pancake.

Hal put his cup down, got up, picked up his *pheran*, and walked away.

'Where are you going?' Gracie asked.

'I'm going to pee. Do I need to ask?' He left the room.

'I am just telling you it doesn't work, it's not my fault that it doesn't so no point being angry with me about it.' She paused. 'I tried hard enough but eventually living your life on best behaviour defeats you.' Gracie saw herself in a slice of darkened glass where the curtains did not meet: an old woman with a piece of cold Scottish pancake in her hand, shouting after a young man. She dropped it back on to the plate and pressed her forehead into her palm, pushing the butter on her fingers into her thin, fine hair.

Chapter Eleven ~

Three weeks after she started staring at the cracks in the ceiling above her bed Faheema looked down. She turned to her nephew Feroz who was sitting on the end of her bed. He had been there for most of the afternoon, drawing pictures of Allah trees, his latest invention, trees so big that their tops went off the end of his piece of paper.

He had left once when he heard Naseema going back to the kitchen from her afternoon sleep, and he had followed her down, coming back up to sit on Faheema's bed again with a plate, a knife, two small rounds of fresh bread, their polished crusts bumped with sesame seeds, a small lump of butter, and a larger one of apricot jam.

He liked sitting with his aunt. She did not talk any more so he could get on with his pictures without all the questions that his mother and Aunt Naseema asked.

'Why always trees? Why do they go off the top of the page?'

How could they understand? Only Uncle Masood seemed to, and maybe Aunt Faheema because she never asked.

Maybe she was looking for Allah in the cracks over her bed.

Now she was looking at him.

Faheema could smell the bread. 'Can I have some?' she asked.

Feroz looked down at the one small round that was left, and then back at his aunt.

'We could share it?' she said.

He split the loaf in half and buttered it. 'Do you want jam?' he asked, looking at what was left on the edge of the plate.

'No, just butter.'

He passed the bread to her and they watched each other chewing in easy silence.

'Thank you,' Faheema said as she finished her piece. She pushed herself up from her pillow. 'I am going to get up now.'

Feroz was still eating. 'Can I stay here?'

'If you wish.' Faheema was unsteady as she crossed the room.

'Why are you getting up now?' he asked.

'Because there is no reason to lie there any more,' she said as she opened the cupboard and sorted through her *salwar kameez*.

'Why did you go to bed for so long?' he asked, turning his attention back to the trees.

'Because there was no reason to get up.'

'Because Irfan is not here?' he asked, scribbling at the branches of the biggest of all his trees.

'Yes, because of that.' Faheema picked out the clothes she wanted and shut the cupboard.

'But he still isn't here.'

'He's coming back,' Faheema said, looking down and seeing for the first time how dirty her nightclothes were.

'Will he be here for my birthday?'

'When is that?' she asked.

'I don't know the date but my birthday is soon, and Gracie Madam told Uncle Masood that she was going to have a party, and her birthday is around the same time as mine. Papa says she is almost as old as Grandpa. He's the oldest person I know so she must be the second oldest. Grandma says she doesn't know how old she is. Mama says she is older than Grandpa.' He stopped for a moment. 'I don't think I'm allowed to say that.' He looked up at his aunt. 'How old are you?'

Faheema did not reply. She was standing at the window, staring down into the kitchen courtyard at the walnut tree.

'I'm going to be eight running.' Feroz leaned back from his picture. 'I think that's beginning to be quite old. I'm not a little boy now, Aunt Faheema, I'm going to be an artist.' He picked up his picture. 'Look, these are my Allah trees.'

Faheema turned to look and they smiled at each other.

She did understand.

Feroz felt relieved that he had been right about her.

When he lay in the dark the faces that had once eased him to sleep were no longer clear. His cousins' faces interleaved each other, the features mixing and dissolving. All he saw of his father was his beard and his skullcap; the details of his mother's face were fading but he had the sound of her voice, always calling him for food. His uncle's face was still easy to remember, perhaps not so much his face but the way he had stood on the balcony and shouted down after he had run away from Lila. He could still see every part of her: her fingernails, the little white crescents at the base of them, the shape of her eyebrows, the way one wandered a little, the finer hair that caught the light at her hairline, and he could smell the cardamom that she liked to suck, yes, not one detail had slipped.

Within his pool of images he wrapped a pale brown shawl around her. He could see his hand beside her face, and he watched as it moved along the outer edge of the wool and curved down and in to find her skin. Within his created darkness Irfan lay down with Lila and pulled away the pale brown shawl.

The sex he now imagined was not the same as it had been when he used to lie between his brothers in the house by the lake. That had been entirely centred around needing to penetrate, images of himself grabbing and releasing into her body. Now when he closed his eyes he saw her face, how her eyes shut as he lifted the shawl, how her skin felt as he pressed his face against hers. His constant replay had rinsed down the images – purifying them, sanctifying them. He never touched her clothes beyond her shawl, but he would still enter her, biting into his sleeping mat so that he would not cry her name. He lay in the dark afterwards, shivering, isolated, his semen clasped in his hand, listening to see if anyone else had heard.

Whoever was awake knew, but they were used to each other now. For three months they had slept in the same tent, eaten together, prayed together, learned how to fight, and listened to each other gasp in the dark, masturbating to find comfort and sleep on the mean ground.

Irfan could not sleep. In a week he was going to be sent back across the Line of Control with Yasin, his training brother, to join a unit near Uri, a day's drive west of Srinagar. Other boys had already gone, Sidi among them.

Irfan had decided to abandon his unit as soon as they crossed the line, to go home and marry Lila, to bring her into the house to live with his family, her family. He would save her.

And she would save him.

He lay in the dark, changing small sections of his plan again; how he was going to travel cross-country and stay in safe areas along the way, seeking shelter as a militant until he got closer to Srinagar. Then he tightened his focus on the details, the times he would sleep, and when he would move. Each change, every shift pushed him towards the pinpoint of all that he was about to do – the moment when he called out to Lila and she turned to see who it was.

He opened his eyes again in the cold night and looked for her face. She would be at the back of the *dunga* boat, bent over the washing board, her scarf halfway down her head, a single strand of hair swinging across the front of her face as she moved. She would look up to brush it away with the back of her wrist as she heard him call. He could not go further than that because he did not know what he was going to say. He lay and waited for the cold to numb him, submerged in Lila, but he did not feel his mother sensing his return.

Gulshan sat outside the *dunga*, waiting for Lila. It was Friday, just after lunch. She might want to go to the market at the mosque. He had borrowed Farouk's boat, with its canopy and soft seats in case she wanted to go. Farouk had not minded. Gulshan had agreed to give him 70 per cent of any water-taxi money he made on the day.

The foreigner had been in and out of the city for the past week. He was often not on the houseboat. He was often not with Lila. Mr Marvellous, the flower man, had said that the foreigner was moving back to stay in a hotel.

Gulshan had passed The Wonder House slowly every day over the course of the month since he had taken the foreigner to Dal Gate. Sometimes Lila had seen him, and she had waved to him, but he had paddled away into the cover of another houseboat.

She had always looked happy.

Mr Marvellous said that there had been a fight. He had told Gulshan how he had been changing the flowers in the sitting room for Gracie Madam. She had been talking to him about a party and how she wanted so many flowers for it, as many as he could manage. He had been pleased but worried that he would not have enough and that he would have to buy from other growers and pay them too much. Only the chrysanthemums were surviving the frosts, and even they had to be wrapped up, sitting in covered clumps in the sleeping flower gardens.

Gracie Madam did not even like chrysanthemums very much.

This had been Mr Marvellous's worry when the foreigner came to tell Gracie Madam that he would be going back to stay at the Residency Hotel. She asked why and he said that he had been there for a month and that he felt he was overstaying his welcome.

Gracie Madam had asked Mr Marvellous to hurry up, and she had paid him then and there, something she almost never did. He had sat under the back of the boat for a while, listening to their conversation. It had not sounded like a fight but he thought it would be a good idea to make it one for the purpose of the retelling.

It was the version he had given Gulshan. And so the young boatman had borrowed Farouk's *shikara* and returned to The Wonder House.

He could hear her voice inside the *dunga* talking to Suriya. He would wait. The sun was warm as long as he did not stay in the shade of the boats, and his *kangri* was hot against his belly. He pulled his arms in through his sleeves and sat just out of the shadow of the back veranda where reflections floated across its carved ceiling. He looked up at the canopy of the *shikara* to see if it trapped the light in the same way. Ripples ran there too.

Beyond the houseboats, three fishermen were working the mid-water of the lake. They stood up at the front of their boats, sometimes leaning down to bring their full weight behind the paddle, skimming their boats across the water. Then they would stop and remain motionless, staring down through the surface, a six-pronged spear in one hand. They waited, minute movement within their stillness, unchanging profiles, clean and fine-cut above the smudged surface of the water.

There was an explosion of movement. One of them waved his spear above his head, a flicking silver crescent pierced by its prongs. He cried out, thrusting his catch in the direction of the other fishermen. Gulshan stood at the front of the boat, calling out to them, his hand raised in tribute.

Lila and Suriya came out of the *dunga*. Lila shouted and waved to the fisherman before turning to Gulshan.

He minded that she only noticed him after the fishermen. He did not realize then, only later when he thought back on it.

'How nice, they never catch anything. The fish must be coming up into the sun.' She turned to him.

'It is, it's such a day. Are you going to the market? Such a day to go to the market.' His gesture drew in the lake, the sky and the fishermen.

'Very beautiful, but no market today. I'm going to the other side.'

He stared at her, seeing how her skin was shining. Her mouth seemed wider.

There was nothing to say. He no longer felt happy about the fisherman on the lake.

Lila squatted down beside him. 'How are you, Gulshan?'

Suriya looked over at the boy on the boat and smiled sadly with him, but he did not see her expression as she turned back into the *dunga*.

'I'm okay, and you?' he asked.

'Thank you, I'm well,' she said, and it was another thing he only realized later – the formality in their exchange.

'Can I take you to the other side?' he asked.

'That is kind but our little boat is more than fine. It's not so far.'

'I can still take you.' He lifted the heart-shaped paddle and held it up as the fisherman had held his spear.

'You've got Farouk's *shikara*,' she said.

'I'm working for him.' He turned his half-truth away from her.

'Then you can't have time to take me to other side.'

'I was going that side,' he said, lowering the paddle.

'I have the boat.' She straightened away from him. 'Would you like some *chai* we have just made?' It was only later, when she thought back, that she realized he must have borrowed Farouk's boat in order to take her wherever she might have wanted to go.

'I've just had,' he said, though he had not had anything since the morning.

He wanted to know where the foreigner was. 'Where on the other side?'

Lila arched up, stretching in the sun. If she had heard him she decided not to reply. 'Gracie Madam is having a party two weeks from tomorrow. She would like to ask you and your mother.'

'In the winter?' he asked as he sat down, because he did not feel strong enough to stand any more.

'She insists it must be on her birthday, she will be eighty-one running.'

'So why this year?' he said, looking at his paddle in his lap.

'*Farangis*, they go on the year that has just been. On her terms she will be eighty.' She lifted her face into the warmth, her hands clasped at the back of her skull, her eyes shut.

Gulshan chewed the inside of his cheek.

'Your brother will obviously have to come as he will be bringing us all the vegetables. Could you tell him as well?' She did not move her face or open her eyes as she spoke, neither was there any enthusiasm in her voice as she extended the invitation to Gulshan's brother, Irshad the *subji-wallah*.

Gulshan made a noise in his throat. Lila did not ask him

why as she would usually have done, nor did she open her eyes. She curved in the light, allowing his concentrated attention to wash over her. She waited until she heard him begin to move away, his paddle cutting sadly down into the water. She waited until she sensed that he was about halfway down The Wonder House.

'You will come, won't you, Gulshan?' she called after him.

He lifted one hand off the wooden shaft in a motion that was neither acceptance nor refusal.

She hurried back to the *dunga*, collecting a shawl and her *pheran* as she bent over her mother.

'I'm going across to Shalimar Garden side,' she said as she kissed Suriya's cheek.

She had turned away before her mother had a chance to sign to her. Suriya's hands were raised in question as Lila walked away, covering her head with her shawl as she replied. 'He's moving to the Residency. He needs a translator for the afternoon. We'll be back before dark. They made him pay in advance for the hotel but Gracie has made him promise to come back and stay tonight.' She ran out into the sunlight and down the duckboard.

Suriya banged two pans together to stop her, to bring her back, but Lila kept running.

Hal was outside the entrance of the houseboat with his bags. He saw Lila and Masood at the same time. The two men acknowledged each other silently over the head of the girl halfway between them. They raised their hands to each other and Lila turned to see Masood, his arm in the air as he stood at the gate, part way between his own meadow and The Wonder House garden. She stopped on the path, closer to Hal than to her cousin.

'I'm moving out, you know,' Hal called over her head to Masood.

'So I have heard.' Masood opened the gate and came through.

The cricket match behind him in the meadow paused mid-over in case there was anything said that would need to be passed on. All three of the people on the path noticed the quiet beyond the gate, and they waited until they were close enough to each other for their voices not to carry.

'Are you leaving now?' Masood asked.

'I was going to, but Gracie wants me to stay tonight so that we can do some more arguing about the party.'

'That's why I have come,' Masood said.

'She's going to argue with you too?'

'Who's going to argue with me?' asked Gracie from the side entrance.

'The rebels.' Hal sat down on his backpack.

'You go away, you've got people to meet. Masood and I will have a quiet conversation.' Gracie flapped her hand at him. 'Go and see your major and report back. I'll have Lila put your geyser on in a couple of hours.'

Masood understood that Gracie had not realized that Lila was going with Hal. The girl moved quickly down the boat before Gracie had time to ask her for anything. She ducked behind the *dunga* and headed around the back to meet Hal at the gate.

Masood jumped across the sill into the houseboat, knocking Gracie off balance. She leaned back against the corridor wall.

'Who is he going to see?' He was very close to her.

'Someone at Shalimar Barracks.'

'Why?'

'I'm not sure, Masood, ask him. He's writing about "the disappeared". I am assuming that he is going to ask for the army view.' Gracie pushed herself away from the wall and turned towards the sitting room.

'But he said he was writing about you?'

'Obviously not interesting enough, am I?' She stopped in the dining room. 'Come on, it's too cold here.'

He followed her. 'Does he know about Irfan?' He stopped at the entrance to the sitting room. 'I asked you not to talk of the boy.'

'Come in, come in and shut that curtain, it's too cold for all this drama and posturing.' She sat down and pulled a rug over her knees.

Masood closed the curtain in the doorway and came to stand beside her. 'Does he know?'

'No.' She fiddled with the rug.

'He's a journalist, he must have asked more questions? What army man is he going to see?' He bounced one fist on top of the other.

'Masood, I have not told him about Irfan, I doubt Suriya signed him on the matter. I have no idea what Lila has or has not told him and I have no idea who he has gone to see. He's moving back into town. The minutiae of his life is no longer my affair.' She patted the rug down hard around her legs.

'He said no name? Did you hear him saying a name of who he is going to see?'

'No, I did not. Will you stop? I don't know who he has gone to see.'

'Could Lila have told him?' His fists drummed harder.

'I don't know, how would I know? They're always

sneaking about together. How the hell do I know what they whisper to each other?'

'Did you hear her say anything?' His voice was getting thinner.

Gracie looked up. 'What's the matter? What are you worried he's going to do?' Her irritation cut across each word.

Masood stepped back and folded down on to the sofa in front of her. 'They came to the house at Eid. They threatened me. It was the same group who took our neighbour and his sons.'

'The one who died?'

'The same.' He stared down at his hands in his lap. 'He was a major. He wanted Irfan to report to the checkpoint. I told him the boy was with relatives in Delhi. I had papers made in Kudji's boy's name, fake papers, and another cousin went to the post with them.'

'Do you think they know?' Her voice softened.

'I don't know. I go to the checkpoint every day and watch for the major.' He worked his palms into his eye sockets, the movements fast and hard.

Gracie pushed herself up from her chair and reached across to take one of Masood's hands. He pulled back but she held on and sat down beside him, spreading the rug across both of their knees. They sat side by side for an hour, Masood with his other palm pressed into his eye as he cried.

They crossed Nagin towards a burnt-out shell that had once been a club, Lila paddling, Hal watching.

She told him how invaders had torched the building in 1947 and the lake people had watched the flames reflected in the lake for two days as the bridge tables had burnt. Some had been braver and had sneaked closer to look through the shattering windows at where the British had amused their wives and mistresses, blurring the edges between the two with gin. Now it had been requisitioned by the army.

As she spoke, she watched across the water for the canopy of Farouk's *shikara*, and for Gulshan. Hal looked at the soldiers who looked back from over sandbags at the lake edge of what had once been the club's garden. It was a blank patch decorated only with rusting army fragments scattered over the indentations where rose beds had once been. Two old *chinars* still stood, the sandbags and soldiers sheltered by their great girths.

When they were halfway, Hal turned to face her. 'Can I do it? Can I try?' He pointed to the paddle.

Lila laughed. 'Why not?'

He stepped carefully down the boat to change places with her, but she did not move.

'Please let me try?' He stood over her.

'Sit.'

'Where, in your lap?'

'No.' She smiled down into the boat and shuffled along to make a narrow space for him.

He squashed himself in beside her and the soldiers stared from behind the sandbags.

His first strokes were good so he pulled the blade harder. The boat veered. He paddled backwards to set them straight and they stopped in the water. Digging down again he cracked the knuckle of his lower hand against the side of the boat. He said nothing, holding his breath and bending lower. They veered again. Lila's arm moved behind him, and her hand wrapped round the paddle beside his. She turned the blade vertical in the water and drew it in towards the edge of the boat, then, lifting it up and out, she made the same small movement again. They straightened. She let go and withdrew her hand.

Hal turned to look at her. In a more balanced place it might have been his hand that had pulled the blade in against the side of the boat to help her. He would have said something as he did it, something encouraging, but as a way of marking his action, and then he would have kissed her, a full-stop, an appropriate balance, in any other place.

She was silent beside him. He dug the paddle in again and the boat slewed. The soldiers laughed behind the sandbags, calling out directions to Hal in Punjabi.

'You're perhaps finding it rather cold here?' Major Kumar asked as he opened the door into his office.

'The days are okay, the nights are cool.' Hal was not sure whether to go through or wait to allow the major to go in before him.

Lila stood behind both of them, Hal's backpack beside her. The officer waved Hal through, and then waited at the open door, unsure about Lila.

'She is my translator,' Hal said.

'I think we will not need a translator for this.' The major was polite.

'I was hoping to be able to talk to some of your men and I was not sure how comfortable they would be with English.'

'My men have fought above 18,000 feet on the glacier, they have defended their country and lost many of their colleagues this summer, they have been without leave for an over-extended period. They are many things, Mr Copeman, but they are not Kashmiri-speakers.'

'I was thinking of Hindi, sir,' Hal replied.

'She speaks Hindi?' The major seemed surprised.

'I speak English, Hindi, Urdu and Kashmiri,' Lila said from the other side of the door that the major still held.

'Very good, very good.' He stepped away from the door and it closed a few inches. 'I hope you will not find this rude, Mr Copeman, but this interview was arranged with your good self. I was not informed of there being any other persons with you.'

'I'm sorry, I should have told your office.'

'Will Miss . . .' The major looked at him.

Hal looked towards Lila through the gap in the door. He did not know her surname.

'Miss Abdullah, sir,' she replied.

'Very good, would Miss Abdullah mind if she waited while we carried on with the interview.' He indicated two plastic chairs against the corridor wall outside his office. 'I will send for someone to get her tea.'

'I won't need tea, thank you, and I will wait.' Lila turned away and sat down in one of the chairs.

'You will excuse us then.' The major closed the door and turned to Hal. 'Please do sit, please be comfortable. Would you take some tea?'

Hal sat down.

'Very unusual having a female translator, and very impressive that she has so many languages. Her English is really very good.' Major Kumar smiled.

'She was at one of the best schools in Srinagar at a time when most of the teachers were still Pandits, I believe.'

'Very good.' The major sat down behind his desk. 'Would you like tea?'

'If you are having some then I would be happy to join you.'

'And perhaps we can tempt our young friend on the way?' Major Kumar picked up the receiver of one of the telephones on his desk.

Hal did not reply. The tea was ordered.

'So, Mr Copeman, what it is you want to know?'

Hal sat forward. 'I appreciate that many of my colleagues in the press are more interested in getting martydom stories from the families of militants. I am not. I am trying to establish every point of view. So, I would like to know how the army feels about its position in the Valley, post the Kargil conflict, post the coup?'

The major pushed himself into the back of his chair and folded his hands on the desk in front of him.

Lila listened to their voices, a little of Hal's, more of the major's. She heard the orderly's footsteps from the far end of the corridor of the old house and watched him carrying the tea towards her, his expression concentrated on a jug of milk in the middle of the tray. He did not acknowledge her as he stopped to knock at the door. For a moment the voices inside were clear again as the door opened and closed.

'Are you satisfied with the efforts of conciliation between the people and the security forces?' Hal asked as the door shut.

'Do you take milk and sugar?' replied the major.

'Both please, one sugar.'

They sat in silence as the major watched his orderly put the strainer over each cup and pour hot milk in first from the little jug.

'Do you know why we put the milk in first, Mr Copeman?'

'No, I don't think I do.'

'When you British started drinking tea you made your cups of the very finest porcelain, like egg shells, and so thin that the hot tea could crack them. So the milk went in first to stop the porcelain from cracking.' Major Kumar got up and walked around his desk. His orderly hovered as he picked up one of the cups and dropped in a teaspoon of sugar. He stirred the tea. 'Though I think perhaps our barrack tea sets are not quite of this quality.' He smiled, passing a solid regulation cup and saucer to Hal.

'Is that a parable?' Hal took the tea.

Major Kumar returned to his desk and sat down slowly before replying. 'You could say that, I suppose, the Valley the cup, we the milk, Pakistan the tea.' He folded his hands on his desk again and looked at Hal's notebook.

Hal did not write. 'It could just as easily be seen the other way around, you being the tea in first, Pakistan, the milk second.'

'Not my tea, never that way in my tea.' The major asked his orderly to offer tea to the woman outside, but it was explained that he had only brought two cups.

He was waved away as he put a plate of biscuits on to his officer's desk. Major Kumar offered them to Hal, who refused with a raised hand. Looking at the biscuits, the major put them down without taking one. They slid, one tipping over the edge to balance between the plate and the desk. The major stared at it in silence.

He answered the rest of the questions as though he was at a briefing. Hal could not find a way to reach beyond the formality. It was only as he got up to leave that the tone changed. The major had just refused to answer a question about a recently reported attack on a group of village women. It had been reported that the security forces were to blame. The major sat rigid as Hal spoke, his fingers lined up on the edge of his desk, but as Hal gave up and got up to leave, Major Kumar's hands dropped.

'This is a conflict and there will be atrocities on both sides, that is the nature of conflict, Mr Copeman. You will be told stories by the people here that will make monsters of the army. There are mistakes, but then these are always exaggerated to such an extent. The insurgents take these stories and turn them from sad but inevitable errors into great big disasters.' He got up from his desk. 'But I would still rather have my job than yours.' He extended his hand towards Hal. 'I simply follow orders, you have to try and find the truth.'

Hal shook his hand.

'Where are you staying in Srinagar?' Major Kumar asked, closing the interview.

'I've been staying in a houseboat on Nagin with Gracie Singh.'

'The old English lady, we hear about her now and then, she makes complaints sometimes,' he paused. 'She's on Masood Abdullah's land?'

'I think that is the understanding.'

'And you will be here for some more time?' The major drummed an index finger against the finer hairs in the middle of his moustache.

'Yes.' Hal paused, looking down to gather up his pad and pen. 'For a while.'

'Very good, so be free to contact me again if there are any other questions that you have.' The major moved to the door.

'May I speak with some of your men?' Hal asked.

'I think in the circumstances, Mr Copeman, that it would not be a suitable idea. Your translator is a Kashmiri woman.'

They parted politely and Major Kumar nodded to Lila as he opened the door.

He watched the young man and the girl walk away down the corridor. He saw their profiles for a moment against a lighter square on the wall where there had once been a painting of a pop-eyed Raja, before this summer house on the lake had been requisitioned as barracks.

The girl was pretty, prettier than usual even. She walked a couple of steps behind the man. Major Kumar remembered how his wife Nitu had walked a few paces behind him when they had been engaged. He assumed the man was sleeping with the girl, though he had not been sleeping with Nitu during their engagement; kissing, not sleeping, but so much kissing, and . . .

Sashi Kumar remembered the dazzling sight of Nitu's dark hair falling on his pale trousers as she had bent her head into his lap for the first time.

He closed the door to his office and sat at his desk with his head in his hands.

He would have to delay another house search at the Abdullahs on Nagin until the journalist had gone. It would mean checking.

He picked up one of the receivers on his desk.

The second winter snows began as two figures passed between stretched rolls of razor wire at the entrance to the barracks. Fat clouds dropped their weight down around the man, the woman, and the soldiers at the gate. The man turned to the woman as they were let out. He saw snow settling in her hair around the edge of her shawl and on the front of her *pheran*. The flakes that fell on her face left drops of water. She unfolded something from the bag she had been carrying and passed it to him.

'I have been carrying your *pheran*. You left it in the sitting room.' She held it out to the man.

He stopped, put down his pack, and took the *pheran* from the girl, brushing his hand against her arm as he did.

The doorman at the Residency Hotel watched the man and the woman as they got out of a rickshaw. He did not move to help them as they pulled bags out from beside the driver. He paused before he opened the door to them. The man was a foreigner but he was wearing a *pheran*. It was the same green serge as the one she wore. He had seen the man before. He had stayed, he was the one who had come back with the police. The woman, the girl, was new.

Lila stood beside Hal as he checked in. She held his backpack open for him as he searched through every side pocket and pouch to find his passport.

'You will want single or double occupancy, sir?' asked the clerk behind the register.

Hal asked for single and the man half-closed his eyes and stared at Lila from blank white slits.

'And you are checking in now, sir?' he asked, pulling at the cuffs of his baggy grey jacket.

'I've booked for tonight so I'm taking my stuff up, but I won't actually be staying until tomorrow.' Hal was searching through his passport for his visa number. He missed the clerk's expression.

'It will be counted as a full night's tariff if you are placing personal belongings in the room, sir.'

'That's fine, I paid when I made the reservation. I'm sure my bags will be very comfortable.' Hal looked up and saw the clerk watching Lila. 'We'll take the stuff up now,' he said, dropping the pen onto the register under the man's nose.

The thin clerk turned slowly to look at the clock behind him on the wall, then at the watch on his wrist. 'What time do you have, sir?'

'It's quarter to twelve,' Hal replied, looking at the same clock on the wall.

'Is that the time you have?' asked the clerk.

Hal looked at his watch. 'Just about, maybe your clock's a few minutes slow.'

'Our check-in time is midday, sir.'

'Good, then we will sit and wait for twelve minutes.' Hal stepped back and sat down on a plastic sofa behind him. It squelched as he sat. He began to laugh.

'That won't be necessary, sir,' the clerk said flatly. 'We can take you to your room now.' He banged his hand twice on to a bell beside the register on the desk.

Two boys who had been watching from the corner of the grey reception pushed themselves away from the wall.

'It's fine, we can manage this, but it would be great if you could send up some coffee. Your coffee is so good.'

'Thank you.' The clerk bowed his head. 'Will that be coffee for one or two, sir?'

'Lila, would you like coffee?' Hal turned to her.

'Yes,' she said.

'Coffee for two then, please.' Hal got up and went back to the desk. He held out his hand to the clerk. 'A key, please.'

The clerk and the two bell-boys watched them walking away along the corridor. None of them moved.

At the door of the room Lila put Hal's camera bag down and pulled her hands back into her sleeves. 'I haven't had coffee before.'

'Don't you like it?' he asked, fiddling with the key in the door.

'It's not something Kashmiris drink much.'

'Cultural or religious?'

'Perhaps a bit of both. *Kawa* is so much a part of the Valley, and *chai*'s the alternative. Some people put coffee almost in the same category as alcohol.'

'The demon caffeine.' Hal humped his backpack into the room and up on to the nearest bed of the two.

'You have a good view,' Lila said from outside the door.

The old polo ground spread beyond the window.

'Why did you say you'd have it then?' he asked.

'Because I never have.'

He looked up. 'Come in,' he asked her. 'Please.'

She did not move. He went to her and picked up his camera bag from her feet. He could read the tension in her body through her *pheran*.

'Don't try it if you don't want to.' He swung his camera bag on to the bed beside his backpack and went to the window. 'Yes, it is a good view.'

The snow was beginning to smudge the edges of the people on the street below. A man at the nearest corner of the polo ground was raking the late falling chinar leaves, trying to move faster than the snow, but it was settling on his small pile, a transparent veil over the shape of the leaves.

'It takes a millimetre of water to make an inch of snow,' he said as he watched the man with his rake. He felt Lila move behind him.

'If I like coffee it will be the third thing.'

'The third?' He did not turn around, but stood very still, staring down at the man fading into the snow below.

Lila stopped on the inside of the door and leaned back against the edge of it. 'Taking alcohol and coffee,' she paused and sniffed. 'And going about the city with a man who is not my relative.'

That had not been the third thing she meant.

Hal reached out his hand behind him. Lila looked at it and straightened away from the door. She pushed her hands out through her sleeves but tugged them back in as she heard sounds in the corridor. Hal heard the waiter after she had, and his hand remained, extended out behind him, until the man with the coffee knocked on the half-closed door.

There was only one chair in the room. The intruder walked between Lila and Hal and, balancing the tray in one hand, he stooped through the bathroom door to pick up a plastic washing stool. He put it in front of the chair with the tray on top. The smell of coffee and unwashed feet came with him. He stared at Lila as Hal signed the bill. He was young, clean-shaven and overt. He waited beside Lila until Hal came to close the door. He retreated very slowly.

'Why should I tip him when he managed to be judgemental about putting down a tray?' Hal lifted the table and the tray closer to the end of one of the beds. 'Come and try the coffee.' He pulled the chair out for Lila.

She did not move.

He stood back from the chair and took off his *pheran*, folding it carefully on to the second bed. 'The snow's getting heavier. We should leave soon.' He poured two cups of coffee.

She laughed and started to take off her *pheran* as she crossed to the chair. She seemed to change her mind as she sat down, and left one side pulled up in the same way as the charioteer carters in the city.

'Do you want to try it black or with milk?'

'What do you think?' she asked.

'I think.' He picked up the metal jug. 'That I want to ask you something else.'

They both stared at the jug in his hand. He dropped it back on to the tray.

'Forgot it would be hot,' he said, his fingers flailing in the air.

She stared at his hand.

'Lila, could you think of leaving Kashmir?'

She made a silent shape with her mouth and he saw the ridges and ground-down plains of her teeth, the way her tongue sat behind the lower row.

'This thing we hurl ourselves at, this love, I've spent most of my time backing away from it. I thought it meant being trapped.' He looked down at the hand that he had burnt. 'But I watch you and how you move in your world. There's so much possibility . . .' He reached his smarting fingers out to her and she held them to her face with both of her hands. 'Would you think about coming with me when I go?' He watched her face crumple. 'We could take your mother, and Gracie, put The Wonder House on the Thames.' He tried to reach his arms around her but he knocked over the pot of coffee as he moved. It filled the tray and began to seep over the edges and down on to the carpet.

He had been sitting with one leg tucked up. It was numb and it gave way as he tried to get up, bumping the table. Spilt coffee drained off the tray and all down the side of his lifeless leg.

Lila covered her face, her middle fingers gripping her nose, her index fingers at the edges of her eyes as she laughed. He took her hands and bent down over her, laughing and touching her, sliding over her skin, longing to taste her.

They did not even manage to take off any of their clothes. The man who had brought the coffee listened in the corridor, enjoying his angry arousal as he heard the foreigner making love to the Kashmiri woman.

'How do you get clean in the winter?' Hal asked through the half-closed door as she undressed afterwards to wash.

'I use one of the bathrooms on The Wonder House,' she replied, breathing through her mouth so that she did not have to inhale the smell from the alley.

'I've never seen you going in.'

'I do it when people aren't around. Gracie knows.' Lila had taken off all her clothes and was running water into a bucket, this time allowing the water to make as much noise as it needed to. She saw her naked back in the mirror and pulled her *pheran* back on.

'Does your mother do that too?' he asked.

'No, she only washes behind the *dunga*. We have arguments about it. She thinks it's wrong that I use the bathrooms.' She watched the hot water pounding into the bucket.

'How do you argue with a mute?'

'She can shout very loudly in her own way.'

'Can I come in?' he asked.

There was no answer. He pushed the door gently and saw her thin arms reaching down to turn off the tap, the steam from the bucket rising around her.

'You're beautiful. Do you see that when you look in the mirror.'

'I can't see anything.'

He stood behind her and saw their dark shapes in the steamed glass. He lifted her *pheran* over her head and she did not stop him, and he saw the scar on her shoulder clearly for the first time. He reached out to touch it. 'What's that?'

'Nothing.' She pushed his hand away, and then stopped, the tips of her fingers resting against the back of his hand, passive. 'It happened in the old city.'

'When?'

'Sometime after the coup. It was a bad time.'

'Who did it?' He stood helpless in front of her.

'Some men.'

'Why?' He reached back towards the scar.

Lila folded her arms around her body and bent her head. She cried so quietly that it took Hal a moment to realize. He lifted her face gently and bent to kiss the livid raised star of skin, his tears on her shoulder. She stepped away from him and into the bath, pulling the shower curtain across. He watched as she poured jug after jug of water over herself, the curtain pulling in and sucking against her hip. He reached out to touch her as she washed the curtain away with another jug of water.

~~~

Every detail of the meadow had been rubbed away by the still-falling snow. Hal slid on the path to the lake and Lila bent down over him. He touched her face as he got up but they did not speak.

She went silently to the *dunga*. He called out to Gracie. It sounded loud and over-enthusiastic against the rolling silence of the landscape. Gracie called back from the sitting room. He shouted that he would be there in a few minutes and turned away, placing his feet again in the footprints that he had just made on the duckboard.

Lila tried to move quietly around her mother in the *dunga* kitchen. Suriya watched from over the mortar and pestle, following her daughter's unnecessary journeys between the pans and the potatoes, the stove and the egg basket. Suriya's only movement was to reach up and turn on the radio at twenty-nine minutes past six. When Hal called from the other side of the blanket at the entrance Lila disappeared into the room beyond the kitchen. He waited before putting his head through.

'May I come and listen to the news with you?'

Suriya rubbed some loose hair away from her face with her shoulder, twitching her head in a gesture of uncommitted acceptance. He squatted down opposite her, pulling his *pheran* over his knees.

His stomach cramped as he cleared his throat. Suriya stared at him to stop him talking as the headlines looped the world together: Bangladeshi tension, a prime ministerial wife's lack of tact in a speech to disabled children in the North of England.

'Amazing how much damage is done in one sentence,' he said as the prime minister's wife fell from grace.

Suriya split cardamom pods with her thumbnail and pushed the seeds out into the mortar.

'That smells wonderful.' He watched her crushing the seeds into the masala. 'Suriya?' he asked.

She looked up but continued to grind.

'I'm asking if you would let me marry Lila?'

The life in her face fell away into the mortar between her knees.

Chapter Twelve ~

The snow fell for three days in the Valley, along the border, and on the other side.

The diminishing sounds of a sleeping room were boxed in by white silence. Pale light separated bodies from boots, the short from the tall, those on their backs from those humped on their sides. The year's first full moon drew out the neutered forms of the landscape, making shadows and shapes. There was enough light to read by.

He knew that he would not be able to leave without being heard. Different rhythms of breath marked varying depths of sleep. His friend Yasin kept moving beside him, his leg twitching and tensing under thick greasy blankets.

There had been a pile of them at the back of the room, bedding that the farmer had said they could use. His face and the tone of his voice had a set to them, an empty flatness like the snow on his farmland. They had met it in other villages, the same expression. No one denied them entry but the heavy blankets they were given, and the food that they demanded, neither warmed nor nourished them. Irfan could feel the hard grey goat meat they had eaten pushing out from behind his diaphragm, as lumpen as he felt under his cold blanket, surrounded by the breath of sleepers and those who watched from behind closed eyelids.

Yasin's leg kicked out again, catching Irfan's thigh.

Now he should go.

Holding his breath he pushed the blanket away.

'What are you doing?' Their commander sat up, the rifle that had been lying across his chest now in his hand.

'I have to go and piss,' Irfan whispered.

'It'll freeze your dick,' said the commander, not bothering to whisper.

'Not much to freeze.' Irfan heard himself, his lying confidence. He did not know that it would be so easy. He had learned well.

'Don't tread on anyone, we're all trigger happy when we get woken up.' The commander lay down again but he kept his rifle pointing at Irfan. 'Write your name in the snow.'

Irfan made a whispered sound, padded with camaraderie that he did not feel. Sitting on his blanket he laced his boots as slowly as he could. The breathing around him deepened, except for the commander who watched each movement of his fingers on his laces in the washed light. Irfan reached under his blanket for his *pheran*.

'Don't bother with that.' The commander shut his eyes as he spoke.

Irfan recalibrated. Without his *pheran* he would freeze. He would have to move much faster to stay warm, he would lose more energy, and he would tire more quickly.

Shrugging studiedly at the commander's closed eyes, he folded his *pheran* lengthwise and wrapped it across his shoulders. Yasin's leg thrashed again as he started to get up. He put his hand on his friend's thigh to push it back towards the other leg, saying goodbye through his palm.

'Take your gun,' the commander said with his eyes shut. 'No safe house is safe enough.'

Irfan did not reply.

'You don't want to get shot when you're pissing, do you?'

Irfan bent down again to pick up his gun from under his blanket.

Snow had sealed the door and he had to use his full weight to open it. As he did a shaft of freezing air woke some of the others. Edging through he shut the door and leaned against it. He stepped through the snow to a point on the outside wall that he thought would be roughly level with where the commander lay. Pulling his water bottle from where he had tied it around his belly under his *kurta* he dribbled a little into the snow, pouring carefully. He stopped and restarted, forming the 'I' of his name with the drops. He stopped again. He was going to need the water.

The land flowed down from where he stood, a flat field, one thorn branch fence, then down and away, flat, still, fast, easy snow. He began to run, stuffing the bottle back down his front and grabbing his *pheran* from around his shoulders.

It hit him with the feeling of being punched in the back, just at the soft point of the neck between the base of the skull and the first prominent vertebra. He was a little beyond the gap in the thorn fence and he threw himself as far as he could, the way they had been taught. Snow closed in around him as he rolled. It came down in a clean line from above where he fell, pushing him down, wrapping and covering him until it continued to flow over him as he crashed into the ice and rock of a frozen stream at the bottom of the hill.

He lay in the water. There was no pain, nothing at all, water under him, snow above him. He thought he was asleep as he lay between them but he could still sense the light behind and above him. Turning over he found himself under a hole in the snow and below a portion of tree; branches that were moving in a wind that he could not feel, shedding their crystals down towards him, caught by the moon, separate and spinning, each one perfect. And silence, white silence in which he could hear them as they spun, their shards of sound joined together into a single pure note.

This was death, he thought. Then he felt pain. It shoved at him from where a bullet had cut a clean shallow channel in the flesh between his shoulder and tricep, and he knew that he was alive. He wondered whether it had been his commander who had shot at him, or a soldier, and also why there was no one shouting in the snow, looking for him.

He began to crawl down the stream. There was a taste in his mouth, the same as when he had first listened to Sidi shouting at them in the courtyard of the house with the blue window. When he vomited it was with the same force as he had after seeing Singh the Sikh, Batapa, Lal and Gupta scattered among the remains of the bunker. He wiped his face with snow, scooping some into his mouth to take away the taste of bile and blood, and he packed some into his shoulder to stop the bleeding. The pain knocked him back down. He lay still until he could breathe more easily. Then Irfan got up and began to walk to the right of the moon, directly south. An ibex watched from a ledge, propped on its front legs, soft ears below thick-ridged crescent horns.

Hal went back to The Wonder House to see Gracie the day the snow stopped falling.

'Were you claustrophobic here?' she asked as he sat down.

'I'd never lived on a boat before.'

'It's not as though it's small.' She waved her hand. 'I've had eight people staying here and no one was cramped.' She turned in her chair so that she could see the whole of his face. 'We only need eighteen inches of space you know. Have you never lived with anyone before?'

Hal looked at her. 'What do you mean?'

'We only need eighteen inches of space around us to feel comfortable. You've had yards of the stuff here.'

'I stayed for a month, it seemed so long to . . .' he paused. 'To be a guest.'

Gracie snuffled against her sleeve.

'I'm sorry, I need to be in the city for the story I'm doing now.'

'So I see. You're done with me then?'

He leaned back into the sofa. 'You've told me your story.'

'How convenient, and now you're on to worthier things, heavier-hitting stuff than the old remnant on Nagin.'

'Is this blackmail from the lady of the houseboat?' He moved towards her.

She took one of his hands between both of hers and bounced it on her knee as she spoke. 'I'm going to be eighty at the end of next week. You're not going to be done with Kashmir before then, are you? This party, first time for years.' She looked down at his hand in hers.

'Of course I'll be here. It's still so cold, though.' He

paused. 'For a party.' He understood why her language had narrowed, reverting again to her spoken shorthand of limited conversation.

'Of course it is, but I'm coming over all maudlin and wondering how many more birthdays there will be.' She closed her eyes for a moment. 'I've had some staggering birthdays during my life here. Jitu used to plan things if he wasn't working on a case.' She pushed her thumb hard between the bones of Hal's index and middle finger. 'We went to Mysore for my twenty-fifth I think it was. A cousin of his was the Maharajah's prime minister. It was the last year of the war so we weren't supposed to be partying, but Mysore was the swing king. He gave the best.' She looked around the room. 'There's a picture of us all somewhere. It was up on Chamundi Hill, twinkly lights all the way up to the little palace on the top. Jit's cousin flirted with me so much that Jit threatened him with an elephant stick, and some foreign woman got so drunk that she danced on the big Nandi bull on the path on the way down.' Gracie sniffed hard. 'Total sacrilege. I'm not sure she wasn't arrested. Some stupid girl who didn't know.' She looked back at Hal. 'And by the time we got back to Simla the rumour had preceded us that I was the tart who had flaunted herself on the sacred bull. Some people thought it was funny but the official lot took it very seriously. Jit made me stay in for weeks until it died down. We had some of our worst fights then.' She turned her face to the ceiling. 'Even though he'd seen that other girl dancing on the bull it was as though he really thought I'd done it.'

'Why did they think it was you?'

'Because it usually was me that did that kind of thing.' She said it with a mixture of sadness and pride.

'I'll stay as long as you don't flaunt yourself at the temple on Shankaracharya Hill.' He wanted to take his hand away now. He had come to talk to her about Lila and he knew that he was going to fail.

'What a good idea. You can help me create some erotic number, the dance of the very thick shawls.' She did her little girl laugh. 'You can help me plan it all. If we have all the *bukharas* lit it'll be warm enough, and I thought we could have a few braziers on the roof so people could go up there if they want to, and fairy lights, lots of those white ones, can't bear the coloured ones, so vulgar.'

'Who are you asking?'

'Everyone, absolutely everyone.'

'Will they approve of it?' he asked.

'I'm not asking for approval, I'm just asking them to come.' Gracie smacked both her hands on to her knees. 'We need to make lists. You're the writer, you write them, come on.'

'I haven't lived with anyone, by the way,' he said.

Gracie smiled.

They wrote lists of things until after it was dark. She called Suriya and demanded the key to the cupboard, and then insisted that she could not drink alone, that he would have to stay. He sat with her, thinking that he might still find a time to talk about Lila, perhaps between her first and second glass.

He had still not said anything when Suriya brought supper. She set it for them on the low table in the sitting room, in front of the *bukhara* because it was warmer than the dining room. As she moved around the room she stayed as far from Hal as she could.

He knew Lila was away. The fishwife's niece was having a baby. She had told him about it the day they had gone to see Major Kumar, and how she was going to help when the time came for the delivery. When Gracie had called him he understood that it was because Lila had gone for the birth, so that they could be kept apart.

When Gracie insisted that it was too late for him to go back to the city, he knew that it was because she had realized Lila would not be back that night. He agreed, thinking that he might find a way of telling her in the morning. He had assumed that Gracie would have known from Suriya, but by the time they went to bed Gracie had drunk enough to cut through any pretence, and still she had said nothing.

He lay on his back in the dark with the door jammed shut with a folded edge of the inner curtain, and he listened for sounds on the duckboards to the *dunga* boat in case Lila did come back.

No one came.

As he wandered towards sleep he felt himself falling off the edge of the present into a heightened version of when he had made love to Lila in that room. He could see her, every part of her in the light, not hidden by layers of clothing, and he watched as he directed himself into her, opening her with a tenderness that made him cry out in his sleep.

The sound of the glass in the sliding window woke him and he pulled his door open to see Suriya carrying Gracie's morning coffee tray. There was only one cup. He wished her a good morning and she nodded without looking at him. He offered to hold the tray for her but she passed him without giving any sign. He stood in the doorway of his room and waited as she put the tray down in front of Gracie's door and knocked, and as she went in he heard Gracie asking her if he was awake. He called out to her down the corridor.

'Come and join me then, young man,' she called back.

He grabbed his *pheran* from the end of his bed.

Suriya was pouring coffee, the tray set out on one end of Gracie's bed. He waited until she had finished before he sat on the other corner.

'Would you like some?' Gracie asked.

'I would, please.'

'Get me another cup, would you, and have we got any biscuits?' she asked.

Suriya shrugged.

'Maybe not, I probably don't need any. Do you think I'm putting on a bit?' She turned to Hal, lifting her chin as she asked, smoothing the crêped skin away from her jawline.

'It's hard to tell in the cold when you're all rugged up.'

'Wrong answer.' Her head flicked towards him. 'There is only one answer to that. You've got a sister, haven't you? Didn't she tell you these things?' Gracie pushed herself up on her pillows, stretching her neck up a little further.

'She probably did but you asked me a question and I gave you the answer. It's a male habit, you see.' He looked down into the coffee, inhaling the smell, wanting to taste it but not wanting to drink it while Suriya was still in the room.

'Snappy this morning, what's the matter with you?' Gracie patted the bed closer to her.

He stayed where he was sitting. Suriya waited by the door while Gracie decided whether or not to have biscuits. He looked from one to the other and straightened as he inhaled.

'I'm sorry, I slept badly. I'll behave now.'

'Good, no biscuits, Suriya, the kind gentleman tells me I am a podge, just more coffee please.' She went on patting the bed to coax Hal. 'We can make more plans for the party. I've been pondering on the rum problem. Some of this lot drink but I'm not sure that any of their friends or relatives know that they do. I was thinking about making two kinds of hot punch, one with rum, one without, same colour, though, so if someone wants to have a nip without others knowing he could get away with it.'

'I did not say you were fat.'

Gracie ignored him. 'Did it at a party for some Mussulman clients of Jit's once. Thick of winter in Simla, high as kites the lot of them. Best party they had ever been to. Not sure we could or should lead the Abdullah ladies down that particular route, though.'

Suriya opened the door and left.

'Will they really come?' Hal asked.

'Some of them, maybe Naseema and Kudji, probably just before the start to have a look. Then they'll flap off back to the house and tell the others about all the wicked things going on at The Wonder House.'

He was listening for Suriya's footsteps retreating down the corridor. He heard the glass in the door. They sat in silence for a few moments. Hal straightened.

'I would like to take Lila with me,' he said.

'To the party?' Gracie folded her hands into where her lap was under the blankets. 'Why would you want to do that, she'll be here anyway.' She spoke as though she was talking to a child, and she looked up at Hal with a smile as brittle as her tone.

He stared at the carpet and they sat in weighted silence.

'Why did you educate her so much?' he asked.

'What do you mean?' Gracie bit back.

'Sending her to the best school, teaching her to love books, literature, great writers, poets.'

'Never poets, not poetry.'

'But why?'

Gracie looked up. 'Because she was a bright girl.'

'And so that meant you could play God, educate her and pull back her horizons, and then expect her to go on being your servant?'

'And what are you going to do? Play the movie hero and take her away from all this?' Gracie's hands jumped in her lap under the blankets. 'What are you proposing, Hal Copeman? How does your particular variety of a happy ending work?' The pain in her face tugged at the edges of her eyes and her mouth. 'You don't just play with people's lives like that.'

'Who are you telling?' he asked.

Gracie reached out from under the covers and took one of his hands. 'Both of us.'

The entrance glass rattled.

'You're not to say anything in front of Suriya,' she commanded.

He was going to say that he already had, but he stopped as Suriya knocked on the door.

Gracie kept her in the room while they had coffee, fussing over little things that did not need to be done. He waited but she kept finding another task, a problem with one of her bedroom shutters, that she needed new batteries for her torch, that one of her top blankets felt damp.

He got up and told her that he needed to get back to the city. She did not try to stop him from going. When he bent to kiss her cheek she leaned away from him on the pretext of looking for something on her bedside table. He stood in the doorway for a moment, trying to find something to say that might breach the gap. He just said goodbye.

'Lovely to see you, my little family loves seeing you. Come back soon, come again and help with the party plans, we'd like that,' she called over Suriya's head as the little mute woman gathered the cups back on to the tray at her feet. Gracie's tone was the same as the one she had used earlier, as to a child, cracked and fragile.

'Thank you, I will,' he said as he turned away.

'So many weeks since we have met,' Mohammed the tailor called out as his friend made his way up the hill from Dal Gate. 'What can it be that keeps you so stitched to Nagin side?'

Masood raised his hand. 'Life, my friend.'

They laughed.

'Are you well? Are the boys well? Is Sahida keeping good health?' Masood asked.

'All are well, inshallah, and your family, all are well?'

'We have had better times.' He embraced the tailor.

'You will have *chai*?'

'Why not?' Masood replied.

'It is too cold for the step perhaps, or I can call for another *kangri*. What do you say?'

'I have.' Masood pulled his *kangri* out from under his *pheran*. 'Let us sit out a while. We are all shut in so much of the time now. These coals could be warmed though.'

'My head says you are right, my bones disagree, I will get cushions.' The tailor called into the interior of his shop for cushions, a brazier and *chai*. 'They say there is going to be a party on the *farangi*'s houseboat.'

'They say, well they are right.' Masood sat down on the step. 'Who did you hear this from?'

'Mr Marvellous was talking in the bazaar, showing off about how many flowers he was going to have to get for The Wonder House.'

'Salman never could keep a thing to himself.' Masood clicked his tongue against his soft palate.

'Like a woman, chat, chat, chat,' Mohammed laughed.

But Masood did not. He thought of all the women around him, of the times he had watched Naseema holding secrets in her heart, Suriya in her silence, and Lila behind her lovely eyes.

A boy brought cushions and a small brazier with a pair of metal tongs. He helped Mohammed on to the cushions and put the brazier down between the two friends, passing the tongs to Masood before going back in to get *chai*. Masood tipped the coals from his *kangri* into the brazier and arranged them around the sides, turning them with the tongs in the flame.

'You hide your laughter, what is with you?' Mohammed adjusted himself on the cushions and settled his *kangri* back inside his *pheran*.

Some of the coals were beginning to glow in the flame. Masood plucked them out and put them back into his *kangri*. 'Nothing of importance. I have not been sleeping so much and this cold seems to be biting right into my core.'

'It's ten years now, just about exactly ten years since all of this started. That must be planted somewhere in our hearts, cold hearts, colder bones.' Mohammed rubbed his temples.

They watched a group of soldiers below them on Dal Gate, stamping on the pavement, their bodies hunched into their khaki parkas, cigarette smoke mingling with their breath in a constant cloud above and between them.

'The Rashtriya Rifles are celebrating today. They had a big catch,' Mohammed said.

'They did?'

'A group of militants in a safe house up near Kargil, quite a big group. Apparently they had come in from Azad on some big mission.' Mohammed called inside again for the chai.

'When was this?'

'Just yesterday, it is a bad thing for the city.'

'Why, what happened?' Masood felt as though he was being strangled.

'The leaders were foreigners, but all the younger ones were boys from Srinagar. You know the halal shop nearby Shah Hamdan mosque?'

'Ibrahim Zafrooza's place?' Masood forced his voice to be even.

'The same. His boy Yasin is one of those they shot. He was at the same school as your nephews. Is this not so?'

'He was,' Masood said to the last of the glowing coals. 'I remember him, a good boy. How do you know all of this?'

'Sahida is a cousin of his mother.'

'I am sorry.'

'It is not so much our sorrow, I maybe met with him four or five times.'

The tailor's boy came with two glasses of tea.

'You will take some bread?' Mohammed asked.

'Thank you, no.'

'Has the cold taken your stomach as well?' Mohammed took a round of bread from the tray and broke it, passing half to Masood.

'Really, I have no appetite.' He put his hand up to stop the bread that was being pushed at him. 'Were there other names that you recognized?'

'A couple, but not people I knew. Boys from families I had heard of, nothing more than that. They seem to have all gone across together. They say one of them had run away before the raid.'

'How do they know that?' Masood burned his finger as he nudged a coal in his *kangri*. He flicked his hand in the air, swearing with a vehemence that surprised Mohammed.

'Quiet, my friend, it was not such a bad burn.' Mohammed took his hand and examined the speck of white skin that was pushing away from Masood's index finger. 'So much of noise over such a tiny thing?'

'The farmer they were staying with turned them in. Militants had been using him as a place to stay above Kargil for many years. He told the army that he had seen one of the group running away in the night, and that he had heard gunfire. They did not find a body.' Mohammed scooped some wet bread into his mouth from his glass. 'This is happening more now. It is getting harder for the militants. People up there are tired of being pushed around. All that crop failure because of the cordite poisoning from the summer war.' He looked up at Masood. 'The government is not compensating them. The militants are demanding shelter and food from them, and the security forces offer them bounties for the militants.' He paused. 'I wonder what we would do, my friend?'

There was something oblique in his question. Masood had been wanting to confide in his friend. It was one of the reasons he had come to see Mohammed, to ask his advice. He stuck his blistered finger in his mouth instead.

'So, they will all be having extra rum at the Rashtriya Rifles tonight.' Mohammed nodded his head again at the stamping group below. 'And how is your nephew doing in Delhi, which one is it?'

Masood took his finger slowly out of his mouth. 'Irfan, it's Irfan, he is well.'

'He has been gone some time now?' Mohammed looked closely at Masood.

'These business courses are not over so quickly.' Masood examined his fingertip in detail. 'He has much to learn, he has only been gone these three months plus.'

They sat together while they finished their tea. Masood did not accept a second glass but he waited long enough so that it would not seem as though he was hurrying away. Mohammed watched him walking away down the street and he was pleased that his friend seemed more purposeful now than he had when he had arrived. He felt that he had done Masood a service, though he knew his friend had not told him everything.

Faheema noticed Masood's distraction.

It seemed to her that she heard and felt things now that the others did not notice, as though a protective membrane had been taken away from inside her ear, and a layer of skin stripped off her body. She imagined the kitchen knives cutting into her every time she peeled or chopped vegetables, and when any of the younger children wailed it felt as though the sound pierced right through into a tender space behind her eyes.

When Masood came back from Dal Gate her brother-in-law's bursts of movement spoke a language to her that she listened to carefully, following him around the house as closely as she could without him noticing.

Masood waited for his middle brother so that they could walk to prayers together. As they made their way along the road in the evening mist he asked Ibrahim if he was pleased with Faheema's progress. The answer was interrupted as the bread man and the coal boy juddered past on their rounds. Ibrahim stopped again as they met a group of Koran students from the mosque school at the end of the road, their adolescent beards tucked down into their prayer shawls, their skull caps squarely planted on their heads, their eyes downcast. The brothers bowed to them and they bowed back, both parties continuing towards the mosque together in silence.

As he prayed, Ibrahim wondered why his brother had asked him about Faheema. Everyone acknowledged that she had not moved from her room for nearly a month before getting up again, but the brothers seldom asked about each other's wives. They asked their own wives for the news of the other women if it was about something too delicate to be bandied about with general family chatter during afternoon *chai* in the kitchen. News of pregnancy, miscarriages, postnatal depression and marriage squabbles moved across pillows behind closed bedroom doors.

Why was his brother asking him when he should have asked Naseema?

Ibrahim noticed that he was out of step in his prayer line and he dropped to his knees.

~~~

Mr Marvellous, Salman, sat down in the corner of his floating garden in the early light of the following morning and cried into the frozen ground. His first big order for over a year and now the hardest frost of the winter had cut through his blanket covers, freezing the weave into solid woollen chrysanthemum tombs. More than half of the flowers had fallen under the weight of the icy blankets.

And now there was a rumour that the floating gardens were going to be towed away to stop Dal Lake from being silted dry.

His father, his grandfather, his great-grandfather, every Mr Marvellous had grown their show-pony blooms on the floating gardens behind Dal Lake. Everything would be ruined now. How would he survive? How would he feed his children?

Faced with these insurmountable problems, the fourth Mr Marvellous saw no other course than to squat in the corner of his frosted floating flower garden in the morning light and to weep.

His wife watched him from the kitchen of their house on the bank beyond the hump-backed line of island gardens. She pulled on her *pheran* and picked up two *kangris* from beside the stove. She went to her husband, pushing *kangri* under his *pheran* without speaking. The flowers fell in different directions all around them, shot down by the frost in anonymous disarray.

'We can buy from the flower men at Pampur. They will not have been affected, it is always a few degrees warmer down there. My brother will get us a good price. We can get other flowers too, not just chrysanthemums, other ones that

Gracie Madam likes, and then maybe you can charge a little more.' She bent down over her husband. 'Instead of making ten times what you would make that week you will make perhaps four times.' Mrs Marvellous squatted down, rolling from one instep to the other to find her comfortable balance. 'This is not so bad.'

Mr Marvellous tried to sniff in the trail of tears and mucus that had threaded itself between his nose and his chin. 'This was my plan.' He snorted out what he had not been able to sniff in.

His wife did not move beside him.

'I am weeping on other matters. They say they are going to take our gardens to stop the lake from being silted up. How will we live then? We survive ten years of militancy and savagery from the Indians and now they will take my livelihood as well. Is this not reason to cry?' He raised his hands towards the skies. 'Do you hear me, Allah?' And flicked his eyes to see if his wife was watching.

Her expression was practised and opaque. They sat together in hunched silence, looking at the dead display.

'Does this news come from our state government?' she asked.

'It does, right from the top.'

'And when has anything ever happened in any hurry from them, whether from top or bottom?'

'This was my thought as well, but they will make noise now to please the complainers and then it will all be quiet again.' Mr Marvellous stood up. 'Call the boys to come and help me, we can save some of these and sell them cheap at the bazaar.'

Mrs Marvellous got up after her husband and went back

inside to wake her sleeping sons. She stopped herself from minding that it was she who had solved the immediate problems rather than her husband. She would tell her sister later, and they could share their stories, as they always did.

Mr Marvellous made a show of trying to resurrect some of the blanketed chrysanthemums. He looked over this shoulder mid-effort to see if his wife was inside the house. She was. He went back to retrieve the *kangri* she had brought out for him, grateful that she was smart enough to give him answers, but stupid enough not to realize that she had done so. He did not choose to think further than that point to the unmapped possibility beyond. He hunched down over his *kangri* again and waited for his sons to come and help him with the frostbitten flowers.

Suriya was waiting for Lila at the gate from the meadow. She had been watching for her through the *dunga* window. Gracie had already called her three times to find out whether Lila was back from the fishwife's niece.

The top layer of snow had frozen in the frost and she could hear the crunch of her daughter's feet through the crust from two hundred yards away. She rushed down the duckboard, her arms stretched wide, making tiny marks below the frozen surface as she ran on the balls of her feet. Suriya seldom ran, especially in the snow.

She reached out over the gate and touched her daughter's face. Lila pulled back a little, surprised by her mother's open display outside the cocoon of the *dunga*. As she opened the gate, Suriya was pushed back, but she moved around to hold her daughter in her arms, folding her head down on to her shoulder so that Lila had to bend her knees to stop her mother from having to stand on her tiptoes. For a moment she was stiff in Suriya's arms. She had only been away for two days but she was being held as if she had been gone for so much longer. Suriya kept holding her tight, one hand wrapped around her back, the other on the side of her head, pressing it down towards her heart.

When she did not let go, Lila pulled back again.

'*Ama*, what is it?' She stood away from Suriya to look at her properly. 'What happened?'

Suriya shook her head. She took Lila's hand and pointed her towards The Wonder House, and followed her to the entrance. She flicked her chin up to ask a question.

'She had a girl,' Lila now put her hand to her mother's face.

Suriya looked down.

'She's lucky, it was all easy, a straightforward labour, she has a little head so there was hardly any splitting.'

Suriya did not look up.

'*Ama*, please be glad. The mother cried when she was told it was a girl, the fishwife made so much noise you would think someone had died. Not you too, *Ama*, you have a girl too.' She dropped her hand from her mother's cheek.

Suriya pulled her arms back into her sleeves.

Lila stamped the snow off her feet on the edge of the duckboard. 'Why do you have to be the same as them? What's the matter with all of you? We hold this place together, not the men, not the big brave men waving their guns about – we do.' She thumped her hand against her chest. 'Women like you, *Ama*, have kept the Valley knitted together. And what do the men do?'

Suriya stared at her daughter.

'These men that you all pray you will give birth to, they shoot each other now, and our children.' Her hand dropped. 'And us.' Lila stood halfway up the duckboard looking down at her mother's small form in the snow below her. 'Is that what you wanted, *Ama*, did you want me to be a boy too?'

Gracie was in the corridor just beyond the entrance glass. She had heard it all, her face in her hands. As Lila came to the sliding window, she turned and stumbled back towards the sitting room.

Gracie had never asked herself the question that had rolled around all of her conscious edges since Hal had left. It had come as he had bent to kiss her goodbye and she had pulled away. Since then it had been throwing her in and out of sleep all night.

What had she done? it asked. What had she done?

Lila stopped at the side entrance and stared at the latch, sensing her mother calling to her.

She had witnessed a birth, the first she had been so close to, and instead of a celebration of life it had been a disappointment to all of the other women, even the fishwife's niece, who had carried the tiny thing inside her. The thrill of the baby's first angry shout of life had been obliterated as soon as her tiny hips had emerged from her mother.

Lila had cried as she had walked home, and she had not known whether it was because she had been the only one to be delighted by the baby, or because that little bloody thing had presented herself as a minute screaming catalyst for Lila.

Enough.

She stepped over the sill into the corridor outside the kitchen galley. She knew that her mother was still waiting in the snow but she did not turn back.

'What was all the shouting about?' Gracie asked as she heard her at the sitting room doorway.

'Why are you out of breath?' Lila asked her.

'Just a little breathless.' Gracie adjusted the rug around her legs.

'Were you listening?' Lila came around her chair to face her.

'It was hard not to.'

'So why are you asking me?' Lila curled down in front of the *bukhara*, letting the heat slide around her back. 'Or do you want me to translate in case you missed any of it?'

Gracie closed her eyes. 'Do you want to go?' she asked.

Lila sat down on the floor at the old woman's feet and put her head against her blanketed knees. They sat for a while and then Gracie put her hand on the side of Lila's head, and pressed the girl to her.

They sat for a while in the safety of silence.

Gracie called Lila again in the evening as the last light dropped down behind the poplars at the end of the Abdullahs' garden. Suriya and Lila were in the *dunga*. They had not communicated since the morning except in the shared gestures of passing pots and spices between each other. Lila was crushing cumin, coriander and chilli seeds to mix with flour, the cumin to smooth the roughness of the chillis. Suriya was working with garlic and onions, chopping them together so finely that they mulched under her blade.

They were trying things out: Lila, a dusting for meatballs, Suriya, a different binding for her pakora mix; things for the party, for Gracie to try. Suriya switched on the radio as Lila went to Gracie.

'What time do we get power back today?' Gracie was waiting at the side entrance.

'Not until nine this evening,' Lila replied.

'Don't use the generator. We need to save all the diesel for the party.' Gracie stepped aside to let Lila in over the sill. 'Even if we're supposed to have power someone will make their disapproval known by making sure we get cut off.'

Lila turned back to the door.

'That's not what I called you for. I need your help. Are you in the middle of something?' Gracie asked.

'We were experimenting.' Lila turned again. 'Things for the party for you to try.'

'Just a few minutes before the light goes.' Gracie started for her room.

Lila followed.

An old wooden-banded suitcase from among the collection that had been under Gracie's bed since 1977 sat in a square of late light in its own circling cloud of dust.

'I managed to drag it out, not bad for an old thing.' Gracie stood beside it with her hands on her hips.

'It's filthy,' Lila said, turning back through the bedroom door.

Gracie stood looking at the lettering on the case that had sat under her railway seat on her first journey across India to Jitu in 1939.

It smelled of trapped time and naphthalene when they opened it. It made Lila turn away but Gracie did not seem to notice as she pulled off layers of powdery tissue paper.

'When did you last open it?' Lila asked.

'Think we packed it up when I was pregnant. All the stuff I brought with me to India and probably decided I wasn't going to wear again. Sealed up for over half a century.' She brushed mothballs away. 'My mother made me bring that, dreadful thing, isn't it?' She pulled out a dark green coat with a balding fur tippet around the collar. 'Being the Yorkshire lass she was she couldn't quite imagine a place where a girl would not need a good thick coat. Never wore it.'

'Wouldn't it have been good for the Simla winters?' Lila took the coat from Gracie. She liked the way it nipped in at the waist and pushed out again into a skirt.

'Think I'd packed it away by the time we moved, not sure. Maybe not.' Gracie burrowed down further.

Lila stood up and put the coat against herself. It was the right length for her. 'Were you taller then?'

Gracie looked up. 'Look at you,' she smiled. 'We just used to wear high heels all the time. It's a pretty shape isn't it, long way from a *pheran*.' She waved Lila over to the full-length mirror on her almirah door. 'Here we are.' She unfolded a dress from the suitcase, a plain black sheath of raw silk. 'Quite the thing then. My mother bought it. Think she really thought it would snare me a nice young officer in Poona on the mess cocktail circuit. It had to be this big secret from my father. She must have spent months of housekeeping on it.' Gracie held it up, running her hand over the material. 'Only wore it once to my first big thing at the morgue on the river. I thought I looked so glamorous. I was so proud.' Gracie stared at the black silk in her hand. 'She hated it, she told Jitu I looked cheap in it.'

'Who?' Lila asked.

'Jitu's mother. He loved me in it but he wasn't brave enough to stand up to her. He asked me to wear it when it was just us but I'd already packed it away.' She held it out

again. 'It doesn't look so dated, you know. I dreamed about it
last night, woke up with this crazy idea that I'd wear it to the
party.' She flapped it at Lila. 'Look, look.'

'Look at what?' Lila put the green coat down on a chair.

'Imagine me being able to fit into that now, elephant in a
babydoll.' She threw the dress at Lila. 'You have it.' She
slammed the top of the suitcase down. 'Help me.' She held
out her arms to Lila. 'Help me up.'

Lila lifted her up from behind, her hands cupped under
Gracie's armpits.

'I need a drink.' Gracie pushed her fists into her eyes for a
moment. 'Get the key from your mother, would you?' And
she left the room.

Lila watched Gracie go, standing beside the suitcase with
the black dress she had been given over her arm. Gracie
stopped halfway down the corridor.

'Can you get rid of that stuff for me, Lila, don't think I
really want to see it again. The dress, though, keep that, and
that terrible old coat if you want.' And she walked on,
supporting herself with the wall.

The hut was in the same place, almost in the middle of the
walnut grove, though it was harder to recognize it under the
anonymity of snow.

Irfan stood at the edge of the grove watching the road,
waiting to see if there was anyone there. He waited until the
light had almost gone before he moved in among the trees.

The hut was where the boxes were kept in the autumn
for storing the walnuts, and for the night-watchmen during
the time when the nuts were almost ready to pick. In a
different time he had sat in the shade of one of its walls,

eating samosas that Lila had made for him and his cousins, their fingers black from picking. The walnut grove was where this circle had begun on the bus ride that had been a surprise.

Boy to man, he thought, though he felt cut adrift.

Snow was banked up around the hut. The windows were boarded up with wooden slats, and six longer pieces had been nailed across the door. He used the butt of his rifle to jam in behind the wood and lever it away from where it had been nailed into the frame. The sound scratched and jarred. He ducked down to see if anyone had heard.

No one came.

He made a fire from the wood that he had broken away from the door and burned it in a metal bucket that he found under some broken boxes in the corner of the hut. There was enough to warm the hut so that he could have slept, but he did not.

He had not eaten for three days. The wound across the back of his shoulder was making him increasingly weak. He could hardly use his hand any more, and now he had a fever that pushed him randomly between icy rattling spasms and engulfing heat. He had forced himself to keep drinking water. He sucked snow as he sat by the fire and then boiled up as much as he could drink in an abandoned tiffin tin with a broken handle that he had found with the fire bucket. He burned his hands on the edges of the tin, but he kept boiling up more snow and drinking it.

His mother had taught him to drink water when he had fever, so much that he felt that he would burst, and then it would be enough to wash the fever away. So he kept drinking until the taste of the boiled snow in the tin made him retch. When he ran out of wood to burn he curled up around the heat of the metal bucket and tried to remake the shape of Lila's face.

It was the day of the party.

Mr Marvellous delivered the flowers before Gracie was awake. He lined the buckets up on the stairs of the veranda, more chrysanthemums than she would want, but most of them were white, that would calm her. And he had got some roses too, pink ones with flecks of white on the petals, quite like the snow, he thought. He had wrapped them in old shawls on the way from Pampur to Nagin, to protect them from being bruised on the bus, his sons fighting to get the whole back row so that they could lay the flowers out on the seats.

Here they were, a whole staircase of them, and not one from his own gardens, not one, but he had still got a better price than he had hoped, and his brother-in-law had been happy about the business. He sat back on the seat in his empty boat and admired the display.

Such a show for the time of year. Quite an achievement.

'*Asal.*' Lila appeared at the corner of the veranda, leaning around the edge from the duckboard.

'They are,' Mr Marvellous smiled. 'And is madam still sleeping?'

'She is, and I don't want to wake her. It's going to be such a long day. Can you wait for some time?' she asked.

'If you can offer *chai* I can wait.'

'I am offering,' she smiled.

'Then I am waiting in all patience,' he smiled back.

As he waited, Gulshan came with the lamb and chicken

that had been ordered from the butchers at Dal Gate, and Farouk slid in beside them with dried fruits, nuts, and the bread that Gracie had asked him to collect.

'She is still sleeping,' Mr Marvellous told them.

So they all waited, making a semicircle of their boats around the veranda steps, sharing *chai*, blowing into their hands as Lila reheated their *kangri* coals in the *dunga* kitchen. They talked about the bits and pieces of news from the city, but they were buoyant enough in their day not to linger on the story of boys from Srinagar being killed near Kargil. They did not know any of the boys, except perhaps by sight. Their conversation turned back to the party without Irfan Abdullah's name having been raised.

Farouk and Mr Marvellous talked of past parties: the naming of The Wonder House when Gracie had danced on a table, and when the Abdullah boys had held a swimming race across Nagin lake, and Gracie Madam had given a silver cup as the prize; Masood's wedding, only Farouk had been to that one; another Nagin houseboat family party, when the eldest son had got into the academically elite Indian Institute of Technology, and they had celebrated for three days.

Each one they talked about had been before Gulshan had been born, or when he had been too young to remember. He was happy to watch Lila moving to and fro along the duckboards with *kangris* and *chai*. She looked so delicate, almost transparent, and he could stare at her without her knowing as she walked away from them down the full length of the houseboat. Mr Marvellous and Farouk watched him trail her with his eyes as they talked, but for once they did not tease him.

Gracie woke late with a sense of panic pressing down on her upper chest about all the things that still needed to be done. When Lila brought her coffee, she rambled through the mental lists she had been making.

'And what about the flowers and all the supplies we ordered?' she asked as Lila pulled the eiderdown back over the bed that Gracie had thrashed away during the night.

'Mr Marvellous, Farouk and Gulshan are all waiting for you. They've been here for over an hour.'

'Why didn't you tell me?' Gracie put down her coffee and started to push herself up.

'Because they are happy gossiping like old ducks and waiting for you, they haven't got anything else to do.' Lila picked up Gracie's coffee cup and handed it back to her.

'If we have all the *bukharas* on full blast do you think it'll be warm enough not to have to wear *pherans*?' Gracie took the cup.

'Perhaps.' Lila sat down on the end of the bed.

She stayed with Gracie while she made a few final lists of things that she had already made lists of, and that had already been done.

From the bank at the top of the meadow it was as though he was looking at a children's illustration: moon blue snow, the trees of The Wonder House garden prickling with white lights, the whole roof of the boat a canopy of the same white lights threaded above braziers that were being lit by two figures as he watched.

Hal stood and waited, knowing that the perfection was seeing it from the outside, from the remove of the meadow bank, and that once he was inside the innocence of the long view would get lost in the individual stories of the night, played out among the rum punch, and Suriya and Lila's lamb and chicken kebabs.

Two female figures moved along the main duckboard of The Wonder House. They pulled the front of their *burqas* back down as they reached the gate into the meadow. They did not see Hal as they stepped cautiously through the snow up to the garden gate with its chinar leaf handle, their heads bent towards each other as they talked.

Faheema watched Naseema and Kudji from the upper window of the house, from her sons' bedroom. She watched Hal as well, and everything beyond him. She searched for movement, for changes in shape, for anything that she might recognize. She too had heard about the shooting of the Srinagar boys up near Kargil, and she had also heard that one of them had run away before the raid. So she stood in the dark, watching the details of the meadow below, trawling with her heart among the moon shadows and swinging fairy lights.

Gracie wrapped herself in shawls that she had not worn since before Jitu's death: brilliant *jamovars*, month upon month of layered embroidery that sat like paintings around her shoulders. They smelled of long-locked trunks, so she sprayed them with the sticky sediment from the bottom of an old bottle of scent. It made it worse, so, ignoring the smell, she put on jewellery that she re-explored as she took it out: an emerald choker that Jitu had given her when they got married, the earrings to match that he had wrapped in a napkin on her breakfast tray just after Hari had been born, and her engagement ring, the biggest of all the emeralds. She closed her eyes and tried again to jam it over the swollen joint on her left finger. It did not fit so she pushed it on to the little finger of her right hand, beside her wedding ring. She looked up at herself in her dressing-table mirror.

'Okay Gracie Singh, here we go, razzle-dazzle 'em,' she said to the slightly unfamiliar face that looked back. Her lipstick was beginning to bleed into the fine lines around her mouth. She turned away from the mirror and took two aspirins for the headache she had had all day. Then, opening her bedroom door, she called for Lila.

Chrysanthemum heads had been laid out all over the floor of the houseboat throughout the day. As Gracie had picked her way through, frustrated by the disorder, Lila turned away smiling each time and Gracie asked what was going on.

Now she saw. They had been garlanded on to the fairy lights, each white flower lit by its own small spotlight, and then looped across the ceilings. On either side of all the doorways were great copper pots, polished to a low glow with lake mud, filled with water, the surface of each thick with roses, their petals lit and shadowed by candles that floated among them. Braziers were by each window, their stands wound around with more garlands, the heat bringing out the scent of the petals. Gracie stood, enchanted. She reached out and touched Lila's face as the girl almost ran past with a plate of samosas, the hot pastry triangles piled up on a bed of chinar leaves, deep burnt reds that Lila had gathered from the winter piles as the party had been planned.

Gracie did not even have to face the moment she hated, the beginning when there was nobody there and the fear crept in that perhaps no one would come. There was already a group at one end of the sitting room admiring the garlands of lit flowers above them, wondering how they had been done. Gracie opened her arms and walked towards them, a tide of warmth rising up through her. Gulshan was in front of her, holding a tray filled with glasses. She winked, he nodded. It was the rum punch she wanted. She took one and crossed the room with a sense of weightlessness to greet her first guests.

Enough people came to make it a party, but not as many as Gracie had hoped would defy the cold and the sullen mood around the lake. Masood knew that he could not stay as long as she would have liked because Naseema had made it clear, during her brief appearance with Kudji, that members of the Abdullah family were only present as the mark of a landlord's respect.

He sat in a corner with other houseboat owners, discussing the woes of the lake. He complimented Lila on how good the lamb, the chicken, and the hot samosas were each time she passed. He had just stopped Gulshan to take another kebab from him as Hal came in. Both he and Gulshan watched as Hal kissed Gracie on both cheeks, admired her *jamovars* and the beauty of her jewellery, and put a small package into her hands.

Hal pulled back a little. She had smelt odd when he kissed her – of dust, age and a cloying scent that overrode everything else. He told her that she looked radiant.

'Thank you,' said Gracie. 'I wish you would stop giving me things. Is it diamonds this time?' She turned her laughter to the other people in the room.

Hal bowed. 'No, just Hemingway.'

'Bullfighting, I hope.' Gracie dropped the package down on to a table beside her. 'Come and see the roof, Gulshan has been so clever with the braziers, come and have a drink, and what about these glorious flowers?'

Masood went on watching as she waved Gulshan over with his tray. She passed a glass to Hal and led him through the room. They reached the bottom of the stairs in the corridor as the head of Srinagar University library department arrived with his wife.

'How lovely to see you, you must think my reading days are over I'm such a rare face among your hallowed shelves these days.' One hand played with her hair. 'How is it at the library?' She waved Hal up to the roof as she led her new guests into the sitting room.

He climbed up and stood between two of the braziers, looking up through the white lights, trying not to make the other small groups of people uncomfortable with his proximity. A man from the tourist office was explaining lake-dredging to a young round-faced history teacher from Eve Garden Girls School. Her parents hung at the edge of their conversation from the other side of the brazier. Hal had met the teacher with Lila, and the man from the tourist office had been to The Wonder House several times so that Gracie could quiz him on various subjects over tea. He waved. Hal nodded to him but backed away.

Three men Hal had not seen before had drawn together around another brazier. They spoke in Kashmiri but there were enough words in English for Hal to knit together their subject, though not the detail.

They were discussing alcohol.

'They say wine is the worst, then vodka. You drink those

things on an empty stomach and you won't want to wake the next day,' said one.

'Rum's the one to take, I have heard that it can even soothe inflammation in the gut,' said another before taking a good gulp of his punch. 'Maybe this is why she has made it so far? Pickled in rum at the age of eighty plus.'

They laughed.

Hal turned away, making a silent stand against what he understood to be their disrespect for their hostess. They did not notice. Below him Lila was coming from the *dunga*. She was wearing her *pheran* with a shawl wrapped and tucked in around her neck. There was something about her hair but it was indefinable from the roof. She was carrying a plate, her face veiled by the steam that rose from it. He raised his hand to her but she did not see.

Hal counted enough time for her to get to the sitting room before going back down the stairs. He waited behind the crewel curtain that separated the galley kitchen from the corridor.

Gracie was calling out as Lila came back through the dining room and she replied as she reached the entrance. Hal whispered to her.

'Why are you hiding here?' she asked.

Now he could see that her hair was rolled up into a pleat, lengthening the line of her neck. A few strands had pulled free and were lit from behind.

'I love you,' he said.

They stared at each other until Gracie's voice called out again to Lila over the layers of conversation.

'I have something for you. Can I come to the *dunga*?' he asked.

'No, my mother is still cooking.' She turned back towards the sitting room. 'I'm coming,' she called to Gracie. 'The bedroom you used.' She turned away as she spoke to him.

He waited in the dark on the end of the bed that he had slept in for so long, in the same place where he had sat during his first power cut on The Wonder House, worrying what Lila had seen below his towel when she had come out of the dark carrying a lantern.

Under the white garlands Masood and the head of the fisheries research department and his wife were discussing the weather when Lila came back with more food.

'*Chilla kallan*! Abdullah, first time we've had this proper heavy snowfall since the insurgency began, wouldn't you say?' The man from the fisheries spoke in English because Gracie was close to their conversation. 'Don't you think, Mrs Singh, good to have *chilla kallan* again?'

Gracie nodded and passed a glass to Masood. He had been drinking the soft punch, but he knew, as she passed the glass to him, that there was rum in this one. She handed two more to the fisheries man and his wife.

'Please, no more "Mrs Singh". It's Gracie, and so good to have a fellow party drinker,' she said. 'You know your wife is one of the few women brave enough to take a drink in public around here.'

'That is because she is a wild woman from Delhi,' said the fisheries man, and he smiled proudly down at his short, round, smiling wife.

'And I'm a wild woman from Yorkshire, so I think that gets me off too.' Gracie raised her glass to Masood.

He lifted his to his lower lip and smelled the rum. He longed to be brave enough to face Naseema's silent condemnation of a little alcohol on his breath. He kept the glass close enough to his face to inhale the flavour. Lila held a plate of chicken tikka out to him, her eyes down.

There was something, some change, he had been trying to discover. He raised his hand to refuse her offer. She turned away and he saw. It was her hair, pulled up in an unfamiliar way, exposing two fine curves of sinew on either side of the back of her neck. He looked down into the glass in his hands and then took a sip, closing his eyes as the warmth cut down his throat and into his chest. Gracie was watching him. She smiled and began to enjoy her party even more.

She sat down on the bed beside him in the dark, and then got up again to pull the curtains open. A speckled wash came in from above and below, the lights on the roof and their reflection from the water. Lila unwound her shawl and then lifted her *pheran* over her head.

Hal released a sound, part pain, part revelation.

She was wearing Gracie's black dress and her body appeared from its bias cut like a brilliant invention.

'Please, marry me, Lila.'

'Why? Because you like the dress?' she laughed.

He started to get up but he could not find his balance. He sat down again and took a small white packet out of his coat.

'This is all I could find. Some crazy lake silversmith made an Irish love-knot ring.' He opened the paper and held the little ring out to her. 'Will you?'

He sat in front of her with the sense that his whole body was falling into the space between them. Only Lila listened for voices in the corridor. She took the ring and looked at it in the palm of her hand, this perfect circle of possibility. As she put her *pheran* back on she sat down beside Hal. She pulled threads from one of the blankets on the bed and pushed them through the ring. Then she held the suspended love-knot out to Hal.

'Can I wear it like this for now?' she asked. 'Until they know.'

His hands shook so much as he tied the two ends behind her neck that he made a bad knot, but it was enough to hold the little ring. She took both his hands and kissed his palms and then the tips of his fingers.

'We have to go back now.' She wrapped the shawl around her neck.

'Is that your answer?'

Lila stood in front of him and kissed his palms again. '*Meri jaan.*'

And she went.

Masood had just one glass but his guilt made it seem more. He ate as much lamb as he could because he thought the spices were perhaps strong enough to mask the smell of alcohol, and it was so good, much more flavour and moisture than usual. He wanted to thank Gracie, but he did not want her to know that he was leaving. He waited in a group on the edge of the dining room until he saw that the corridor beyond was clear, then he slipped away.

Irfan watched his uncle putting snow into his mouth, spitting it out, and then taking another mouthful. He looked so small as he crossed the meadow from The Wonder House to the garden gate. Irfan was surprised by the strength of affection he felt for this man who seemed so reduced now. The young militant remained crouching down behind the tree where the madman who thought he was a *Pir* usually sat, his hands raised to his heaven. And, like the madman, Irfan did not feel the cold as he watched his uncle spitting out his guilt as he picked his way through the snow.

When he saw Lila moving from the *dunga* to the houseboat his whole body froze. She seemed to have light around her, and he felt each of her steps on his heart. He shivered as she stamped snow from her shoes when she reached the duckboards with plates of food in her hand.

They must be her samosas, smoky with cumin, walnut-picking samosas.

People began to leave when Gracie asked the man from the fisheries to help her move the low table in the middle of the sitting room so that they could dance. It was not until most of the remaining guests had gone that she remembered that her record player had not worked for more than five years.

'We could have played Suriya's sacred radio. Imagine the drama?' she said to Hal when he and the fisheries man and his wife were the only guests left.

'Take a turn with me, young man, and we can pretend that this fine gentleman and his good lady are the London Philharmonic playing a fancy foxtrot just for us.' She held out her arms to Hal.

The fisheries man and his wife became an orchestra, their bodies soft and their faces pink from the rum as they mimed violins, trumpets, drums and flutes. Hal took Gracie in a gentle waltz around the low table that they had not managed to move. Then he and the orchestra sang a version of 'Happy

Birthday'. As it finished, the head of fisheries research department and his wife bowed and took their leave.

'Do you want me to help you to bed?' Hal asked Gracie after they had gone.

'I'll manage. Call Lila, will you?' She slumped into her chair. 'Will you come tomorrow on my birthday because I will be feeling depressed? Or is it already today?'

'It is. Happy Birthday to you, Gracie Singh, and of course I'll come. I've some people to see in the morning, I'll come in the afternoon.'

'Busy, busy you. Good party?'

'It was, very good.' Hal sat opposite her for a moment. 'What does "*meri jaan*" mean?' he asked.

'It's Urdu, rather over-egged poetic way of saying "my life".' She paused. 'As in "you are my life", why?'

'And is the houseboat name because of Kipling?' he pushed on as Lila's answer unfolded.

'Of course.' She straightened up a little.

'Of course. I'll call Lila on my way out.' And he got up quickly and bent to kiss her before he left.

She still had the same strange smell.

He did not have to call Lila. She was waiting in the corridor where Gracie could have seen her if she had turned around. He smiled into her and her hand went to the thread around her throat. He touched the back of her *pheran* as he passed, and leaned towards her saying, 'goodnight and thank you' to her in a voice that did not sound like his own. His mouth was against the curve of her temple as he spoke, and he walked away in awe of the erotic simplicity of how her skin had felt against his lips.

Gracie woke with the sense that the morning was a different shape. She was so thirsty but there was no water by her bed.

Lila always put water there.

She reached for the clock, keeping her head on the pillow because when she tried to lift it she felt sick and off-balance. It was just after eleven o'clock.

Lila and Suriya had let her sleep too late.

She called out into the silence, but only silence came back at her. She began to feel angry and it gave her the impetus to get up and pad around in the curtained semi-darkness looking for her slippers, her dressing-gown, and then her *pheran*. She needed to pee and she needed water.

As she sat on the lavatory she realized that she did not feel sad about being eighty, just angry that she was thirsty and unattended on her birthday morning. So she sang a little of Porgy and Bess and wondered where her boots were so that she could go out and find the girls.

She found the boots in the galley kitchen tucked under the stairs to the roof. Both sideboards were loaded with glasses and dishes from the party. Of all the food there were only two samosas left.

They had been so good, and the lamb too. The girls had done something different with them. She thought maybe she had forgotten to thank them enough at the party. She would tell them now.

It took three attempts for her to push the entrance door open, and the freezing fog that poured in made her call out again, an irate bellow, at having to make so much effort. She wanted to lie quietly, drinking hot coffee, and perhaps have some biscuits, the chocolate macaroons that Lila got on Thursdays when they were fresh from the baker on the edge of the vegetable market at the end of Maulana Azad Road.

She took small steps down the duckboard, trying to use the frozen edges of other people's footprints to find a grip. Rotting chrysanthemums loomed out of the mist at her. She called out again into the thick air, and for one last time at the top of the *dunga* duckboard before pulling the double blanket aside.

Suriya and Lila were lying together, almost curled around each other.

'What's the matter with you two, did you get drunk last night?' Gracie stepped into the *dunga* kitchen for the first time in three years. It was not until she was next to Suriya's radio that she saw that both of them were dead, the dark seep of Suriya's blood mixing with her daughter's, fanning out all around their heads on the *dunga* kitchen floor.

Chapter Thirteen ~

England, August 2002

He had kept death away behind carefully constructed barriers, thick walls that he had begun to build as a boy, standing beside his mother at his father's cold funeral. He had known then that he would have to take responsibility for her end. Beyond this his own death had been the only other one he knew he had to accept.

He had not expected to have to arrange a cremation for a woman who was older than his mother and no blood relation, but that was what he had just done.

For Hal, the acuteness of his time in Kashmir had ended when Gracie called him at the Residency Hotel on Maulana Azad Road the morning after her party. Suriya and Lila's murders, the return of Irfan Abdullah, the chaos of that day, and the days that followed, had been reduced to a series of logistical decisions. And one of those had been to take Gracie away from the constant sound of wailing. Among the half-formed images of the mourners who had come to The Wonder House in the days following the deaths he had seen just a numbness at another loss for a people who knew no other way. One face stood out, one expression – Masood's stricken emptiness when Hal had told him that he was taking Gracie to England. As someone who had been made so aware of his foreignness it was Hal's response to a world that was no longer subject to the rules of logic.

Now he stood alone in the Chapel of Rest on the London Road, just outside Brighton, and stared at Gracie's coffin. He wanted to feel something that mattered, but all he could manage was an exhausted disgust at the smell of stale life that sat between bunches of factory-seamed flowers in black marble vases, placed at her four corners.

They laughed about it once, the idea of her funeral. It was as she had struggled through pneumonia during early spring two years before, just after he brought her back to England. She looked so small and pathetic in the bed in the hospital beside the sea that she refused to acknowledge.

'Why?' she said when he told her to have a look.

It had been as they had driven along the seafront the first time he took her out for the day from the retirement home on the London Road.

'I never wanted to see it again. I waved it goodbye in 1939, why should I be pleased to see it now? I'm only here because I've lost everything I love. I hate it.' And she smacked the palm of her hand against the car window so hard that Hal had swerved.

When a cold turned into pneumonia he sat with her in

the hospital, and she asked him if she was going to die. He had lied.

'But of course I'm going to die, maybe not immediately but quite soon. England encourages one to die. Kashmir makes one want to defy it.' She lifted her chin with what remained of the spirit that she had brought with her from Nagin, folded among her cardigans and shawls into those suitcases that smelled of moth balls and old tissue paper.

For Hal and Gracie loss had become a personified presence that sat between them in the silences they shared.

'I always want to sing rude songs at funerals. Do you think there is anything profound in that?' she said out of the blankness.

That was when they laughed.

Now it just seemed sad.

When he went back to the Chapel of Rest to collect her ashes he had to wait while they attended to someone else who had come to pick up all that was left. He had read somewhere that you were unlikely to get just the ashes you were expecting, that it was more likely to be a mixture.

Gracie would not relish being mingled with the other old folk from the corridors of the retirement homes of the Worthing to Brighton strip. Hal smiled.

He sat in the waiting room among more seamed flowers and copies of *Hello*, the *Radio Times* and *Reader's Digest*. This was only the second time he had ever really noticed the latter, the little magazine of dentists' and undertakers' waiting rooms. It looked different sitting on a glass table under a spray of fake cherry blossom, and seemed to have fitted better with the anachronism that had been the world that Gracie had created on The Wonder House.

He picked up the top copy from the pile. It was more than two years old, a cover story of a man who had survived ten days in a pot-hole in North Wales. Lila had been alive when it had come out. He had not even met her then.

This familiar, the one that had returned with him from Kashmir, settled back down inside him, a thick wedge of weight that had made its home between his heart and stomach. He turned the magazine over so that the smiling face of the rescued pot-holer went front down into the jaws of a white shark on the cover of the next edition on the pile, and he opened his wallet to check his ticket again for his train time. He still had three hours.

The man who brought the urn to him had such an expression of earnest gloom that Hal wanted to shake his hand and congratulate him. He wondered what it would be like to deliver pots of people all day long. It seemed understandable that this man had a rim of dandruff around his collar and psoriasis between his eyebrows, but Hal could not stop himself from drawing back slightly as the undertaker reached out and put a practised hand on Hal's shoulder as he passed him the urn.

'Did your mother-in-law show a preference for where she wished her ashes to be scattered?' he asked in a kindergarten teacher's voice.

'She did.' He had put that Gracie was his mother-in-law on the forms, an instinctive response.

'That's nice.' The undertaker smiled, his mouth in a straight line.

'I suppose it is.' Hal looked down at the urn. He was holding the last fragments of the life that had changed his. He took a step back, feeling suddenly sick.

'Perhaps you should sit for a while. Can I get you a tea?' asked the undertaker.

'I'm fine.'

'I hope you've got someone with you? You're not driving, are you?' the man asked.

'I'm getting the train and I've got a taxi waiting for me here.'

'That's good, very sensible of you, and very sensible of your wife to get you to come, if I may say, terribly hard for daughters.' He folded his hands carefully and gave his straight-line smile again.

'She's dead.'

There was not even a beat.

'May I extend my condolences to you,' said the undertaker, his hands still folded.

'Thank you, I think I'll go now.' Hal paused. 'Is it possible that you could send the bill on?'

'Please don't think about that now, Mr Copeman, we have all your details, it's not something you should even consider at the moment.' He crossed in front of Hal to open the door. 'Now you go safely and it's been a pleasure to meet you.'

'I'm sorry but I . . .'

The undertaker put his hand up. 'Please, Mr Copeman, I understand.' He closed his eyes and nodded his head in a way that made Hal want to push him away. He smiled instead from a conditioned reserve.

He took Gracie to a coffee-chain café in the Lanes and put her on the counter in front of him. He watched the tourists traipsing in and out of antique shops over the small knob on the top of her grey-streaked marble urn; the Mercury model from the classical Roman selection, as against the Greek or French lines. The names of the styles had seemed so absurd. Who cared?

A boy with a line of spots down each cheekbone collected Hal's mug. He was not concentrating, sweeping absently across the counter among cups rimmed with drying milk froth and a half-eaten blueberry muffin squashed into a napkin. He was watching a trainee at the hairdresser's across the road. She was sweeping up hair cuttings and her tight black T-shirt moved as she bent over the broom. She was enjoying the attention.

'Shit, really sorry, is that . . .?' The boy focused as his hand brushed against Gracie.

'My mother-in-law, she won't mind, she likes younger men.' Hal smiled as the boy flushed deep red around his spots.

'God, sorry mate, are you going to scatter her here?'

'Not right here.' Hal passed his cup.

'Did she want to be scattered here?' asked the boy. 'I mean not here, as in right here, but in the sea here?'

'No, not at all. She wanted to go back to where she came from.'

'Where's that then?'

'In India, right up in the mountains, Kashmir.'

'Blimey, your wife Indian then?' the boy asked.

'No, she was Kashmiri.'

'Was? Oh sorry, I mean . . .'

A man with the flatly important tone of a manager called out.

'Sorry, I'm going to get bollocked now. Good luck with it, I mean with her.' He nodded to Hal.

He carried her back to the sea front to get a taxi. He

laughed out loud as he walked past a chocolate shop with whirls and twirls around its name: '*Choccywoccydoodah*'. He held Gracie up to see and it seemed as though he was losing all sense of balance.

At the front he crossed the road and sat on the seawall for a few minutes. There were still people on the beach, dug into the pebbles, their striped windbreakers planted against autumn, their trouser legs rolled up as they lay resolutely in the thin sun. He lifted her to the sea and tried to smile because it would annoy her so much.

He knew that he was not doing very well. Every time he found himself in a new situation his reaction was to wonder how different it might be if he was sharing it with Lila. His sister had said once that it took a year to recover from every year of a big love. He had known Lila for two and a half months. He had made love to her twice, and he was still trying to share his life with her over two years after she had been killed.

'I'm sorry you're bringing the wrong girl back with you,' Gracie had said to him as he had led her on to the plane for London ten days after her eightieth birthday.

He pulled her urn into his chest as he sat by the sea and pressed it into the place where his heavy familiar was pushing back down on his stomach wall.

It was a different place he came back to with Gracie's ashes, not in any dramatic way, but in the detailing, as fine as the cedar carving on the boats; it was the way people spoke and held their heads.

Nagin Lake had been cleaned, the rumps of encroaching weed had been pulled up. Some of the floating gardens had gone, towed away by bilious speedboats, the same ones that had once taken tourists water-skiing beside the Mughal gardens on Dal Lake. Between Nagin and Dal the lotus gardens were in flower, their waxy petals lying on the water, quietly, silkily cheapening the imported water lilies that bloomed so easily through the lake seasons. Gathered boatmen at Dal Gate lay in the shade of their canopies, sleeping in the heat, their feet and hands trailing in the water, so still that minnows hovered and darted. Fingers and toes flicked in sleep and clouds of tiny fish wheeled away.

As the freeze of winter had sealed everyone inside, so the damp late August haze now pinned them supine, draped across boats and walls, houseboat decks and withered lawns. They sought the air on the lake with the same deliberation that they applied to curling around their *kangris* in the cold.

Hal had rung from Delhi. Masood had said that he would meet him at the airport.

It was thirty-three degrees when he flew back into Srinagar. The security was the same, though everyone moved more slowly. The man at the registration counter had a closed face. He took Hal's documents and read them over three times.

'Your last wisa was journalist wisa, why are you on tourist wisa now?' he asked.

'I've come as a tourist.' Hal tried to take his passport back.

'Mr Coopmin, we have an election here in one month, we are not permitting journalists in with tourist wisa.' He pulled the passport back.

'Can I speak to your manager?' Hal asked.

'I am manager.'

'Good, well that saves some time then.' Hal snatched his passport and opened his backpack. 'I believe your elections start in late September. It is now 29th August and my flight back to London is on 9th September, at least two weeks before your elections start.'

'Show me ticket.' The man leaned over the counter.

'I am trying to.'

The foreigners' registration manager watched as Hal pulled things out of his pack and fanned them out around himself. The ticket was almost at the bottom. He put it on the counter and began to repack while the man turned each page with slow interest.

'And you will leave Kashmir on what date?' he asked when Hal looked back up from his pack.

'Would it have been easier to ask for my ticket back to Delhi?'

'Mr Coopmin, you did not say you had such a ticket.'

'I do, here it is.' He passed over the domestic flight ticket and watched as the manager turned the pages as slowly again.

He walked out into the heat between lines of police who, one by one, looked first at his shoes and then his pack. Masood's face was not among those bobbing beyond the barricades. He walked to the edge of the parking area and waited in the shade of a guard hut. A dog and a girl wearing glasses and a pale green *salwar kameez* waited with him, each keeping a silent distance from the other. A boy on a motorbike with the same eyes and mouth as the girl came to collect her. He looked at Hal's shoes as the girl perched sideways behind him.

He had forgotten that militants wore good boots, and that

he was almost dark enough to pass as a Valley man. He had forgotten that Kashmiris looked at a man's feet before they looked at his face. Zamruda had told him, Lila had told him, Major Kumar had told him, and he had still forgotten. He raised his hand to the girl as they rode away. She just stared back.

Masood was half an hour late.

'I didn't know you drove,' Hal leaned in through the passenger window of the little blue Maruti.

'Of course.' Masood reached his hand out to Hal.

'I don't remember seeing you driving.' Hal shook his hand, realizing now how little he knew about Masood.

'It was a hard winter then, too much of ice and snow for my driving skills, such as they are. Welcome back to Kashmir.'

'Thank you. How are you, how is everyone?'

Masood got out of the car to take the backpack from Hal and put it on the seat. He bowed his head. 'Your mother, your sister, they are well?' he responded.

'I think you could say so, though they might not agree.' Hal smiled. 'It's hot.'

'Yes, too hot.' Masood got back into the car and leaned across to open the door. 'It is cooler on Nagin.'

They drove in silence to the city. As they turned on to Maulana Azad Road Hal wound the window down further. He was finding it hard to breathe.

'You will forgive me if we stop for petrol. I was getting so late I did not want to stop on the way to the airport.'

Hal nodded.

The petrol station was just the other side of the Residency Hotel.

'I think I'll walk a bit.' Hal began to get out of the car.

'Just two minutes, so sorry, we will be on our way to Nagin.' Masood jumped out of the car and shouted for the pumpman.

Hal pushed into the back of his seat, closed his eyes, and concentrated on the smell of petrol fumes. Masood's English was not as good as it had been, not as easy or fluent. He remembered him sitting in the corner at Gracie's party, how he had watched Lila as she had moved through the room with a plate of food, samosas, how they had both watched her.

Turning to look for Masood he caught him in profile, bending beside the pump to check the spinning figures behind the smudged glass. He was a good-looking man underneath all the labels; the beard and skullcap, his moustache shaved back to stubble, every line of his body muted by the fall of his kurta pyjama. Gracie had told him of the young Masood, clean-shaven in the time of jeans and whisky, before the Valley had closed in on him. Hal's former lack of interest in the younger Masood had been under-pinned by the presence of Lila between them. Now he felt himself drawn towards this man in the vacuum that she had left.

The older man bent to get back into the car. It seemed to be quite hard for him but he masked it with a grace that again Hal had chosen not to notice before.

'So sorry, I have great trouble with my back now.'

'I can see.'

They looked at each other before Masood started the car again.

'Dr Hamid is an old fool. He gives me exercises that give

me so much of pain that I cannot even stand to do them
now.'

'Thank you for coming to pick me up.'

Masood turned to him as he pulled out from the petrol
station. A bus squawked and swerved.

'Oh, sorry, sorry.' Masood looked back at the road and
they drove on.

They left the car at the edge of the lake, on the opposite
side to The Wonder House, beside the burnt-out Nagin
Club where the soldiers had watched Lila teaching Hal to
paddle a *shikara*. They were still there behind their sandbags,
their holey socks and baggy underwear hung out to dry in
the lower branches of the chinar trees above them. They
stared at Hal as they had before, different men under the
same netted helmets, with the same moustaches.

Farouk was waiting for them, his boat pulled up on to
the bank. He was crouching beside it, sucking on his
hookah. He did not get up until they reached him at the
water's edge, but then he embraced Hal with an intensity
that surprised him. Farouk's face looked as if a bit of air had
been pumped into the hollows that had sucked in from his
cheekbones.

'You look well, Farouk.' Hal smiled into the old boatman's
eyes.

'Yes, thank you, sir, things are not so bad now as last time.'

All three of them made a performance of getting Hal's
fairly small backpack on to the boat. Farouk held out his
hand to Hal to help him on to the boat but they missed.
Masood bent gingerly to push them away from the bank. For
a moment he seemed to be about to step on too but, as the
prow slid, he leaned back to get his balance.

'I will take the car back to the house. Shall I see you later at the boat?' He raised his hand.

'Fine.' Hal lost his balance and fell back across the full width of the seat.

Farouk laughed from between his remaining front teeth.

Masood looked at his watch. 'It is now time for you to take lunch. There is a new man on the boat who will take every care of you. I will come down perhaps around four. Does that suit?'

'Yes, that suits.' Hal righted himself.

Farouk back-paddled out into the lake and Masood waved.

Two soldiers leaned a little further out over the edge of their sandbags to watch as the boat pushed away. A grebe dived away from the boat, streaming past them under the water, bubbles of oxygen threading away from its feathers. A smudge of tiny fish zigzagged away from the arrow of its beak.

'It's so clear now.' Hal leaned over the back of the seat to face Farouk as the old *shikari* swung his boat around.

'It has all been cleaned. This is good thing, the lake is clean and the tourists will come back when the election is passed off well.' Farouk scooped a handful of water across the back of his neck. 'People are swimming in it again. Maybe a time will be when we can make *kawa* from the lake again also.'

'Kashmiri *kawa*.' Hal held up his hand. 'Green tea, cardamom, cinnamon, almond flakes.' He folded down his fingers and thumb and stopped. 'What have I forgotten?'

'Saffron,' Farouk replied.

'Of course, the secular stigma.'

Farouk sighed without understanding and turned the boat towards The Wonder House.

From the middle of the lake it looked the same, except that a cotton awning had been stretched over the wooden frame on the roof where the criss-cross canopy of white lights had hung at Gracie's party.

'Why didn't they put him in prison?' Hal asked.

Farouk stopped paddling and looked up from the water. 'No person was asking for a case to be put.'

'Everyone knew he did it.'

Farouk looked at the paddle in his hands.

Hal stared straight ahead at The Wonder House. Someone was moving about in its shade, a short stocky man in *kurta* pyjama, his curled lamb's wool hat still on his head in spite of the heat.

'It was family matter.' Farouk pushed the heart-shaped blade back down into the lake.

'A family matter.' Hal's voice was empty. 'Who's that?' He pointed to the man on the roof.

'That is Moqbool. He will look after you.'

'He will look after me,' Hal repeated.

The old boatman lifted his paddle out of the water and laid it across his knees, the lotus-petal blade tipped slightly down so that water would not run between his legs.

'Many people have died. The father of Masood, Ibrahim and Rafi, Old Lotus Valida, a little girl who was born to Rafi and Kudji in spring but with hole in her heart, my brother's wife and my nephew shot in the street in the night with others in crossfire between militants and *jawans*. Many people have died since when you were last time in Nagin.'

The words and names moved around Hal, some with faces, others as blank figures he could not remember: Masood's father, the silent man who had sat in the corner of the winter sitting room as he drank tea with the Abdullah brothers, the morning Masood had found him wandering in the meadow.

The old man had been suffering from what they called Valley depression. Masood wanted Hal to talk to his father about his youth in Kashmir before Partition. The old man had brightened for a moment as he spoke of taking Britishers for summer treks into the mountains, about how much they had laughed. Then he was silent as he sank back down into his sense of loss.

Hal saw again the bow of Masood's head when he had asked him about his family.

'He probably didn't want to be alive any more.'

'Who?' Farouk asked.

Hal had not meant to say it aloud. He shook his head.

Two women moved towards the *shikara*, squatting on the fronts of their lily leaf-loaded boats. As they came close, Farouk called out to them. He told them to leave the man alone, but they did not stop. One of them had two water lilies in her hand, bound together with their own dripping stems. Allowing her boat to bump against them, just next to Hal, she held the flowers out to him and water from them ran off her arm and down into his lap. Everything about her was confident, the way she had snapped the cellulose of the stems within their sheaths at intervals so that she could wind them around the flowers, her steady balance on the furthest forward point of her boat as she leaned across to him, and her exposure. Except for a rose-patterned scarf that had slipped back from her hair, no other part of her face or head was covered. She did not look down as she offered the lilies to Hal, but presented them straight to him, her head bent a little to one side to find his eyes. He looked at her and saw the lighter brown of her eyes within the darker rim of her irises. Her pupils did not flick, nor did she blink. He thought she was begging and he held his hand up to turn down the lilies, but she pushed them at him even harder, using the other hand to keep her boat pulled in close to the *shikara*. Once she realized that he was not going to take the lilies, she put them carefully into his lap and spoke to him in Kashmiri, her eyes holding on to him. He did not understand.

'What's she saying?' He turned to Farouk.

He looked at the woman and she nodded to him. 'She is welcoming back to Kashmir the man who was to be the husband of Lila Bibi,' he replied.

Hal saw the lilies in his lap and the woman's brown eyes, darker than hers, but as strong. He took her hand, wet from the flowers, and put it to his cheek. She laughed and pulled away, turning and talking to the other woman. She pushed away from the *shikara* and their loaded boats moved behind as Farouk began to paddle again.

Hal looked at the lilies.

'They wanted money as well,' Farouk said.

Hal kept looking down at the flowers in his lap because he could not reply. Water from the stems was seeping into his trousers and he began to smile. He was returning with a bunch of lilies clutched to him to hide the damp patch around his crotch. Gracie would like that.

Within the boundaries of The Wonder House he had expected to find shadows that would smother him. He stood just below the veranda on the front deck, waiting for the sarcophagus of cedar carvings to close in around him, but only heat and light bounced off the underside of the ceiling.

It did not feel like sacrilege when he sat on the cushions where he had first seen Gracie. They had been re-covered in a pattern of winding poppies, almost identical in Hal's memory to the ones that had surrounded Gracie in her chair, fading away around her. The curtains in the doorway were the same. That was as far as he could go for now.

Moqbool offered to bring his lunch out into the shade of the veranda. He took Hal's pack and disappeared away along the running boards, grunting as he swung the bag. His heavy-footed progress stopped for a beat as he hacked and spat among the lily pads by the entrance duckboard.

No essence of Lila.

Hal closed his eyes and watched the same rippling light behind his eyelids as played on the carved ceiling of the veranda.

He would stay there for now, the rest could come later.

The over-spiced lamb that Moqbool brought sat heavily in his stomach and Hal fell asleep in the still of the early afternoon. The houseboatman left him until he saw Masood coming down the meadow, and then woke Hal by clearing his throat, spitting into the water from where he stood between two veranda struts.

Hal's neck was stiff from lolling on his shoulder. He rolled his head against one of the cushions, conscious that he had been asleep with his mouth open and that there was a line of spittle across his chin. He wanted Moqbool not to be there.

Masood called out to him as he stepped up on to the running boards. Moqbool plumped cushions around the two

men as they settled opposite each other. They talked about
the heat and the grand scale of the clean-up of the lake until
Moqbool went to make tea, and then they ran out of things
to say.

Two boatmen came towards the veranda from different
directions. They paddled faster as they realized they were
both heading for the same prey. Masood and Hal watched as
the *shikaris* pushed through the heat haze that disintegrated
the lines of all that moved on the surface of the water.

'The lake sellers are coming.' Masood raised his eyebrows
in the direction of the approaching boats, as though the
effort of lifting his hand was too much in the heat.

'Would they be offended if you told them that I'm not in
the mood to shop?' Hal pushed his head back into the
poppies.

Masood leaned out over the carved lotuses. 'No sale here,'
he called to the jeweller and the shawl-seller.

The jeweller edged closer. 'There is always a sale, brother,
let me just show.'

'Leave us, will you.' Masood leaned over further.

'Come brother, just give us five minutes each,' called out
the shawl-seller before changing to English. 'Hello, sir,
welcome to Nagin,'

'He is Gracie Madam's friend. He has brought her back
from England,' Masood spoke to both men.

'She came back? We thought she would not come back.
She is here now. She always bought from me, this is fine
news,' laughed the shawl-seller.

'She will not buy from you now, he has carried her dust
back with him. They burned her in their way.'

The salesmen were silent.

'So you will kindly leave us for some time?' Masood asked again.

Neither of them replied but allowed their boats to nudge together and drift away from The Wonder House, their heads bent towards each other as they talked.

They could not see the foreigner properly because of where he was sitting on the veranda.

If he was the bearer of Gracie's dust he must be the same man who had started the chain of events that had led to the murders of Lila and Suriya Abdullah.

One of them got up when they were a little further away and turned back to The Wonder House. He raised his hand as though in farewell to Masood and the other man, but it was not that, he was shading his eyes from the sun to see better.

The shawl-seller asked the jeweller if it was the same man. The jeweller said that it was, the tall foreigner who had stayed at the houseboat during the winter of Gracie Madam's party and the murders. They went on talking about it for a while before paddling on together, discussing the test cricket and the recent engagement of the jeweller's son.

'We might have less interruption if we sit inside,' Masood said as the lake sellers edged away.

Hal lay down among the cushions. 'Okay,' he replied after a pause.

Masood slid open the door to the sitting room.

It was as it had been the first time Hal had been there. Even the air had its same flavour. He had to wait on the sill to separate the shadows from the furniture after the bleached light of the veranda. The Mughal poppies on her chair were as faint as he remembered, more so perhaps, the chair replaced in its summer corner, away from the *bukhara*. The table beside it still had a stack of *Reader's Digests* balanced on the cross between the legs. He counted down six issues and pulled out the edition with the pot-holer on the cover.

'All are present and correct, except that Kudji has taken copies from the time Gracie Madam left. This is not a bad thing, is it? They stopped coming some months after you went from this place.' Masood stood beside him.

'I wasn't counting, it was something else.' Hal pushed the magazine back into the pile.

'And have you found it?'

'I have.'

'We can sit here.' Masood pointed again to the two sofas on either side of the room.

Again they sat facing each other among the rocking patterns of light and Hal told Masood about the cremation and Gracie's will.

'We argued about her will a lot. She had this idea that I would come and live here after she died and just watch my life drift across the surface of Nagin.'

Masood sat listening, very upright, his hands folded in the dip of his *kurta* between his thighs.

'I think she thought I would be happy here until I managed to make her understand that it would be purgatory for me.'

Masood moved his head. 'I am forgetting, what is purgatory?' he drew the word out into four separate parts.

'A place of purging, a personal hell between heaven and hell while they decide how bad you were and where they're going to put you.'

'You will have to forgive me, my English has slipped in

these two years past.' Masood was looking down at his hands. 'No Gracie school madam to correct me.'

'Well, school ma'am and I established purgatory, so she changed her mind and wanted you to have the boat.' Hal moved forward on the sofa.

Masood looked harder at the shape of his hands in his lap, the way his fingers crossed one over the other, and for a moment he saw Gracie in the unfocused space around, offering him the box of neatly stacked India Kings from the desk, bending to unlock the cupboard, leaning through the window sill, hollering for Suriya or Lila. Hal watched him sitting, his eyes half-closed, his hand clenched in his lap.

Moqbool came with tea, thumping into the room. He had made *kawa* in a thermos instead of a samovar, and the lid fell off as he poured, spilling tea, cardamom pods, wet cinnamon bark and almond shavings into the cups, the saucers, and all over the tray. Masood and Hal watched in silence as he righted the cups, adjusted his fur hat, picked up the tray, and took it all away again.

'It is not a boat with good luck.' Masood looked around the sitting room. 'She came here to mourn and now you will leave her dust here.'

'So what does that mean? You don't want it because of that?'

'Not so much for that, there are other reasons beside.' Masood turned back to Hal, focusing on his shirt buttons, closing down any line of enquiry.

Moqbool returned from the galley kitchen with the *kawa* repotted. They watched as he poured two cups with studied deliberation, adding a teaspoon of sugar to each and stirring them slowly before passing the first to Masood, the second to Hal.

'No saffron.' Hal looked down into his cup.

Masood was about to say something and then seemed to change his mind. 'No saffron, you are right, it is expensive now.' He paused. 'A bad harvest these past years.' He bent over his cup. 'When were you thinking to . . .' He looked up. 'How to say?'

'What? When am I going to scatter her?'

'If this is the right expression?'

'When the wind is blowing in the right direction for her.'

'May I come and share this with you?' Masood put his cup down and folded his hands back into his lap.

'I hadn't really thought about making any deal about it.'

'I see,' Masood said.

'Do you think I should?' Hal asked.

'I am not Christian so I am not clear on your customs.'

'Neither am I.'

Masood straightened. 'You are not Christian?'

'No, I mean I suppose I'm Christian. I'm just not sure about what you do at the scattering of ashes. The funerals I've been to were with boxes for burying.'

'You suppose you are Christian?' asked Masood.

'I just don't have the conviction in Christianity that you have in Islam.' Hal drank. 'I love this stuff.'

Masood was troubled. He picked up his cup again and turned it in his hands. 'You are not sure what you think as a Christian but you come to scatter Gracie Madam's ashes.'

Hal did not reply.

'And why do you think I have so much conviction in my religion?'

'Because you wear all the clothes and most of the time when I saw you here you were on the way to the mosque, or coming back from it.' Hal leaned forward, resting his arms on his knees.

Masood looked back down into his cup. 'Some of it is belief, but much of it is fear.'

In the silence Masood drank some of his tea, put his cup down and got up from the sofa. 'So we wait for the wind to blow the right way?' He reached his hand out to Hal. 'You will send Moqbool to tell me when it does?'

'I will.' Hal got up and shook his offered hand.

'Moqbool will look after all your needs. Would you like veg or non-veg supper? He does roast duck very well.'

'Duck, is that from around here?' Hal asked.

'It was shot by my nephew this morning,' Masood smiled.

Hal stared.

Masood hurried through the explanation: 'The son of one of my sisters, his name is Mushtaq.'

'Duck sounds good,' Hal said.

'I will tell Moqbool as I go.'

'Thank you, Masood.'

Both men knew that it was the first time that Hal had used his name.

'And you will have the boat,' he added.

'What will you do if I do not? You cannot take it with you.'

'You could sell it and then it would be towed somewhere else,' Hal shrugged.

'I think she is supposed to stay here.' Masood bowed his head as he left.

'Thank you,' Hal said for the second time.

~~~

He fell asleep again in the late afternoon, stretched out along the sofa, his head lifted up by cushions so that he would catch the first of the evening air on the water through the open windows. He woke as the light changed. Moqbool was standing at one of the open windows. He could have been there for some time, or just a moment. He nodded as Hal opened his eyes.

'I think I should go for a walk, Moqbool, this jetlag is knocking me about.'

Moqbool nodded again, unsure of what he meant.

'What time for supper, sir?' he asked.

'Whatever suits you, Moqbool.'

The houseboatman looked confused.

'It's just after six-thirty now, half past six, how about half past eight?'

'Half past eight for dinner,' Moqbool repeated.

Hal's centre of gravity shifted as he walked down the duckboard to the grass between the flower-beds on either side of The Wonder House garden. They were both full of white chrysanthemums. He stopped to find balance in the disorder that he was calling jetlag.

Two cricket games were being played in the meadow, leather on Valley willow. The game nearest the gate of The Wonder House stopped for a moment as he came through. White capped and *kurta*ed players turned to face him as he crossed one edge of their unmarked pitch. He heard the game resume behind him as he walked away.

Under his almond tree on the bank, where the meadow dipped down to the lake edge, sat the mad *Pir*, but he had hair now, and a skullcap. Hal remembered him on the frozen ground in the winter with a shaven and uncovered head, and now in the heat he was thatched and capped. He looked so much younger with his head of hair, boyish, childlike.

The madman turned as he heard someone approaching. Hal had not remembered his eyes either, how they fixed and held.

'You are back now,' said the *Pir*, not in his chanted singsong, but in a flat speaking voice, and in English.

'Yes, I came back.' Hal nodded to him.

'All are gone now,' he said.

Hal wanted to look away.

'She was with a knife at her neck. She was going to kill her so she died.'

Hal sat down hard on the grass. 'What do you mean?'

'Too close. Bullet in one side, out of the other, and in again.' He pressed his index fingers into each of his temples and then pushed one of them into the same place on the side of Hal's head. 'Bullet from assault rifle passes through two skulls if fired from so close.' He kept his finger to Hal's temple. 'And from there on.' His other hand made an arc into the grass beside them. He looked down at his finger in the dried grass.

'You saw?' Hal pulled his head away. He asked again. 'So you saw?'

The boy-man looked up slowly from where his finger was in the grass, its top joint bent back because he was pushing so hard into the earth beside him. He stared at Hal, but his eyes seemed to be without a point of focus, the pupils blown wide so that they were only rimmed by a fine band of flecked teak.

For a moment Hal wondered if the mad *Pir* was blind, but from the way he moved, the way he had pushed his finger into Hal's temple, he could not be.

His hand arced back up from the earth and his body followed the same curve. He pushed the full spread of his palm into Hal's face.

'Over now, go back, she has no need of you.' His full weight knocked Hal backwards. 'I watch over her.' He pulled back, returning to his place under the almond tree, humming to himself, the starkness of his eyes behind hovering eyelids, his head to one side, as though he was singing to someone else.

Hal scrambled away, forcing himself not to run, trying to find breath.

He sat on the veranda as the sunset played out, but he did not notice.

She came back in threads, each one almost breaking as it strained towards him across the water, so fine that alone they were invisible. It was only as they met and twisted that she became tangible among them; her feet on the running board above his head, her thick grey socks, the big toe knitted separately to the rest; the movement in her throat as she had swallowed whisky from the glass that he held to her mouth; her hands moving around her head as she adjusted her shawl, dancer's arms in two such familiar curves; how she jutted her shoulder as a statement of irritation; the sense of her moving behind him as she had reached to draw the paddle in towards the side of the boat to stop them from slewing; the shape of her in the dress she had worn under her *pheran* at the party, the celebration in her face as she had stood in front of him.

He reached out to hold on, moving from the seat to the steps of the veranda. Opening the gate he went down to the water, his right hand in a tight fist. And then he rested the back of his palm on the water and his fingers opened.

Every moment he had held on to had been separated from the next by his inability to act, his failure to reach her and hold on to her because he had not known that she would go. The weight inside began to dissolve as his hand pushed down into the lake. He threw cupped water into the air, creating light through the drops as they bounced back up from the surface. They left skittering bubbles where they fell.

The ripples did not spread out in smooth circles but seemed to be moving away from him in a line. Across the lake a kite played with a boy on the roof of a houseboat, pulling him against the low rail as it fell in limp curves on the slow air of the day, then arcing again on cool drafts that pushed up from the surface as the sun left.

Hal watched their dance for a while, and then he called for Moqbool and asked him to go up to the house and tell Masood that there was some wind on the lake. He unpacked Gracie from the bottom of his bag and went up to the roof. He waited at the edge, as close as he could remember to where he had been standing when Lila had come up the staircase behind him on that New Year's night.

Masood came and Hal heard him on the stairs, pausing at the top.

'Do you know why she called it The Wonder House?' he asked, facing out towards the lake.

'From the writer, Kipling, from him,' Masood replied.

'Did you read *Kim?*'

'No, only thing I read of his was the poem we had to learn at school, "If", all about being pukkah British and stiff-lipped.'

Hal laughed. 'The Wonder House was the museum in Lahore. It was the repository of the fragments that made up Kim's brief childhood.' He did not see Masood nodding behind him. 'This was the museum of her life.'

The boy across the lake flipped forward as the kite tugged. Hal took the lid off the urn and, stepping right to the very edge of the roof, he leaned out and shook Gracie on to the lake. They watched in silence as some of the dust fell straight down while a finer layer floated further away. They both looked about for something that might manifest her passing, but no hawk flew and no cloud made a particular shape that could be interpreted as being anything but a cloud. Just the boy and his kite moved on the other side of the water. They waited in uncomfortable silence.

'Should you not say some small prayer?' Masood asked.

'I don't think so.'

They looked down to where grey streaks of ash had fallen on to the water. One of the scrawny ducks from further down the lake pushed out from under The Wonder House and shuffled through the ash with her beak, trying to clear a tiny feather that had stuck in one of her nostrils.

'The mad *Pir* says he saw the murders,' Hal said as he watched the duck.

'How so?' Masood felt embarrassed to be watching Gracie Madam being snuffled by a muddy duck. He looked around for something to throw at it.

'I saw him under his tree in the meadow this afternoon,' Hal replied.

Masood found half of a broken wooden clothes peg and threw it at the duck. She scooted back under the veranda.

'This is not possible.'

'What do you mean?' Hal asked.

'He died from pneumonia the winter after you took Gracie Madam. He would not come inside until he had tea from Lila and he would not hear us when we told him she was no more.'

'So who's the new mad *Pir* then?' Hal turned to face him.

Masood brushed the dirt left by the broken clothes peg from his hand. 'Another boy who is not straight in the head now.'

'Who?' Hal's voice fell off the question.

Masood stepped back. 'My nephew Irfan, he has not been straight in the head since that time.'

Hal saw it as it might have been: Suriya bending over her sleeping daughter in the dark to cut away the Irish love-knot ring that he had tied around Lila's neck. He saw Irfan watching Suriya with the knife against Lila's throat, and he saw him raising his assault rifle in panic.

Epilogue ~

A boy called Ahmed Abdullah hanged himself in September 1975 from a lower branch of a cedar tree at the edge of a clearing in a forest that looked up to Haramukh, the sacred peak.

He had been there with his sister only a few weeks before. Ahmed had made her wrap her arms around the trunk to feel the tree's warmth through the thin cotton of her *kameez*. He had told her that it had been marked to be cut down. She had kept her face against the bark, listening to her brother's words, and when she had let go she had pressed her lips to the place where her cheek had been, and he had bent and kissed her, holding both sides of her face in his hands. Her skin had been the most beautiful thing he had ever touched.

Ahmed hanged himself because he was in love with his sister. He used the rope that was tied around his mule's neck to strap timber to her once it had been felled. He got up on her back and threw the rope over one of the lower branches of the tree with a sense of purpose that, even in his abstracted state, he realized was clinical. He did not even pause as he tested the knot before putting the carefully tied noose around his neck, settling it against his skin inside the collar of his *kurta*, aware only of the rasp of his breath.

He knew that his mule would not walk away, however loud he shouted, so he simply stepped off her rump with the image of his sister's face as he had held it between his hands.

Ahmed's mule waited under his juddering body as he spun slowly on the rope that had been around her neck, and she did not move when his body emptied down the side of her hindquarters.

Ahmed's sister waited until the sun was almost all the way down the edge of their *dunga* boat before she went to look for her brother.

Suriya knew where to go. Ahmed had told her that he was going to fell the tree that he had shown her on the edge of the clearing. She saw his mule first, still standing below one of the lower branches of the cedar. She could not understand what the mule was standing under until she was close enough to see that it was her brother.

She stopped speaking. Even her wide-mouthed screams of pain were silent as she gave birth to their daughter in the early summer of the following year.

In September 1977 Gracie Singh bought cedar timber to build a houseboat. The merchant was so happy to have sold the lengths from the hanging tree that he had cut, even though it had been marked with a red cross as bad wood. He had kissed the money that she had paid three times, and he had felt a warmth for the foreigner, even though she was an infidel.

Acknowledgements~

Much has disappeared, and many have died in Kashmir since this story began. It is written in their memory. In Kashmir such thanks to the Wangnoo family, to Salaama, Moqbool, Parveena, and to those officers and men of the security forces who do operate within the parameters of a moral code that it is possible to maintain within conflict.

On the way to publication enormous thanks to Elizabeth, and then to Clara, Toby, Morgan and Elisabeth for their trust. And to those who have been the scaffolding that has held me in place, loving thanks to Lisa, Gautam, Susie, to Rajiv, my mother Sally, Johnny, my sister Emma, and to Richard, in gratitude for all the space you gave.